I0671854

ZAP BANG

STORM SEEKERS 3

BY

CHRIS KRIDLER

Copyright ©2014 by Chris Kridler

All rights reserved. No part of this book may be reproduced or transmitted in any form or by any means, electronic or mechanical, including photocopying, recording, or by any information storage and retrieval system, without permission in writing from the writer and publisher.

Published by Sky Diary Productions, Rockledge, Florida

Learn more about the author and storm chasing at

ChrisKridler.com

Cover design and photo illustrations by Sky Diary Productions

Original A-10 image by U.S. Air Force

Paperback ISBN: 978-0-9849139-8-5

First edition

ELECTRIFICATION

J ack wanted nothing more than to ignore the phone ringing at his desk in the dark, cavernous, nearly empty launch control room. He had a weather experiment to run. But only a few people had this number, and the call could be important.

Lightning flashed outside as he picked up the receiver, and his hand tingled with the sharp sting of electric shock.

"Damn!" he said, dropping the phone with a clatter. The grad student next to him laughed. Jack knew better. Lightning Safety 101: Don't use a corded phone in a thunderstorm.

He picked up the receiver anyway, determined to get off the line quickly. "Yes?"

"Is this NASA?" came a creaky voice.

"No," said Jack, already knowing this wasn't a call he wanted to take as he scrolled through the sensor readings on his monitor.

"Are you sure? This ain't the launch center? I want to report a UFO."

"I'm sure," he said. "Try 911."

"I need NASA! This is a warning from the universe —"

Jack hung up and rubbed his hand, trying to recover his focus. Even with two weeks on the job, focus was elusive after his months-long escape to Florida and one too many naps by the ocean.

"You got zapped, didn't you?" asked Daryl, one of the grad students who rotated in each day — or, at least, whenever storms were expected. "I thought these phones were shielded."

"Lightning finds a way," said Jack.

Outside the quiet building at Cape Canaveral, one of several devoted to the launch of rockets, the strobing thunderstorm grew louder. It promised good results for the sensor experiment Jack had been hired to run by a wealthy, some said wildly eccentric, patron who had yet to reveal himself in person.

Maybe the boss was odd, but Jack had to admit that it felt good to work again, especially when working meant hearing the sound of thunder. Unfortunately, Jack and Daryl had to watch the lightning on TV.

From a borrowed corner of the launch control room, with its tiers of computer desks ascending behind them, they monitored a movie-theater-size screen on the wall. Flanked by digital countdown clocks, it displayed multiple camera views that showed flashes illuminating the empty launch pad. Beyond the pad lay the Atlantic, dark and seething in the storm.

On the desk in front of them, computers showed the data their six lightning sensors gathered with each strike.

"It looks like it's picking up everything tonight," Daryl said.

"That's because we cranked up the sensitivity," Jack said.

"Oh, yeah," said Daryl, a pale ectomorph with spiky blond hair who must have to wear a coat of armor to avoid getting burned in the Florida sun. None of the students seemed particularly informed about this project; the Florida Tech professor who was funded by their benefactor kept sending them Jack's way. He guessed they were too busy drinking, screwing and occasionally studying to keep track of this little experiment.

Jack sighed. Those were the days. He was thirty-two and had spent at least as much time drinking as he had chasing women, but lately, his customary pleasures had been less than satisfying. Maybe he'd been in Florida too long. He needed to get back to Oklahoma and chase some storms. In a month or so, he thought, it'll be tornado time.

For now, Florida's severe season took the edge off his craving. March was a good month for storms, and this was when their billionaire backer, whom Jack knew only as Dr. Y, had wanted to test his prototypes. After a smattering of bird-fart storms earlier in the month, the elements came together in earnest today, powered by a low-pressure system over the Gulf and a branch of the jet stream dipping over the peninsula.

Jack stood, stretched and watched the big screen with a mix of awe and frustration as a lightning crawler danced across the black sky. He wanted to be out there. The numbers and lines on the monitors jumped up as the sensors mapped the location and voltage of the bolt. The high-ceilinged room resonated with the thunder that followed.

Rockets were rarely hit by lightning these days, mostly because of protection on the pad and stringent weather criteria for launch. But monitoring was essential; transient charges could work devious damage on sensitive satellite electronics. If you missed a strike and failed to check for problems, you could launch a billion-dollar piece of space junk.

On a launch day, this building would be teeming with engineers abuzz with the excitement of shooting a rocket to space. Jack had been given a tour on just such a day, arranged by their benefactor, who hadn't bothered to show up. Word had it Dr. Y watched the liftoff as he dangled from a parachute over nearby Titusville.

Jack had been thrilled by the fiery power of the launch, a barely controlled explosion topped by meticulously engineered hardware. But nothing enthralled him as much as a storm.

The lightning increased in frequency. The images of the launch pad on the gigantic wall screen flashed in stuttering bursts of white as the lightning protection system — the surrounding towers and wires — shielded the empty space where a rocket would await launch.

As Jack watched, a bolt hit the ground, and a tree of lightning burst skyward from one of the towers.

"Upward lightning!" he noted with enthusiasm.

"So what?" asked Daryl, who'd been sneaking glances at the texts dinging on his phone.

"So it means the tower initiated the lightning, and it was probably a positive bolt. I thought you were studying meteorology? And would you put that goddamn thing on stun?" Jack asked as Daryl's phone dinged again. Oh, great, he thought. Now he sounded like a crabby old man.

"Huh? OK," Daryl said, pushing a switch on the phone. "Sorry. Anyway, I'm not studying lightning. I'm focusing on water resources and flooding. But I need some extra credit, and my prof needs his funding from the bizarro billionaire, so here I am."

"Lightning kills more people in Florida than flooding does. You might want to pay attention."

"Chill, dude," Daryl said.

Jack wondered if he'd been this much of an asshole. Probably. "So what have you heard about our bizarro billionaire?" he asked.

"My prof tells me he monitors his pet experiments in progress. Live. Like Big Brother. He might be watching us right now."

"He must really like lightning, then," said Jack. "Because we are less than exciting."

He sat again at the desk, typing in his observation of the upward lightning and punching return, entering it into the log. Jack kept a running journal of his observations to enhance their data and, in part, to entertain himself during these long sessions on watch. His phone buzzed in his pocket, and he glanced at it briefly: a text from a girl he vaguely remembered after a night of rum cocktails at a local watering hole, followed by a depressing encounter in her shabby bungalow with her noisy cat mewing outside the bedroom door. He'd have to block that number.

He looked up in time to see a blast of white light overwhelm the cameras.

"Whoa!" Daryl said. The thunder trailed by several seconds, since the launch pad was four miles away.

Jack was already scanning the data. "We might've gotten a direct hit," he said.

"Awesome!"

"Not awesome. Look. This sensor is reading low," he pointed out as another bolt hit nearby. "Actually, one is dead, and three of them look off. It reset the sensitivity back to factory settings, if you will."

"Then I guess it worked. You know exactly where the lightning hit!"

"Not exactly." Jack tried to restrain his impatience. "We have to look at the data. The bolt may have hit the ground and traveled. It may have struck above the sensors — four of them are right under the protection towers."

"Your job, not mine," Daryl said with relief as Jack punched in a new journal entry.

"What is your job, anyway?" Jack asked.

"To make sure the computers are running when you go pee. Hey, if you do, can you get me another Mountain Dew from the machine?"

"Why don't *you* go?"

"Great idea. I'll be back." Daryl tucked his phone into his pocket and sauntered off into the shadows.

Jack shook his head and paged back through the data from the big strike. This would be fun to analyze. But not as much fun as being out there to watch it. And any other data they got tonight would be next to worthless now that half the sensors weren't calibrated and one was fried.

He jumped when the phone on the desk rang again. This space was kind of spooky at night, and the electronic warble was sharp, echoing in the empty room. It was probably Daryl, lost on his way back from the soda machine, Jack thought. Or maybe it was another UFO nut. He picked up the phone more gingerly this time, hoping the shock had been a fluke.

"Jack Andreas," he said.

"Dr. Andreas, so nice to speak to you at last," came the oddly pitched male voice. What was that accent — 1930s Hollywood? Jack didn't recognize it.

"May I help you?"

"That will be telling. This is Dr. Y. So you know about upward lightning?"

Their benefactor? Or, as Daryl called him, the bizarro billionaire? He must have been reading the journal entries as Jack was punching them in.

"I know a little," Jack said.

"Your old friend Professor Malik says you know quite a lot, and as a storm chaser, you might be just the fellow to help me with a project I'm working on. Could you come see me tomorrow to discuss it? I'm not far away."

"I — sure, I don't see why not," Jack said. "Your sensors are going to need work anyway."

"I saw that, and they are just a sideshow, my boy, a sideshow. I'll send my people out in the morning. No need for you to stay another minute. You'll come for drinks and dinner tomorrow, won't you? I'll have my car pick you up."

"I'd prefer to drive," Jack said.

"If you must, of course. I'll have my assistant email you the address. We'll buzz you in at the gate. See you at seven."

Jack hung up the phone. He'd been happy to get this little job. The money from his last consulting gig was running out. But he wasn't sure he was ready to deal with an eccentric billionaire.

Daryl wandered back into the room, soda in one hand, phone in the other.

"Anything new?" he asked.

"Go home," Jack said. "God called. Show's over."

❧

JACK DROVE his Volare wagon south on A1A past Patrick Air Force Base as the late-afternoon sun gilded the ocean on his left. The shallow waves looked exceptionally blue today, careening into turquoise as sunset neared, glinting in the light. He could smell the salt air through his open window and wondered if he would miss it when he returned to Oklahoma.

He turned west on the Pineda Causeway, enjoying the feeling of soaring as he crested the bridge, and took the exit for Merritt Island.

As he turned south, the light immediately thickened under the growth of hoary oaks, their branches shading the road like wizened arms. He wended through the curves of Tropical Trail, watching the Indian River Lagoon appear and disappear through the trees on his right, and the sun reached for him through the gaps. As the island narrowed, the water became a steady companion, almost always in view, its bank studded with boat docks that accompanied the larger and larger houses on his left.

He checked the address again on his phone but kept the GPS voice off. He wanted to enjoy this ride in quiet, savor the peace before whatever awaited him beyond the gate at Dr. Y's.

Gate? It looked more like a fortress. He pulled into the wide driveway and faced an eight-foot-tall, spiked, black wrought-iron fence. Its wide gate, incorporating a design that evoked forked lightning, was flanked by tall, elegant stone posts.

An island of flowering bushes and short palms grew in the middle of the driveway, camouflaging another post with a keypad. Jack leaned out the window and pressed the intercom button. He felt someone watching him as he waited and looked up, noticing small cameras atop the gateposts.

"Dr. Andreas?" came a woman's voice, tinged with a light Jamaican accent. "I'm buzzing you in."

The gate slid open, and he eased the car through, following a winding avenue of pavers toward a structure he could barely make out through the trees. The house seemed to grow as he approached, unfolding into a contemporary, three-story stucco mansion with a broad portico flanked by two long, curved, one-story wings embracing a circular courtyard. Jack parked on the edge of the wide court, near a detached garage with four doors that easily could hold twice that many vehicles. No other cars were in view. This was a driveway made for a Mercedes or BMW, not his shabby green 1977 Plymouth.

He emerged and smoothed his tan cotton canvas blazer, which he wore over a light-green collared shirt that picked up the color of his eyes — an unusual concession to civilized attire, given he was meeting his employer. He'd even shaved. But he hadn't given up his jeans. It was just cool enough to wear these layers; soon, the heat would triumph over fashion.

The light was fading here among the oaks, diverse palms and flowering plants — hibiscus, bougainvillea, plumeria, oleander. He'd learned that much from his aunt's botanical books at her vacant Cocoa Beach condo, where he'd been staying since late summer. The rest was too exotic for him to identify.

Jack paused at the water feature at the courtyard's center. The fountain was dark granite, rectangular, topped with an unusual sculpture mounted on a pedestal. The clear acrylic block, about two inches thick by eighteen inches square, was set on edge like a window, and water spilled under it. The shifting colored light that shone beneath it revealed a pattern inside the block that reminded Jack of a branching tree reaching toward the sky. And then he realized what he was looking at.

"A Lichtenberg figure," he murmured, reaching out to run

a finger over the smooth surface as the changing colors illuminated each delicate branch. It looked like a lightning crawler frozen in ice.

"So now you know my taste in art," came a voice from nearby, the same strange tenor he'd heard on the phone, tinged with British or Ivy League or something Jack couldn't identify.

"It's beautiful," Jack said, looking up at Dr. Y. He was surprised to see a man of barely five feet tall, with gold wireframe glasses and curly, reddish-gold hair that had thinned to wisps in the center. His rotund form was clad in a vintage Hawaiian shirt, long white shorts and leather sandals. So much for dressing up.

"Nothing that a five-million-volt particle accelerator won't do," said Dr. Y with a grin of tiny, numerous teeth. "Or lightning, if you're unlucky enough to be hit by it. I prefer a more controlled situation. That's why I let the artists play in my lab sometimes."

"I want one," Jack said in a rare moment of acquisitiveness.

Dr. Y chuckled. "Perhaps we can arrange that as part of the payment plan," he said. "Won't you come in?"

Jack walked up the few shallow steps to the wide patio, past the columns, and shook the man's hand before entering through the double wooden doors. Dr. Y closed them with a soft click behind him. Classical piano played from hidden speakers that reverberated off the marble floors and through the seemingly endless open floor plan. A sunken living room before him led to a wall of sliding glass doors that opened onto a pool, terrace, vast backyard and, seen dimly through more trees, the Banana River Lagoon on the other side of the island.

"River to river," Jack noted.

"It cuts down on neighbors," said Dr. Y. "Elena?"

"Right here," came the response from a female figure click-clacking down the dim passage on the left, which curved away to mysterious destinations. When she emerged into the light of the living room, Jack blinked at the sight of an elegant woman with ebony skin and tightly cropped black hair. "I can show him to the game room while you get ready," she said, islands in her consonants. She wore business attire — black slacks, a white button-up blouse and low black leather heels with silver buckles. "I'm the assistant," she said to Jack, flashing him a bright smile. "I emailed you? Come with me."

"Go on," Dr. Y said. "I'm preparing a little entertainment before dinner, and I need a few minutes to make the cock-tails." He grinned again and walked quickly in the opposite direction.

"Sounds ideal," Jack said. Cocktails would go a long way toward lubricating this peculiar evening.

Elena briskly led Jack back the way she'd come. The soft notes of the piano music echoed off the marble floors, marble walls, marble everywhere. Halfway down the wide corridor, a staircase spiraled up to rooms unseen. Wide windows offered views of the lawn and river on the right; doorways lined the hall on the left. Elena pulled a phone from her pocket and tapped the screen a few times. Recessed lights above them came on.

"Very sci-fi," Jack said.

"You have no idea." She stopped in front of a dark wooden door, opened it and gestured Jack inside. "I'll be back in a few minutes to get you." She whirled and was gone.

"Damn!" came a voice from inside. He couldn't see from where, at first, as the room had a narrow entrance that opened up into a dream man cave. Or perhaps a gentleman's cave. Rock music played in the background, and the look was warmer, more vintage. A bar of rich, dark wood with six stools, all with wooden backs and green leather seats, stood to his right, illuminated by antique chandeliers. A generous liquor selection lined the old-fashioned mirrored bar back; the door to a glassed-in, refrigerated wine pantry could be seen to the bar's right. On the far left of the room was a low platform topped with three antique chairs, the kind where men used to sit while their shoes were shined, that made for perfect viewing of the ornately carved, green-felted pool table at the center. Next to the chairs were a few blinking pinball machines and a glowing jukebox.

Beyond the pool table was a roomy, round alcove with comfy chairs, a large television that hung on the wall, and more west windows. The pink and orange light of sunset revealed a figure standing in the shadows, fringed with fire.

She stepped into the pool of light cast by the stained-glass lamps hanging over the pool table, holding a cue stick, evaluating him with cool gray eyes.

"At last, you've arrived. Just when my luck was running out," she said, gesturing to the table, now empty of everything except the eight-ball. "Want to play?"

Jack felt a prickle of recognition and a more insistent rush of attraction. She was dressed more casually than he, in a soft, black, wide-necked T-shirt with long sleeves, loose jeans and black sneakers. Her brown hair fell just above her shoulders in a modern cut. She wore little makeup, and he noticed her faint freckles, her strong but soft cheekbones. Her slight smile showed one dimple more persistent than the other. Not perfect, but a natural beauty, Jack thought. And somehow familiar.

"I'd love to play," he said, withholding his name as she had done. This encounter felt delicate. Who was she? Was she working for Y, too?

"Beer?" She leaned her cue against the table, walked over to the bar and, behind it, opened what had looked like another wall panel to reveal a large refrigerator.

"Of course," he said.

She grabbed two, popped off the caps with an opener mounted behind the bar and walked out to press a cold bottle into his hand. It was Florida Beer's Swamp Ape. She looked him in the eye with an expression that suggested she was withholding something. Maybe a laugh. "Want to break?"

"Sure. Rack 'em up."

Jack had spent enough time in bars to become a fair pool player, though his victories were often owed to lax bar rules and drunken opponents. This woman seemed more or less sober, though she took a healthy swallow of her beer before setting it down on the bar. She rescued the balls from the pockets and popped them into the correct triangular configuration. Jack went to a cue rack on the wall and shopped for a weapon, trying to figure her out. He knew one thing. He wasn't going to be beaten by a girl.

Armed with an elegant stick from the collection, he turned back to the table and put himself behind the cue ball. The woman leaned against her cue, watching him, making him nervous. Why? Women didn't make him nervous. He hit the white ball hard, and it scattered the rest with a clatter. None went in.

"Wide open," he said, stepping back to let her have a look. She circled the table, found a shot she liked and bent low to execute it. Jack thought he could see the bar's chandeliers glitter in her eyes as she sunk the three in a side pocket. She moved on to the one and banked a shot to drop the yellow orb into the corner. Then she barely missed the seven as she tried to use another ball to hit it into the next corner, where it rattled and was still.

"Damn," she said, as she had when he'd entered the room earlier.

"Looks like a pretty good run to me," he said, trying to pick the easiest stripe.

"I can do better."

She's a driven creature, he thought. It was only pool. He targeted the eleven and managed to get it into the pocket opposite the corner where her seven stood guard, then failed to hit the thirteen into the side pocket. She picked her next target and proceeded to sink four balls in a row as he drained his beer and admired the graceful way she bent her body over the table. She left only her pesky blue two, and she put the cue ball where he'd have to possess magical powers to sink the ten, his most likely target. Nonetheless, he drew on geometry to concoct an unlikely scenario — a double bank shot — and got the damn thing in.

"I knew you were lucky!" she said, though why or how, he didn't know. And his luck ran out on the next ball.

"Almost lucky enough," he said as she circled the table and picked her angle.

"Sometimes a little luck is all you need. Though skill helps." Was she showing off? Or teasing him? She dropped the two in two seconds, then turned to the eight ball and called the farthest corner. She drove the cue ball into the eight with a satisfying thwack and grinned as it popped into the pocket.

He raised his eyebrows. "Where'd you learn to play like that?"

"I learned more in the Army than how to fly a helicopter. No hard feelings, Jack?"

She knew his name. And what was that about a helicopter?

"You have me at a disadvantage," he said. His slightly wounded male pride was salved by her smile.

"You really don't remember me, do you?" she asked. "Maribeth Lisbon. Helicopter pilot?"

The match of his memory struck and fired. He remembered her eyes, the debris strewn over the field, the adrenaline of the moment and that same powerful allure, then as now.

"Holy shit," he said unceremoniously. "Uh, your hair was longer, I think."

"You do remember." She looked pleased. "And yours was shorter?"

"Yeah, letting it get a little shaggy," he said, running a hand through his dark mane.

"You gave me your card. I kept it, kind of as a good luck charm. You showed up after the crash, and I just sort of associated it with the fact that I was still alive." She'd retrieved a canvas satchel from behind the bar, and from it, a small, black wallet; out if it, she pulled his wrinkled card.

Jack laughed. "But you never called," he teased, glad he finally knew who she was.

"Luck brought you to me," Maribeth said. "I never really expected to see you again. Luck doesn't work like that."

"Only this time, it did," Jack said, and he reached out and shook her hand. Her grip was firm and comfortable and electric. "The next question is, why are you here?"

"It's a long story. Let's just say I think a lot of luck will be required."

Just then, Elena came through the door. "It's time," she said. "Time for cocktails and acts of genius."

❦

ELENA LED them back through the corridor, to the living room and through its French doors to the thickly landscaped terrace and the lagoon-shaped pool. It was nearly dark now, but tiki torches cast a flickering glow over the water, the waving fronds of the palm trees and the adjoining tiki bar, decorated with carved masks and a roof of thatched palm. There was just enough light to make out a strange machine on one side of the patio and, in the pool, a round figure in a black wetsuit doing the sidestroke. Dr. Y stood up in the shallow end when he saw them.

"Excellent!" he said. "Time for Mai Tais. Colin?"

Colin, presumably, appeared from another door beyond the bar. A thin, pallid, well-groomed fellow, he was dressed in what Jack considered hotel tropical — a bland Hawaiian shirt that matched his khaki pants. He held a tray laden with cheese, crackers, fruit and something fried that smelled delicious. This he placed on the bar, exchanging it for a tray already loaded with drinks in tiki mugs, each garnished with a bunch of mint and a straw. He offered the cocktails to Jack and Maribeth first, who each took one, and then to Elena, who waved him off. She was on her cell phone and had retreated to a lounge chair near the bar to conduct business.

"Sir?" Colin said in an English accent to their host, holding up a mug that looked like an escapee of Easter Island.

"Afterward," Dr. Y said.

"Yes, sir," said Colin, retreating once again to the house.

"I pay extra for that accent," Dr. Y said, making Jack wonder if Elena's accent cost extra, too. And Dr. Y's wasn't exactly average. Maybe Jack could earn a few extra bucks by ginning up some exotic dialect. Say, Arkansas.

"You all should stand back," their host continued. "Head over to where Elena is. That should be sufficient."

Jack complied, taking a sip of his Mai Tai and its heavenly layers of rum and juice and grabbing a bite off the tray before heading to the far end of the patio. The nibble was a crab rangoon, he discovered, and a damn good one. No fake krab with a *K* for Dr. Y.

Maribeth picked up a couple of pieces of cheese and crackers and joined him in the shadows, shooting him a questioning look. Jack shrugged.

"All right!" said Dr. Y, who half-swam to the edge of the pool and put on a crinkly, shiny cap and shoulder wrap that were sitting there. "And they mock tin-foil hats!"

"Is he going to do what I think he's going to do?" Jack said, more to himself than anyone.

"What's he going to do?" Maribeth said.

"I thought you might like a little demonstration before we talk," said Dr. Y, who was adjusting his Jiffy-Pop attire. "Besides, it gives me a chance to play with my Tesla coil."

"That's a fucking big Tesla coil," Jack said under his breath, surveying the machine at the end of the pool. A box a few feet square was topped by a cylindrical tower perhaps ten feet tall. It had a large head, like a doughnut lying flat, that would be the envy of any robot. From it extended a slender pole that curved over the center of the pool.

Dr. Y laughed. "I heard that, and yes, it is. I wanted you to appreciate the power of a direct hit by a hundred thousand volts. My headgear and the salt water will help protect me."

"As long as I don't have to do this later," Jack said.

"Not quite." Dr. Y donned a long, steel glove that looked like medieval chain mail, clamping to it a cable that came up from under the water. "Besides, this is at most point-one percent of the power of a real lightning bolt. Elena?"

"Yes," said the assistant, who was now off the phone and standing next to them with a control box whose wires snaked into the shadows.

Dr. Y had made it back to the center of the pool, trailing the underwater cable. "Count down and throw the switch."

She counted aloud, perhaps to be clear to everyone when to be scared out of their wits. Dr. Y sank into the water so that only his nose, eyes and metallic cap were exposed.

" . . . Three . . . two . . . one . . . now," Elena said, flipping a switch.

A brilliant bolt of manmade lightning arced from the Tesla coil's wand to Dr. Y's raised, gloved hand.

Jack took an inadvertent step back.

"Holy shock therapy, Batman," Maribeth whispered.

The bolt danced from the end of the wand to the end of Dr. Y's fingers, until he lowered his hand into the water. Then, ever shifting, the manufactured lightning appeared to shoot through his head and into the pool.

Intellectually, Jack knew what was happening. The metal and the salt water were distributing the charge, with the cable as a backup. But it still made him want to jump into a car or some other structure to avoid getting struck. He'd had close calls with tornadoes, but lightning made him truly nervous when he chased storms. You never knew when it was going to hit you until your hair was standing on end and it was too late.

Dr. Y raised his hand, and the bolt again attached itself to the glove before Elena switched it off.

There was a collective exhale from the audience, the release of held breaths.

"I'm not sure if we should applaud, but that was off the chain," Jack said.

"Off the chain *mail*," Maribeth quipped.

"Thank you, my dears," said Dr. Y, who walked up the pool's sloping concrete beach while removing his glove and headgear. "I wanted you to know how intimately I view the subject of lightning. It is my obsession. It's why I've called you here. Now, enjoy the drinks — my specialty, you know. I'm going to change, and then we'll talk."

Dripping and resembling a bipedal sea lion, their host padded down a sidewalk that curved along the house toward another unseen entrance, and Jack and Maribeth wandered over to the Tesla coil. Jack held up his mug and clinked it against hers, admiring her eyes in the light of the torches.

"Here's to insane employers," he said.

She raised one eyebrow and took a sip through her straw. "Give him a chance," she said. "He's spent a fortune on a research plane. I know, because I've been training to fly it for months. I have a feeling you might find this fun."

"I suppose you're not going to tell me more."

"I don't know everything yet."

"You know how to survive," he said. "I have a feeling that might come in handy."

"Stop it," she said with a wry half smile. "You're jinxing me."

He watched her walk over to Elena as he took another sip of his drink. Then he wandered back to the tiki bar, where he sat on a stool, had another crab rangoon and observed the women as they talked and joked. They must already know each other, he realized. Maribeth had said she'd been training for months.

Colin wheeled a cart laden with food from his secret lair

toward a half-hidden part of the terrace on the other side of
the pool. Jack followed him through the palm trees and saw,
lit by more tiki torches, a round wooden table adorned with a
tropical-print tablecloth and place settings for four. There
were candles, flowers and, thanks to Colin's ministrations,
bowls of colorful salads, vegetables and rolls. "The kebabs will
be out shortly," Colin said to Jack, vanishing again with the
cart.

"Dinner is nearly ready," came Dr. Y's voice down the
walkway. "Come along, ladies, come along. Ah, Dr. Andreas,
you've found the dining room," he said as he stepped into the
clearing, flashing those tiny teeth again. He wore a different
Hawaiian shirt, long shorts and sandals and carried a Mai Tai.

"You can call me Jack."

"Yes, I *could*," said Dr. Y, sounding doubtful. The women
appeared in the clearing, and Jack eyed Maribeth as she sat
opposite him, with Elena between them. "I suppose you may
wonder why I go by Dr. Y," the scientist said to Jack, "and it's
not a play on 'Doctor Who,' though that is one of my favorite
shows."

"It has crossed my mind," Jack said.

"It's my rather fanciful name," said Dr. Y, taking his seat.
"Percival Yzaguirre." A dim bell rang in Jack's brain; he'd seen
the name increasingly mentioned in articles about energy,
technology and large fortunes. "A mother from England," Dr.
Y continued, "where I received some of my early education,
and a father whose father was from Mexico. They met here.
The great Melting Pot of outlandish names. I certainly didn't
wish to be known as Dr. P."

"Maybe if you were a urologist," said Maribeth.

"Ha!" said Dr. Y. "Perhaps, my dear. But I'm not that kind
of doctor. Physics is my game. I started with NASA — I knew

your father briefly at Goddard when I was just out of school."
He nodded toward Jack. "A brilliant fellow. Retired now, yes? I
trust you have his genes."

Jack was taken aback by the mention of his father and even
more so by the comparison. He didn't like to think of himself
as anything like the man he barely spoke to, the volatile alco-
holic he still blamed for the wreck that killed his mother so
many years before.

With effort, Jack kept his reply neutral. "I'm no geneticist.
Meteorology is my game," he said, gently mimicking Dr. Y.

"Ho ho! Yes, indeed. Point taken," said their host. "Well,
my dears — ah, here's Colin with the kebabs — I've brought
you here to discuss a research project that I plan to launch
this spring in Tornado Alley. As you know, I'm fascinated by
lightning, and to that end, I have used my own money to have
a slightly used A-10 Warthog expertly refitted to conduct
lightning research. The one they also call the Thunderbolt. If
the National Science Foundation can have one, why not me?"
His eyes twinkled as Colin served up the food. "I am especially concerned with upward lightning. You know a bit about
this, Dr. Andreas?"

"Lightning produced by tall objects. Essentially, lightning
that shoots up rather than down."

"Indeed, and here's the rub — we still know so little about
it," Dr. Y said.

"But lightning hits tall objects, right?" Maribeth asked.

"Yes," said Dr. Y, "but tall objects also can produce upward
lightning when there's a strike nearby. I happen to care about
this very interesting area of research not just because I am
fascinated by lightning, but because I have a considerable
investment in wind energy. In our future. Wind produces
almost ten percent of our energy now, but it could be so much

more. The largest of these wind farms holds hundreds of turbines, and wind turbines generate far more of this sort of lightning than anyone has anticipated. Perhaps ten to a hundred times more attachments than we thought."

"Attachments?" Elena asked.

"Points of attachment are, essentially, where the lightning hits," Dr. Y said. "The damage can be significant."

"Because of the blades?" Jack said.

"Yes, in part," answered Dr. Y. "How do you get adequate lightning protection on spinning blades? But the frequency is also a concern, because these towers are generating upward lightning, not just receiving downward strikes. And there are even more questions. What kinds of chemicals are all these lightning strikes producing? Could they be hazardous? How are trace gases transported by the storm, and what are the effects? What about lightning that fires from tall buildings in cities? What sort of additional dangers can it pose?"

"And I'll be flying into it," Maribeth said.

"You'll be flying into the storm, but you'll be protected from lightning strikes," Dr. Y said.

"You'll have my tin foil hat ready by then, I'm sure," she said.

"Ha! Of course, my dear," he said with a smile. "Your plane may trigger lightning, but what it will do is study the bipolar nature of lightning bolts and a little chemistry with sensors and cameras. A thoroughly documented bipolar strike initiated by the airplane would be very desirable. For so long, the discussion has been of positive bolts and negative bolts. But what we're coming to realize is that lightning has positive and negative ends. And, of course, we also want to photograph upward bolts with high-speed cameras."

"You don't want me in the plane, do you?" Jack asked.

"Oh, no," Dr. Y said. "That's a one-woman job. I need someone to run our mobile research on the ground. Chase the storms. I hear you have a bit of a knack for that."

If only he knew, Jack thought. "Tell me more."

"The trick will be catching the storms in my defined areas of research," said Dr. Y. "We have free rein to operate in two main areas in Kansas and Nebraska where there are wind farms. I'll have radar and instruments in each to measure various criteria and map the lightning in three dimensions. When storms are in those areas, we'll operate the plane as well. This is my highest area of interest. However, on days when the storms are elsewhere, we can do mobile lightning research and photography. If you're available, we'll spend the next two weeks here going over my plans. Are you available, Dr. Andreas?"

"Definitely available," Jack said as he glanced at Maribeth and caught her eye. Amusement danced across her face before she looked away.

"Excellent! I have a team of technicians and engineers working on the sensors and cameras," said Dr. Y. "Let me go over some of what we're looking for . . . "

Jack heard the physicist but kept watching Maribeth as she listened to Dr. Y. The firelight of the torches lit the pleasing angles of her face, and her gray eyes held a blaze of excitement as she absorbed the details of the research. A most unusual storm-chasing partner. This, Jack thought, is going to be an interesting spring.

AURELIUS ZANE KNEW his career was in the toilet when he saw the vehicle he'd have to drive for the new TV show.

Sure, he'd snagged the drone tornado footage he'd wanted for his last epic documentary, but it came at a great cost, and though his debts were not as titanic as once they were, the credit card bills kept coming. And no one really gave a damn about his old show after they saw the incredible human tornado probe flown by his now-co-host, Brad Treat, in the documentary miniseries produced last year by Aurelius's former paramour.

"I just want you to know I'm slumming between gigs," Brad had said when they'd met up for the first phase of *Zany Weddings* on the west coast, "and I'm getting paid twice as much as you are."

Sure, the show was named *Zany Weddings* to play on Aurelius's surname, and to try to separate itself from the other nutty nuptials crowding the cable networks, but the production company thought snagging Brad was a real coup. And so the star, Aurelius Zane, had become the co-star.

Aurelius fumed, but he'd made a gamble and lost, and this might be his one chance to resurrect his career as Adventurer Deluxe. As he meandered into his late thirties, he'd been wondering why he did it at all. Was it the thrill? The fame? He'd started to realize it wasn't so much about the grandeur of nature. The prospect of facing the austere plains of Tornado Alley again was almost painful, no matter how many twisters they might see. Especially in this vehicle.

The silver *Zany Weddings* production van was OK. It followed the hosts around in their quests to get couples married in crazy situations — on top of a volcano, whitewater rafting, diving on a wreck, jumping out of a plane, or in the lion enclosure at a down-and-out zoo. But the company wanted the transitional shots to look good, so it had wrapped the large, white SUV driven by Aurelius and Brad in such a way that it resembled a wedding cake, especially with the highly decorated layers they'd added on top. At the summit was a small sculpture of a bride and groom in hiking gear, as if they'd just climbed the mountain of a car. "ZANY *Weddings"* was emblazoned on the sides in a mix of brash capitals and elegant script. The cake car was even more obnoxious than the proliferating fleet of storm-chaser tanks on the road.

Aurelius had tried to explain to the producers that getting a couple married in front of a tornado wasn't as simple as scheduling a weekend shoot. They would have to find the tornado first. The company, which saw this episode as the one that would clinch ratings, agreed to put a few weeks into it, provided the crew could pick up one or two weddings in between. There was a couple who wanted to get married while riding an angry bull in a rodeo in Texas and another who wanted a pagan rockabilly wedding at Carhenge in Nebraska. There would be a lot of driving.

Fortunately, Aurelius's colleagues had driven the wedding cake car and production van out from L.A. to Oklahoma City, and Aurelius had flown in after two weeks off — mandatory while Brad hosted a science show on a sea voyage to Antarctica.

After a night in a modest chain hotel, Aurelius drove the cake car to Will Rogers Airport on a sunny, chilly May morning to pick up his co-host, the crew van close behind. Most brides chose spring for its pleasant weather, but this was also prime time for tornadoes. For their bride, Aurelius hoped the skies would produce the latter.

"It's great to see you again," he said as he helped Brad load his bags into the SUV, but his tone said anything but. "How was your flight?"

"There were many flights to get here from Argentina, but

mostly I sat in first class, so I can't complain," Brad said. "Besides, flight attendants really like me."

"Your shirt *is* a conversation piece. Have you changed it in the last two weeks?" Brad had taken to wearing T-shirts everywhere that said "I fly into tornadoes." Usually, it evoked a reaction along the lines of, "Hey, you're *that guy!*" followed by women squealing and men buying him beer.

"I had to wear coats in Antarctica, genius," Brad said in his nasal tone. "And I have several of these shirts."

Aurelius knew that fact all too well. Brad's wardrobe was driving him crazy. Aurelius opted for a long, double-breasted black jacket, worn open over button-up shirts. Combined with his floppy, dirty-blond hair, it gave him what he saw as a touch of drama. The men were physical opposites. Aurelius was fair and brawny; Brad, with his dark buzz cut, was tall and scrawny.

"We're supposed to head out directly and pick up our couple," Aurelius said as they got into the cake car. "The cameras are on."

"Of course they are," Brad said, looking around the car's cabin and noting the colony of electronic eyes rigged to record their every move. He shifted his body almost imperceptibly, getting into broadcast attitude.

Aurelius swallowed his irritation and did the same as he drove them out of the airport, the crew van close behind. He reached over and tapped the laptop computer mounted between the seats to be sure their GPS navigation was on. Then he nodded toward the one camera that streamed a wide-angle view back to the production van so that his co-producer, a reliable young woman named Danni, could monitor the action.

"The couple are Polly Ann and Tyler," he said loudly

enough for the cameras. "They already live together, but this is a first wedding for both of them."

"That's unusual."

"At least on our show," Aurelius said, recalling the grocery clerk who'd been married four times already when she stepped into the lion's pen with her true love and hair stylist. It had been the clerk's, and their show's, first lesbian wedding. "Also unusual, as you know, is that this wedding won't be held in a set place. The couple have a license for every state in Tornado Alley, because we'll have to get it done wherever we find a tornado. And we can't bring a whole wedding party with us."

"Just the essentials," Brad said. "Our crew will act as witnesses, and the reception will be spontaneous. Who's going to marry them?"

"They're marrying each other, of course."

"Ha ha," Brad said, attempting to act as if he were amused and failing. "Who's administering the vows?"

"I am," Aurelius said. "I've passed a very difficult five-question quiz online and become an officiant in the Digital Church of the Light-Emitting Deity. I'm fully authorized to marry anyone."

"The Church of the L.E.D.?"

"It's one of the top twenty Internet churches," Aurelius said.

"Congratulations," Brad said.

"I do whatever is necessary to accomplish my goal, whether it's climbing over hot lava or chasing a typhoon —"

"Just don't fly into a tornado, OK?" Brad said. "That's my job."

Aurelius gave him a sidelong glance as they headed west

and noted with annoyance Brad's wicked smile. "Why don't you tell me more about what that was like?" he prodded.

"This show is about making people's extreme wedding wishes come true," Brad said. "Let's stick to the story of Polly Ann and Tyler."

For someone who was so into trumpeting his feat, Brad sure didn't like to discuss the details, thought Aurelius.

They talked about the couple's obsession with severe weather for the cameras, then lapsed into uncomfortable silence for the last thirty minutes of the trip. Several miles off the Interstate, well west of Oklahoma City, they rolled up and down low hills, trying to follow GPS navigation to the couple's home.

"This looks less than promising," Brad said as they passed a dilapidated trailer park.

"We aren't here to judge," Aurelius said, thinking the trailers were at least roomier than his Pasadena apartment. "Anyway, we have another turn before we get there."

"Where is this place?" came Danni's voice over the CB radio. Aurelius wasn't unhappy to have her as his fellow field producer. She was efficient and made it easier for him to handle his co-star duties. At least he was a producer, even if his star had been outshined. He needed the money.

"Somewhere past these cows, I think," Aurelius said into the radio as they made the turn. A cluster of brown cows stood watching them from behind a fence, swishing their tails. They stared hard at the confectionery car, looking as if they might enjoy a slice of wedding cake.

"Kinda creepy," Brad said.

"You can't fly into a tornado and then be scared of cows," said Aurelius.

"Don't be ridiculous," Brad said, less than convincing.

Aurelius made a mental note of Brad's bovine fears as they came upon the end of a driveway at the bottom of a hill. There was a barn-shaped mailbox and no immediate sign of a house.

"We turn here," Aurelius said into the radio.

The two vehicles climbed the driveway, which curved around the hill, and they found themselves facing a circular parking area next to garage doors that were built right into the slope. A long row of shallow windows peeked out of the hill above the garage, and bits of structure stuck out of the grassy ground. There was modest landscaping, too — a couple of trees and patches of flowers. A gravel walkway of pale yellow river rock extended from the parking area and up to a door built into the side of the hill.

"Is this a Hobbit couple?" Aurelius asked.

"What?" asked Brad.

"Underground house. Don't you ever see movies? Read books?"

"I've been busy," Brad said pointedly.

They all disembarked. Danni and shaggy Scooter carried cameras, and the black-clad, fortysomething audio man, who in his other life was a DJ known as Vinyl, held a microphone boom.

"Time to knock," said Danni, a redhead with a pixie haircut and a flat Illinois accent.

The crew followed Aurelius and Brad up the hill, and they made a big show of rapping the horseshoe doorknocker five times.

A beaming little blonde threw the door open. "Honey, they're here!" she said in a classic Oklahoma twang, and almost instantly, a stocky young man, barely taller than the diminutive Polly Ann, was at her side.

"Well, howdy and welcome!" said Tyler.

"Tyler and Polly Ann, are you ready for your Zany Wedding?" asked Brad. While a lackadaisical host, he seemed to relish saying the big line.

"Hey, you're the badass who rode into that tornado!" Tyler said.

Aurelius sighed in exasperation.

"OK, cut," said Danni. "We've got to do this again with me inside. You kids mind?"

Kids, Aurelius thought. Danni, made even more youthful by her fine features, was barely older than the couple. Hobbits, meet your elf producer. And get ready for a long three weeks.

❧

EVEN IF MARIBETH weren't comfortable flying the A-10, she'd never admit it. Never admit weakness. The Army had taught her that. Or rather, being in the Army as a woman had taught her that. Any hint of weakness could have meant the death of her career, before she decided to leave on her own, that is.

The truth was, she was quite comfortable with the Warthog, though she hadn't flown warplanes for the Air Force. She'd flown helicopters for the Army in Iraq — nothing like this compact, chunky tank-killer.

And then, after she'd learned to love chasing storms in a helicopter as a civilian, the TV station had dumped her. It didn't matter that the accident hadn't been her fault; her bosses just didn't want to crash any more expensive hardware. They'd wished her well and spent the insurance money on another news van.

She loved helicopters, but she had never stopped flying

planes. Fixed-wing aircraft had been her first love as a girl, and flying just about everything had been her second job with her father's company. So when a headhunter came to her dad shortly after the helicopter gig ended, asking if he knew any pilots who could fly a private jet for a corporate bigwig, she decided she might like the travel. It turned out the jet she was hired to fly was Dr. Y's.

"I've been looking at your resume, Ms. Lisbon," he'd told her after a couple of months, visiting her in the cockpit during a runway delay on a foggy San Francisco evening, "and you have some unusual skills."

"If flying is unusual," she said.

"Only if you do it wearing a cape," he joked as he leaned against the cockpit doorway. He made a habit of chatting with his crew. Always informal, he wore one of his vintage Hawaiian shirts, though she knew for a fact he'd just come from a business meeting. Money talks more than clothes, she supposed.

"I'm looking for a pilot used to dealing with unusual circumstances," he continued, "and it seems to me you qualify." She briefly imagined him running a private air force somewhere when he added: "I've managed to acquire a retired warplane for a little weather research project of mine. Have you ever flown an A-10?"

She'd tried not to let him know how excited she was. "I've been around them. I'd need some training, but I'm sure I can do it."

Her quick response might have exceeded her actual confidence, but the mission seemed like just what she needed. She was already burned out from being constantly on call for these smooth, stormless cross-country flights. Except for one jaunt to Hawaii, the travel had been less than exotic. As much as she craved normalcy after her military life, routine bored her, and she found her days too often empty. This mission could fill the chasm. And so she'd been paired up with an instructor and a simulator and spent several intense months preparing for an adventure that was almost a reality.

Now she felt the plane's power ensconce her as she flew over the area where the hills of eastern Kansas started to flatten into the pancakery most people associated with the Land of Oz. The state's elevation increased toward the west, but a driver would mostly see the plain. From her perspective, she could see much more — countless channels, wet and dry streams, carving out the state's meager peaks and valleys.

It wasn't the fastest plane, but it was solid and responsive, especially after the retrofit. The gleaming cockpit had all the technology the original model didn't. This is my office, she thought, hurtling through the air at a modest three hundred fifty miles an hour at ten thousand feet. The altitude meant she didn't have to wear the bulky oxygen mask a fighter pilot might, just a boom mask — essentially, oversize sunglasses with a microphone attached to a helmet, the same kind the Blue Angels stunt pilots used.

She turned to the west, heading back toward Salina and the wind farms beyond. This was a test run, yet another test run, as Dr. Y and the team tried to work out all the problems they'd been having with their experiments. No storms awaited her on the horizon, just isolated, puffy cumulus clouds, tinged with gold as the sun declined, and the brilliant white of cirrus clouds, heralding an approaching front. She spied a sun dog to the right of the sun, a splash of refracted color in the cirrus's ice crystals.

Below her, a ring of six high-speed cameras and wing-mounted instrument pods, holding gadgets from a radiation detector to a current sensor, took the place of weapons, and hundreds of pounds of electronics and servers were mounted in the belly. They were accompanied by ballast to make up for the removal of the A-10's massive gun, which weighed some four thousand pounds when fully loaded, so heavy that the plane's balance depended on it.

The bubble canopy had been hardened with a fine, nearly invisible metal mesh to shed dangers such as lightning and hail, and that meant she couldn't eject as a wartime pilot might. That was OK with her. This seat was a lot more comfortable, and she had no plans to eject. The only enemy firing at her plane's armored skin would be Mother Nature.

The one thing about the Warthog that made her cautious — not nervous, she reasoned, cautious — was the turbofan engines. They could easily suck in hailstones, and that would be a bad thing. The plane could survive a lightning strike, she reasoned, but perhaps not a hail barrage. She didn't plan to test its hail endurance, either. It's all about controlling the input, she thought. Control your environment, and you control your destiny.

On the panel, a mounted tablet computer indicated a video call from Maribeth's teammates on the ground. Linked to the plane's newly installed satellite Internet connection, the tablet let them circumvent the more formal radio communications she used with the airfield. The satellite link also let them transmit real-time sensor data to the ground, but not the data-hogging video they would be shooting.

Maribeth tapped the screen. "Go ahead," she responded through the microphone in her helmet as Dr. Y appeared.

"How's it going up there, Ms. Lisbon?" asked Dr. Y, who appeared to be in his office at the hangar, its walls covered with lightning photographs. He wasn't usually on the horn. She wondered what was wrong now.

"Nominal so far. You?"

"I'll have Fred explain," he said.

A younger face framed by shaggy, rusty hair and a beard pushed into the frame, his voice faster, Southern and much more frustrated. "The starboard high-speed camera's pictures are fucked up again," Fred said. "Looks like they were painted by a blind man."

"I thought Monet did OK," Maribeth responded.

"It's a goddamn mess, but we'll fix it," said Fred, vanishing off-screen.

"Oh, that boy's language," said Dr. Y, back on camera. "We're going to have to take it apart again. It's another delay, I'm afraid. At least a day."

"Well, we don't have Jack yet, do we?" she asked.

"He's coming in time for tomorrow's severe weather, which, unfortunately, my airborne cameras will miss. My engineers and I are going to work on the bad one and fine-tune the other gear while Jack and Fred take the van out and give those ground instruments a whirl. Perhaps you should go with them, my dear. They'll need a woman's gentle hand."

"You mean you want her to kick our asses into gear," she heard Fred saying in the background.

"Whatever gets us there," Dr. Y said with a smile. "Come back to us, Ms. Lisbon."

"I live to serve," Maribeth said. And gently kick ass, she thought, whenever required. As the call ended, she took a moment to savor the waning flight, the peace above the fray. Chasing storms in a vehicle would be frustrating, she thought as she banked around, leaving the setting sun behind. There was no direct flight to a storm on the ground, just roads that never went where you wanted them to go. And Jack would be in charge.

Jack had intrigued her during the two weeks of briefings in Florida. On the surface, he was absolutely the opposite of men she thought she liked, or should like. He was clearly accustomed to having women fall all over him; she'd seen it when the team had gone out to dinner one night by the river, when servers and random women made a point of showing him how available they were. He deftly and politely ignored them without ever losing the thread of his conversation with her. When it came to the work, he was commanding in everything that had to do with weather, but she had to admit that his authoritative approach seemed justified: He really *did* know just about everything about weather. She'd started out wondering if he was like those men she'd met in the service who wouldn't hesitate to steamroll you to get their way. But she came to realize he offered his expertise only when it was required; otherwise, he stepped back and let the mission proceed, listening to everyone else along the way.

It was confusing to see him again, to rethink her first impression, after her brief encounter with him after the crash last year. He'd seemed so kind then, a calming voice in an anxious moment, but that assessment was colored by the fact that she'd just narrowly escaped death. In Florida, he'd seemed different, on his own beam, wrapped up in the technical aspects of their project, at least at first. And then she realized he was paying a lot of attention to her.

It dawned on her that her curiosity about him, which, she was sure, was both innocent and well-hidden, could endanger their working relationship. So she put up her walls again fast.

She was unaccustomed to men knocking on her door. They saw she was all business; there was usually a reason for that. Like this time. She was a pro, and she wanted to do a professional job. But as professional as she was in everything, she was an amateur with someone like Jack, and she sensed he was anything but amateur when it came to women. All of her alarms went off when he was around, along with a faint and not altogether unpleasant buzzing in her nerves.

Up here, such personal discomfiture never seemed to matter. She was flying. She was part of something infinite and perfect. She pulled her microphone aside and popped a cinnamon mint from the tin she kept in one of her pockets. In the coral-gray light of fading day, she reluctantly said goodbye to the sky and headed back toward the airport.

JACK PULLED the rumbling Volare up next to the hangar and tried to resist the urge to get out and kick it. The aging wagon had broken down in Mississippi, and it had taken a day to get the new starter, if new was the proper word. The part had to be overnighted from a Kentucky junkyard. Jack didn't care about antique cars beyond a distant admiration, and his was far from collectible. But for all its ugly angles, it had been remarkably reliable, and that's all he wanted. It had to break down just as he was trying to haul ass from Florida to the Alley to chase the first big storm system of the season.

He'd ended up driving all night to get to the rendezvous in Salina, knowing that he'd probably end up driving a few more hours to today's target, which he put in northern Oklahoma. At least they didn't have to stay among the wind farms today.

Dr. Y's email said they had to give the van's cameras a work-out, and that was exactly what he planned to do. He'd get their lightning, as long as it was as close to the tornadoes as possible.

Jack grabbed his backpack, exited the car and stretched. His driving muscles were out of shape. It was all that outdoor time in Florida, walking, bicycling. The tedium of the drive made him acutely miss his forsaken cigarettes, but without them, he knew he felt better than he had in a long time. At least physically. Mentally, he wasn't so sure. He missed the simplicity of his youth, his grad-school years, pursuing storms and women, usually in that order. Now his chases were complicated by the need to make a living, and his liaisons were complicated by a concern that he might actually feel something, after the painful demise of an intense affair last year. In Florida, he'd managed to quell most of his qualms with the salve offered by the occasional beach bar girl. He didn't want to acknowledge that, increasingly, they bored him.

It was time to simplify again, he told himself. Simplify. Chase. Seek and ye shall find. It was May, spring, warm, and full of clouds and promise. And he was already so sleep-deprived, it felt as if he'd been chasing for a month. He felt wrung out and wrinkled, and he was way past needing a shave. He shook his head, trying to clear his mind as he walked toward the large building, with its white metal walls and brick trim.

"Dr. Andreas!" Dr. Y called out, hastening toward him from the wide-open doors of the hangar. Even here, he wore a Hawaiian shirt. "Welcome! You know how to cut it to a sliver, don't you?"

"Car broke down," said Jack, shaking Dr. Y's hand and

following him into the vast, echoing space of the hangar. Just inside the doors, Jack stopped, halted by the sight of the A-10 Warthog at its center, a gleaming weather research plane with a history of blowing up tanks. Painted on its nose were eyes narrowed to angry slits and an open mouth full of teeth, but the massive gun those teeth would normally clench had been replaced by an instrument pod. Five guys and a woman in blue jumpsuits were working on the plane's guts, with parts and gizmos laid out all over drop cloths and carts on the floor. The tinny tune of a country-pop song complemented the sounds of their clanking tools and echoing voices.

On one wall was a row of lockers and doors. Jack spied the lightning research van parked in an opposite corner, a white whale of a chase vehicle.

"Is the van ready?" he asked.

"Fred's got it as ready as it can be," said Dr. Y. "He's going with you, of course, and Ms. Lisbon will be riding along, as well."

"Maribeth?" Jack was simultaneously pleased and concerned. "You're still fixing the plane?"

"The plane is fine. It's the cameras. Or if it's not the cameras, it's one of the other sensors. I want it all working when we have storms in the target area. Are you quite all right?"

Jack had put a hand over his eyes as a wave of fatigue swept over him, complemented by a touch of dizziness and nausea. "Coffee," was all he said.

"You'll find the lounge well-equipped. We even have espresso."

"Even better." Jack looked forward to caffeine, followed, he hoped, by tornadoes. He trailed the physicist to a door off the main bay.

The lounge was a comfortable room whose door kept out the noise of the hangar. In here, a couch and a few comfy chairs shared space with a desk, a refrigerator, a vintage Operation Thunder pinball machine, and a coffee table. A television mounted to the wall showed a muted meteorologist in a sober suit pointing out the areas of highest risk for storms. Under the TV was a table laden with a deluxe coffee-brewing robot, a platter of hearty sandwiches, a bowl of fruit and half-empty boxes of doughnuts.

"Will you marry me?" Jack joked as he put down his bag.

"Ha ha! I'm not the marrying kind," said Dr. Y, making his way through to his office, one of two attached to the lounge.

"Neither am I," Jack said as the door closed behind Dr. Y, though he suspected they were avoiding different destinies. He loaded the espresso grounds into the machine and pressed a button to get his high-test brew before grabbing a ham sandwich and collapsing into the desk chair.

He'd quaffed the espresso and half the sandwich when the door to the hangar opened and Maribeth stepped through it, dressed in jeans and a flattering stone-green blouse that shifted her gray eyes to jade. It was unbuttoned just enough to reveal a hint of pale skin curving down toward an alluring valley. He tried to focus on her eyes so he wouldn't get caught admiring the rest of her. He'd done a lot of that in Florida, sidelong glances and surreptitious scans, and he'd almost memorized her. She'd been completely immersed in the work, with rare flashes of humor, though he thought he'd spied her regarding him with curious stares when she thought he wasn't looking. He'd worked hard to bring her out, and the less she said, the more he felt he understood her. Her obsessiveness was both intriguing and familiar, and he wanted to get inside it. Tap that drive.

"I was wondering when you'd get here," she said, looking a little tense.

"We'll have time to get to the target area. I need to review data one more time." He took another bite and reached into his backpack for his laptop, setting it on the desk and powering it on.

"We have a lot to test today."

"Fear not," Jack said mildly. "It shouldn't be an early show."

A shadow of annoyance crossed her face before she assumed her usual composure and sat in a comfy chair across the room. "Fine," she said. "Sorry. I think Fred has infected me."

"He can't be as hyper in person as he is on Skype."

"Oh, more," she said, finally smiling.

"Sandwich?" he gestured to the platter.

"I had breakfast." She glanced at the hands of the wall clock, which said 11:10 a.m. "Doesn't feel like lunchtime yet."

"Eat while you can. Every chaser knows that. Or you'll have to survive on roller food." Though Jack had to acknowledge that the occasional gas-station taquito made him happy. Snacks of last resort confirmed that he really was on the road, his favorite place to be.

"I've never actually chased storms on the ground, you know," Maribeth said. "It was always in a helicopter."

"Really?" Jack felt a little rush of delight as he swallowed the last bit of the sandwich and looked over the growing tornado possibilities displayed on his screen.

"Chasing from the sky is way cooler," Maribeth said with authority.

"Oh, no," he said, turning his gaze to her, observing her surety. He made a mischievous determination to crack it. "You don't get it. You can't until you're breathing in the dust of the inflow. You're practically a chase virgin."

"Bullshit. I've seen dozens of tornadoes. Maybe hundreds."

He smiled at her wrinkled brow and slight frown. "Not like this," he said. "This is going to be fun."

THE SPORT-UTILITY WEDDING cake rolled north on U.S. 183 toward the target area with cameraman Scooter in the back, the future bride and groom in the second row of seats and the television tornado chasers up front, letting the young couple do most of the talking. Brad sat sideways in the passenger seat and watched them, nodding, as Aurelius drove and eyed the scene in the rearview mirror.

"Oh, I am such a fan of yours, Mr. Treat," said Polly Ann, looking suitably adorable in flowered shorts and a low-cut yellow blouse that matched her blond locks.

"Call me Brad."

"I have watched every single episode of your storm show with the Bubble," she gushed.

"Dozens of times," said fiancé Tyler.

Polly Ann smacked him playfully on the shoulder. He winced. "Oh, you watched it with me," she said before turning back to Brad. "As soon as I heard you were hosting *Zany Weddings*, I was like, I just have to be on that show and meet you! So that's when I proposed to Tyler."

"I do like a woman who knows her own mind," Brad said. "Tyler's a lucky man."

"Oh, stop," Polly Ann lilted in that Oklahoma twang. "But yes, he is. I mean, I'm a lucky girl. We both love storms so much."

"So much that we built our bunker home so we could hide from them," Tyler said, though they'd covered this ground the day before with their TV tour of the house. "Polly Ann's terrified we're gonna get hit."

"Now, that's not totally true," she replied, "but it is true my mama and daddy's house got destroyed in Moore, and I see no reason not to be safe when we can be. But because of you, because of what you went through for science, I would face any fear, Mr. Treat. Brad, I mean."

Aurelius glanced at Brad, who wore a satisfied smile, and felt a tickle of discomfort. In the rearview mirror, Tyler's expression reflected his own. He hoped the cameras weren't picking it up, too — the faint scent of groupie.

"We're starting to get some nice cumulus clouds now," Aurelius said, trying to change the subject. "We're getting closer to the target area."

"You can tell from all the chasers," Brad said.

It was true. Already, they'd been passed by a handful of cars sporting antennas and decals, and they'd seen more than a few chasers hanging out in small towns along their route. Those who had noticed the *Zany Weddings* vehicle — and who hadn't? — could be seen laughing. The increasing numbers of chasers sporting extreme team names and logos suggested that recent deaths and media lamentations would have little effect on how they chased. After all, Aurelius was still willing to drive into the worst of it, if it meant his show would be better, and no one was going to tell him any different.

"What's all this?" Brad asked as they approached the water tower that rose above Seiling, Oklahoma. Across the street was a gas station lot clogged with chase cars and chasers, many of them milling around a boxy truck wrapped with psychedelic graphics showing storm clouds, lightning and a rainbow, with winged sandwiches flying through a cerulean sky over fields of French fries. It had a big, open service window in the side. Aurelius slowed to see signs on the truck advertising sandwiches, fried chicken, soup and wraps under the words "Chuck's Wagon."

"Oh, I've heard of that!" Polly Ann said from the back. "It's a food truck! It's been traveling all over, but the owner was interviewed on the local TV and said he's going to be catering to storm chasers all season."

"No kidding," said Aurelius.

"Brilliant," Brad said. "I'm hungry, and we need gas. Let's stop."

"Good idea," Aurelius said, wondering if those words would ever pass his lips again where Brad was concerned. The food truck was a good idea, too. Chasers were always starving, always hanging out in places where they were unlikely to get a decent meal, and almost always finished their chases long after most restaurants had closed. He couldn't imagine anything more dull than playing chef to the chasers and missing the storms, but perhaps he could use the owner for a bit of decent television.

"Danni, we want to stop and check out the food truck," he said on the radio.

"We were just talking about that," she replied. "I saw a YouTube video on this guy. He's a trip."

"But can he cook?" Aurelius asked no one in particular.

He parked the wedding cake under the overhang and started fueling. The van found a spot elsewhere and discharged the rest of the crew, which split to film the chasers, chase cars, Tyler and Polly Ann. Some chasers wandered toward the cake car, while a number of them recognized Brad and gathered around him, shaking his hand. *Bubble. Bubble.*

The word floated on the air, bouncing up through their inquiries and conversations. *Everyone* knew about the Bubble and Brad's daring flight into a tornado. Toil and trouble, Aurelius thought, feeling strangely anonymous; Aurelius, who'd starred in TV adventure shows before Brad knew how to shave. He concluded his transaction, straightened his jacket, ran a hand through his hair and made his way through the crowd to the food truck.

The last couple of chasers were leaving the window with their sandwiches and drinks and gave him a nod as they walked by. While the unseen proprietor lingered in the darkness in the depths of the truck, Aurelius looked it over. Condiments sat on the ledge, including exotic hot sauces, sea salts and honey, next to a mottled-blue-glazed ceramic cup stuffed with business cards. He pulled one out. The bright white, heavy cardstock felt smooth under his fingers. On one side, there was a quote in an elegant serif type attributed to Rumi: "This is love: to fly toward a secret sky, to cause a hundred veils to fall each moment. First to let go of life. Finally, to take a step without feet."

Aurelius idly wondered if this was the best message for someone selling food. The other side of the card had the words "Chuck's Wagon" and a square QR code that, one assumed, would lead to a website. No name. He pocketed the card.

"Are you Chuck?" he called to the figure in the shadows, getting impatient even at the momentary wait.

There was movement and, in a trice, a wiry man of medium height appeared at the window. His tanned face was creased from what looked like decades in the sun, though his age was indeterminate; his hair was long and gray, a disorderly array of waves, braids and dreadlocks. His eyes were wildly blue, almost clear, the irises lined with a thin dark edge, the pupils points of burning coal. His T-shirt was covered with clouds, and a strange tattoo that looked like a red tree branch crawled down his right arm.

"Please," the cook said in a textured, spirited voice. "I am Charles. There is no Chuck here."

"Well, I just assumed," Aurelius said.

"When you assume, you spit in the face of possibility," said Charles.

"I thought you just made an Ass out of U and Me."

"That, too. What do you seek, my friend? For I do not think you are hungry for fried chicken."

"Well, maybe a sandwich," said Aurelius, wondering what Chuck, er, Charles was getting at and perturbed by his presumptuous hippieness. "How much?"

"Everything has a price," Charles said with a smile that showed numerous teeth. "Sometimes we pay for what we think we want with our happiness. But you can buy a little happiness with my food. There's the menu." He made a sweeping gesture that ended with him pointing to a blackboard that listed the specials of day, interspersed with chalk drawings of lightning bolts.

"Um," Aurelius said, trying to make sense of the cook's pitch, "I'll take the turkey cranberry wrap." He handed the money to the serenely smiling Charles.

"Get anything good?" came a voice at his ear as Charles turned away to minister to the sandwich. It was Danni, camera in hand.

"I hope so," said Aurelius. "I'm really not sure."

"Chuck?" Danni called out as the truck's proprietor popped up again holding a wrap and homemade potato chips in an open-faced cardboard box.

"Charles, please, my dear. Here you go, young man," he said, handing the food to Aurelius and holding him still with that transparent gaze. "I will see you again. You are a seeker, and I know how to find things."

"All chasers are seekers," Aurelius said, shaking him off, his self-possession returning.

"Yes, but few of them ever know what they've found," said Charles with a little bow. "Now, mademoiselle, how may I assist you?"

"Charles, I'd like to do a little interview with you for our show," Danni said.

"Anything to spread the word," said the cook as Aurelius escaped around the corner, out of sight of Charles but still within earshot.

"Can you tell me your last name and spell it for me?" she asked.

"Names are powerful things, so all I can give you is my legal name. It's Smith. Really, you can look it up," he said. "I am widely licensed to operate this traveling shrine to the spirit of the sky."

Peeking around the corner, Aurelius watched Danni smile as she held the camera in Charles's face. "Tell me how you came to open your food truck, Mr. Smith."

"I was once like many of you, chasing after the storm, trying to find the tornado. Because, in my youth, the storm found me. It cleaved me. It opened me to the possibilities of the universe. It sent me on a journey, a journey that took me through many experiences, many lives, and long before all your technology, many chases, many dreams."

Many drugs, Aurelius thought.

"And so," Charles continued, "I found the storms, and I found much more. More than I could share, more than one cloud, one storm, one moment. One day, as I contemplated how to reach into the hearts of those who had followed in my footsteps, who had filled the roads with their cars and their noise, I realized I had a way. I would feed them. I would feed their souls. I would take my chuck wagon on the road and feed these pioneers, and perhaps lead some of them to the promised land."

Danni shifted the camera, and Aurelius saw her step back and adjust the zoom. "Do you consider yourself religious, Mr. Smith?"

"Religion is only the icing on a very large cake. Do you consider yourself a cake seller, mademoiselle?"

He must have gestured to their ridiculous vehicle, because Danni looked over her shoulder at it and laughed. "I can't even bake a cupcake, Mr. Smith. I hope we see you again on the road."

"Oh, I can guarantee it. I am destined to see again your friend hiding around the corner. He has questions for me."

Aurelius was embarrassed. How did Charles know? And why had Aurelius hung around, anyway? He didn't have any questions. He just had a goal. To get this show on the road, to get some thrill-seekers married, and to make it good enough so he could get his career back on track. All without throttling Brad. He stomped off toward his co-host, who was still surrounded by chasers, and didn't look back at the truck.

"We're going," Aurelius shouted at him on the way to the cake car.

"But I didn't get any food."

"Eat cake," Aurelius said, getting in the driver's side and slamming the door behind him. He didn't know why he felt so ruffled. He looked down at the box of food, still untouched in his hands, and set it on his lap so he could pull the paper off the wrap. He took a bite and felt, just for a moment, his whole body relax into the taste of turkey and cranberry and sprouts and magical aioli. It was *really* good.

❜

ONCE AGAIN, Jack was on the road, chasing storms in a boxy white van, but this one represented a new species of the many research vehicles that had carried him into the path of supercells. This one, like the others, had an anemometer and other conventional weather instruments mounted to the roof, but it also had an electric field meter, a digital oscilloscope, and light sensors that would trigger the ultra-high-speed camera.

Inside the back, there was barely enough room for two people to work around the computers and gear, but Fred, the chief engineer, had insisted on giving him a tour before they left the hangar.

"You did read the documentation?" Fred had asked him.

"I read it, but there were a lot of pages. I'm more of a hands-on guy," Jack had responded. He'd studied the camera in depth during his time in Florida, but it was more fun to make Fred crazy.

"Bullshit, *Dr.* Andreas," Fred said, saturating "Dr." with sarcasm and delineating each syllable of Jack's last name, *An-DRAY-us*. "What the fuck do you think you're doing here? A scientist doesn't go into an experiment half-cocked."

"I try to go into every situation full-cocked," Jack said with an innocent expression. He yawned. This briefing was more than his lunchtime caffeination could support.

"Wake up and pay attention."

"I thought Southern guys talked slow."

"Do you think I'm slow? Don't answer that," Fred warned.

"Where'd you get that accent, anyway?"

"Where I come from, it's not an *accent*. It's the way people talk. North Carolina. Asheville."

"The mountains. Nice. What brings you to the prairie?"

"Work, you idiot. I thought you were from Virginia. But you sound suspiciously like a Yankee."

"Northern Virginia," Jack admitted. "And it's been a long time."

"Ah, the soulless suburban wastelands. That explains a lot. Now, this camera shoots high-def at 25,000 frames per second," Fred said, not missing a beat. He pointed to the floor of the van, where a boxy gadget was mounted on a two-foot-square metal platform. Covering the camera was a clear dome that reminded Jack of an astronaut's helmet in an old B-movie, or a delicate Victorian bell jar meant to display flowers and butterflies.

"That's going to be fun in a hailstorm," Jack noted.

"It's impact-resistant, dingleberry. So we'll slide open this panel" — Fred reached up to the ceiling and pulled aside what would be a sunroof on a less geeky vehicle — "and pop in the platform. I can do it myself, but it's nice to have help," he said, giving Jack a pointed look.

Jack took his cue and helped Fred push the platform with the camera up through the hole and lock it into place with pivoting brackets. A sealed tube brought wires from the dome into a control box inside the van that allowed them to link the camera to the triggering mechanism, adjust its angle of view and see the results on a monitor.

"Isn't it awesome?" Fred said with admiration. "I call it the Ghost."

"Should I ask why?"

"It's cool, Andreas. It needs a cool name. And it makes lightning look completely fucking otherworldly. Now shut up."

Jack had seen high-speed lightning footage before, but at 25,000 frames per second in high definition, the Ghost would slow down each step of a lightning bolt in excruciating detail, stretching the flashes of a few seconds into several minutes, allowing the scientists to read and interpret every nuance as the firebolt danced toward the ground — and toward the sky, as Dr. Y liked to remind them.

"We can't do this while we're moving, I take it," Jack said, already foreseeing halting his tornado chase so they could document the lightning. He had to remember this was work. This was science. He wasn't chasing entirely for pleasure.

"We prefer not to operate it while we're moving, but we can drive with it on if we have to. We'll mostly park to use it, and that will give us a chance to use the other cameras, too." There were five additional specialized cameras, as Jack had already seen, with varying frame rates and purposes. Though they could be taken outside, mostly they'd stay inside, operating from their mounts atop a metal bar. A panel on the right side of the van folded down to create a window that gave the cameras a good view while sheltering them from most of the rain.

Jack's favorite window was on the other side of the van, toward the back. It was a bubble window, another option for a mounted or handheld camera. Jack liked it because, from the outside, it made the vehicle look a little like a 1970s conversion van that might hide crimson shag carpeting, a mobile bar, a leopard-skin bed and a bitchin' stereo system.

Instead, the interior sported un-groovy white metal walls and a black rubber floor. Only a modest logo for Dr. Y's research division — a flask with a lightning bolt in it and a Y coming out the top — decorated the outside of each door.

Now, with their Kansas base far behind them, Maribeth drove the van toward their target in northwest Oklahoma. There, fluffy white cumulus clouds bubbled. They stretched upward and pushed against the cap — the layer of warm air above them — and collapsed, exhausted, not yet able to break through. Jack could identify with their fatigue.

He consulted a laptop computer mounted between the front seats and eyed the shifting dewpoints that denoted the approaching dryline, a likely trigger for the storms he expected. It was a volatile setup, with a strong low moving out of the Panhandle, a lifting front, perfectly directed winds and the Oklahoma air, juicy with Gulf moisture, heating quickly in the afternoon sun.

"This would be a lot faster if we flew," Maribeth said.

"If only you had a helicopter," Jack said.

"The station decided helicopters weren't worth the investment anymore," Maribeth said ruefully. "And Dr. Y won't let me have my plane back."

"Not yet, goddamnit," Fred said from a short bench in the back, the only seat among all the gear, where he consulted another laptop attached to a mount that rose from the floor.

"There, there," Maribeth said with a small smile, "I'm sure they'll fix it sometime before next season."

Fred sputtered with more cursing, and it was clear to Jack that the pilot enjoyed teasing the engineer as much as Jack was starting to enjoy teasing her. Her smile was a rare prize, and he was ready to spend all his quarters for another chance to win the game.

"So you're going to shoot anybody who gets in our way today, right?" Jack asked.

"Are you saying that because I was in the Army or because I'm a Texas girl?"

"Does it matter?"

"In the Army, we carried guns because we had to. In Texas, you just do it on principle."

"So you're packing?" Jack couldn't suppress his surprise.

"Of course not," she said innocently. "We're in Oklahoma." The corner of her mouth lifted, and he wondered if she'd be kidding if this were Texas.

"So, uh, did you fly combat missions in Texas? I mean, Iraq?"

Her dimple disappeared. "I supported combat missions."

"Who'd you support?"

"Infantry."

"How?"

She shot him a look of impatience before turning back to the road. "We started out doing security for the living areas, but the helicopters we flew did better than the Apaches in the desert. We could take off and land in the sand, we could fly with the doors off, we could see better. So our squadron followed the division as it bounced from city to city up to Baghdad. I'd scout for trouble, call in the artillery and the Air Force, walk them in on targets."

He could tell this wasn't her favorite subject, but he was too curious to stop. "Did you do that the whole time?"

"Similar stuff on my second deployment, but more work outside the city, near Tal Afar. The enemy had figured out they could set up a wall of ammunition just to see what they could get. If you flew low, you got hit — so we didn't fly low. We'd provide recon with a video camera."

"Ha," Jack said. "And then you became a helicopter chaser. Still shooting video."

"There's a certain logic to that," Maribeth said.

"So why'd you leave the Army?"

"Are we close to the target area?" she asked, ignoring the question. "Or a town? I could use a rest stop."

"Me, too, goddamnit," Fred said from the back, his drawl-on-speed made more emphatic by the bucket-size travel mug of coffee he carried around. "Do you have a bladder of iron, Andreas?"

"Take it easy, guys. There's got to be a place around here somewhere," Jack said, pulling up the mapping software on the laptop and risking a sidelong glance at Maribeth. Her face was impassive as she drove, closed, as impenetrable as a concrete door on a bunker. You could hide from a tornado behind that face, he thought. "We're almost at Seiling. Stop at the first gas station, and we'll assess."

Maribeth pulled the van into a Shell that already had a half dozen chase vehicles in the parking lot, and while Jack filled the tank, she and Fred went in search of bathrooms. For the third time today, he reached for a cigarette and remembered he didn't smoke anymore. There was something about chasing that brought the craving back in earnest. Or maybe it was the two farmers gabbing and smoking as they leaned against their pickup truck on the other side of the pumps. He inhaled their secondhand smoke and found it, at first, nostalgic and satisfying, then almost disgusting. What the hell was wrong with him?

At least he still had an appetite for beauty, as quirky and tough as it might be. Maribeth headed back to the vehicle with a granola bar in one hand and a root beer in the other, her brown hair blowing in the strong southeast wind, catching red highlights in the sun, her blouse rippling, her face again relaxed, betraying nothing of their earlier conversation.

"Go ahead in," she said as he put the gas cap back on. "I'll park it."

"OK, thanks." He gave her a smile, hoping he hadn't pissed her off. He liked her. She had a cool facade that hid a slow burn, a core of strength and energy. She was steady and sharp. And she could talk about the weather in the best possible way. He'd had worse chase partners, that was for sure.

Business accomplished, he shopped in the convenience store until he found pretzel sticks, which he deemed slightly better than processed meat products in his comparison of cigarette-shaped foods. He also bought a bottle of Coke for the caffeine. His sleepless night on the road clawed at his consciousness. It was like being drunk, only without the pleasant side effects.

Outside, he watched the chasers come and go. Most were hanging out, awaiting nature's decision. The road was busy with them, too, buzzing by in both directions, from cars to SUVs to a vehicle shaped like a wedding cake. There's no way that's a chase vehicle, he thought, but the "ZANY *Weddings*" label on the side made him wonder. Another truck wrapped with graphics of storms and flying sandwiches rumbled by, too. Labeled "Chuck's Wagon," it looked like a food truck, a strange sight in this small town. He considered the pretzels in his hand and decided to watch for the truck down the road.

Jack leaned against the van and gazed up at the more and more populated sky, the skeins of woolly vapor there, and calculated how long he had until the clouds blew the lid off the troposphere. At least long enough for a twenty-minute nap, he thought.

"Hey, Fred," he shouted into the open door behind the

driver's seat, where his compatriot was playing with the rack of cameras. "Any blips on radar yet?"

"Just checked. Nothing. We'd better get something today, damn it. If we don't, I'm holding you personally responsible. This may be the last chance to give these cameras a whirl before the real research starts."

"Nature will deliver, Fred. I'm going to catch a few Z's. Where's our driver?"

"Leaving me alone, unlike you."

"Touchy, touchy," Jack said. He looked around and saw Maribeth on the edge of the parking lot, talking on her cell phone. He thought he heard her say, "I'll be careful, Dad," as she wandered away. It struck Jack as funny. She'd survived a lot worse, hadn't she? Well, maybe. With war and tornadoes, it all depended on location, location, location.

He saw a small, matte-black hatchback filled with high school kids pull into the lot. The four boys talked excitedly as they got out and started roaming among the chase vehicles, taking special note of an armored chase car, a knockoff of a famous one. As the teens chatted with its owner, Jack got into the van's front passenger seat, leaned it back and shut his eyes. The chatter and the uneven drone of passing engines and the warmth of the spring day seeped quickly into his sleepy senses, pulling him deep into a dark, tenuous place, where everything depended on the undependable, where the wind was his only transport, and where he was soon lost, gratefully, in a funnel of mist, unsettling and irresistible.

EVEN BEFORE SHE hung up with her dad, her phone rang again, and she made her apologies and switched calls.

"Dr. Y?"

"Ms. Lisbon, how are things?"

"They haven't killed each other yet," she said as she wandered back toward the van and caught sight of an unconscious Jack through the open passenger window. "Looks like Jack is catching a few winks while Fred tinkers. Despite the bitching, I suspect they're having a good time."

"I know you'll keep them on track, my dear," he said.

"I don't think you need to worry. Jack may act nonchalant, but he wants the storm more than anybody. He spent most of the drive talking about the forecast."

"How does it look?"

"Violent," she said, walking across the lot and scanning the sky. She'd done her own forecast that morning and was sure they would see powerful supercells, if not tornadoes. "I can't remember the last time it felt like this in Oklahoma, and the clouds show it."

"Take care of yourself and, of course, my van," he said with a chuckle. "I'll leave you to it, but check in when you have something to report."

"Will do," she said. "Later." She hung up and breathed in the heavy air. It reminded her of Florida. The deep moisture and the heat lay upon them like a thick blanket, with the persistent wind offering the only relief from the oppressive afternoon. It made her uneasy. The official forecasts echoed her worries, exhorting people to keep their radios on so they could hear warnings, telling them to stay off the highways at rush hour. She hated to see people in danger, and her enjoyment of the storms was derailed whenever she anticipated a day like this. She'd seen enough suffering.

Phone in pocket, she wandered back to the van and leaned against the front fender on the passenger side. Why there? So she could watch Jack, unobserved. She liked being around him, but she didn't like the way he was digging at her, tickling her funny bone, asking questions. Did she? She evaluated the strong jaw and nose, the dark, messy hair, the wrinkled black T-shirt wrapping his lean, sinewy frame, his innocence in repose. She'd never been able to observe him this way, not in the two weeks in Florida. No time. Which isn't to say she hadn't been watching him.

She couldn't deny her interest in Jack. She didn't need his moves, his cockiness, his damn good looks. But she was starting to like them anyway. He reminded her of some of the good guys she'd known in the service, rare friends who let her be one of the boys when she needed to be without making note of it, which was the whole point. Maybe she was having flashbacks, here among the storm chasers, the heavily branded teams crowding this small town, the almost entirely male army of storm geeks and adrenaline junkies and eagerly budding media whores. She'd seen enough of media, too, to want to sign off on all of it. But she did have an attraction to the sky, and this mission fulfilled every part of her, or almost every part.

And then there was Jack, sleeping — not a prince, the flip side of the fairy-tale princess, but the first man who'd interested her in a long time. Her last boyfriend was a flaky guitar player, and she'd been in control of that relationship, if she could call it that. Which is to say, she hadn't exactly been emotionally invested. After her scare in the helicopter crash, she'd ended it. She didn't need any more pointless entanglements.

She laughed at where her thoughts were headed. Jack? Ridiculous. Wake him up with a kiss and you'll see the prince's true nature, she thought. But even as she mocked herself for the idea, it intrigued her, and she felt her face get warm.

Maribeth sensed a flash of motion around her, the cars, the chasers on the move, and looked up at the sky again to see one of the cumulus towers expanding like a giant mound of vanilla ice cream, scoop on scoop, white on white as it exploded upward, breaking the cap.

"Damn!" she said, annoyed at herself for her reverie. "Jack! Fred! It's time!"

Jack stirred in the seat and leaned up sleepily to look out the front window at the burgeoning storm. "Oh, yeah, baby. Now that's an alarm clock," he said in that warm, mildly deep voice, and he flashed his green eyes at her with a grin. She answered with the smallest smile possible.

Fred hopped out of the van and squinted up, and even he seemed delighted. "Terrific!" he said, then looked stricken. "I gotta pee! I swear, I'll be quick as a bunny on a date," he yelled as he dashed toward the gas station.

Maribeth and Jack laughed, and she felt her self-possession return. It was good to be back in action.

"Plot a course," she said as she hopped in the driver's side.

"With pleasure," he said, banging on the keyboard of the laptop, and the word *pleasure* made her sigh, a tiny sigh that only she could hear.

CHARLES DROVE his less than sporty food truck among the salmon run of chasers heading northwest of town. He soon dropped off the main highway onto a grid of rough roads that would stair-step toward the growing storm — or storms, as others were starting to form south of the first, with even more intensity. He didn't want to get in the way of these storm seekers, these misdirected dreamers, but he wished to be nearby, to share his energy with them, or his wisdom, should they choose to seek it. And if they didn't, he always had his fine curried chicken salad with grapes and sesame seeds.

Despite his calm center, even he felt the excitement of the building storms, and more than anything, he wanted to be near the lightning. He felt a kinship with its power, its randomness born of ultimate order, its seemingly fragmented expression of a great whole — the global electric circuit, the current that even in fair weather flowed from every blade of grass, every molecule of water, every heart and soul on Earth up to the ionosphere. The current flowed around him, around everyone, and he was part of it, perhaps more than most. Scientists still grappled with how to reveal the global electric circuit in numbers and equations, but they knew it was there, and they studied it from land and space. He studied it with his unquantifiable mind. Charles did not need the numbers to know it was around him. He felt it in each rumble of thunder, even bore its mark on his skin.

Charles had traveled far, seeking out the ganglia of this great electric nervous system that enveloped the world. In turn, he sought friends, women, artists, mystics, scientists, exploring their connection to the circuit, to one another, seeking the commonality that linked them. He had come to believe that the unifying factor was the circuit itself and that their connectivity was more orderly than anyone could imagine. All were on a path determined by a shimmering fate shaped by this flowing power. He was so much closer to it than the rest; he understood it; he took it into his body and made it a part of himself.

He had once chased storms in his pursuit of answers and

Nature. She teased him like a woman before revealing her true connection with him. He continued to be her vessel, sharing, as he traveled, the questions that might help the seekers find answers. He longed to feed these chasers wisdom, to help them understand that what they sought should not be thrills or fame or money but enlightenment. Even the scientists did not truly understand what it meant to be enlightened, a fact he knew all too well. He saw them with their whiz-bang gizmos, their spinners and sensors. He saw the fleets of cars brandishing antennas. He saw the white van with the flask-and-bolt logo and its window like an eye and briefly feared the analytical forces that trespassed upon his mystical journey. For nothing that they could theorize or feign to prove would even touch what he had learned so far.

In this, what he saw as his fourth and possibly final life, he was sure that ultimate enlightenment was near. He would bide his time, and in time, he would know it was time, *the* time. And time would become meaningless. And in a flash, all would be clear.

WHAT NEITHER AURELIUS nor Brad would admit but knew at some level was that neither of them was much of a forecaster. Both had chasing experience and a degree of operational knowledge, but in the past — Brad as a tour operator and then a TV star, and Aurelius as a frequently filmed adventurer — they'd been able to rely on a ringer. For *Zany Weddings,* they didn't have a pet meteorologist, so both surreptitiously scanned web discussion groups and Facebook posts to find out where everyone else was going.

Now, as they drove with the crowds moving northwest out

of Seiling, Aurelius hoped their fellow chasers knew what they were doing.

It was Brad's turn to drive, and at Danni's suggestion, Polly Ann rode shotgun. Danni insisted the bride's fangirl gushing would make good television. But it just made Aurelius — and Tyler, he suspected — more uncomfortable. Aurelius and Tyler were stuck in the second row of seats as Brad monopolized her, with camera guy Scooter in back.

"We have to choose our storm wisely so we can get our shots of you getting married in front of the tornado," Brad told Polly Ann. "And with a storm like this, we have a great chance of getting you hooked up right away."

The stars in Polly Ann's eyes were going supernova. "Well, that would be great and all, but I hope we get to chase with you more than a day!"

"I hope so, too, but we have to go for any opportunity, as I learned when I flew in the Bubble," Brad said, citing his triumph once again.

Polly Ann and Tyler emitted sighs, hers dreamy, his impatient. Aurelius felt a need to connect the couple again for the sake of the show. And to get the cameras off Brad.

"How did you two meet, Tyler?" he asked.

Tyler's face softened a bit. "Poll" — it sounded like "Pawl" — "was in my freshman English class in college. We ended up studying together, because we had to memorize all the meters and rhyme schemes of all these poems."

"So poetry brought you together? That's so romantic," Aurelius said, believing in his heart that it really was. He still fancied himself a romantic hero and could appreciate the importance of poetry in wooing a maiden.

"Well, not exactly," Tyler said.

"We kept cutting class and getting ice cream together!"

Polly Ann exclaimed. "I hate poetry. We ended up dropping the class, and the next semester, we took a bowling class together instead. Tyler throws a bowling ball like — like he's making thunder! How could I resist that?"

"I'm not a bad bowler myself. We should make time for a couple of games," Brad called back to Tyler.

"Let's see if Poll and I can get married first."

Under Tyler's civility was the unmistakable timbre of jealous anger. Aurelius hoped he could defuse it or get them hitched fast. He knew it would be incredibly lucky to get them married today. Their storm now competed with three others, shoulder-to-shoulder and growing like linebackers on steroids.

"We have to figure out which storm to chase here," Aurelius said.

"I think we're doing just fine with the first one," Brad said. "It's not like we're the only ones with the same idea."

Aurelius eyed his phone, looking at the blossoming radar and the dots on Spotter Network, which showed the location of chasers who elected to broadcast their signal.

"A few of the chasers are targeting that southern storm," Aurelius said. "Usually that's a fair bet."

"What, don't you trust me?" Brad asked, subtly sarcastic.

Polly Ann beamed at him. "Oh, I trust you. I know you're going to get us right to the tornado. But you can take your time."

Aurelius cringed again. "There's an intersection up here where we'll have some road choices. We should stop for a minute and think about it."

"If it makes you feel better," Brad said, suggesting he thought little of the idea.

"It's good strategy," said Aurelius. He felt some of his flash and confidence return in the face of Brad's smugness and turned on his deepest commanding voice. "Stop."

Brad caved to the alpha-male vibe and turned right onto a dirt road, driving a half mile from the busy highway, up a gentle hill and past a grove of trees for an optimum view. The production van was right behind them, and once they parked, there was again a flurry of cameras and microphones as the crew captured the thoughts of the young couple and their hosts.

Danni filmed Aurelius expounding on the weather, then took him aside.

"Hey," she said. "Is it my imagination, or are you and Brad a little, well, hostile? You guys got along great on all the previous shows."

"It did seem that way, didn't it?" Aurelius said, noncommittal.

She smiled. "It's actually totally fine with me. It might even make for a better show. Add some tension, you know? Especially since we might be trying to get this tornado shot for a month."

Aurelius felt a shiver of horror. "I thought we only had three weeks?"

"Maybe," Danni said, still smiling.

"You're joshing me," he scolded. "If we do this right, we might get to see our tornado today."

They both turned at the rumble of another vehicle. A white van pulled up about thirty yards behind them on the dirt road. A woman and two men got out, chatted and pointed at the sky.

One of the men looked vaguely familiar to Aurelius. It took a moment before he put it together. It was that guy who was on the Bubble crew when Brad pulled his stunt. Aurelius remembered him standing there that day, but mostly he remembered trying to convince his old paramour Wynda that Aurelius was the one who needed to fly in the Bubble. He'd been under the impression that Brad wasn't keen to do it. And then — well, the rest was history. Still, he wondered if this fellow might tell him more about what went on that day after he left, maybe fill in the gaps that Brad didn't like to discuss.

Aurelius patted Danni on the shoulder. "Give me a minute," he said.

"Not too long," she said, looking west toward the storms.

"We have a moment. They seem to think so, anyway," Aurelius said as he walked toward the trio.

"What do you think you're doing?" It was Brad at his elbow, out of breath from running to catch up.

"Just saying hello to some fellow chasers."

"That's ridiculous. We have to go. That thing could produce a tornado, and you have to marry the Charmings over there."

"We have a moment," Aurelius repeated. "I would have thought you'd like to say hello to your old colleague." He looked sideways at Brad and saw that, without a doubt, the opposite was true. Interesting.

"Hail, fellow adventurers!" Aurelius said to the trio. "So nice to see you again." He reached out and grabbed the hand of the startled dark-haired fellow. "Aurelius Zane, if you recall."

"I recall," the man said, waiting in vain for Zane to recall his own name before he relented. "I'm Jack. This is Maribeth and Fred. We're just figuring out our next move." He paused. "And this is Brad Treat," he added for the benefit of his colleagues.

"It sure is," Fred said with a mix of interest and bewilderment. "I'd almost forgotten you were on that crew."

"Just the forecaster," Jack said, looking at Brad with a sardonic expression.

Brad turned purple. "You," he said to Jack.

"I see you've learned your first vowel," Jack responded without emotion.

"*Pffft,*" Brad sputtered. "We've got to go." He tugged on Aurelius's arm.

"So soon?" Aurelius shrugged him off. "I thought we could talk about old times."

"We don't have time to talk about anything, even with TV stars," said Fred, heading for the van. "We've got to get going so we can set up. Come on."

The woman said nothing, but she appraised Aurelius and Brad keenly before getting behind the wheel.

"Gotta go," Jack said with a smile, getting in and slamming the door. The van made a three-point turn and took off as Aurelius and Brad walked back to their vehicles.

"That was strange," Aurelius said.

"You're strange," Brad said, still fuming. "It's time to chase. I say we stick with the big one. It's dominating the line. And then we can get our tornado and this damn wedding and get out of Oklahoma and on to rockabilly rodeos or whatever's next."

"I bow to your fame and expertise," Aurelius said with a flourish, letting his jacket flap dramatically as he did, indeed, bow, an entirely mocking gesture. And he thought about what he would ask Jack the next time they ran into them, because it was Tornado Alley, and one thing a chaser could be sure of was running into other chasers. Especially ones Brad didn't want to run into, if Aurelius could make it so.

❦

FRED WAS the first one to point out the car behind them as they jogged west, on their way to the southern storm.

"They're right on our ass. Is there no way to avoid storm chasers at this point?" he asked.

"Not at any point," Jack said. He turned to look through the small rear windows and spotted the matte-black hatchback. "I don't think they're chasers, per se. Those are the kids who were salivating over somebody's chase tank at the gas station."

"They're the last thing we need today," Fred said. "Why aren't they following the goddamn tank?"

"Because," Maribeth said, "when the tank left, there was already a news crew following it. Maybe three's a crowd."

"Where'd they come from?" Jack asked. "I didn't see them behind us when we left Seiling."

"They must have been mixed up in all the traffic," Fred said. "I guess they waited on the main road after we turned to get our view and then pounced on us when we came out. Why us, anyway?"

"Maybe we have just enough instruments on the roof to look serious," Maribeth said.

"We can't waste any more CPU on them," Jack said. He was tired of thinking and just plain tired as he tried to interpret the radar loop playing on the laptop. "Not our problem. This storm is our problem. It seems to be moving slowly east. I want to get on it before it starts cranking and decides to turn south or otherwise complicate our lives."

"Road?" asked Maribeth.

"South, soon," Jack said. "I'll say when."

He pulled up the mapping software, trying to clear his

head. He grabbed his Coke from the cup holder and drank the rest of it, hoping the caffeine would kick in. Only adrenaline propped his eyes open now as he watched their storm fight for its place. As what was currently the tail-end Charlie, at the southern end of the line, it had an uninterrupted flow of moisture delivered by the strong southeast wind. He liked the look of its convection, the burgeoning clouds, whose edges looked harder and more serious than those on the other storms clawing upward to the north. But would it keep growing or meld into a line? The upper-level winds suggested it would sustain itself, but only time would tell.

Time. It was close to 6 p.m., with plenty of daylight left. They would try to film lightning no matter what time of day it was, but darkness might aid their official quest, as long as they were positioned well. On the way, he thought, they might get to see the storm produce something a little more interesting. He took a few more seconds to evaluate their options.

"OK, I don't really like doing this, but I don't think we're going to have a paved road before we're way too far west," he said. "Let's take a left on this next farm road and see if it'll get us south to our east-west option."

"Done," Maribeth said, slowing down and taking a left by a ramshackle farm that had a couple of shaggy ponies in its pasture. He liked that she didn't point out the obvious — if they'd been more sure of their storm, they could have driven west right out of Seiling. But this was one of those things: Almost every chase involved going in a circle at some point.

The ride immediately got rougher as the van bumped along the part-dirt, part-gravel surface.

"What the fuck?" Fred exclaimed. "The cameras! Please! Take it easy."

"I never take it easy," Maribeth said. Jack saw the half smile again but wasn't sure if she was kidding.

He glanced back. Choking on their dust was the little black car. He was relieved for all their sakes that no rain had yet hit this road; judging by the ruts, it would produce large puddles at best and tire-sucking mud at worst. The landscape was fairly flat, and he had a broad view of the storms as they played for dominance. Theirs looked better and better as the base grew darker and, it seemed, closer to the ground. A few ragged tendrils of cloud lowered and lifted under it, pendulous and ominous, suggestive of rotation. There was more rain, too, and if they didn't hurry, they would be caught on the wrong side of the core. The radar signature echoed red, with hints of pink — likely hail. As he evaluated its likely size on the VIL, the weather radio sounded its earsplitting alarm of doom, making them all jump, and declared a severe thunderstorm warning for the whole line.

"That's a big goddamn area, isn't it?" Fred asked. "We could set up just about anywhere."

"Two issues with that," Jack said. "One, if you set up right now in front of this line, you won't have a lot of time to fine-tune your gear and get your shots before you're overtaken. Second, if we get south to the best storm of the day and get out of the rain, we're going to have an unimpeded view for the cameras and a lot better lightning." And, he hoped, they'd see whatever tornado it might produce.

"And you might get to see your tornado," Fred echoed his thoughts. "But I take your point and agree with you. For now."

Jack noticed Maribeth smile and felt a little lift himself. They were doing this, he thought. They'd be a good team, right? He let himself imagine what being a team with Maribeth might be like, late at night, in a quiet hotel room, and then jerked his attention back to the storm. Not now, for Christ's sake. His brain was all over the place. He popped open his bag of pretzel sticks and stuck one in his mouth, sucking off the salt, to get his mind off smoking and sex and other momentarily unattainable things.

The one thing he felt most confident about attaining today was off to his right and looming larger, setting itself apart from the line. The unshackled storm showed hints of striations and a lowering base that took on the shape of a massive flying saucer as they approached. If there were aliens inside, they plotted carnage. The supercell's gray-green color deepened and darkened and flowed into a remarkably smooth, round ship of cloud that sported an increasingly insistent lowering.

Oh, yes, Jack thought. It was spinning, and it was swallowing the sky.

"NOW, DON'T GET TOO CLOSE," Danni said over the radio. "We have to set up the shot. Use your best judgment."

"We will," answered Aurelius, wondering how good that judgment was. He was back in the passenger seat, with Brad driving and the future honeymooners in the second seat. They'd just navigated around Woodward, still aiming for the storm in the middle of the line.

"Tyler and Polly Ann," Aurelius said, "we may be heading for your wedding. Scooter there in the back is going to focus on you right now, and so am I." Aurelius picked up the small video camera he kept stowed up front for the big moments. "This is an important part of the show — talk about what this is going to mean to you now that we're so close to getting your dream wedding."

"This doesn't even seem real," said Polly Ann, who appeared to be genuinely amazed through the viewfinder, not just reality-TV-amazed. "We've been chasing storms for one day, and we might be on the verge of getting married in front of a tornado!"

"Honey, are you ready?" Tyler asked. "We've been dreaming about this for eight months."

"I know, ever since we saw the ad for the show!" she said.

That will be cut, Aurelius thought. Aloud, he said: "Tyler, could you talk about your feelings a bit here? I know it's not easy, but the audience wants to know what you're thinking right now."

"Um, OK." Tyler looked uncomfortable but composed himself, grasped Polly Ann's hands and turned his brown eyes to her blue ones. "Polly Ann, you know why I want to get married in front of a tornado, right?"

"I think it's because I wanted to, isn't it?" she asked, sounding confused.

"Partly," he said. "But it's also because I want you to know that no matter how stormy things get, I will always be there for you. I will be your shelter in the storm. I'll be your storm cellar, baby. I will always keep you safe, until — until we see the rainbow."

"Oh, Tyler!" said Polly Ann, tears coming to her eyes. "You are my storm cellar! That is so sweet! I'll be your — your water supply. Your emergency rations! I'll keep you alive, darlin'!"

The metaphors were getting a little strange, Aurelius thought, but the couple seemed sincere as they kissed for the cameras and sat back.

"I think we're ready," Tyler said.

"Yes, we sure are," said Polly Ann, who still held Tyler by the hand. "When are we going to get there?"

"I'm working on that," Brad said.

"Oh, I know you are. Thank you, thank you, thank you for making this possible!" she said.

Thank us when we get a tornado, Aurelius thought. He put the camera down, because right now, it wasn't looking so great. The middle storm, the first that had formed and kicked the chasers into gear, loomed large but had also become a high-precipitation bomb, dumping heavy rain and hail, judging by the radar and what he could see with his own eyes. It also seemed to lack the revolving structure of the southern storm, which was now far out of reach but still in view in the distance.

"Don't you have some wedding clothes for this?" Brad asked.

"Yes, we have some quick-change outfits for when we think it's time," the bride said. "Do you think we should put them on?"

"It wouldn't hurt," Brad said. "This storm is looking mean, and we might not have much time to set up when we stop."

Aurelius wondered why he was in a hurry. It didn't appear the storm was about to do anything. And then he realized that Polly Ann was stripping in the back seat as Brad enjoyed the view in the mirror. At least she left her undergarments on, Aurelius thought as he averted his eyes, but he hadn't anticipated this part of the process. For all the other *Zany Weddings*, the couples had dressed in situation-appropriate clothing in advance.

"See, I'm ready. I told you it was fast!" she said.

He looked back to see her in a short, low-cut satin dress

with a branching lightning bolt sewn in silver sequins across the front. She wore white sneakers with silver laces and a jaunty, miniature white top hat sprouting a lace flower and more sequins, held in place by a pair of sparkling hatpins. "See, so the wind doesn't blow it off!" she explained as she pointed out the rhinestone-encrusted spikes.

"Fascinating," Aurelius said, unnerved by the weapons-grade hair accessories. "You look fine too, Tyler." All her fiancé had done was change into a black and white bowling shirt over his black shorts, but it seemed to complement her highway-ready getup pretty well.

"Not exactly a black-tie affair, is it?" Tyler noted with a grin, looking happier now that the wedding seemed near.

"Should we set up soon?" Danni asked over the radio. "It looks like we're getting close."

They were quite close, actually, and lightning sparked above them in the storm's anvil, followed by a long, low rattle of thunder.

"Might as well," Aurelius responded. "We'll at least get some B-roll, just in case the tornado doesn't happen."

"Ye of little confidence," chided Brad, who found a likely side road with a wide spot where they could park and get a view. Pretty ranchland rolled away from them to the west, flanking a decrepit old barn surrounded by wildflowers, making a lovely background. For what, Aurelius wasn't yet sure.

CHARLES HAD BARELY MOVED his food truck, except to get a slightly better view of the storm. He fed a couple of chasers who happened by, then closed the window. He had entered what he considered his atmospheric zone, on a farm road southeast of Woodward, awaiting what Nature would bring. Though he always drove himself just within the reach of her rage, he then let what would happen, happen. He didn't fear the hail or wind. And he knew in his heart it would not be a tornado that embraced him. It was the global electric circuit that sent signals all around him, that would tell him when it was the right moment to commune with it again. He was patient and, as always, he was humble before Nature's power.

He wore a ratty straw cowboy hat and stood outside, facing the line of storms. He could see the undulations of the cells embedded in a great line of churning clouds. He could feel the anger, Nature's tantrum as she lashed at the imbalances of air and water and electricity that she so wanted to correct. Even in this chaos, her expressions of order emerged in beautiful spirals, in a consistent system, though its manifestations appeared infinite in variety. Each storm was an elegant expression of energy, a release of physical power, of metaphysical ecstasy.

He stretched out his arms, singing words that were not words, calling upon Nature to reveal to him her will — to embrace him, to take him to a higher plane, to bring him to the edge and then push him over it. He had faith that, in that virtual space, he could fly. He felt his molecules become one with those in every living thing around him. Birds sang nearby, happy amid the growing turmoil, complementing his tune. Each tender green stalk in the young wheat field next to him bent and rose with the wind, bowing to the storms as if they were the source of all things holy. He felt the same way; of all of the levels of consciousness he'd explored, of all the places he'd seen, of all the people he'd met, no phenomenon put him so in touch with the orderly chaos of Nature as did a storm.

Today, though, as he faced the maelstrom and closed his eyes to feel the shifting wind, the dropping temperature and the fine raindrops on his face, he felt a darkness he rarely saw in her, a sadness that she would express in the most violent way possible. This storm, he grasped, would not be the maker of his destiny, so he hummed in harmony with the wind, trying to soothe the goddess and to ease the pain of those she would punish.

"THE PAVED ROAD isn't going to do it, either," Jack said as they came up on the east-west route. "We have to get farther south."

"And west, right?" Maribeth said, eyeing their target out the window. "We could go west first."

"It'll cut us off. We're not in a plane, or did you forget?" he teased.

"I'm trying to forget, but it's not working. We should be OK if we go south. We'll do all right as long as the road doesn't get any worse." She crossed the paved route and kept going.

"How could it possibly get any worse?" asked the frustrated Fred from his bouncy seat in the back. "We need to get into position. Please. Before I barf."

"At least airplanes have barf bags," Maribeth noted.

"Stop saying barf," Fred said.

"You started it," she responded.

"Children," Jack said. "Another couple of miles. Then we should be in good shape."

The storm sucked in the daylight that dared linger around it, though a deep orange glow in the recesses underneath confirmed the sun still hovered above the horizon. They were just about parallel with the supercell now, and Jack could make out a well-defined wall cloud under the flying-saucer base, spinning, extending fingers toward the ground.

"Funnels?" Maribeth asked, her voice flat and intense.

"Yeah. I think it's going to go multivortex."

"Those idiots are still behind us," Fred said in disbelief and, Jack could hear it, worry.

"They must think they can handle it," Jack said.

"Maybe they can't," Maribeth said.

Jack looked back, then front toward the storm. "What are we supposed to do about it? Call their mom? We have to go. If they have any sense, they'll get out of the way."

"Demonstrably, they do not have any sense," she said, looking in the rearview mirror.

"Look," Jack said, feeling the fatigue and excitement and the contagion of worry they carried. "We have to focus here. We'll be fine, and so will they." He was mesmerized by the now-chunky funnels lowering and dancing toward the surface, only to lift, indecisive. A bolt of brilliant cloud-to-ground lightning hit between them and the wall cloud, a message from the intense updraft. "It's going to do it," he said.

As they passed an east-west dirt road, he saw two chase cars on it blasting east, away from their position and farther from the storm. Chasers, chasers everywhere.

"Jack, we need to set up," said Fred, sounding even more concerned.

"You're right. We'll go a little farther, just to make sure. Look for a spot."

Maribeth said nothing, but she glanced in the rearview

mirror, noting the black car, and slowed at a wide spot next to a wire fence and a rusty old bathtub-turned-trough.

"Angle the van so the cameras face the storm," Fred commanded. No one was polite now.

Maribeth wheeled the van into the space next to the tub. "Not ideal for a getaway, but we'll manage," she said, forced composure in her tone.

"Why would we need a getaway?" Jack laughed, giddy, as he hopped out of the car. A large funnel pushed toward the ground from the storm's base and seemed to dig in, whipping up a whirl of dust not a mile from their position. The black car passed them and stopped a hundred yards up the road.

"I need you in here, Andreas!" Fred called out.

"Oh, shit," Jack said. His fatigue had turned into a kind of euphoria, fanned by the adrenaline and the tornado. He ran around and climbed in the side door. In a moment, the Ghost was locked into place.

"I don't think we'll use the other cameras yet," Fred said. He still sounded nervous.

"First tornado?" Jack asked.

"Yes, goddamn it, but that's not why," Fred said. "We're too fucking close. We're going to have to move in a minute. Now get out there and monitor while I activate everything."

"We're fine," Jack said, but all he could think about was the tornado. He hopped out. In the two minutes he'd spent inside the van, the fat funnel had multiplied into a carousel of sometimes two, sometimes four and five funnels ripping into the dirt. The motion was astonishing, and the wall cloud itself was almost riding on the ground. The storm was like an angry animal, alive and brimming with fury, volatile, unpredictable. Even the individual vortices were huge, tornadoes in themselves, spinning rapidly around the center of rotation. When the funnels merged, their violence would be unimaginable. The whole thing was about to wedge out. Maybe they were too close to get the lightning shots they wanted. But just one more minute . . .

He reached into the van and grabbed his Nikon off the floor. He shot a series of photos and then some video with it, entranced by the storm. The tornado was getting bigger.

"What do you think?" he asked, looking up for Maribeth, but she wasn't there. She was — there she was, running back from the direction of the little black car.

"I told them to get the hell out of here, but they just laughed at me. Little pricks," she said as she ran up, out of breath more from anger than anything, he thought.

"Isn't it incredible?" he gestured toward the tornado.

"It's OK," she said. The dust was lofting and rolling around them in waves. She coughed. "Is this what you mean by breathing in the inflow? I'm not finding it that attractive."

"It's *OK*?" Jack sputtered in disbelief.

"I'll grant you," she said, her hair blowing straight out in the wind, her eyes narrowed in the face of the billowing dirt, "it's impressive. But I don't like the motion on it, Jack. I've seen plenty of tornadoes, even if they were from the air, and I can tell you that it's coming in our direction. And those little morons —"

"It seems to have more of an easterly component."

"When's the last time you looked at radar?" She had her phone out and was tapping it quickly. "Shit. It's already turned northeast, Jack. You probably can't tell because it's changing shape. We need to go, now."

"I can always tell," he said with confidence. "Don't worry — we can easily get ahead of it and drop south."

She held out the phone with the radar image so he could

see it and looked at him steadily, those gray-blue-green eyes as mercurial as the storm. "The river, Jack. The Canadian River."

Clarity came to him then, a knife through his tornado ecstasy, and he pictured the map, just as she must be envisioning her usual aerial view. The Canadian River cut off all their southern escape routes for miles. He turned and took another photo of the tornado, now one thick and widening cone. The storm was an eerie mix of turquoise and brown, seeming to shudder in its rapid rotation.

He turned back to her. "You have a point," he said.

Maribeth spun on her heel. "Fred, we're going!" she called as she climbed into the van.

"I want to get the camera in!"

"No time!" she said.

Jack got in, too, and struggled to close his door against the wind as the storm inhaled. He gaped as the tornado seemed to fill the western horizon outside his window, getting bigger. Maribeth hit the accelerator and spun off to the south, toward it.

"What the hell are you doing?" Jack said. "Turn around! East! Go east!"

"In a second," she said. She pulled up next to the black car, where the teens were outside filming the tornado with their cell phones, taking selfies and woo-hooing. She honked her horn and pointed in the opposite direction, toward escape, when they looked up. They waved her off.

"Idiots," she said.

"Go," Jack said. "We can't wait."

"Idiots!" she said again. She honked the horn multiple times, urgently, and did a rapid three-point turn before hauling ass north on the rough dirt road.

For the first time in a long time, Jack felt as if a chase was getting out of control. Maybe it's the exhaustion, he thought, but no — he leaned over and peered past Maribeth to take in the sight of the ferociously rotating tornado. It had become a massive bowl of dust, whirling on fast-forward, and it wasn't getting any smaller. Colossal vortices emerged and vanished in the huge, rotating wall of darkness. He looked back and saw, in the distance, following headlights. The kids in the black car. And behind them, the dust, the hot breath of the beast, beginning to eat the road.

2

THE SNAP

Maribeth felt her anger transform into something more familiar, an exercise in control, as she evaluated the situation and lay on the accelerator as hard as she dared on this dreadful road. She shot north, then took the first east road to avoid the core. Still, a few hailstones banged on the roof and the windshield, and one left a nice ding in the glass in front of Jack.

"The Ghost!" Fred called out, his anxiety evident.

She glanced in the rearview mirror. He was clutching his beard with both hands and looking up. Behind them the world was a hell of dust and darkness and furious motion, and she could barely make out the headlights of the teenagers' car as it tried to follow them.

"Did it get hit?" Jack asked. She realized he was talking about the camera. His face bore no trace of the flippant daredevil of a few minutes before.

"I think it's OK," Fred said, "but I'll feel a lot better when I'm sure we're out of the hail."

"We have bigger problems than hail," said Maribeth,

expressing what they would not. The intense winds buffeted them as the circulation neared. The van shimmied as they bounced forward. The dust around them took on a dull roar.

"Oh, god," Fred said.

"I know," she said.

"No." His voice was jagged as broken glass. "They're gone."

"What?" she asked sharply.

"I can't see the headlights."

"It's all the dust," Jack reassured them, but he didn't sound convinced, either. "They're probably fine. Maybe they took another road."

Maribeth felt sick. But this was no time to second-guess. She had to get them out of there.

"I think we should go north," she said.

Jack glanced at the laptop. "Do it," he said. "The river curves up in front of us anyway. We might be fucked if we stay east. Go north."

"The hail!" Fred said. "The Ghost!"

"How impact-resistant is that snow globe, anyway?" Jack asked.

"How big is the hail?" Fred asked in a squeaky voice, all his bluster gone.

"As Maribeth said, we have other problems. But we'll probably avoid the baseballs."

They hit a north farm road, and Maribeth turned hard. The van bounced through a water-filled rut with a horrible groan and kept going. Intermittent hailstones the size of golf balls banged on the roof. The van slid on the muddy surface, with the tornado seeming to keep up with them. Was it overtaking them? Maribeth was used to seeing them from the sky, with a 360-degree view and a straight line of escape whenever she felt it was time to leave. She was starting to wonder why anyone drove anywhere at all. The dust had thinned, but the darkness behind them seemed thicker and more menacing. She couldn't see anything back there.

"Just another mile or so," Jack said. His voice was quiet, scary. "You can do it."

That's when she knew how close it was. The van fishtailed and hit another pothole, and for a long second that dragged into two, she felt a strange lifting feeling, a distant cousin of flying. And then the van's back wheels slammed onto the ground and she was driving for her life.

Small debris and tumbleweeds flew past them as she pressed the pedal to its limit. Amid the thunder and howling wind, they shared the silence Maribeth heard passengers experienced on a doomed airplane, when they knew they were going to die. She'd been in hairy situations before, been close to that moment herself, but this was new. She'd accepted death in the past, accepted it ahead of time. It was part of the deal, flying over Iraq. She'd buried so many friends. She used to think of herself there with them. It made it easier, imagining it had already happened, that she'd already walked through that door of shadows. Here, in the middle of Oklahoma, she wasn't ready to go yet. She had the stubborn thought that there was a lot more she wanted to do.

"It's 60! It's 60! Turn right!" Jack said.

His voice broke her from her grim trance, and she realized the wind wasn't quite so violent. And they were coming up to a paved route. She turned right, breathing again, and felt one small tear form in the corner of her eye. She ignored it, still driving as fast as traffic would allow. Because here, there were many more cars than they'd seen in the past several minutes, all pushing as quickly as they could to the east, mostly chasers, fleeing.

"I think we're OK now," Jack said. "It's wild. It's massive on radar, but you can't even see it. The dust is ridiculous." He paused. "I never thought I'd say this, but I think I'm through chasing this one."

"Think we can still get some lightning shots?" Fred asked. "Dr. Y will be pissed if we don't get anything, especially when he sees the storm reports."

"Yeah, OK. We can do that in front of the line of storms. It's all lighting up. But — I think we could use a break." Maribeth knew he was talking about her. "We could go north for a bit and just get out of the path. Take 281 out of Seiling."

"I hate that town," Maribeth said with sudden vehemence, and Jack laughed. She could hear the relief in the sound. She sensed it for a moment, too, then felt herself sucked again into that black space inside, where the little car had vanished into the storm. "Do you think —?"

"We can't know," Jack said.

"Look at the socials," Fred replied. "It'll be there first."

"I don't do that shit," Jack said.

"All right. I will." Fred tapped on the laptop in the back and spent a few minutes scanning the feed. Then he closed the computer. His silence was loud. Maribeth looked around, at the cars in front of her, their headlights lit in the creeping dusk stirred up by the storms to the west.

"Someone just came upon the damage path and found two demolished cars," Fred said. "There are a couple of photos. One looks like a post office Jeep, of all things. The other one — it's hard to say, but it doesn't look good. Emergency vehicles are getting to the scene now."

Maribeth felt her anger overtake her, and she slammed her

hand against the wheel one, two, five times. It stung, and she liked that it hurt. She could feel that pain, understand it. It was of her own making. This other thing, this loss, this emptiness sprang from something she could not change. And her helplessness made her furious.

"Want me to drive?" Jack asked in a gentle voice.

"Shut up," she said. They were all silent as she drove into Seiling and turned north, knowing she could not drive or fly away from the dreary horror of this day.

NORTH AND WEST, the crew of *Zany Weddings* had set up its cameras to capture an entrancing view of the gloomy and globular storm that crawled toward them over the rolling landscape. They'd done a couple of quick interviews with the engaged couple, and Aurelius had brought out a small leather book into which he'd pasted the Church of the L.E.D. wedding rites, which he'd printed off the Internet. He was ready if the storm was, but they couldn't see anything that suggested it was going to produce a nuptial tornado.

"It's pretty rain-wrapped," Brad said, stating the obvious.

"It's tornado-warned," Aurelius noted, more to say something exciting for the cameras than to express any sort of optimism. "We might see something as it gets closer."

"It's already on top of us," noted Danni. She and Scooter had covered their cameras with nylon wraps as a few drops of rain began to fall, and Vinyl sat in the crew van, listening to something other than their chatter, judging by the way he was rocking his headphones. Tyler and Polly Ann huddled under an umbrella, looking miserable.

Danni was right. The wind had picked up, and the sprinkles became a steady shower.

"Let me check the radar again," Aurelius said. He popped into the van and pulled up the radar image on the laptop. There was still a tornado warning, but he saw on the loop that although the storm had vigorous rotation when it passed over Fort Supply Reservoir, not far to their west, it had all but fallen apart.

He stepped outside to give his report. "It doesn't look good, and there's no sense in just standing here and getting wet." He heard a strange slapping sound behind him and turned around. "What was that?"

"Hallucinating again?" asked Brad. He was smiling malevolently when the next fish hit him in the head.

"Ow!" Brad exclaimed, echoed by Tyler's "What the hell?"

Aurelius caught sight of another flash of scales beyond Brad amid the sprinkles, then more and more, accompanied by the faint scent of algae. The fish fell around them in a bombardment right out of a surrealist painting. They whacked the vehicles and hit the ground, where the poor creatures worked out their last breaths in the red Oklahoma dirt.

"Film it!" Danni screamed. She reached into the van and cuffed Vinyl on the earphones, jarring him out of his trance. "Film it, damn it!"

She and Scooter snapped into action, and Vinyl stuck his microphone boom out the open door of the crew van. Aurelius admired their utter inconsideration of the biblical implications of this catastrophe, even as he felt a slimy creature smack him in the shoulder.

"Looks like a crappie to me!" said Tyler, who'd turned his umbrella upside down and was trying to catch what he could, leaving Polly Ann screaming. She ran to the cake car and dove in.

"Crappie?" Aurelius asked.

"Crappie bass! Oh, look, a catfish!" It had landed neatly in the umbrella and looked quite taken aback.

Danni laughed in delight, breaking the cardinal rule of the invisible cameraman, but Aurelius couldn't blame her. This was insane. He looked up to catch a foot-long walleye on the nose. His left nostril started bleeding as Tyler picked up the fish.

"I'm out," Aurelius said, jumping in the cake with Polly Ann, who looked out the windows in stunned disbelief as her future husband jumped from spot to spot, trying to catch more fish. Brad cowered next to the crew van, covering his head, trying to find shelter that wasn't there. Aurelius found a fast-food napkin in the glove box and stuffed it in his nose to stanch the bleeding.

"What does this mean?" asked the mystified bride, her dress spattered with water. If any fish scales had marred her attire, they were neatly camouflaged by the sequins.

"I believe there was a tornado, only we didn't see it," Aurelius said. "It passed over the lake and picked up the plague of fish you see before you."

"This is really weird," she said in a dazed voice. "Maybe God doesn't want us to get married."

In moments, the downpour of fish ended, followed by a deluge of rain and nickel-size hail. The remaining cast and crew hurled themselves and their belongings into the vehicles. Tyler was the last one in, his dark hair dripping, with no less than seven fish in his umbrella.

"Hey," he said, muddy and grinning. "Y'all got a bucket?"

JACK HAD LET himself doze off just once as Maribeth drove them north and east into the evening. They made a pit stop, drove east again, then north into the middle of nowhere, and parked in a dirt lane just off a gravel road. They were west of Enid, with plenty of space between the research van and the approaching line of storms. The lightning was vigorous, constant, snapping to the ground and scattering up through the clouds, talking back and forth, tapping out a luminous code in the darkness, accompanied by the rising and falling sound of percussive thunder. The cameras were operating, even the Ghost, which, after a careful inspection and a thorough dusting, Fred had declared operational.

"Unfortunately, I think it blew its wad on less than ideal bolts," Fred told Jack as they stood outside, leaning against the van, eating pretzel sticks and watching the storms.

"What do you mean?"

"It responded to the light trigger and clicked on, but the lightning it recorded was about as pretty as a frog in a banana pudding."

"So record some more," Jack said.

"Where do you think we *store* HD video at 25,000 frames per second?" Fred asked. "The goddamn hard drives are full. Both of them."

"It might be worth looking at later," Jack said, though he was thinking more about the tornado footage he'd shot. He wondered what everyone else saw. What those boys saw.

"I'm going to call my wife and see if she can get my kid on the FaceTime," Fred said, sounding glum. "They're an hour ahead of us. Might be asleep."

"How old is your kid?"

"She's eighteen months." Fred's tone turned wistful. "An angel with blond, curly hair." Jack marveled that this sentimental dad was the same temperamental engineer who'd been yelling at him half the day.

"Just watch that potty mouth," Jack teased him.

"What kind of fucking monster do you think I am, Andreas? I don't curse in front of my *child*." With that, Fred let slip a small smile and disappeared into the van. And Jack dropped his bag of pretzels through the open passenger window and went to find Maribeth.

She'd made herself scarce after they'd come to a stop, and he hadn't wanted to bother her. Or rather, he had really wanted to bother her, but he wasn't sure his need to talk to her should trespass on her need to be alone. Not until now.

She wasn't within the soft glow cast by the van and its gadgets. He stepped beyond it, a few feet down the lane. Since the adrenaline had worn off, his body had relaxed into sleep deprivation, wearing it like an old slipper, and the world hovered somewhere between wakefulness and dreaming, especially in this shimmering darkness. It took a moment for his eyes to adjust, and then he could make out the grassy verge, a field with a low, stone wall, and strange shapes beyond.

He walked several feet, looking for a gap in the wall, and found it — a broken iron gate, half off its hinges, swinging in the wind. It creaked as he pushed it aside, rusting under his hands.

Above him, he could see stars, innocent sparks that would soon be overtaken by the black and explosive storms to the west. Ahead, he made out a few shapes in the dim light, some squat and low, some tall and thin, mismatched and spread wide apart. One separated into two, the second fluid in its motion, and he recognized the shadowy curves of Maribeth.

She stood still as he approached, reminding him of a deer poised for flight. But he wasn't a hunter. Was he?

"What is this place?" he called out softly.

"A cemetery," she said. "Maybe a family plot or an old churchyard. Though it seems disorderly. Spread out. I don't know."

"Half the stones are leaning," he said, keeping his voice low. "And there aren't very many of them."

"And the shapes are so different, you know? That one's an obelisk. This one's square. Feel this." She reached for his hand, a gesture that so startled him he almost withdrew, but he let her lay his fingers up against the stone. "Feel how rough it is," she whispered. "Marble, I think. Old."

"Weathered," he said, turning his hand over so he could grasp her fingers. "The wind and the rain, wearing them down for all these years."

"They haven't surrendered yet," she said.

He didn't want to move, didn't want to break whatever spell was being woven about them, somewhere between the starlight and the distant lightning.

"That was my nickname in training," she said in a self-mocking tone. "Never Surrender."

"I can believe that," Jack said, edging closer to her, leaning against the stone, his arm barely touching hers as he settled in next to her, shifting his hand, still holding on. They stood for several seconds that way. Jack listened to the wind in the rough grass around them and the distant thunder.

"I just keep thinking if I'd gone back," said Maribeth, "or said something different, or stopped earlier . . . "

He ran his thumb over her hand. He meant to soothe her but found desire in the warmth and texture of her skin. There was something about her, something he'd been resisting, something real and something hidden behind her jokes, her frank manner. She had a presence he rarely felt in women, a force to reckon with, a defiant spirit, a molten core under her sometimes frosty exterior. More simply, this close to her, he wanted her. He pushed the craving down, addressed her distress.

"A million intersections," he said. "A million ways to change the future. But you can't change the past. Maybe none of us can change anything."

"I refuse to believe that."

"Never surrender," he teased.

He thought he saw her smile. She withdrew her hand and crossed her arms, but she didn't move away. She radiated heat, leaning against his shoulder, or rather allowing him to lean against hers in the cooling wind of night.

"Once I think a certain way, it's hard for me to change," she said. "It's always been that way. And in my mind, I am always going to see myself leaving those boys back there in the storm."

Jack spoke low, barely louder than the wind. "You tried twice. They ignored you. It's just too bad they didn't take you up on it. You're a hero."

"I'm not that. I hate that word. That's a word politicians use to talk about us, but they don't know what it was like. They don't understand what we had to do."

They weren't talking about the tornado anymore. Jack wasn't sure what to say. So he stayed silent and studied her strong profile, those cheekbones, the gentle illumination of her eyes as lightning cast its spectral, shifting light upon them. She was looking at the storms and something beyond, something she didn't want to see, would always see.

"*I* know you," he finally said. "Real heroes are pretty scarce, but you're the closest thing I know to one."

She looked him in the eye, her expression skeptical. "Better save it for Superman," she said. "Comic books. That's where the heroes are. Fighting for the right in Technicolor leotards." She punched him lightly in the arm. "Bam, pow."

"Zap, bang," he said in the same playful tone, elbowing her arm in return, just as lightning capered across the western sky, a spectacular, forking firework of light.

She gasped. "Did you make that happen?"

He reached for her hand. This time, he didn't let go. He had never been more tired, more awake.

"Zap, bang," he whispered, leaning in to touch his mouth to hers. Her supple lips molded to his, tenuous, as if she might vanish with the next lightning flash. The moment was so electric, so fleeting, that he shivered when she broke away. He opened his eyes. Headlights had flooded the scene.

"Damn," she whispered, echoing his thoughts, as she looked up at the truck stopping by their van. She squeezed his hand once before walking toward the truck. He still felt the heat of her fingers, her lips, a stirring in his body. He wanted more.

He followed her up the lane and saw Fred hopping out of the van.

"Turn off those damn lights, will you?" Fred yelled at the driver. "You're going to completely fuck up my photography!"

The headlights went off, and as Jack got to the vehicles, he recognized the truck as Chuck's Wagon. His stomach rumbled. He could use something other than pretzel sticks.

A side panel on the truck popped open, revealing a counter and a modestly lit kitchen beyond. "I'm so sorry to disturb you, but I thought you might like some dinner," said the long-haired, slender, sun-creased driver. He smiled, unperturbed by Fred's fury. "Hello, my friends, hello!" he greeted Maribeth and Jack.

"Hello," Maribeth said warily.

"I could so use a sandwich," Jack said. He couldn't help himself. Fate had sucked earlier today, but at least now she was bringing food to their bumper.

"I highly recommend the curried chicken salad," the man said. "It's rather late, so I'm not cooking right now, but I have some excellent cold cuisine."

"Who are you?" asked Maribeth.

"Charles Smith, at your service," he said. "Are you hungry?"

Her caution eroded at his friendly manner. "Starved," she admitted. "I'll take one of those chicken salad sandwiches."

"Me, too," Jack said. "Fred!" he called.

Fred looked sheepish on the edge of the road. "Do you have peanut butter?" he asked. "I have this crazy thing for peanut butter."

"I have a peanut butter, blueberry and bacon sandwich you simply must taste," Charles said. "It will take you into another dimension."

"That sounds so weird I have to try it," Fred said. "I — thanks for stopping."

"I'm here to replace what the storms have taken out of you," the cook replied. "I'm here to feed your stomachs and your souls. Did you find what you sought today?"

They were all silent for a moment. Jack, finding the question disturbing on multiple levels, looked at Maribeth.

Fred rescued them. "We are now. Lightning."

"You seek lightning?" Charles asked, his face brightening

as he took payment from Fred and set about assembling their sandwiches. "Then you are rare among the nomads."

"How so?" Fred asked.

"Most of them seek the violent expression of Nature's tantrums," he said, "and not the balance implicit in lightning, the restoration of order." Jack tried to keep his inner skeptic from laughing. He didn't want the crazy guy to lose it altogether and stop making his sandwich.

"I can tell you do not see the global electric circuit as I do," Charles continued, with an eyebrow raised at Jack, "but I also seek the truth in lightning. And so does your boss, I take it?"

"Our boss?" Fred asked, more guarded.

"I saw the 'Y' on your van. Why is always a good question to ask. And when. Timing is everything." Charles looked pointedly from Maribeth to Jack and back to the sandwiches, which he wrapped in white paper. "And sometimes what we see as perfect timing or luck, good or bad, is really destiny manifesting itself. It shows we are on the right path toward our purpose, even if we don't know what that purpose is."

Jack felt uncomfortable. What the hell was this guy talking about? He yawned. He was still so tired. He took his sandwich and bottle of water, determined not to think about it any further, at least not tonight.

"Thanks," Jack said. "Lucky you found us."

"Destiny brought me here," Charles said. "Destiny fills your bellies tonight. Destiny will bring me to you again." He closed the side panel, and a minute later, he popped up in the driver's seat. The truck went on its way, lumbering into the darkness.

Jack took a bite and closed his eyes, letting the grapes pop in his mouth amid the salty-sweet combination of chicken and curried mayonnaise. He wasn't much of a gourmand, but this was special. He opened his eyes and smiled at Maribeth, who looked equally happy with hers. She gave him a thumbs-up. Was there a new light in her eyes? He was too fatigued to tell, but he found himself hoping that gleam was more than his imagination.

Fred was heedless of anything but his dinner. "I don't know about destiny," he said between bites, "but this is one fucking great sandwich."

MARIBETH TURNED down Fred when he offered to drive the van to Enid for the night. She felt it was her job to get the crew secure and rested. They could get back to central Kansas tomorrow in time for her to fly if the plane was ready; they'd know in the morning. Jack had been sure there'd be more storms to chase.

They were all exhausted, especially Jack. As soon as they started rolling, he drifted off, still paying the price for his overnight drive. Maribeth noticed Fred was out, too, when she looked in the rearview mirror.

They'd been through a lot in one day, but not as much as some. The massive tornado had destroyed a few structures on the farmland where it had cut its path, according to the radio, including the home of a ranching family who'd survived in a cellar. And there were reports of five deaths in automobiles. No details were given, and Maribeth didn't want them. Now soft pop music played, almost indiscernible above the road noise.

Driving while the others were asleep gave her a chance to think, a chance she didn't necessarily want. She felt alone in the near silence, driving in the light rain; alone, except for the palpable presence of Jack in the passenger seat. Jack, who'd broken through her defenses in the cemetery. She didn't think they were that easy to breach, but her alarms were quiescent as he got close to her, first with words, then his kiss. There must have been a reason she let him in. She was loath to admit it, but her body wanted to take that kiss so much further than her brain did.

She was disciplined about things like that. She made logical choices. In the Army, she'd stayed away from any relationship that might be trouble for her career, which meant she'd stayed away from most of them. There was a boyfriend at home for a while during that time, a friend with benefits, and there'd been one or two guys otherwise, but they hadn't meant much. She didn't need the trouble.

And oh, boy, here was trouble. How was she going to keep this excursion professional with her body wanting to go full throttle and her brain slamming on the brakes? She had forgotten the pressure of desire, had shut out its chaotic energy. She preferred order, machines that did what she told them to do. She liked quiet nights and peaceful dawns over the clouds. Maybe this impulse was just a manifestation of being alone too long, or of proximity syndrome; Jack was here and available. Fred was too young and married; Dr. Y was too old and, she knew from flying him in the corporate jet days, had more than one handsome fellow available for botanical garden tours and nights at the opera. Hell, she was older than Jack by a couple of years, as she knew from reading his resume. Besides, it was only a kiss, and there was no telling if anything like that moment would come up again, or if it was a moment of weakness on either part. It was a moment, that was all. A moment of wind and lightning and stars.

She gave her head a shake and stretched as well as she

could in the van's seat without letting go of the wheel. This line of thinking was foolish nonsense, and the situation was absurd. She belonged in an airplane, not on the road with a sexy storm chaser and his profane engineer sidekick.

Not wanting to wake Jack, she leaned over to the laptop and used the GPS software to map the route to the hotel. The last several miles slipped by like water, flowing in the darkness, punctuated by the passing of misty headlights and occasional lightning flashes from the dying storms, as her mind returned again and again to the kiss — just as, again and again, she tried to shut it out.

She pulled the van into the hotel parking lot just before midnight. The roll to a stop jarred her passengers, and they stretched and looked around, wide-eyed as prairie dogs.

"This is definitely better than the places I stay when I'm chasing on my own," Jack said of the upscale chain hotel.

"Dr. Y doesn't want us bringing bedbugs back to the hangar," Fred joked.

"Don't even say that word," Maribeth said. "I can put up with just about anything except for the idea of invisible insects sucking my blood while I'm sleeping."

"Tiny vampires, feasting on your succulent skin," Jack said in a whisper, looking diabolical.

"Stop it, goddamn it," Maribeth said, stepping out of the van and heading toward the back to get her bag.

Jack met her back there. "Their tiny jaws chewing on your tasty toes," he continued.

"Seriously? Are you sure I'm not packing a gun?"

"It won't protect you against the evil little creatures and their blood-sucking tubes," said Jack, his tone suggestive.

"Are y'all done?" Fred asked, elbowing his way between them to get his own bag. "Give me the keys."

Maribeth handed them over, and Fred closed the back door and hit the lock button until there was a honk.

"There's a lot of hardware in there," Fred said quietly, "and I don't want anything to happen to it. You should hear the alarm we've put on this thing. It's absolutely ridiculous. It would give a sloth a heart attack."

"Oh, I like sloths," Maribeth said absently, slinging her bag over her shoulder and heading for the doors. "They're cute."

"Not as cute as those little bugs under a microscope," said Jack, walking next to her. "Now that's cute."

"Are you going to shut up?" Maribeth said, but this time she couldn't help but laugh.

"At your service," Jack said, opening the door for her. Fred followed, and they went to the counter and underwent a grueling check-in process that consumed the little energy they had left. Then it was upstairs to their rooms, which were all on the same green-wallpapered, floral-carpeted hallway.

Fred found his first, and Maribeth followed Jack to the other end of the passage.

"See you at the continental breakfast," Maribeth said softly, so as not to wake the other guests, as she stopped at her door and slid the key card in the lock. Before she could go in, Jack leaned close.

"See you then, unless you need protection from the creatures of the night," he whispered in her ear. "Or a sip of bourbon. Call anytime." His impish smile seemed like something more than a joke and, she had to admit, almost irresistible.

"Thanks," she said, mustering a dry, confident smile, and closed the door behind her.

JACK AWOKE from a nightmare into a nightmare, a nightmare of noise, a nightmare of being dragged from sleep just two hours after having been awake for thirty-nine. It was a howling sound, an electronic scream, not quite a tornado siren, though that was the sound haunting his dreams. This wasn't a siren, but it was definitely an alarm.

"The van," he said in sudden realization and sat bolt upright. He felt like shit. It didn't help that he'd capped his endless day with two generous pours from the bottle of bourbon he kept in his bag. Robotically, he donned his jeans and threw on the sour T-shirt he'd worn the day before. He stuffed his bare feet into his high-tops, grabbed his key card and ran downstairs and out the front door before realizing he had no way to shut off the earsplitting alarm. He'd have to wake Fred.

There was no need. Fred stumbled out the front door of the hotel, too, in sweatpants, flip-flops and no shirt at all. With his scruffy beard, pasty skin, furry chest and bedhead, he strongly resembled a lost vagrant. Lights went on in several rooms, and someone shouted, "Turn it off!" from a second-story window.

"What's happened to it?" Fred asked wildly. "Did someone break in?"

"First turn off the goddamn alarm," Jack growled. "Do you have the keys or whatever you need to turn it off?"

"Oh, yeah," Fred said, looking in his hand and seeing the keys there, as if for the first time. "Here." He extended the fob toward the van and pressed a button.

The electronic caterwauling abruptly ceased, leaving a vacuum of near-silence — the hushed sounds of wind, insects and a distant train. The rain had stopped. Jack looked around. Lights were going off again in the hotel, and he fought back a wave of queasy fatigue so he could help figure out what was going on.

Fred gingerly stepped toward the van. Jack followed his lead, and moving in opposite directions, they circled the vehicle, looking for signs of trouble.

"Glass looks fine," Fred said. "Doors look fine." They started pulling on handles until they'd tried them all, before Fred unlocked the back, hopped in and did a quick inventory. "It's all here," he said, getting out again. "I think maybe we dodged a bullet."

"Well, something set it off. It wasn't the wind. Was it?"

"No, it's not that sensitive."

Jack badly wanted to go back to bed, but the mystery bothered him. "Let's take one more look, just to be sure," he said.

They walked slowly around the van, examining it from top to bottom.

"What the fuck?" Jack heard Fred say from the passenger side.

Jack walked around to meet him. "What is it?"

"Look," Fred said, pointing under the van. Next to the back wheel was a fish.

Jack tried to process this image. Something made it especially weird. "Why does it have duct tape on it?"

"Does it?" asked Fred, just as baffled.

"Look." Jack reached under the van and carefully pulled out the fish by the tail. Two strips of duct tape were stuck across the front and back of its foot-long body, trailing long, sticky ends that had picked up dirt from the parking lot.

Fred stared at it for a dazed minute, and then he started laughing.

"I appreciate this is funny-strange," Jack said crossly, "but why is it so funny-ha-ha?"

"Someone is fucking with us, my friend," Fred said. "This is a classic. My fraternity loved this one."

"You're a frat boy? And what are you talking about?"

"Engineering fraternity," Fred said, waving off the question. "Sticking a fish in the wheel well. It's a classic practical joke. We'd notice the smell in a day or two."

"But why? And why didn't it stick?"

"I guess the alarm scared them off before they could get it done. As for why — random act of idiocy?" Fred speculated. "I don't know. Got any enemies?"

Jack mulled the question. "Not sure. Do you?" he asked.

"Fuck no. I'm lovable as a kitten in socks," Fred said. "But just in case, I'm going to move the van up by the front doors and ask them to keep an eye on it. There's a security camera up there, too. I think it'll be all right. I'd sleep in it, but —"

"No," Jack said. "We're both exhausted. Move it and go to bed. I'll see you in the morning."

"Oh, shit," Fred said. "I left my hotel key in the room."

"They'll get you another one at the desk," Jack said. "That's one of the lesser disasters of the past twenty-four hours."

"True," Fred acknowledged, getting into the van and cranking it up for the move under the hotel's concrete marquee.

Jack looked around and wondered if Maribeth had heard the sound. Hell, Santa at the North Pole had heard it. He looked up at the second floor, about where he thought their rooms were, and saw a curtain fall back across a window. Discretion, the better part of valor, he mused.

He walked slowly back toward the hotel, still holding the creature by the tail, looking around, trying to figure out why they'd almost ended up carrying a rotting fish to its final destination. Was this a random prank? Some kind of anti-storm-chaser thing? Or karma?

At the door, he dropped the fish into a trash can. A strange shape caught his eye. It was a vehicle at the far end of the parking lot, almost hidden by the shadows, with a peculiar stepped box on top, like a turret. He had trouble making it out. Another storm-chasing tank? They were everywhere. You'd think kids would want to target something like that instead of their modest research van. He'd read that one of the more famous chaser tanks didn't even have air conditioning. A dead fish would have been putridly effective in a tin can like that.

There was no use speculating now. The prankster wouldn't be unveiled tonight. Jack climbed the stairs to his room, ripped off his clothes and collapsed into bed, where he drifted into dreams of heavy clouds and beautiful women, draped in mist, their arms outstretched in ecstatic flight.

AURELIUS FOUND the *Zany Weddings* team in the lobby of their Enid hotel, complaining that the breakfast room was already closed.

"About time you got up, princess," Brad said as Aurelius approached the cast and crew. Brad sat on the arm of a love seat; on the other end, Danni was curled up like a cat. Polly Ann sat on Tyler's lap in a chair, while Scooter and Vinyl shared a couch with their heads back and their eyes closed. Baggage lay about their feet.

"Plenty of time for today's chase," said Aurelius. "And I feel very well rested, thank you very much."

"I didn't get a lick of sleep after that alarm went off," said

Tyler, who'd added a cheap foam cooler to his belongings. He sure loved those fish, Aurelius thought.

"That was god-awful loud," Polly Ann agreed.

"I think I'm still deaf from it," Brad said.

"You must have sensitive ears," said Aurelius. "Either that, or you were right next to it. Adventuring around the world has taught me to sleep through most noise, though I confess that it did make me roll over." Truth was, he'd been awake for an hour after the alarm, consumed by an unfamiliar anxiety and loneliness, and in his moment of weakness had penned and sent a lovelorn email to his former paramour, Wynda, the fiery British producer. Who knew where in the world she was now? In the light of day, he hoped the email had gone astray. He'd burned that bridge a year ago.

"So was there a fire or something?" Tyler asked.

"Clerk told me it was some storm chaser van," said Danni, whose short red hair was still wet and spiky. "They thought it was a break-in or something."

"Which one?" asked Tyler, peering into the parking lot.

"It's gone. It left before I got up this morning, and I was up early," she said, ever cheerful. "I'm the only one who didn't miss breakfast."

"Hey, look," said Brad, "maybe it's our lucky day after all."

Outside, a colorful truck pulled up on the edge of the lot, and Aurelius realized with trepidation that it was Chuck's Wagon.

"Oh, yeah!" said Scooter. "Breakfast!"

"Load up your stuff first," Danni called to them as they jumped to their feet. "I already checked them out," she told Aurelius as they headed outside. "Why don't you get your bags and join us? And then we can talk strategy. At least we got some decent B-roll yesterday. Those fish were priceless."

She grinned, slung a bag and camera case over her shoulder, and headed outside.

Aurelius was in less of a hurry, but he knew they'd have to get going if they were going to get to the Kansas target area. He reluctantly headed upstairs to his room, grabbed his bags and went downstairs to drop off his key card. A few minutes later, he hovered several feet away from Chuck's Wagon as the others placed their orders.

"Could you grill up a fish for me right quick?" Tyler asked Charles, who was making egg sandwiches for everyone else.

"I don't stock fresh fish, young man, but I do an excellent eggs benedict, if you want to get fancy."

"I have the fish right here," Tyler said, popping the lid off the foam cooler he'd been carrying around. "I have seven of them. Wait — six? I thought there were seven."

Charles peered over the counter and looked into the small cooler. "Are they fresh?"

"Just, uh, caught them last night," Tyler said, and the others laughed.

"They fell out of the sky," Polly Ann said. "I think they're devil fish."

"Maybe they're just fallen angels," Charles said. "How about this. You give them to me, and I'll clean them and keep them on ice. If we meet again tonight, you can have a divine fish fry on me — as long as I get to join you."

"Well, I don't know," Tyler said, frowning into his treasure of fish and ice cubes.

"We don't want those smelly things in the vans," Aurelius said. Better to get rid of the fish now. He'd find a way to avoid Charles later. "Give them to the professional."

"Ah, my friend Mr. Zane, isn't it?" the cook called out as he took the cooler from Tyler.

Aurelius blanched. He hadn't told Charles his name. But then again, perhaps the cook knew him from television. He straightened up, remembering his reputation, and stepped toward the truck.

"It is I," he said with something of his old grandeur.

"And you are hungry," Charles said, handing out paper-wrapped sandwiches and cups to the others. Aurelius caught a glimpse of fluffy eggs, cheese and bacon nestled between croissants, and he felt his stomach rumble. Rather than argue, he decided to order and leave as quickly as possible.

"I'll have one of those," he said, "with cheese and spinach, if you have it."

"I'm glad to see you're eating your superfoods," Charles said as the others drifted away, eating and talking. "It is my belief that a spiritual journey requires a strong body as well as a strong mind." He turned and cracked an egg onto his griddle, where it sizzled pleasantly, and sprinkled seasonings on top of it. He brushed the inside of the croissant with butter and put it on the hot surface, too. The simple, delicious aroma made Aurelius think of home and Sunday mornings at his parents' house in Pennsylvania. He hadn't seen them in so long, but there was a reason for that. He was an adventurer. He was meant to roam the world, seek out nature's extremes wherever he could find them, and film them for posterity. But then, there was the bubbling egg and the smell of warm bread, and a mental snapshot of his mother sitting at the kitchen table, smiling, holding a cup of coffee and watching the songbirds outside at the feeder.

Charles used a spatula to flip the croissant out on the counter next to his stove, laid on the egg and a slice of the farmer's cheese that one of his signs advertised, and layered on the bright green spinach leaves. He capped and wrapped the sandwich and turned around to hand it to Aurelius.

"How much?" Aurelius asked.

"My gift," Charles said.

"But yesterday you told me everything had a price."

"Yesterday, you wished to feed only your body. Today, you wish to feed your mind."

"That's absurd," Aurelius said, taking a bite of the sandwich and finding himself deep in flavor, seasoned by a distant memory. "Do you have orange juice?"

"Certainly," Charles said, taking a bottle from his refrigerator, filling a sturdy paper cup and handing it over. "Squeezed this morning."

"Really?" Aurelius said, letting wonder get in the way of his determination to avoid talking to this strange fellow.

"Of course," Charles said. "If it's worth doing, it's worth doing well. It's worth appreciating the little moments. They have the biggest flavor. The big moments are too often lost in the rush of time, and we spend too often trying to get back to them, or trying to create them again, when they are already gone and yet always one step beyond our reach."

Aurelius nodded, but he wasn't entirely getting it. He was wrapped up in the taste of his breakfast and, with it, the fresh scent of the air after last night's rain and the sun beginning to shine through the scattering clouds. Sun and heat for the storms. And for a moment of light and warmth. The sandwich was gone. He drank the rest of the fresh, lively juice and looked at Charles again, not sure now how to take him. The man was a rumpled and wrinkled wizard. A great cook. An eccentric who probably didn't know what he was talking about. Still, it didn't do any harm to be friendly.

"Thank you," he said, putting his trash in Charles's outstretched hand.

Charles dropped it behind the counter and smiled. "I'll see you later this evening, perhaps," he said, "with your fish. And we'll talk some more."

It seemed to Aurelius that Charles was doing all the talking, but he nodded. "Be safe today. We're heading to Kansas."

"I've already plotted a course on the yellow brick road," Charles said with an enigmatic smile, and he shut the window, completing again the truck's mural of psychedelic storms and winged sandwiches.

"I'M AFRAID YOU'RE RIGHT," Dr. Y said as the video clip on the laptop concluded. He was seated at his desk, with Fred and Jack standing behind him. "It's not all we hoped, but it's an excellent test. What's the status of our video lab?"

"The guys will have it set up by end of business today," Fred said.

"Good, because I want to see what the Ghost gets on the big screen once it captures some upward lightning. I think the storms will actually intrude on the southern research domain today, so we might have a chance. Jack?"

Jack nodded. He was slightly less tired than the day before, after a few scant hours of sleep, but he was hardly alert. Instead, he was on edge and eager not to fuck up today as he increasingly felt he had fucked up the day before.

"We should get some action along I-70, maybe even right here in Salina," he said. "But I think we might have to go as far west as Hays for initiation."

"When the storms fire, we'll have Ms. Lisbon take off, and

we'll have the instruments activated throughout the wind farm," said Dr. Y, who tapped through more video and images taken by their other cameras last night. "In fact, I'd rather like to come along with you today, if I won't be in the way. Since there's a seat available."

Fred and Jack exchanged glances. One didn't say no to the boss.

"Whatever you like," Fred said. "It's your wagon. You might have fun."

"Oh, I'll be there for more than fun," said Dr. Y, closing the laptop and spinning around so he could look at them. His face conveyed his amusement. "Don't worry; I'm not going to spy on you. I have another little experiment I'd like to try. At any rate, I've chased storms before." He sighed. "Ah, my misspent youth."

Jack wondered just how misspent Dr. Y's youth could be, given he'd managed to build an almost unthinkable fortune in technology, much of it by the time he was thirty. All Jack had done by thirty was lose count of how many women he'd slept with and finally get his Ph.D. Two years later, he was still never sure about his bank account, but at least this job would tide him over — if he didn't screw up again.

He and Fred hadn't said anything to Dr. Y about their close call with the tornado, but Dr. Y already seemed to know a lot about their chase. He must have talked to Maribeth. Jack didn't get the sense she'd ratted them out — more like confided in Dr. Y. That was an interesting friendship, Jack thought. He felt an unexpected pang of jealousy, though he was pretty sure Dr. Y didn't swing that way. It was their confidence that interested him. He'd had a tiny, breathless view of what that kind of intimacy might be like last night with Maribeth, and it was strange to him, strange and enticing. He'd never met a woman to whom he really wanted to tell everything. Jack wasn't sure most were equipped to shine a light into the dark corners of his mental subbasements.

"We should leave by one, just to make sure we're in position," Jack said, putting himself to the task at hand.

"Thirteen-hundred hours," Dr. Y said with a smile. "That's how our pilot calls it. I'll be ready. Get some lunch. Great catering today!"

Fred and Jack left his office and headed to the hangar through the lounge, ignoring the feast of sandwiches, salads and desserts. Around the A-10, workers buzzed, finishing preparations.

Fred seemed nervous. "What the hell does he want to hang around for?" he said. "He should be back here, running the show."

"You mean you don't want him looking over your shoulder," Jack said. "I don't really get it, either, but maybe his experiment will be interesting."

"Or crazy," Fred said. "Now, you didn't hear that from me, but have you seen the pool thing?"

Jack laughed. "You mean when he shoots lightning through his head? Yeah, nothing crazy about that."

Fred grimaced. "I've got to make sure the hard drives and batteries and everything are squared away on the gear," he said. "I've doubled the storage on the Ghost so we can record longer, too. Why don't you go make yourself useful? Do a forecast or something."

"Sure thing," said Jack as Fred walked off, but he had already done an exhaustive forecast. The front that had helped kick off the storms yesterday had lifted north, and the low had deepened and moved only slightly east. The air over central Kansas was largely untapped, warm and moist and explosive.

He was sure there'd be storms, but for once, Jack didn't worry about whether he'd see a tornado. Yesterday's brutal encounter had blunted his insatiable appetite. The thrill had been trumped by a terrible respect. The disquiet was fading already, and he knew he'd want to see a tornado soon, but he felt different. Ready for something more. Perhaps this research could lead to something, a chance to do some good.

He wandered toward the A-10, its painted-on snarl lively in the lights of the hangar, its teeth ready to take a bite out of the sky. Its square tail looked unwieldy and formidable. The bubble canopy was flipped open. Maribeth sat inside, conferring with a guy in a jumpsuit standing on the top rung of the telescoping ladder that allowed the pilot to get in and out. She caught a glimpse of Jack and nodded, said a few more words to the tech and climbed out of the plane. Jack met her at the bottom of the ladder.

"Everything OK?" he asked.

"Essentially. The important stuff is fine. And by that I mean the stuff that will keep me in the air, which I deem a priority over the radiation detector."

"It's always good to know when you've been nuked by lightning," Jack said.

"Maybe so, but it's not like I can do much about it, and I'd have to get hit first. I'll be fine. Everything else is ready. I'll fly low and slow and hope I get lucky over the windmills."

"We'll be looking for you," he said.

"I'll be hard to miss," Maribeth said. "Not many A-10s flying over central Kansas in a thunderstorm."

He realized they weren't really saying anything, that they were dancing around what happened last night, but despite her deflection, he felt closer to her than he had just twenty-four hours ago. She was flushed and excited for the imminent flight. Her brown hair was pushed behind one ear, showing off brass-tone earrings that layered gears, wings and a propeller, very steampunk. Her brown Doc Martens boots could kick anyone's ass, except they were covered with — flowers? Yes, flowers. She didn't have her flight suit or G-suit on yet, but she wore an olive T-shirt with her jeans that shifted the color of her eyes from gray to smoky green. *Zap, bang,* he thought. And she smelled good, too.

"What is it?" she asked, breaking into his increasingly private thoughts.

He broke off his roving stare. "Oh, uh, there's lunch," he said. "Want some?"

Maribeth laughed. Was that the beginning of a blush? "You're weird," she said. "OK. I have a few minutes. My work is done, at least until my job *really* starts." They walked toward the lounge amid the clanging, hissing noises of the hangar.

"Does flying this not terrify you, just a little bit?" Jack said, waving at the Warthog.

"A little fear is healthy," she said, "but it's better than being in a car. Obviously."

"On some days, yeah," Jack said, wincing at the allusion to yesterday.

"And you're not scared by tornadoes, I take it?" she asked.

He shrugged. "If you're scared, it means you have something to lose."

"And you don't?" Maribeth had that serious look again, as if she was concerned for his well-being. He wasn't used to anyone being concerned about his well-being.

"What about flying the helicopter?" he asked, avoiding the question. "Was that scary?"

"Enjoyable if you stayed away from the hail. And amateur drones, of course." They exchanged a knowing look.

"Or gunfire," he said.

"I hope there's no more of that," she said as they entered the lounge. "I'm here, right?"

"I'm glad," he said, not wanting to scare her off, wanting her to keep talking. He picked up a plate and started filling it with food. "Did many women have the job you had? In the Army, I mean."

"Some."

"That's cool. For some reason I pictured you alone among the guys. I bet you made some good friends."

"Eventually," she said, picking out a turkey sandwich and fruit from the spread, along with a bottle of water.

"What do you mean?"

"I mean, I didn't have many friends at first. There were so few of us — women, I mean — it's like we were always competing. And we were always upset when one of us let us down. I mean, if we saw a woman not living up to standard, we'd think, shit, she's ruining it for all of us. The guys, most of them, they assumed you were a lesbian or a slut or a bitch — "

"Sounds like a great porn movie," he interrupted, "'The Bitch, The Lesbian and The Slut.' " Holy shit, did he say that out loud? His lack of sleep had dangerously loosened his tongue.

To his relief, she laughed. "Or a French art film. Anyway, I was going for *bitch*." She gave him a brief, mischievous glance as she sat in one of the chairs.

"Impossible," he said, returning her smile. He took a bite of his ham sandwich, a good one with melty Swiss cheese and brown mustard.

"Mostly not a bitch," she acknowledged, "except when I had to be. And sometimes I had to. You're fighting for respect all the time. I always felt like I had to prove I'd earned what I'd earned."

"Did people judge you like that?" He imagined her struggling to fit in, to show her worth, which was becoming more and more obvious to him. The idea of her being discounted just because of her gender angered him.

"Some of the men had prejudged us. Not all, but — anyway, I could be just as bad. I was always on guard, always worried about what we women looked like as a whole. It took an older pilot, a woman at the end of her career, to help me figure out that it was OK to be friends with other women. Some of us would get together in a tent and watch *Sex in the City* on a five-inch TV just to talk and kind of remember what it was like to be a girl."

"It must have been strange to watch four dolled-up women strutting around New York City in skyscraper heels while you're waiting for your next combat mission in the desert," Jack said.

She took a bite of a bright red strawberry, a somewhat distracting operation as the juice moistened and reddened her lips. "It seemed exotic, but it also seemed kind of normal. I craved normalcy. And I enjoyed the escape. It was a relief from the pressure. A break from always playing with the boys. Not that I don't like playing with the boys — I've always been that way. But it wears you out, always being on guard, coming up against the bravado all the time. Guys like you."

"Hey!" he exclaimed.

"You know what I'm talking about. Women communicate differently from men. And we think more, too. You — well, men — assume we're so emotional, but it's not the case. Men make snap decisions in stressful situations. We reason it out first. I saw it in combat all the time."

"I never thought of it that way," Jack said, taking a sip from his cola. "I just — act, now that you mention it."

"So think first today, OK?"

"I'll do my best."

Maribeth watched him for a moment. The scrutiny made him uncomfortable.

"This is an obsession with you, isn't it?" she asked. "Nothing gets between you and that tornado. I saw it in your face yesterday."

"I may have had a lapse in judgment yesterday," he admitted. "But chasing has always been like that for me. I've always wanted to get close, and even when I fail, I want to keep doing it. I don't get the people who chase for one or two years and disappear. I don't get the people who want to quit the chase before sunset and go have dinner when there's more light in the sky, more storms to see, and then lightning after dark. I don't understand walking away from it. But then there was yesterday. And those kids."

"Death changes you." She sounded calm, but her voice betrayed a long acquaintance with mortality.

"Yesterday was one of those reminders," he said. "I don't know. Maybe I've fooled around too long. It's good to be doing research again. I hope some good will come of it."

"As long as you don't try to drive into another tornado," she said. "I expect to see you and the van in one piece when the day is done."

She wasn't joking. She was serious again, her wide eyes fixed on his. She had a way of looking at him that made him question himself. Her gaze, so clear, suggested mysteries he wanted to solve.

He popped open a bag of potato chips and offered her some. "I always aim to make it to the next tornado," he said.

"A laudable short-term goal." She took a chip.

"I'm full of them," Jack said, his thoughts wavering between contemplative and carnal as they chatted and shared the bag, as his fingers brushed hers, as he tasted the salt and wondered when he would have a chance to kiss her again.

❧

"GREAT BEND," Aurelius said. He drove north on a minor road that had just taken them over the Oklahoma border into Kansas. A line of healthy cumulus clouds bubbled to the west — a long north-south line, neatly defining the dryline.

"Wichita," said Brad.

"You can't chase in Wichita," Aurelius said. "You'll be sitting in rush hour traffic if you do get a storm, and that's not where you're going to get a storm."

"It's in the middle of the moderate risk."

"That's because the entire area is going to get storms eventually," Aurelius said, "and the Storm Prediction Center is covering its — bases," he said, avoiding the more crass word in deference to the cameras. "Besides, Wichita is way too far east. If you're going to get a tornado, you want to get it from an isolated storm, and that'll be to the west."

"Since when do you know so much?" Brad demanded.

Since I read the SPC discussion this morning, Aurelius thought, but aloud, he said: "Try a little logic, Brad. How long have you been doing this?"

"Long enough to have flown into a tornado. And you?"

Aurelius had no answer to this riposte, but he heard no further objections when they made it to Route 160 and he took a left.

"My wedding dress looks a little rough after yesterday,"

Polly Ann said sadly from the back seat, where she was perched in a denim miniskirt, red halter top and sandals, just scanty enough to be perfect reality-TV attire.

"And my shirt stinks like fish, so I had to dig out one of my backup bowling shirts in case we need it," Tyler said.

"Well, you can't smell your clothes on camera," Aurelius said. "I'm sure they'll be fine."

"And you look wonderful no matter what you wear," Brad said to the bride, shooting Polly Ann a grin. His open flirtation wasn't just embarrassing; it was seriously bad for the show, Aurelius thought, and it had to stop. He glared at Brad, who now stared at one of the in-cab cameras and spoke.

"We're on our way to marry these two in a real whirlwind wedding with our prettiest bride yet," Brad said brightly. "And a groom who's almost as handsome, even if he does smell like fish."

"I do not!" Tyler said.

"But you just said —"

"I said my *shirt* smells like fish, and it's in the other van in my bag," said the offended groom. Danni must be thrilled, Aurelius thought.

"If you say so," Brad said with a charmless laugh. "I have keen senses, but my sense of smell isn't one of them."

Neither, thought Aurelius, is your sense of propriety or timing. "It's still two hours to Great Bend, so you might as well relax, everyone," he said, trying to defuse the tension. "We'll make a pit stop in Pratt and go north."

It was already two o'clock, and he hoped the storms would wait until they got into position. He wasn't sure how much more of this in-car chatter he could stand without weather to distract him. The adventure was leaking out of his life fast. What happened to his days of shooting typhoons while neck-deep in storm surge, of narrowly avoiding pyroclastic flows, of cave-diving in airless catacombs? Wasn't there something more to life than playing second fiddle to Treat the Terrible?

He reached between the seats, into the finely crafted, distressed-leather satchel that had added some eight hundred dollars to his credit-card debt, and pulled out a package of Ho Hos. He ripped it open with his teeth and bit into one of the comforting logs of chocolate-covered cake. The white swirl in its center looked up at him, as if to ask whether there wasn't more interesting rotation out there, or if he might not be going in circles, or whether he could get better nourishment than these cunning little snack cakes. Since when did snack cakes have a mind of their own? He put them into the cup holder, disgusted with himself. Since when did he have a mind that strayed from the path, a road of which he'd always been sure, the highway to danger, to Nature's worst tantrums?

Of *course* Nature had tantrums. Look at any TV show, and you'd see she'd been called worse than temperamental. She was Angry, Furious, Extreme, Deadly. And he wanted to take the fight to her and, of course, capture it all on film. Or did he? He looked in the rearview mirror at the, for the moment, unhappy couple, who gazed out different windows, and then at Brad, who made faces at himself in the side mirror as he checked out his profile.

Oh, Nature, Aurelius thought. You fickle wench. This relationship isn't working out.

He picked up the unfinished Ho Ho and, with a sigh, took another bite of its soothing, cream-filled vortex.

MARIBETH STOOD in the wide-open hangar doorway and watched the van leave with mixed feelings. She had no desire to chase a storm in a vehicle again anytime soon, though it was interesting chasing with Jack. He'd almost convinced her he knew everything about tornadoes until his miscalculation in the path of the Oklahoma wedge. Everyone screwed up sometime, she thought.

She wondered if she had screwed up, too, by letting him get under her skin. Because he was definitely getting under her skin. She must have sloughed off her tough hide in Florida like one of its lizards. He'd been around her for a couple of weeks in the subtropics, learning about the mission, and while their interaction hadn't been as intense as it had the past couple of days, she had a feeling he'd been working on her then, too. She just hadn't realized how deeply he'd slid under her scales with his charm and physical presence. That brief, breathtaking kiss in the graveyard had seemed so natural, so inevitable.

She hated herself for letting it intrude on her thoughts now, just before her first real chase in the Warthog. But Jack wasn't making it easy. When he'd left just now, Jack had enclosed her hand with both of his for a few seconds longer than was necessary. At first, he'd said nothing at all. Just flashed those damn green eyes at her.

"See you tonight," he'd finally said, which sounded much more fraught with gravity than the other guys' handshakes and good-lucks. He'd released her with the barest hint of a smile and one of his armor-piercing stares.

"This is bullshit," Maribeth told herself, not for the first time, and spun on her heel to return to her plane. Now was the worst part. The waiting. Though the A-10 was good for five or more hours in the air with the extra fuel tanks, Dr. Y wanted to wait until they were sure storms were in the works before they let her go. She understood, but she'd feel better in action. Like a stream, she constantly tumbled forward, living through motion; being forced to eddy in a tranquil pool was beyond frustrating. The waiting gave her time to think, and she didn't need that right now, nor the strange, warm feeling she still had after Jack held her hand as he told her goodbye.

IT WAS 4:30 P.M., and at a desolate intersection south of Hays, Kansas, that begged for an impeccably dressed Cary Grant to be dive-bombed by a crop duster, Jack, Fred and Dr. Y waited for the first storm to fire.

The cumulus clouds were not as densely seeded as they'd been the day before, but they looked promising against the blue sky, growing fatter by the hour. The crew had been at this intersection for close to two hours, occupying their time with a Frisbee and adjustments to their gear. Now Jack fought back the irritation of waiting by sitting in the passenger seat and paging through the data. He'd already virtually memorized the last hour's maps and models, but they changed often. At this point in the chase, he would rely on experience and his eyes, but the computer provided a distraction as he fought the urge to doze in front of his boss.

Fred and Dr. Y were in the back, adjusting the sensitivity of the light meter that would trigger the Ghost, tinkering with the other cameras and fielding phone calls. It was Dr. Y who fielded most of them, many via video chat, heedless of the data required. That's what being rich does for you, Jack thought. It lets you do whatever the fuck you want. That would include buying an endless supply of vintage aloha shirts like the one Dr. Y wore today, this one with the islands of Hawaii on it.

Rolling the end of a pretzel stick around in his mouth, savoring its chunks of salt, Jack tried not to pay too much attention to the calls. Still, he couldn't help wondering about Maribeth and her plane. They were supposed to give her the green light when the first storm was born, but there was nothing yet.

At least she was waiting in a hangar with access to catering and a bathroom. He'd already watered a bush outside twice.

"She can't stand not doing anything," Dr. Y said as he got off his latest call.

"What?" asked Fred, who was reseating a battery in the camera they'd been working on.

"Ms. Lisbon. She said to tell you both that she expects you to get a storm started by five, or she will personally make your lives a living hell when you return."

"Like mine isn't?" Fred said as he fought with the tripod mount on the bottom of the camera.

Jack grinned, imagining Maribeth's impatience. "Did you tell her that we've decided to call it off and wait for tomorrow?"

"Oh, no," Dr. Y said. "That wouldn't offer nearly enough suspense. I told her we expected storms to initiate well after 8 p.m."

"Ha!" Jack said. Even he was more optimistic.

"But then I took it back," confessed Dr. Y. "I couldn't torture her like that."

"She may not have to wait much longer," said Jack, peering out the window. "I think we have a critical mass of raindrops." The drops weren't falling on the glass; rather, they were a few miles to the west, coalesced into an almost transparent rain shaft that fell from the most bellicose cloud. It had assumed an aggressive, mounding appearance and had started to sprout an anvil. The late-afternoon light cast the young cell's bubbling convection in sharp relief, its roiling edges tinged with saffron.

"Now that's a pretty picture," Dr. Y said, looking to the west and then at the laptop in the back of the van. "I see a few showers on radar now."

"They're all starting to go," Jack affirmed, looking to the north- and southwest at the cumulus clouds that had been cooking there all day. They were, one by one, pushing up and through the warm layer above, on their way to maturing into thunderstorms. "I still like ours the best, but we'll keep an eye on them. This one's right on the nose of the dryline push, and it has some real meat on it."

"Don't make me hungry," Fred said. "It seems like everywhere we go, that food truck pops up. But not today, of course!"

"Food truck?" Dr. Y asked with interest. "I've read something about a storm-chaser food truck."

"It's run by this strange guy who calls himself Charles, even though the truck is called Chuck's Wagon," Jack said, still eyeing the growing cloud. They'd be fine for a few minutes here as it matured.

"You can't judge a man for being strange without walking in his shoes," Dr. Y chided with unusual forcefulness. "I'm sure he's no stranger than I am."

That wasn't a comparison Jack wanted to make. "So, are you going to call her?" he asked instead.

"Ah, an excellent idea," said Dr. Y, agreeably distracted now that his research could get underway. "Time to unleash the Warthog."

THE LATE-BLOSSOMING Kansas storms had done the *Zany Weddings* cast and crew a favor, giving them more time to get into position. Aurelius had convinced them they should wait at Great Bend, though a lot of chasers were gathering farther north, near I-70, as evidenced by the marching dots on Spotter Network. He figured that if a whole line of storms went up again, they could catch the southernmost cell and get their tornado.

The team needed a break, so they weren't that hard to convince when he spotted a sub shop. There, as most of them grabbed sandwiches and drinks, Danni took him aside in the parking lot and asked him what was going on. She'd been monitoring their van via the streaming video link and wasn't pleased with what she saw.

"I can't help it if Brad is an oaf," said Aurelius, who had become adept at hiding his own oafishness from the cameras.

"The squabbling is kind of fun for the show," Danni admitted, "but if he succeeds in screwing our bride, I'm going to cut his dick off."

Aurelius's eyebrows shot up at this uncharacteristically violent language from the always buoyant Danni. She didn't appear particularly bloodthirsty, but he knew it was time to start taking Brad's attitude seriously.

"I'll talk to him," he promised her. As co-producer, he liked her management style, calm and direct. Though her hair kept reminding him of his long-lost Wynda, this young woman was nowhere near as mercurial. Still, she might not be someone a man wanted to be around if she had a knife. He hurried off to find Brad.

The Twister Tracker was inside the sub shop, signing the T-shirt of the girl working the register, his Sharpie straying onto one mound of her ample bosom as another girl in an apron filmed the procedure with her phone.

"I am never going to wash this shirt," said the pretty young clerk. "I just cannot believe that you flew in a tornado. I am nowhere near that brave. I run to the cellar."

Brad, wearing another "I fly into tornadoes" T-shirt, smiled as he lifted the pen just shy the summit. "It's not a job for everyone," he said lightly.

"Brad, a word?" Aurelius called.

Brad looked up in annoyance, then composed his face so his fan wouldn't notice. "Sure, Zane."

The girls at the counter looked at Aurelius curiously, perhaps with vague recognition. That was his fate. Vague recognition. Why was he out here at all? He motioned Brad into a booth and spoke low, so only Brad could hear.

"You have to stop flirting with Polly Ann," Aurelius said.

Brad looked up as the register girl set a soda cup in front of him. "And I brought you a straw," she said shyly.

"Thank you, sweetheart." Brad smiled, his eyes following her small, curvaceous body as she returned to her post.

"Brad," Aurelius said.

"What? I have no idea what you're talking about."

"You're coming on to Polly Ann. This shoot is a major chunk of this season's budget. We can't let it go to hell because you want a piece of the action."

Brad looked shifty. "I thought sex sells."

"In this case, marriage and a lifetime of devotion sell, both of which have nothing to do with sex," Aurelius declared. "Don't screw this up for us."

"Don't you mean, don't screw this up for *you?* Look, Zane, people will be watching to see me and the storms, especially in the Tornado Alley episode. Whatever happens, it's going to sell. And people love drama."

"Some people still want honor," Aurelius said. "The other dumb wedding shows on TV get the ratings because, even though they know it's all fake, people believe deep down in their hearts that you can find true love by mixing one moron with a bunch of sex-starved singletons. Our show has more going for it. We have actual couples who love each other in the presence of terrific natural disasters and exotic locations. We don't need your — your shenanigans to ruin it for us. For the audience."

Brad slurped on his straw and put down his cup. "Let me give you some advice. There is no point thinking about the audience. I thought you already knew this. When I first met you, you seemed to get it. The point is to think about yourself. If you believe in yourself and do whatever you want, the audience will believe in you. The audience will follow. And I don't give a shit about ruining your show, Zane, because this is *my* show."

Aurelius sat with his mouth agape, but no sound came out as Brad smirked, got up and walked out the door.

"Young lady?" he finally called to the register girl. The other one was tapping on her smartphone, probably uploading the autograph video. "Could I have a Pepsi, please?"

"OK. That'll be a dollar fifty," she said. No free drinks for Aurelius. "You are so lucky to be working with Brad Treat," she continued as she walked the soda over to him. "What's he really like?"

"Hmmm," he said, handing her two dollars, taking a steadying sip of the cola and drawing on his knowledge of wildlife documentaries. "You know how rabbits are sleek, clever and fast? Handsome creatures." She nodded. "Well, he's like the stinky weasel who stalks and kills cute little baby rabbits by dancing around them and sinking his teeth into their necks." Aghast, she watched him as he took his soda out the door and into the glaring afternoon.

The rest of the crew stood in the parking lot, trying to see over the buildings to get a glimpse of the western sky. A clear view was nearly impossible, but to the northwest, he spotted a few storms pumping fists of cloud into the gray-blue of late afternoon. *Way* to the northwest. If they had any hope of filming this wedding today, they were going to have to fly.

MARIBETH FOUND the hours of waiting dreadful. The plane had been outside the hangar and fueled for hours. She'd played about twenty games on the pinball machine in the lounge while obsessively checking radar on her tablet computer, and when the word finally came, she'd stowed her bag in her locker and packed her flight suit's pockets with her wallet and her certificates, a tiny flashlight, a tin of mints, a handheld GPS unit, her phone — off as always during a flight — and a small notebook that contained emergency and regional airport information. Though if she needed that, she didn't even want to think about how screwed she'd be.

She donned the G-suit over the flight suit, climbed aboard and did her checks with the help of the ground crew. At last cleared by the tower and ready to fly, Maribeth eased the A-10 into position and began her taxi. She compensated for the offset nose wheel as she headed down the runway and, once again, got the familiar sensation from the sluggish turbofan engines that this beast might never lift off as she accelerated.

Then, seemingly at the last possible moment, she was airborne and climbing.

Her instructions were to approach the storms and fly a pattern around, under, into and in front of them, especially when she was over the wind farms. She turned toward the west — the ailerons let her turn this thing on a dime, if there were any dimes to be had up here — and smiled as she took in the breadth of her view.

There were half a dozen distinct cells elbowing one another along the horizon. Judging by the radar Dr. Y's team had added to her display, the biggest storm by far looked as if it would ride along and just north of I-70 into the realm of their experiment. The supercell dominated the air around it, and the only storm to its south had shrunk and been subsumed into a flanking line of feeder cells sucking on the warm, moist inflow carried by the southeast wind.

At top speed, she could be on the storm in less than fifteen minutes, but she didn't press it. Cruising at about 300 knots, or 340 miles per hour, she'd be there almost as fast. This was a very different target from what the Warthog was designed to hit. She would not be plowing rounds into a tank here. She would play this rendezvous much more delicately, flying close enough to get her readings and images and going into the storm as necessary, without putting the aircraft in jeopardy.

The A-10 was very different from the helicopters she flew in Iraq and then as a TV-station chaser, but fragments of those experiences flashed in her mind as she advanced. The adrenaline summoned them. She closed her eyes for a moment and willed them away, especially the unbidden images of murky, dusty raids in Iraq, the blaze of gunfire and the smell and the noise and the radio, the knowledge that someone waited on the other end of the fire she summoned, someone she had never met and would never have a chance to meet, a threat, a man with a gun, or maybe someone else, a person who'd become a paper target, a necessary loss, disposable in the machine of war.

She shook herself out of her dark reverie and blinked, swallowed, focused on the plane, checked her gauges, made sure everything was right before she closed with her objective. Emerging from the line was a beautiful storm, a Titanic amid a handful of fishing boats, a flagship in silvers and greens with a ragged, rounded appearance. It grew by the minute, darkening, subtly spinning, a supercell with — there it was — lightning.

She took a deep breath. The instruments were running. The high-speed cameras beneath her were ready to trigger. All she had to do was fly, and fly well. She could do that. Today, she wasn't hindered by wheels and gravity and earthbound chaos. She had wings.

"THIS IS CHAOS!" Fred shouted from the back as the van, driven by Jack, hurtled north on a gravel road through the hail core of a minor storm that had formed almost over their heads. They were trying to get into position on the big one, the one that seemed likely to roll over their target, the fields of giant wind turbines.

"This isn't chaos," Jack said as hail the size of nickels, punctuated by a few golf balls, hammered on the roof and windows. "This is a picnic." At least compared with yesterday. With the rush of the chase and all this racket, he was definitely awake. As he looked for new dings, he noticed the chip they'd earned a day ago on the passenger side of the windshield had become a crack and had grown by a couple of inches.

"At least the Ghost isn't sitting on the roof right now," a mildly excited, happy Dr. Y remarked as the hail thinned in favor of lashing sheets of rain.

"That's the truth," said Fred. "Yesterday —" And then he shut up, just in time to avoid revealing how much in jeopardy the hideously pricey camera and its housing had been as they fled the tornado.

"Still," Dr. Y said as he leaned forward and looked up, "I'd prefer to be in the clear air so we can set up to shoot the lightning."

"I'm working on it," said Jack. While raindrops still spattered the windshield, they'd entered a slice of sunlight between the updraft of the southern feeder storm and the big beast to its north. Jack glanced at the vertically integrated liquid readout on the radar app on the laptop and noted that getting into the hail core of the northern storm would not be such a good idea.

"Cannonballs," he muttered.

"Hmm?" said Dr. Y, taking a look at the radar himself. "Yes, you might want to get east. If you think it's best."

Jack wasn't sure how to take his boss's gentle guidance, but so far, it hadn't been bad.

"A couple of turns, and I'll have us at the Interstate," Jack said. "We can take that a little ways until we find a good exit where we can get a wider view." It almost hurt to say that: wider view. They were not in perfect position now, but they were close, and that's where he most liked to be.

The storm was shapely, with thin, frothy layers executing a slow spin over the mostly flat landscape just to their north. Hard, bubbling convection above those tiers soared in globular corkscrews toward the sky. Over their heads as Jack turned east, the mammatus-lobed anvil spread out in front of them and cast a broad, dark circle over the world, enlivened with sparks of prickly lightning.

There wasn't a wall cloud on the storm, yet — no lowering to indicate a nascent tornado — but with the obvious rotation, he wouldn't be surprised to see one soon. He took a breath and reminded himself why he was here: to shoot lightning, to take readings, to do science. And that was a good thing. Better than the willy-nilly chasing most of the hordes were doing out here today. Even on these gravel roads, he'd already seen several other chasers.

As he turned north again, almost to the highway, he recognized that he might not get all that far east of the storm if it had its way. Now under the anvil's shadow, they had trouble keeping ahead of it. The supercell was moving fast, maybe fifty miles an hour, driven northeast by the raging river of wind above them. They wouldn't have a whole lot of time to set up. He looked up again, this time scanning for a plane. Nothing was in sight, but that didn't mean anything. She might be flying behind him. She was up there somewhere.

Dr. Y checked his phone. "She's flying a pattern," he said in answer to Jack's unspoken thought. "She's fine."

"Yes, she is," Jack said, and he heard Fred guffaw in the back. That hadn't come out quite right. He reached for a distraction. "So are you going to tell us what your experiment is, Dr. Y?"

"I think you might find it interesting, Dr. Andreas," said Dr. Y, merry behind his gold-rimmed glasses. "It's a lightning tent."

"A *what?*" Fred asked.

"A lightning tent," said Dr. Y. "A portable lightning shelter made with cloth woven with metal mesh and an elevated poly-carbonate floor. I thought I might deploy it today."

"Huh," Fred said. "I guess we could stick it out there while we shoot our footage."

"I don't think you understand," said Dr. Y. "I intend to get inside it."

Jack gripped the steering wheel and felt a wave of unease. A lightning tent? So that was the package the techs had loaded into the van earlier? This was *nuts*. And it was definitely not what he had signed up for — sticking a billionaire into an envelope so he could be zapped like a frozen burrito.

Hell, one disaster at a time, he thought. They still had to get ahead of the storm.

As they reached the Interstate, Jack took the ramp and accelerated east, with the spiraling sky-monster throwing down spears of forked lightning behind him as it filled his rearview mirror.

"SHOULD I CHANGE INTO MY DRESS?" Polly Ann asked from the middle seats as Aurelius drove as fast as he dared.

"Yes, definitely," Brad declared, just as Aurelius said, "I wouldn't rush into it."

"There's no tornado, is there?" Tyler asked, sounding defeated. Scooter was in the back, shooting the video the in-car cameras wouldn't catch.

"Well, there *might* be a tornado," Aurelius said, "but whether we will see it is another question entirely. I'm trying to get us there."

He'd made the mistake of heading west first, not realizing just how fast the distant storm would crank east. Now they were behind the eight-ball as he headed back north, hoping to find a good place to turn and pursue it.

"Storm chasing is really just a big waste of gas, isn't it?" Polly Ann noted in her Okie lilt. "It's never like this on TV. It's like, tornado, tornado, tornado, tornado —"

"True," said Brad, who sat sideways in the passenger seat so he could talk face-to-face with the couple. "Editing cuts out the boring parts. But at least this gives us all time to get to know each other." He leered at Polly Ann, but she didn't seem to notice.

"All the same, even though I can take a few weeks off, it'd be a lot better for me if we got married in the next few days," said Tyler. "This is my busy season."

"What do you do, Tyler?" Aurelius asked. He knew he'd been briefed, but he couldn't remember. Something to do with construction. Maybe this would be good for the show.

"I build storm shelters. Cellars. Safe rooms. It's not really the best time of year to put them in, given all the crazy weather, but when people get scared, the phone rings off the hook."

"Ah," Aurelius said. "And your house is the ultimate storm cellar."

"Nothing as safe as an underground house," Tyler agreed, relishing this unpaid commercial.

The radio crackled. "Aurelius," came Danni's voice. "You hear the weather radio? That storm has a tornado warning on it."

"Shit," Aurelius said under his breath. Then into the radio: "Radar-indicated, or did somebody see one?"

"Radar-indicated right now, but I'd like to get there if we can do it. Faster. Within reason."

He sighed. "I agree. I'm going to take us right up to I-70 and blast east."

"The warning says it's on I-70."

"Yes, but it's already east of Hays, and it's the fastest way. We may have to punch through the back side." The idea of this dangerous maneuver cheered him.

"OK," she said. "You guys are the storm chasers. Whatever gets us there."

Aurelius glanced over at his co-star, who looked a wee bit worried. "Ready, Twister Tracker?" Aurelius asked.

"Um, sure," Brad said. "Bring it on. No risk, no reward, right?" But his eyebrows, which lifted in worry and collided in the middle of his forehead, said anything but.

THE STORMY FLIGHT almost started to feel routine. Excited to be executing her mission at last, Maribeth flew her pattern. The supercell edged over the westernmost turbines, marking the start of where the experiment's instruments were distributed throughout the wind farm. She double-checked the status of the gadgets on the plane and confirmed with the hangar team that it was receiving data transmissions.

Her confidence in the A-10 grew by the minute. It could more than handle the whims of the storm. Even with the bumpy ride, she felt comfortable in her cocoon. Dr. Y's bean counters had marveled at the tight space in the cockpit during a tour of the hangar, but after years of flying, she found it more than accommodating. It wasn't like an F-16, as her instructor had been fond of telling her, where you could barely fit an aspirin inside the cockpit with you. This updated airplane had an autopilot system that helped her if she needed it, and there were cubbies to stow snacks and tools. The A-10 responded to her touch like a good horse to the reins, and the engines' power seemed to transmit itself into her body, exhilarating as she felt more than heard their roar keeping her aloft and intensely alive.

Still, there were plenty of tasks to demand her attention. She was grateful the staff was keeping video calls to a minimum. Communications could be tricky in the storm. At times, the radio buzzed with static as charge built up on the aircraft and dissipated. There'd been no lightning yet generated by the airplane. She'd like to trigger a strike for Dr. Y if she could, trusting that the airplane would do its job and keep her safe.

She'd been in and out of the rain, but mostly she'd kept just to the east of the storm's core, not wanting to tangle with the hail. This was a tough plane that was built to take a lot more than hail strikes, with a bulletproof windscreen and an armored cockpit, but the potential interaction of hailstones with the engines worried her. Hail was the one thing everyone had recommended she avoid, one more thing to remember as she maneuvered around the worst of the storm. With the engines placed high on the tail, debris from the ground was almost never an issue, but debris in the sky? Yeah, that could suck.

She dropped her altitude now that the cell was moving into the domain of the experiment. If lightning struck the turbines or triggered an upward flash, she wanted to make sure the plane's cameras caught it.

Maribeth tightened her pattern so she could stay mostly over the towers with their white, slowly spinning blades. Their red warning lights blinked in unison as the supercell created its own twilight. The sky was an eerie blue-green to her west, and the storm had dreamy striations, rotating tiers of cloud. But she didn't see a tornado. There was so much precipitation, it might have been obscured if there was one.

The cameras did the hard work of recording the bolts, but she scanned the dynamic atmospheric theater with eager eyes. She wanted to see what Dr. Y was after.

There! A CG to her left — a cloud-to-ground bolt — was followed by a blast of light upward as lightning branched from the top of a turbine toward the sky.

"Damn," she said. So that's what upward lightning looked like from the air. It hadn't come anywhere near her, but it was still a thrill, especially from her low altitude. Before she could even think about a bolt hitting her, she saw another CG to her right. It lit up another turbine, but there wasn't another upward flash. Nonetheless, its power was impressive, as it drummed out multiple, white-hot return strokes. Long peals of thunder crackled around her.

This was fascinating. She made her slow circle, hoping for more upward bolts. Cloud-to-ground bolts rained down, some from the anvil, some from the dark heart of the storm. Some struck the turbines, but none shot up.

"Come on, come on," she found herself saying, mesmerized by the supercell's performance.

Rain spattered against the clear canopy above her. As loud as the rain was on its surface, she hardly noticed it; she was too busy looking for more lightning. Another bolt hit the ground, and a crawler of electricity spontaneously shot out from the cloud, its branches spider-webbing across the sky.

"Fantastic!" she said. And then she heard the first raps on the canopy.

She snapped her head up, instantly forgetting the lightning show. Was it just heavier rain? At this speed, she couldn't be sure. The noise had increased tenfold. And then a few good whacks told her what she knew already: She had strayed into the hail.

"Shit, shit, shit," she said, assessing her course, sharply turning to get out of the core as quickly as possible. She felt and listened for anything unusual, anything that might disrupt the thrum of the engines through the plane, as the rapping hail banged on its body and pushed her pulse to the max. Did she hear a sputter, feel a bump? And then the sound was back to the normal rush and hum, complemented by another blast of thunder just behind her.

The sick afterburn of alarm-adrenaline pushed through her veins. It's OK, she told herself, but she felt otherwise — stupid for her inattention, embarrassed by her alarm. A little fear is healthy, she remembered telling Jack. And he said fear was for people with something to lose. She tamed her heartbeat, eased the plane back into its pattern and paid close attention to the supercell, wondering if he was right.

JACK HAD FOUND a perfect low hill upon which to set up and shoot the incoming storm. At least a dozen wind turbines were in view, each more than three hundred feet high, their trios of tractor-trailer-length blades turning intrepidly in the face of the supercell.

Unfortunately, he parked the van just as one of the towers sizzled with upward lightning, in the wake of a cloud-to-ground bolt, and the Ghost, which was still sitting on the back floor, didn't get it.

Dr. Y was outwardly calm, but his voice betrayed his agitation. "You and Jack get the Ghost going," he told Fred, "and I'll activate the other cameras."

The white blades of the turbines gleamed in sharp relief against the slate-gray sky. Earlier, when Jack had driven the van through the sunny afternoon to get into position, they'd passed close to one of these twenty-first-century windmills. The shadows of its whirling blades had swooped over them like birds of prey, ponderous and unsettling, suggestive of the power they harnessed.

The blades around them now moved with the same might, but they cast no shadows, except when illuminated by lightning.

The rain hadn't hit their position in the wind farm yet, so the team had a chance to get clear footage in the darkening sky before they were overrun by the storm. The cell had been tornado-warned, but given they were driving away from it, Jack hadn't seen anything he could call a twister. With all the rain and hail, he wasn't sure he would have, anyway. He pushed the thought from his mind as he helped Fred lock the Ghost into place and activate its support system. Dr. Y had already flipped down the van's side panel and was switching on the handful of high-tech cameras lined up on the support bar. In a mad rush of five minutes, they were up and shooting. The sound of the wind and thunder almost drowned out the van's running engine.

"Would I be insane to step outside right now?" Jack inquired, knowing the answer was yes. The lightning was frequent and close. He'd already decided it might be better to stay inside and keep an eye on the radar, in case they needed to make a quick escape.

"Actually," said Dr. Y, "you could help me deploy the lightning tent."

Jack couldn't believe he actually wanted to go through with

it. "Have you tested this in the lightning lab?" he asked as Fred looked up from the monitors with a frown.

"Once or twice, but I thought it would be more fun in the field. Come along, Dr. Andreas. Nothing ventured, nothing gained."

Everything told Jack not to do it, except this eccentric scientist who was paying the bills.

"All right," he agreed, with little enthusiasm.

They pushed open the back doors of the van, jumped down and pulled the rectangular package out behind them. It was about the length of a guitar case, unwieldy, secured with Velcro straps.

"A bit heavy, I know," said Dr. Y, unfolding the package, cheerful again now that his experiments were running and he was about to turn himself into a lightning rod. "I hope to develop it with lighter materials so people can take it into the field when they're working, in case a storm comes up and they have no protection. Or you could stow one on your golf cart."

"Really?" Jack was barely listening. And he didn't play golf. He looked up with unfamiliar nervousness as another cloud-to-ground bolt hit a mile away. "What are we doing with this, then?"

"Just grab that end and we'll drag it away from the van a bit," said Dr. Y. "And now we do this, and this, and unfold the floor; snap the supports in place, and make sure the tent is secure over the platform — oh, yes, and then I get inside it." He laughed as his thinning curls blew crazily in the wind. "I'll zip myself in."

"I don't like this, sir," Jack said. It was the first time he'd called Dr. Y "sir," but it felt like a moment when gravity was required.

"Nonsense. It's perfectly safe, as long as I don't touch the sides. Of course, not for you," Dr. Y said as he got inside the blue-black, shiny, booth-like tent, which was slightly taller than he was and just over three feet square. "Better get back into the van. Set up one of those little cameras in the bubble window, won't you?"

"But sir — "

"Help Fred. That's an order. Just tell me when it's time to leave. It wouldn't do to leave me here. I haven't tested it against hail. Ah, listen to that!" he exclaimed as a tumbling cascade of thunder resounded nearby.

Jack ran back to the van, cursing eccentric billionaires.

"What the fuck does he think he's doing?" asked Fred when Jack closed the back doors behind him.

"Tempting fate? I guess it's kind of like the pool thing." Jack could hear himself rationalizing as he found the small wide-angle camera, turned it on and used a suction cup mount to affix it in the bubble window, where it had a good view of the lonely tent. "Maybe he'll be all right."

"Yeah, but for the pool, he uses a goddamn Tesla coil with two hundred thousand volts." Fred pulled his rusty beard in distress. "We're talking a hundred million, maybe a *billion* volts. With a *B*. He's certifiable."

"Well, something like ninety percent of lightning victims survive," said Jack.

"Yeah, and most of them have their fucking wiring fried and are never right again." Fred watched out the big window with the cameras as he spoke, and Jack joined him. For five minutes, both of them were silent, chewing on the potential death of their benefactor twenty feet away.

"Maybe I should look out the other window," Jack said. "Make sure he doesn't get hit."

"Oh, you'll hear it," Fred said. "Damn it to hell."

"What?"

"We haven't had a single upward trigger since we stopped. And I think we're running out of time."

Jack shook his concern for a moment and focused on the storm. Its layers had matured into a stack of smooth, massive, atmospheric doughnuts, with a heavy, green precipitation core underneath and continuing convection above. Very green. The peculiar light suggested it had plenty of hail in its coffers and was no doubt generating more in its strong updraft, pushing the icy balls tens of thousands of feet in the air, where they circulated or hovered in the winds until they were heavy enough to fall to earth and beat up unlucky storm chasers.

He stepped over to the laptop between the front seats and looked at the radar. The hail was still massive, and it was coming closer.

Out the front window, which faced south and not directly at the storm, Jack saw another strange sight: Chuck's Wagon, lumbering their way. "Does that guy have a homing beacon on us or something?"

"What now?" Fred asked.

"The food truck."

"I wish I had time for a sandwich," said Fred, a touch wistful. "But I think we need to shut down and get out. And I'm not taking a chance with the Ghost on the roof. You need to check with our fearless leader."

"*Me?*" Jack said. "I've already been out there once."

"Somebody's got to do it, and I have a family," Fred said, sounding amused.

"I may never have a family if you make me go out there and get struck."

"Oh, please, Andreas. Like you're in any hurry."

Jack had to acknowledge some truth in this statement, but

at the same time, it bugged him. Still, the "greenage" was coming, and somebody had to do something.

"Fuck it," Jack growled. "I'll get him."

He went out the back door again and saw the food truck circling and pulling up several feet behind him. The first sprinkles of rain had begun. He ran up to the tent, trying to make his body as small as possible as another bolt hit nearby.

"Dr. Y!" Jack shouted over the thunder. "We have to go. The hail's coming."

"How distressing," said Dr. Y, his voice muffled. "I was just meditating in here. You know, it's almost dark. And the thunder makes an electrifying accompaniment."

"I'm sure," Jack said, looking up and about, feeling like a bird stalked by a cat, ignoring the food truck stopped behind them. "Need help getting out?"

"I think I can manage."

It seemed an eternity before Dr. Y found the zipper. "I've got it!" he called from inside the fabric, just as Jack's hair stood on end and he heard The Snap.

BOOM! The thunder accompanying the sound of super-close lightning battered his ears as he hit the dirt. He breathed fast and hard, not quite sure at first that he'd really escaped the bolt, whose thunder expanded and rolled around him as superheated air exploded along the lightning channel, breaking the speed of sound like the end of a cracking whip. Only luck had saved him. His hair had stood up — he'd been a living leader for the charge seeking to connect to the ground, to complete the circuit — and the bolt had chosen something else: a tussock, a vole, an unlucky fucking bug. A chance in a million. Actually, if he wanted to be scientific about it, one in twelve thousand.

He jumped up, grabbed the outside zipper pull as Dr. Y

fumbled with it, and pulled it down in a flash. He almost yanked the scientist out of his mummy box and pushed him toward the van, dragging the tent behind him.

"We have to put that away properly!" said Dr. Y, stumbling forward and then trotting as the rain increased in intensity.

"We will — in the van," Jack said, climbing in behind him. "Come on," he said, moving to close the doors.

"Wait," said Dr. Y, staring out the back.

In Chuck's Wagon, the driver stared back.

"Now!" said Fred. "The Ghost is in, the panel is up, but we have hail, my friends!"

He was right, and it wasn't small. Baseball-size stones bounced in the grass as Jack helped Dr. Y slam the back doors shut. Jack darted up to the driver's seat and put the vehicle into gear.

"But I don't have my seatbelt on!" said Dr. Y, dropping into the passenger seat as the van lurched forward.

Jack laughed. It wasn't just the irony; it was the thrill of being alive after learning the meaning of fear in that one, stray lightning bolt. He flipped the van around and headed toward the paved road, where he accelerated south to escape the hammering hail.

THE PROBLEM with chasing storms with a group of any size was having to take extra bathroom breaks, even when the storm of the day was dashing away from them. Aurelius would have kept going, but the women were insistent that they stop at a gas station at the Interstate, just as he insisted on driving again, over Brad's protests. Brad had been subtly undermining this course of action ever since Aurelius had mentioned

punching the hail core, and each expression of Brad's displea-
sure had made Aurelius exponentially more keen to do it.
Aurelius had no intention of killing an entire TV crew, but he
didn't see anything wrong with racking up a few hail dents
and scaring the crap out of Brad in the process. If it got really
bad, he'd stop, and the storm would keep moving away, and
they'd still have most or even all of their windows, along with
entertaining footage.

When they at last hit the highway, he cranked the rolling
wedding cake up to its top speed, which was more modest
than it should have been thanks to its wind-resistant tiers.
Aurelius did his best to weave among the surprisingly large
number of cars on the road and catch up with the storm. It
always amazed him to see how many people traveled on the
Interstate highways in severe weather, completely unfazed by
a tornado warning like this one. Surely these truckers, with all
their radios and technology, heard weather warnings. Did they
think their boxy trailers were immune? Perhaps they advanced
because, from this angle, the storm was so pretty, its hard and
bubbling updraft lit up bright orange by the descending sun. A
rainbow, or hailbow, was faintly visible in its precipitation,
which from this distance had a harmless, misty appearance.
Though the radar warned of hidden intensity, there was no
rain here, just a damp road and sunshine — until they caught
up to the storm.

Aurelius was doing his best to do just that, touching
eighty-five miles per hour at times. Polly Ann and Tyler had
executed a quick change into their wedding togs; the sparkly
dress had lost several sequins and had crease marks and a
mysterious blue stain on one hip. The lace flower on the
miniature hat seemed deflated, though the big hairpins still
sparkled viciously.

Aurelius suddenly wanted to do more than annoy Brad; he had a desire to get this silly job over with and move on to more interesting things. And if he could find the tornado that was supposedly in the core, he might have a shot at it.

The weather radio had been issuing so many dire warnings about driving on I-70 that Aurelius turned down the volume. He didn't need the distraction, and he could see exactly where the storm was — almost directly over the highway. It was not just moving northeast; it was growing in that direction, getting bigger and nastier. He could see an occasional lightning bolt from this angle. He had no doubt there were many more to the east. It was so strange how these Plains storms could look so innocent from the west, especially when they were jumping off a dryline. The *Zany Weddings* crew was taking the vehicles from the sunshine right into the maelstrom.

They were almost upon it when Aurelius noticed several vehicles parked by the side of the road. Some drivers must have heard the warnings; at least one car, he noted, had lost a couple of windows, probably to hail. So be it, he thought. For this chase, he had insurance for everything from meteors to sinkholes. Now that would be a headline, he thought: *Intrepid adventurer Aurelius Zane dies when tornado drops him into sinkhole.* He hoped *The New York Times* already had its obituary written. Everybody knows you've made it when you're written up in *The Times*, especially when they do it in advance. Then he remembered that they hadn't interviewed him yet.

"Did *The Times* interview you for your obituary?" he asked Brad.

"What?" Brad turned white.

"You know. They interview really famous people pre-death."

"Oh," Brad said, pulling himself together. "There were a

lot of interviews. Yeah, I think there was something about having a story in the can for my untimely death. I guess they were worried about me flying into another tornado."

Aurelius didn't even have to look over to see the smirk. Damn it! Treat was getting an obit in *The Times?* "Would you like that to happen today?" he replied, just to make Brad wince.

"Now, I love you guys," Polly Ann said from the back, "but I'm not ready to fly in a tornado."

"Fear not, my lady," Aurelius said as the first raindrops and small hailstones peppered the van. "My first job is to get you married in front of a tornado, not flying inside one."

"We're ready," Tyler said, and without coaching, he turned to Scooter in the back and expounded on his devotion to Polly Ann like a pro.

The hailstones got progressively bigger in size, starting with coins: dime-size, nickel-size, quarters, half dollars. Then sports: Ping-Pong balls. Golf balls.

"Aurelius, it's getting kind of loud back here," came Danni's voice over the radio.

"Go ahead and drop back by a mile or two," Aurelius said. "We'll let you know if it gets really gnarly. But we're getting great footage, I think." As usual, cameras were running inside and out, and the wedding cake made for awesome audio as hail pounded its many surfaces.

More golf balls. Tennis balls. Baseballs. Softballs, only not so soft.

The windshield took a hit, and a handsome spider-web crack bloomed in the middle. "Now keep an eye out for the tornado," Aurelius shouted over the percussive racket.

"What are you doing?" Brad said. "Slow down. Let the core pass us."

"But this isn't the main core. This hail is wrapping around the circulation," said Aurelius. "Which means there should be a tornado if you look carefully just off to the left. Ah, I think I see it. Do you? A gray cone in there. Maybe we can pull off a ceremony while I'm driving!"

"Are you crazy?" Brad shouted as Aurelius reached one hand into his leather travel bag and pulled out the book with the rituals of the Church of the L.E.D. He momentarily lost a grip on the steering wheel as he struggled to open it to the right page. He heard Polly Ann gasp.

"We're OK," Aurelius said, enjoying the cacophony as he regained control, accelerated and read from the book. This balls-out chasing was liberating, somehow. "Dearly beloved, we gather here in the bear's cage of a supercell thunderstorm to join these two beautiful people in matrimony according to the will of the Light-Emitting Deity . . ."

"I am not ready!" Polly Ann screamed as the tornado emerged from the rain next to their speeding wedding cake. "I don't want to die!"

"You're not going to die," Aurelius said.

"Zane, stop this fucking car!" Brad screeched, sounding almost as hysterical as Polly Ann.

Tyler was glued to the window, staring at the tornado. "Look at that thing eat," he murmured as the amorphous, ugly cone ripped apart a billboard.

"Aurelius!" came Danni's voice over the radio. "You have to stop!"

Aurelius had forgotten that she could see at least some of what was going on in the car, and as much as he resented her tiny voice of conscience and reason, he felt obligated to obey. He deflated, put down the book and picked up the radio mike.

"All right, all right," he replied, slowing down and pulling onto the shoulder. As he did, the tornado, thinning and still wrapped in the rain and hail that was hitting them, danced like a snake onto the road a hundred yards in front of them and dissipated in a sinuous toss of its hips. A tractor trailer roared by the twister's last vestiges, wobbling but otherwise unharmed. The gods protect fools, Aurelius thought, then wondered if he might also belong in that category.

Maybe he did, but amid the last few smacks of hail and the stressed breathing and piquant smell of fear he finally noticed around him, he felt a hell of a lot better.

MARIBETH COULD HAVE LEFT the hangar an hour ago, but she was still keyed up after her flight. She wasn't ready to be alone, not yet. She'd walked around the plane with the techs, looking for signs of damage and finding little except a few hail dents. She'd written a preliminary report. Then she'd combed out her helmet hair and changed out of her flight suit into civvies — her favorite worn blue jeans, plaid blue-and-green canvas loafers and a soft, dark blue, long-sleeved V-neck T-shirt that felt like a hug.

She wanted a hug, a connection. She was all nerves, all pulse, bound up in angst and ready to burst. This wasn't like her. This wasn't the person she wanted to project. But her brain wasn't listening. She was buzzing. She was shaken. She should leave. She had just about resolved to do so when the research van pulled in, and she sighed with what she realized was relief.

Maribeth walked over to the van as the men emerged. Fred looked tired, Dr. Y pensive, and Jack — Jack was inscrutable, but his green eyes were dark. As they rested on her, they lit up with a spark, a hint of lightning. And he smiled. Wow. That smile. He walked right up to her and hugged her, then disengaged as if he was as nonplussed as she was.

"How was it?" he asked. That hug? Fantastic, she thought, then told herself to get a grip.

While Fred unloaded hard drives and memory cards for analysis, Dr. Y walked up next to Jack, and she found her gears engage, moving into official report mode.

"I saw one stroke of upward lightning," Maribeth said. "The cameras may have caught more, but that's all I saw. Still, I know we got a lot of lightning."

"The Ghost missed the upward lightning," said Dr. Y, a slight frown on his lips. "No trouble?"

"None to speak of," she said lightly, remembering the sound of the hail on the canopy, the charge of adrenaline as she'd listened for any falter of the engines. In a way, she was still back there, reliving that moment in the cockpit. Civilian life had made her soft, she thought. That was nothing. But for nothing, it had been scary as shit.

"I tested my lightning tent, but it was inconclusive," Dr. Y said, closing his eyes and rubbing his brow. "I think I need to turn in. I have a lot to think about." He toddled off toward his office, his flashy shirt a contrast to his mood.

"Did something happen out there?" she asked Jack.

"Yeah," he said. "All in all, a surreal day. Hey, do you want to go out, get a bite or something? I'm still tired as hell, but it'll be hours before I can go to sleep. Um, he did get us somewhere to sleep?"

Maribeth laughed. "Yeah. Pretty good hotel. There are lots in town."

"Oh, I know. This is a major chasing hub. Though my haunts tend to be a couple of rungs below Dr. Y's."

Maribeth regarded him. She didn't want much from him, right? She didn't want much from anyone, nothing so deep she'd miss it when it was gone. Maybe, she thought, I just need to have a little fun.

"Where do you want to eat?" she asked.

"I don't really care," Jack said, "as long as it has a bar."

"It won't have cocktails as good as Dr. Y's, but I think I can hook you up. I think I've scouted every reputable watering hole in town."

"Well, then," said Jack, a glint of mischief returning, "let's find one of the disreputable ones."

"Are you sure you don't want a decent one?" Maribeth said. "Because when I drink you under the table, you're going to want a nice floor to pass out on."

"Oh, honey," he said with a smile, as her internal tough chick compromised all her principles and rolled over at *honey*, "forget what you learned in the Army. Now you're running with the *elite* drinking force."

AURELIUS FOUND that no one in the crew would talk to him as he drove them to their hotel in Salina, except Danni, who gave him an earful once they stopped. Now that his adrenaline had worn off, he was suitably contrite for putting their guests in danger, but he still secretly reveled in his memory of Brad's panic as they courted the tornado.

"At least," Danni said, once it was clear she'd forgiven him, "Scooter says the footage is completely bitchin'. This tornado wedding episode may have to be a two-parter."

They gathered in the hotel lobby after checking in,

discussing where to get dinner, when a familiar figure strolled through the automatic doors.

"My friends!" said Charles, wearing a Stanford T-shirt, his shaman hairdo more moplike than ever. "Did you forget? We have a dinner date. I have the most excellent fish fry picnic ready for you outside!"

The tired crew looked at the wizened chef with skepticism. It was Tyler who finally got them going. "I wondered if you'd find us," he said, beaming. "I've been looking forward to eating my fish all day."

"Devil fish," Polly Ann noted to no one in particular.

"Probably beats Applebee's," Scooter said.

"Fuckin' A," said Vinyl, who'd popped out one earbud to listen to the conversation. Aurelius was as shocked as the others. They rarely heard Vinyl say anything.

"All right, let's do it," Danni said. "We'll pay our share, though, Mr. Smith. Our company has deeper pockets than it likes to let on."

"Some of us get paid in lint," Aurelius muttered, and they all walked outside together.

The rain had stopped, leaving a few scudding clouds. A handful of brave stars shone through the light pollution from the hotels and the nearby Interstate. Chuck's Wagon was set up alongside the grassy lot that adjoined the parking lot. On the lawn, Charles had set out several folding camp stools around an old metal bucket, which burned brightly with a small fire. By the truck was a cooler full of iced beverages, including beer, Aurelius noted with increasing cheer.

"Where do you keep all this stuff?" Aurelius asked Charles as the chef climbed into the truck and behind the counter, where he put together plates of fish, homemade tartar sauce with capers, seasoned fries, and a broccoli salad dotted with cashews, raisins and red onion.

"It's a big truck, and the stools fold flat. The bucket has endless uses. I pick up firewood here and there," said Charles, handing heavily laden paper plates through the big window. "One must always have the means to make a campfire. It is the primal meeting place, the place where we find each other and the universe."

"Or at least the place where you find dinner," said Tyler, who, having taken his first bite, seemed ecstatic to have his fish fileted, battered, fried and ready to eat a day after it had fallen into his umbrella. "This fish is great. I had no idea it would make so much."

"I did have to multiply your catch to feed everyone," Charles said.

That was a funny way to put it, Aurelius thought. "Is there a fish market around here?"

"Of course," Charles said, a twinkle in his eye. "Kansas is well known for its fresh fish."

Was he kidding? It didn't matter. It smelled delicious. Aurelius took his plate, grabbed a bottle of craft beer and sat on one of the stools. Charles handed out the last of the dinners, shut off the bright light inside the truck and came out to join them. He sat in the only available seat, right next to Aurelius, who eyed him warily before taking a bite of the fish. It was light, gently salty and scrumptious. He sighed, stared into the fire and enjoyed the moment.

"You see? You like?" Charles said, digging into his own food with relish as Aurelius opened his eyes and nodded. The others chatted among themselves.

"It's excellent," the adventurer admitted. "Where were you

when I was doing my jungle expeditions? We could have used a cook like you."

"You mean a guide," Charles said, happily forking heaps of salad into his mouth. The flickering fire lit up every crease in his weathered face, recalling a wooden totem in a land far away.

"We had guides."

"Not like me," Charles said. "Though I do not always know the way. Today, I saw that destiny may have new ideas for me, or perhaps they are very old ideas, but I feel I am not yet finished here in this kingdom, where the storms reign."

"Hmph," said Aurelius, savoring a French fry. "How do you know? For instance, how do you know where to go next?"

"If you let it, life will figure out your path for you. Follow the signs." Charles released a long, bullfroggy burp and sighed. "Nourishment for the body and soul." He set his plate on the ground and looked up at the sky. "Nature gave us violence. Now she gives us stars. She is sated, for now."

"I wonder if that's true," Aurelius said, catching a touch of the chef's philosophical mood. "Somewhere, a tiger is devouring its prey, or an owl is grabbing a mouse out of the leaves. I think your Nature is always hungry."

Charles clapped his hands together, as delighted as a child. "Yes, yes!" he said. "But here, on your path, she is calm and welcoming. One never knows one's path until one can look back upon it and recognize it. And then one's destiny becomes manifest."

Aurelius wondered if Charles had a point. When he looked back on his path, from volcano to big surf to wild jungle to hurricane, it was hard to see where it led. But there were highlights. Wynda was one of them. And the journey itself. He liked motion, being in motion. His moments of fame were fleeting shadows now. Perhaps they weren't worth pursuing at all.

He took a swig of beer and put aside all thoughts of his path. "Is there dessert?" he asked.

"I am so glad you asked. Chocolate raspberry mousse," said Charles, a wide, wild smile on his face. "Isn't the present delicious?"

❧

"YOUR CAR OR MINE?" Jack asked as he walked Maribeth out of the hangar and into the breezy, cool evening. Both carried bags from yesterday's tornado chase. She looked different tonight, pretty in her casual clothes, a strange light in her eye. Her cool demeanor had warmed a fraction. He didn't know why he'd hugged her earlier; it just seemed like something that had to happen, a compulsion after a tough day when he'd begun to doubt the sanity of their benefactor. In short, he'd wanted to.

"I don't have a car. Not here," she said. "Dr. Y lets me have a rental when I need it, but I don't have one right now."

"How did you get here? Where do you live, anyway?"

"How do you think I got here?" she asked, waving at a line of planes parked nearby. "And I live in Oklahoma City. My dad moved his business there after — well, I help him with his business, and that's where my last job was, so I have an apartment there. You live in Wishwell, don't you? I thought I saw that on your resume."

"That was before. I moved my stuff into storage when I went to stay in Florida last year. Didn't see much point in paying for my crappy apartment while I was gone, especially when I didn't know where I'd end up."

"So you're homeless," she said pleasantly.

He laughed. "For now. We'll see where I land when this gig is up. I might actually have to get a real job. I don't know. Maybe it's time. OK, here's my car. Oh, shit."

"What?" she asked, before her expression revealed she'd seen it, too: a nice crack in the windshield. "Oh. We did get some hail here before you arrived, but I didn't think it was that bad."

"It only takes one," Jack said. "And the crack in the van windshield is getting bigger, too. Maybe they'll all explode at once."

"How exciting," she said. He opened her creaking door, taking her bag in the process. "Thanks," she added, more softly, as if she was not used to such courtesies.

"Don't thank me yet," he said. He put the bags in the back and got in the driver's side. "You haven't ridden in this thing. It still smells like 1977."

She sniffed as she buckled up. "*Star Wars*. Polyester. A hint of disco."

"Oh, please, no," he said. "Not disco."

"Take me to Funkytown, Andreas," she commanded, and he started the engine and headed into Salina.

Though Jack had been to several of this town's drinking venues over the years, there was usually a stretch between visits, and he let Maribeth direct him. Her first candidate for a disreputable bar advertised "Karaoke Tonight!" on the sign outside, so he vetoed it. They settled on the next best thing: a lounge called Escapades that seemed to be trapped in an identity crisis — part biker bar, part yuppie hangout, part burger joint, all fueled by a jukebox heavy on country.

They found a quiet booth in the corner farthest from the brightly lit pool table. There, a handful of worker bees, men and women, played amid a colony of empty beer bottles, their deteriorating business casual wear revealing shirttails and cleavage. A few creased old gents nursed highballs at the bar, and a biker couple next to the jukebox got dangerously close to swapping tonsils. The walls were cluttered with photographs, movie posters, pennants, roller skates, a nude painted on velvet with Budweiser bottle caps over her nipples, Mardi Gras beads, a photo of skywriting spelling out "Surrender Dorothy," and a large Aermotor windmill fan blade strung with colored lights.

"I was in here once before," Maribeth said. "I think they decorated this place the year your car was built."

"At least ten years before that. And thirty years after," Jack said. "It's got layers, this place."

"If you peeled them, it would probably collapse in on itself."

"All of Salina would be sucked into the black hole."

"And they complain about tornadoes," Maribeth said. "Here comes our waitress."

A woman of some fifty hard-won years, in a black T-shirt, short denim skirt and server's apron, her brown hair knotted in a disheveled bun, came to take their order. Jack and Maribeth consulted the tiny tented cardboard menu on the table and, given their limited choices, ordered burgers.

"And to drink?" the server asked.

Maribeth looked at Jack. Jack looked back and smiled. "Bourbon on the rocks, one big cube or a couple of normal ones, whatever you've got," he said. "You have Knob Creek back there, I think?"

"Make it two," said Maribeth. Ah, so she was going to drink him under the table, or so she'd said. He grinned. "How late do cabs run here?" she asked the waitress.

"In Salina?" she replied. "Uh, I think you can get one at least till midnight. Anyway, don't worry about it. I'll drive you home if I have to. Don't touch the stuff myself."

"Are you serious?" Maribeth asked.

"Sure. You tipped me big that other time you were in here, with the round fellow in the Hawaiian shirt."

Maribeth laughed. "Oh, yeah, I'd forgotten about that," she said as the waitress left. "Well, the damage will be done well before midnight, I reckon." Maribeth turned and winked at Jack, leaning in with a smile, her shirt gaping just enough for him to get a glimpse of the creamy curve of her breasts over a midnight-blue bra. Who was this woman, and what had she done with Maribeth? Her party switch had flipped, Jack thought. He found himself titillated, confused and even missing the serious pilot just a little, but this doppelganger was definitely interesting. And sexy. Allowing a half smile of his own, he looked into her eyes, giving her the stare, until the hint of a blush rose in her cheeks, bringing out her faint freckles. The waitress returned with the two bourbons. No fancy ice cubes, but there were a couple of chunky blocks in there. It would do.

"You can't win," he told Maribeth flat out as he took a healthy sip from his glass.

"You know what they call me. 'Never Surrender,'" she said, downing hers in one guzzle.

"Now that's not how to drink good bourbon," he chided.

"I'll sip the rest. I needed that one." Her eyes had a haunted look for a moment.

"Something *did* happen in the plane," he guessed, holding up two fingers to the waitress so she'd know to bring another round.

"Not really. I had a scare, is all. Got into the hail when I shouldn't have."

"I thought maybe you'd been hit by lightning."

"Not yet," she said, "but planes are pretty good at handling that. Except this one has more electronics than anything I've ever flown, so who knows."

"I almost got hit by lightning."

"Is that why Dr. Y was so weird back there?"

"No," Jack said. "I don't think he even realized how close it was. He was in that stupid lightning tent."

"Is that the portable lightning shelter he's been working on? He actually climbed inside it?" She shook her head. "Sometimes his objective scientist just vanishes when lightning is involved. But it would be a great thing if it actually worked."

"As long as he doesn't have to have an idiot like me to help him get into it. Kind of defeats the purpose."

"You're not an idiot, *Dr.* Andreas," she said as the second round arrived. She looked at him for a long moment, concern in her eyes, as she took a sip. "Did you really almost get hit by lightning?"

"My hair stood on end. That means I was in its sights. It's just random luck I didn't get struck."

"That's close."

"Yeah." He drained his first drink, wanting to keep up. "It scared me."

"Really? The man who knows no fear."

"I don't think I ever put it like that." He smiled.

"Well, no one can say this isn't an interesting job."

"With interesting company."

"Yes, very interesting," she said, taking a sip, her eyes not leaving his. "You're just a heap of trouble, aren't you?"

"What? That's the second time you've called me out. I won't stand for it," he teased.

"That's OK. I don't mind a reasonable amount of trouble."

"Wait — that's from a movie, isn't it?"

She nodded. "Very good. *The Maltese Falcon*. My dad's a Humphrey Bogart nut."

"What's he like?"

"Great movie star," she deadpanned. "Love the voice. Sexy despite his hangdog looks. Or maybe because of them."

"Not Bogie," Jack said in mock frustration. "Your dad."

She chuckled. "Pilot his whole life. Actually Air Force. Made him squirm when I chose Army. Now he runs Casablanca Aviation."

"Bogie again."

"Well, that, and that whole thing in *Casablanca* about getting to Lisbon and the plane to freedom. So the name, Lisbon, and the Bogie connection — he couldn't resist."

Jack held up his glass, and she mirrored him. "Here's to the beginning of a beautiful friendship," he said in a bad Bogart accent and took a healthy sip.

"Trouble," she murmured, drinking with him, still looking at him from over the rim.

"And your mom?" he asked.

She paused. "Dead."

"Oh. Me, too," he said, choosing to be flippant because he didn't like the alternative.

"I'm not going there right now," she said, the bourbon creeping into her voice. She took another sip. The waitress brought their burgers, slightly charred but thick and hearty with a good slice of tomato and melted Swiss cheese.

"Fair enough," he said, not wanting to go there, either, but wondering about her story. Because it was obvious there was a story, and it wasn't like his was pretty, either. They were silent for a couple of minutes, using the burgers as an excuse not to talk. He added ketchup and took a big bite. Factoring in that he hadn't eaten in about nine hours, it wasn't bad. A Kansas cow had not given its life for naught. The fries were skinny, crispy, salty and satisfying, especially when contrasted with the peppery caramel of the bourbon.

"This is pretty good," Maribeth said. "I mean, when compared with the energy bars that keep me going in the cockpit."

"Fuck that astronaut food," Jack joked, wiping his mouth with his thin paper napkin.

"Yeah. From now on, I'm telling Dr. Y he has to have a charcoal grill and fresh burgers ready to go in the Warthog."

"Why stop there? Demand filet. I mean, there is an unlimited budget," Jack said. "He should hire an Oompa Loompa or something to stay in there and cook for you."

She almost choked on her last bite as she guffawed. "I don't think even an Oompa Loompa would fit," she said as she recovered herself. "Maybe we could put him where the ballast is."

"You could drop Oompa Loompas on anyone who annoyed you."

"I draw the line at bombing Americans with Oompa Loompas," she said, and her face flickered from merry to dark in an instant. Then the shadow passed, and she downed the rest of her second drink. She closed her eyes, sighed and opened them again. "I've only had two, but I feel kind of wasted," she admitted. "I haven't eaten much today. I'm waiting for the burger to work."

"You work too hard," said Jack, flowing, focusing on her as he finished his drink, too. He waved again at the waitress.

"How can you know that? You don't even know me."

"I know you."

"Seriously? How long have we known each other?"

"Forever." He smiled. "Remember Florida? All those hours? Dr. Y's staff cocktail parties by the pool? And then the phone calls. The video calls. I know you." And he felt the truth of this modestly buzzed statement even as it rolled out of his subconscious, as it had in the graveyard. The waitress delivered two more glasses of bourbon.

Maribeth seemed unsure what to do with his attention. "I don't know what you know."

"I know enough." He reached across the table for her hand. There was something about her hands that intrigued him. They were neither delicate nor rough, and hers was small in his, but it felt strong. She wore no nail polish and just one ring, a blue star sapphire on her right hand that burned with a delicate white starburst under the single lamp that hung above the table. He rubbed the smooth stone under his thumb, then grasped her other hand and caressed her wrist, tracing the faint tan line that showed where she usually wore her chunky working watch. He loved the way her hands worked, could drive a van out of a tornado, could fly a helicopter or a plane practically into one. Or perhaps it was the heat they generated.

She wrapped her fingers around his. "I have a funny feeling about you, Jack. In bourbon, veritas." She smiled, let go, held up her glass and took a deep sip.

He leaned in, his voice low. "Funny, ha-ha?"

"Funny-strange. Funny. Strange. Something else." She leaned closer to him as she held her glass with both hands, looking down into it, all eyelashes, and he felt her leg brush against his under the table. He felt an ache, a stirring at her touch. What was she saying? Did it matter? Her body said everything. She wanted him, even if she didn't know it, and he knew now for certain that he wanted her.

"I think you're incredible," he said. "But you can call it a funny feeling if you like."

She looked up at him in surprise, and instead of her usual calculating look, he saw something softer in her eyes — questioning, yearning, gray tinged with blue, an unsettled sky. "Are you using your powers for good or for evil, Dr. Andreas?"

"Good," he said without hesitation. "Very, very good."

"Hmm," she said, taking another sip. "I think I may need just one more drink before I can continue this conversation."

"Or we can end this conversation and start another one." He drank down half the third glass, feeling the heady mix of whiskey and fatigue. "You could keep drinking me under the table here, or you could drink me under something more comfortable. And I have a bottle in my overnight bag."

He gauged her reaction to his proposition, felt a shift. She lifted her drink and used her tongue to draw in one of the half-melted cubes, sucking it gently as she looked off into space, thinking, rolling the ice around in her mouth, unconscious of how fucking hot it was to see her lips red and wet like that.

"I'll call the cab," she said, crunching the cube to its doom, pulling her phone out of the canvas satchel she used as a purse.

"I'll pay the bill," he said, getting up, walking unsteadily to the bar and flagging down their waitress. He looked back at Maribeth at the table and couldn't believe his luck. It *was* luck, he thought, or maybe it was timing; she hadn't seemed susceptible to his usual persuasive powers. Or was she? Could he use his powers for good? He smiled at her question. Yes, he thought, I could do anything to be that ice cube. Or to get inside her defenses, to understand why he cared so much what she thought. He had a feeling he should foster this friendship, whatever it was, gently, but greater forces were at work. There was a rushing sound in his ears, a fire in his body, and a jet engine driving him to her.

❧

MARIBETH not only had a strange feeling about Jack; she had a strange feeling about herself. She was melting into a fluid being of bourbon and emotion, an alien in her own skin. She knew she couldn't drink Jack under any table,. but she liked the idea of trying, of challenging him, of maybe letting him win. Her rational self saw Jack as brilliant, wrapped up in his storms, a player, a daredevil. But her instinctual self, which burned sweet with bourbon and the kind of clarity that came only from taking off her safety goggles, saw something else in him, the way she used to see something in rare men she met in the Army — tough on the outside, wide open on the inside, ready to give her a chance to be herself, which was, always, a chance to be her best.

And she couldn't ignore their completely irrational attraction as he sat close to her in the back of the cab, holding her hand, careful and quiet and insistent as he caressed her fingers, her palm, seducing her one digit at a time.

The cab dropped them and their bags in front of the hotel.

"You probably need to check in," Maribeth told Jack. "I've had my room for months."

"Really?" Jack asked as they walked inside and to the counter, where a tiny, shivering chihuahua in a sweater looked on from the desk. The dog sniffed the air, then lay down and closed his eyes.

"That's Chester," the young man on duty said, nodding toward the dog, as he took Jack's ID.

"Some of us have been here so much, Dr. Y's people thought it might be nice if we had a regular place to stay," Maribeth said, reaching over the counter to rub Chester behind the ears. "He could've given us an apartment, but he said Fred and I deserved maid service. I couldn't agree more." She smiled, feeling floaty. She should drink more often.

"Fred?" Jack asked, looking puzzled.

"He has another suite in the hotel. So do a couple of the technical people who are here all the time. Others live in town. The transients get regular rooms."

"Am I a transient?" Jack asked, as the clerk handed him a key card.

"I don't know. Are you?" she teased. "Here, let me see." She looked at the number on his card. "Yeah, you're a transient." She laughed at his mock hurt expression as they moved toward the elevator. "So I guess that means you should drop off your bag in your room and meet me in mine. I mean, since I actually have a table to drink you under." Shit, she was babbling. Who was this drunk girl doing all the talking?

He smiled, that intoxicated, intoxicating smile. "I was hoping you would say that."

The elevator swished open, and they got on board. She hit two and three on the panel. When the door shut, he moved close to her, his heat invading her space, so close she wondered if he would kiss her. She felt herself wanting him to.

"I'll be there," he whispered in her ear as the door opened on two. He practically jogged out with his bags, and she was left leaning against the elevator wall, feeling weak in the knees and drunk with more than whiskey. The door closed, and she climbed to three.

"Oh, what the fuck, what the fuck," she whispered to herself as she hefted her bags and headed down the hall to her suite. "What the fuck am I doing?" Inside, she flipped on the kitchen table light, tossed her bags in the bedroom, used the bathroom and went into the kitchenette for a couple of glasses. Then came the soft knock on the door.

Maribeth hesitated for a moment. She could stop right now. She could face him tomorrow at the hangar and say she passed out. She was exhausted, after all. They had a lot of work to do. But that wasn't her way.

She opened the door.

Jack entered with his bottle of bourbon. He still had on his black T-shirt and jeans, but he'd shed his high-top sneakers and now wore just black socks.

"Forgive my informality," he said, looking around. "I feel like a real transient now that I see your 'room.' It's a damn apartment."

"A suite, that's all. A little kitchen, a living area. It makes it nice when you have to spend a lot of time. I'm not always looking at the same four walls."

"So there's a bedroom," he said with a smile, nodding toward the open door that led there. He placed the bourbon on the coffee table in front of the brown leather sofa. He gestured toward the table that divided the kitchen from the living room, where the glasses sat under the hanging lamp, next to a laptop computer and a wireless speaker. There was also a pile of books, topped by a worn copy of *Fate Is the Hunter*.

"Ice?" he asked.

"Not the fancy cubes you desire, but they'll cool you down," she said, heading to the fridge.

"Maybe I don't want to cool down."

Maribeth smiled and shook her head, grabbed cubes for the glasses. "Trouble, like I said."

"I think you like trouble," Jack said, relaxing on the couch. She was relieved he didn't turn on the TV. Some men saw a remote and just couldn't help themselves, and then hours were lost watching sports and bad sitcoms.

"I'm a pilot. I like smooth sailing." She kicked off her loafers as she walked over.

"You like a challenge. I promise you, I won't be a challenge. I'm a pushover," he said as she sat next to him and placed the glasses on the table. He filled them. The pretty russet liquid danced over the cubes, catching the subtle light.

"A pushover and a challenge at the same time," she said.

"Here's to a good challenge." He lifted his glass.

She picked up hers, lightly touched it to his, then put the drink to her lips, watching him all the while. She couldn't take her eyes off him tonight, his lithe body, his striking features, his glittering green eyes. She wondered how she'd shut out all these stimuli before. She really hadn't, she acknowledged. Maybe it was because she was more than a little buzzed, but she liked that he was so in the moment, wild, an adept flirt who clearly had one objective: her. This was going too fast.

"Do you like music? I can put some on." She put down the glass and got up to tinker with the laptop and the wireless speaker.

"I like music," he said. "What do you have?"

"My tastes are what you might call eclectic. Tell me if you hate this, and I'll put on something more conventional. Something more pop. I don't know what you like." Rock seemed too distracting. She chose her classic jazz playlist and set it on shuffle. She sat down as Johnny Hartman's "Stairway to the Stars" poured out of the speaker in a mellow brew of dulcet vocals and saxophone.

Jack had a strange look on his face.

"You hate it, don't you?" she asked. "I'll switch it. I know nobody listens to this stuff anymore." She started to get up, but he put a hand on her knee. She sank back into the couch, annoyingly willing to obey his touch.

"I love — this is what I listen to when I'm not chasing," he said. He seemed melancholy and pleased all at once. "I can't believe you like it, too."

"Eclectic tastes, like I said. If I'm really cranking on a road trip, it might be Rage Against the Machine." She smiled. "You never know." She took another sip of bourbon and set down her glass. "You're falling behind."

"Right," he said, taking a drink and putting the glass down. "I don't care." He wrapped an arm around her waist and pulled her to him, pressing his lips to hers, his mouth softly opening, his tongue insisting on opening hers, kissing her deftly, slowly, like the sound of the saxophone curling like smoke around the cool piano and the delicate, dark heat of the vocal. He ran his other hand through her hair, holding it at the nape of her neck, and she felt herself collapsing like a star, burning in darkness, consumed by gravitational attraction. She moaned lightly against his lips, still resisting, her arms at her side, but wanting him so.

He released her and looked into her eyes, touched her cheek. "Not my night?" he asked with a bittersweet smile.

Maribeth reached out and brushed his rough cheek in return, searching his eyes, finding their glitter had fallen away to reveal something more real, more powerful. She could say no. She could keep saying no forever to everything and die in control. Fuck it, she thought. She leaned in and kissed him back.

He wrapped his arms around her, responding with twice as much hunger, pushing her back on the couch, kissing her neck, sending waves of electricity over her skin, engendering an ache deep between her legs. She was feeling so much, too much. This was like free-fall, sick, exhilarating, and she wondered if she would recover before she crashed.

❧

JACK MOLDED his body to Maribeth's against the soft leather of the couch. Drunk on the bourbon, high on the jazz, he ran his hands up under her soft blue shirt, reaching to pull it over her head. She, who'd broadcast resistance all along, did not resist this incursion. She'd jumped off her castle wall, he felt it, and he wanted to catch her, to enfold her.

She had so many sharp edges when she was working; now, he ran his fingers along her soft curves, her shoulders, the arc of her breasts above her midnight-blue bra — a pretty lace bra he'd never have predicted. This was her secret identity, a mysterious beauty. He kissed one nipple through the sheer lace and felt it harden, felt her stir beneath him. She watched him, her mouth open, lips dark red, eyelashes pronounced in the shadowy light, and as he traced his fingers over her areola, her eyes closed and her head went back. *Yes.* He slipped the straps off her shoulders and reached around to undo the clasp. He pulled the bra away and marveled at her pale skin, the full, round breasts, as he bent down and sucked and nibbled on one dark peak, then the other. He kissed her collarbone, her neck, her mouth again, tasting the bourbon and her own desire as she kissed him back.

Below, his hands worked on her jeans, the button, the zipper, and he pushed one hand into the loosened fabric. Her underpants were wet, and he toyed with her through the fabric until she moved beneath him. He pulled her jeans down and off, the dark blue underwear, and she was naked before him. He stopped, stared. She was entrancing, surprisingly sensual, her skin flushed, her lips parted. She looked at him with boldness and yearning. She pulled out from under him, stood slowly before him, inches away, a backlit hourglass figure, strong legs, her tousled brown hair barely brushing her shoulders. He noticed her earrings, with their aviator charms, flash in the dim light. She reached out and touched his sleeve, tugging lightly at his T-shirt, and gave him a sexy half smile.

"I think you're forgetting something," she said.

He almost jumped at the literal electric shock of her touch, a spark of static electricity. Transfixed, he stood before her, pulled the shirt off, took off his jeans and socks and underwear. He moved just close enough so her breasts barely touched his chest, skin to skin, breathless at being so close to her. He pressed forward, placed his hands on her hips, kissed her again.

"Bedroom," she whispered.

He did something he never did with women. He scooped her up, cradled her, and she wrapped her arms around his neck as he strode through the open door of the bedroom. He lay her on the bed in the semidarkness, straddled her and kissed her. She spread out her arms, as if she were taking flight. The light from the adjoining room limned her skin with a delicate glow. He took his time, moving his mouth down her neck, her breasts, her belly, her sex. He played with her bud with his tongue until her body rose to meet his mouth, her taste musky, her cleft wet, satisfying evidence of her arousal.

"One second," he whispered as he stood up.

"Jack," she said, but he'd run to the other room, to his jeans, to get a condom. He had it on when he walked back in. Now she lay loosely curled up on her side.

"Protection," he explained.

"Someone here should be cautious. Who knew it would be you?" she said softly, not looking at him.

"What is it?" He wanted her so badly, but he also wanted to understand.

"What is it you do to me?" Maribeth asked, turning her head slightly to look up at him with stormy eyes. "I should have drunk you under the table by now."

"You have. I'm drunk. I'm drunk on you," he said, climbing onto the bed, curling up against her back, spooning her, soothing her, caressing her, building slowly, kissing her neck, her back. Her skin was burning hot. His erection was hard against her, and he almost erupted as she shifted, melding against his body. He reached around her, teasing her again until she groaned. As she relaxed, he pushed between her legs with his shaft, finding her sweet spot. With one intense thrust, he drove into her slick folds.

"Oh, Jack," she gasped, pushing back against him. He wrapped his arms around her and built a slow rhythm, feeling his own detonation near as his breathing came short and fast.

"Mari," he whispered, kissing her neck as she pressed even harder against him, taking him in to the hilt, and he felt her clench and quiver around him as he came, a deep and deliciously excruciating explosion.

As they trembled and stilled, he ran one hand gently over her damp skin while he held her close with the other. She sighed, tranquil against him. He planted trails of light kisses along her neck, her shoulders, loath to withdraw, to leave the warmth of her body. He liked being inside her. He wanted to stay.

MARIBETH AWOKE with a thick head to the sound of someone leaving the bathroom and then the pressure of a warm body pushing down the mattress next to her. It took her half a second to realize who it was, to remember everything, and then it came back with a start. She'd blame her evil twin if she had one. She'd just fucked the cocky storm chaser. How was she going to keep it professional now?

"You awake?" came his voice in her ear. His arms snaked around her waist, as they'd done last night, and he was curled up behind her again. OK, so he was more than the cocky storm chaser. He was Jack. He was . . . incredible. And he was like a human heater against her.

She turned over before he could get any ideas and looked him in the eye as they both lay against the pillows. His dark hair was adorably rumpled. *Stop it,* she told herself. "Pretty awake," she answered him, "considering the vats of bourbon we drank last night."

"You are pretty, awake," he said softly, kissing her neck, running a hand along her hip.

"Oh, no, no, we've got to get to the hangar," she said as she saw the clock: 8:20 a.m.

"Not yet. I don't think it's a chase day. Come on, Mari." He flicked her ear with his tongue, her earring. She hadn't even taken off her earrings. It had all been so urgent then, but now —

"I can't," she said, but she was getting hot all over again as he nibbled her neck and pulled her closer. She mustered all her resolve. "No, I have to get ready in case they need me." She pulled away, sat up with the sheet around her, trying to clear her head. Jack leaned on one elbow and looked at her with a lopsided grin. With his other hand, he tugged on the sheet, revealing one breast.

"Trouble," she said, trying to suppress a laugh. She pulled the sheet back up. He pulled it back down and touched her nipple lightly, circling it with a fingertip until it hardened. "I can't," she breathed.

"Yes, you can," he said, but he gave up and lay back on the pillows. She kind of wished he would continue so she could protest some more.

She inhaled and pulled herself together. "I'm going to take a shower. Alone," she said, warding him off as he opened his mouth.

"You're killing me," he said.

"If I were, you'd know it," Maribeth joked, letting the sheet fall away as she got up and headed for the bathroom.

"Oh, fuck, now you are killing me," he said, gazing after her as she walked by. "Can I use your laptop?"

"Sure," she said, going into the bathroom and shutting the door, feeling what was left of her composure fall away. She turned on the shower and stepped into the flow before it could warm up, gasping under the needles of ice, wondering what the hell she had done.

❦

JACK RELUCTANTLY FOUND his clothes and put them on. He wasn't sure what to make of her reaction this morning, but she looked just as good in daylight as she had last night. He hoped he'd see a lot more of that Maribeth and not the duty-bound woman from this morning, though he liked her, too. Really liked her. And that was kind of new. God, things had gone hot and fast last night. Not that he was complaining. But this whole working relationship thing could be tricky. He stood at the open doorway of the bedroom and listened to the water running in the shower. The bathroom door was closed. He took two steps into the bedroom, two steps closer. Screw the working relationship, he thought, though he knew the work was important to her. He understood and respected that, even as he wanted to rip the door off its hinges and hold her again.

He pushed down the impulse and turned around, went back to the living area, found her laptop. The music playlist had run out, but iTunes was still open, and he took in her modest jazz collection with approval: the stuff he grew up with, listening to records with his mom, and more, favorites from over the years — Miles, Ella, Frank. He sat at the table, closed the program and got to the task at hand, typing in the address for his weather data page on his obscure little website, the one without a home page that hardly anyone ever found. He started clicking through the links to satellite images, surface observations, weather balloon data and the models. If anything happened today, it was definitely out of their research domains, and it probably wasn't worth going to northern Iowa just to test cameras. He should call Dr. Y. His phone was in his room, and even though the suite had a phone, he had no idea what the number was. Instead, he opened his webmail and shot Dr. Y a quick forecast summary, with the recommendation that the lack of weather would probably give them a couple of days to regroup. A response came back almost immediately.

"Agreed. Errands to run today. Data to review. Come in when you wish. This afternoon is fine. Y."

A good day to lie in bed with the pilot. He listened. The water was still running. He weighed his options and decided it might be best to respect her borders. For now. And he needed to get his goddamn car.

He didn't want to just go, though god knows he'd done it plenty of times. This was different. Maribeth was different. He looked around for some way to leave a message. In the kitchen, he found a box of cereal and shook a few Cheerios onto the counter. He rearranged them into a heart and immediately obliterated it. *Really, Andreas? Still drunk?* But he did have the exotic idea that he didn't want last night to be their last. He ate a couple of O's while he thought. Then he shaped the pieces into a passable lightning bolt, shook a few more from the box and made an "XO" followed by a "J." Some breakfast, he thought wryly. He grabbed what was left of his bourbon and headed out the door.

"SO THIS IS how it's going to work," Danni told the *Zany Weddings* crew over breakfast at a local diner. Aurelius chewed on his lackluster French toast and listened. Chuck's Wagon was gone this morning from the hotel, and they'd swallowed their disappointment and headed for the nearest greasy spoon. "Our storm chasers here say we're not likely to get tornadoes for a couple of days, so we're going to go shoot one of our other zany weddings."

"Can we go home?" Tyler asked.

"I'm afraid not," Danni said. "There's just too much driving involved, and it's only a detour of a couple of days. We

have high hopes we can get a tornado later in the week for you
and get you hitched."

"I love a wedding that goes off with a hitch," Brad punned
to chuckles and groans.

"Oh, I get it!" Polly Ann said after a minute and laughed.
She looked at the Twister Tracker with adoration made fresh
by a good night's sleep. Aurelius longed for a boulder to drop
on Brad's head.

"Are you sure we have to go? I'm starting to wonder if
we'll ever get a tornado, and I have a lot of work to do at
home," said Tyler, but the look he was giving his fiancée
suggested he was worried about something other than his
storm shelter business.

"We have a lot of time invested in this shoot," Danni said
firmly, "and like I said, we should have storms in a couple of
days. Right, boys?" She directed her leading question to Aurelius and Brad.

"Absolutely," Aurelius said. "Try to view this as a vacation.
Today, we'll take a rest in town, and tomorrow, we'll head to
magnificent Carhenge."

"In England?" Polly Ann asked in awe.

"In Nebraska," Danni said, her tone somewhat lacking in
enthusiasm.

"But there will be Druids," Aurelius said.

"Rockabilly pagans," Danni corrected. "They have great
tattoos."

"Oh," said Polly Ann, sounding confused. "But we have
today off?"

"Yep," Brad said. "Go nuts. And tonight, you're drinking
on me. I finally got the advance on my book contract!"

There were cheers all around at this news, more for the
drinks than the contract, but Aurelius remained silent,

wondering if Brad would be any more revealing about his flight in the twister if he had to write about it in a memoir. Or, more accurately, tell a ghostwriter about it. Zane's own book, *Life Is an Adventure*, was now frequently seen in bookstore remainder bins for as little as $1.99. But he hadn't written it for the money, had he? Actually, he had. Debt never rested. Yet he still treasured the positive review he'd received from a blogger who specialized in posting photo galleries of international disasters. He was sure that had earned him a few readers, even if they just bought it for the photos in the middle. He took a sip of murky coffee and stared out the window at their rolling wedding cake. The hiker figurines on top looked tattered after their close encounter with the tornado and hail yesterday, as if they'd attempted Everest and failed.

"What is there to do in Salina on a day off, anyway?" asked Scooter, who was devouring his Paul Bunyan Platter of eggs, bacon, sausage, pancakes and fruit.

"Not sure," Danni said. "I'll have to check the tour book. But I'm going to do laundry. And Aurelius is going to get the windshield replaced. Right, buddy?"

"Sure, pal," he said. And while he waited for the repair, he'd write another love letter to Wynda. He'd convinced himself that she wasn't receiving them. After all, he hadn't received a reply, and he'd written two already. It was like writing a journal, an outlet for his frustrations and ruminations and the loopy thoughts Charles had been putting in his head. And, of course, it was a chance to remind Wynda of his fond and steamy memories of their previous assignations. Or maybe it was a form of mental masturbation. Unleashing his libido and his electronic thesaurus on an unattainable long-distance siren seemed a reasonable distraction as his hopes of a life of adventurous glamour dimmed.

"Check this out," Brad said to Polly Ann as he hung a spoon from his nose and snorted like a pig, making the handle bounce up and down. She clapped and laughed, and Aurelius felt the last bit of air leak out of him. They didn't make adventurers like they used to.

❦

WHEN MARIBETH EMERGED from the bedroom, Jack was gone. She'd taken her time, letting cold, then hot water revive her, wash away her dreamy state.

She dressed in khakis and a white blouse buttoned halfway over a white, scoop-neck tank top, then considered the empty suite. It was just as well, she told herself. That was Jack, right? She'd always suspected he was the hit-and-run type. And then she went into the kitchen to make coffee and found his awkward and endearing message written in Cheerios.

A lightning bolt, a kiss and a hug. It sounded like a song from a musical. And definitely not like Jack. She was going to brush the cereal into the trash, but she thought better of it, grabbed a bowl, gathered the bits and added more from the box for breakfast. I shall eat your message, she thought, and then, distracted by a memory of the night before, she let the milk overflow the bowl.

"Shit," she said, grabbing a washcloth to mop up the spill.

She finished her breakfast quickly and used her phone to check her mail. Annoying ads. A couple of newsletters. A message from her dad; all was well. And a status from Dr. Y: She wouldn't be needed today. Screw that. She wanted to know the results of her flight. She grabbed her canvas satchel, filled it with the essentials and went to the lobby to see if anyone could give her a ride to the hangar.

She found Fred just finishing the peculiar egglike matter that was served daily in a chafing dish in the continental breakfast room. He never got his act together enough to purchase groceries for his own suite's kitchen.

"No operations today, thank fuck," he said to her as he got up.

"Is fuck a synonym for everything with you?" she asked.

He raised his eyebrows. "You use it occasionally."

"Not for everything."

"It's convenient," he said as they walked into the lobby. "It has so many meanings, depending on inflection and what it modifies. Like, 'That's a fucking great data set.' Or, 'Would you fucking look at that?' Or, if I'm spelling my name to the more receptive, 'F as in fuck.' Or the classic, 'What the fuck?' Or, 'You are so fucking fucked up.'" He looked at her curiously. "Are you? I mean, fucked up? You look kind of tired today. Not that I'm being rude or anything."

"I indulged a bit last night," she confirmed.

"Oh, really?" Fred loved a bit of gossip. "Dr. Y go on a cocktail-making binge? He didn't look like he was in the mood when he left last night, but he does love a good drink."

"No, not with Dr. Y."

"Oh, now, you didn't go drinking with Andreas, did you?" he scolded in his mountain brogue. "That boy will drink you under the table."

"Funny you should mention that," she said.

Fred laughed. "I wondered when he'd make a move. He mentions you every time we talk. He's had his eye on you since Florida."

"No way," she said. She was either the last to notice everything or in complete denial.

"And how'd it go?" Fred lowered his voice. "You can tell me."

"Please!" Maribeth said. "Do I ever ask you questions like this?"

"No, but we're friends, and you could if you wanted to. It's just that my life is so goddamned boring, you wouldn't want to. So did you have fun?"

"Um." She hesitated, but the heat rose in her cheeks.

"Ah-ha! What is he — all hat, no cattle?"

Maribeth burst out laughing. "Really, Fred. If I answer you, will you stop this line of questioning and give me a ride to the hangar?"

"Very well," he said, looking eager.

"If he were a cowboy, he'd be at home on the range," she said, embarrassed at even this obscurity.

He took a moment to digest this answer, then nodded and smiled as if he understood, then frowned. "I wouldn't call that enough detail to warrant a ride to the hangar."

"Fred," she warned.

"OK, OK," he said. "Come on. But keep an eye on your corral. That boy's a rustler if I've ever seen one."

❧

AFTER HE'D GRABBED sneakers and his wallet from his room, Jack had asked the motherly older woman at the front desk which cab she'd recommend as Chester the chihuahua looked on with a haughty air.

"You're one of the Dr. Y group, aren't you?" she asked, looking up his room number. "I can get you a cab, but if you like, he's got a couple of bicycles here you're welcome to use. He's such a nice man, isn't he?"

"Yes, he really is," Jack said, though he was thinking, *and kind of crazy.* "I think I'd like a bike ride. Where are they?"

So she hooked him up with a decent bicycle, and using the GPS on his phone to navigate, he hit the road for Escapades. The air was pleasantly cool after the passage of the front, though he was heartened to see a few struggling clouds. With more moisture would come more weather, especially when the next system moved in.

It had been several days since he'd been on a bike, and it took him a mile or two to hit his rhythm. Finally, as he pedaled through tree-lined streets, sometimes bumping over brick pavers, his Florida-trained muscles kicked in, and he relished his speed, the breeze on his face and the chance to work through some of the thoughts haunting him. Like the image of Maribeth standing naked before him, then blazing in his arms, the dormant volcano unleashed. The notion was presumptuous, he knew, but he hadn't seen any evidence of that passionate woman until last night. She never talked about a guy stashed away somewhere. Except for that kiss in the graveyard, she'd been immune to flirting, at least until he got some bourbon into her. But he didn't think it was just the bourbon. It was as if she'd made a decision, and he wondered if she had decided to trust him. He liked the idea. He couldn't get past the fact that, glorious fucking or not, he really liked her. He respected her. Now that was a strange feeling indeed.

By the time he got to his car, he was sweating, and his day-old clothes were more than ready for the laundry. Escapades looked even shabbier by day, but he had a feeling he'd always remember it fondly. He put the bike in the back of the wagon, climbed in the driver's seat and drove back to the hotel.

An hour and a half later, showered, with fresh jeans and an Omaha Storm Chasers baseball shirt on, he rolled up to the hangar in his car. The sun, now high in the sky, glinted off the new crack in the windshield. It wasn't too bad. There was no sense in replacing the glass now. Hail season was far from over.

The hangar was quieter than it had been, but a few techs were still around, tinkering with instruments. The A-10's snarl seemed almost like a warning: *Don't mess with my pilot.* Jack had no plans to mess with her, except in the best possible way. He smiled.

"Andreas, nice of you to show up," said Fred, who'd emerged from the research van. It was parked in its corner, all its doors open.

"It's an off day," Jack said.

"You don't *look* like you got drunk last night."

"What's that supposed to mean?"

"I know things," Fred said mysteriously. "You want to check out the footage? We've got it running in the second office — we finally got the video lab going."

"How's it look?"

"We got some pretty cool — I mean, scientifically valuable stuff from the Ghost," said Fred, entering the lounge, followed by Jack, who grabbed a plate and a sandwich off a tray as they stopped outside the door to the second office. "We captured one complete bolt really nicely. It's amazing how long it takes to hit the ground when you break it down step by step. But unfortunately, none of the ground cameras caught an upward bolt, just one from the Warthog. It's not a bad shot, but there's rain in the way, and motion inhibits the clarity, too."

"So you still have some analysis to do? Something worthwhile?"

"Oh, yeah," Fred said. "I'd be delighted, normally. But Dr. Y really wants the upward lightning. I hope we get lucky next time. When is next time, by the way?"

"A couple of days away, I think. Probably farther north this time."

"In the Nebraska domain?" Fred asked, his voice brightening.

"Quite possibly," Jack said, "though conjuring a supercell in one county in Nebraska is like trying to shoot the moon."

"Shall we go in?" Fred said with unnecessary drama, and he opened the door to the darkened office. On tables against the far wall, four monitors were set up. One was probably a seventy-inch, Jack thought, almost a movie screen. On it, he quickly grasped, lightning video from the airplane was playing. And sitting in front of it was Maribeth.

"Good morning," Jack said, bumping Fred out of the way to take the seat next to her. He put down his plate and focused on her face, her subtle smile.

"Almost good afternoon," Maribeth said. "How are you?"

"Feeling pretty good, actually. I got in a nice bike ride when I went to get my car this morning. You see, I left it at this bar last night."

"Oh, really?" she asked, playing along. "What was it like?"

"A real dive," he said, "but there was a pretty girl there."

"Will y'all please stop it," Fred said. "You're too fucking cute. Now check this out, Andreas," and the chatter stopped as the engineer leaned between them and cued up a video from another airplane camera.

"This is the best one," Fred said, standing back to watch the screen. Jack scooted his chair closer to the computer, closer to Maribeth, and snuck his hand into hers.

"Fred, is this the one with the upward lightning?" she asked, withdrawing her hand. Jack heard a bubble in her voice betray her, like a little pop of champagne.

"Yeah, that's it. Here," Fred fast-forwarded through the plane's flight, and Jack got caught up in the dizzying swoops, Maribeth's flirtation with the dangerous supercell.

"Has Dr. Y seen this?" Jack asked.

"Came and went already," said Fred. "He's seen almost everything. He said he had some research to do. OK, here we go."

The bolt started off-screen, a slow-motion burst of light as recorded on the high-speed camera.

"Frames per second?" Jack asked.

"About 12,000," Fred said. "Shut up and look. Here it is!"

In the wake of the cloud-to-ground bolt, the upward flash initiated from the top of the wind turbine, a bright branch shooting toward the sky, flanked by two lesser branches. Those also branched upward, building a fleeting tree of light, as twigs of dazzling staccato bolts shot up between the limbs. The brightest branch pulsed, clawing at the cloud, as the other branches widened, scattered and dissipated in the darkness of the storm. It was beautiful, but Jack could see why they weren't satisfied. The rain dimmed the footage, and at one point, part of the branching was off-camera as the plane moved. So much luck was involved in this project, he thought, and half of it was bad.

"See those recoil leaders? Those strobing flashes that look like they're bouncing back?" Fred said. "Classic on these positive bolts."

"Why exactly does it fire upward?" Maribeth asked.

"Usually, tall objects initiate a positive leader as lightning looks for somewhere to go," Fred said. "That is, a negative leader from the storm induces positive charge on objects on the ground. The field is enhanced at the tip of the tall object — in this case, the turbine."

"How far up does the leader reach from the turbines?" she asked.

"That's one thing we're working on, but from a tower, five hundred meters isn't unlikely."

"Much higher than a typical ground leader, then," she said.

"Definitely," said Fred. "But that's just during a normal downward strike. Sometimes in a storm you have a horizontally stratified positive charge region — basically, it causes a lot of positive cloud-to-ground bolts instead of negative ones. A positive leader goes down and connects, and you get a rapid return stroke that causes a cascade of electrons upward."

"A negative return stroke," Jack said.

"Yes," Fred said. "The negative deviation causes an upward positive stroke from a tall object — lightning-triggered upward lightning, all because lightning hit nearby. Actually, it doesn't even need to hit nearby. It could be fifty kilometers away. And it sucks for the turbines, or skyscrapers, or whatever tall object is around. We've found that towers can be exposed to lightning ten times more frequently than random objects on the ground thanks to this upward initiation."

"And I'm flying through that airspace," Maribeth mused. "I'm not too worried about the lightning, since planes survive lightning all the time, but I'm wondering if my risk is enhanced here. Not that I mind," she added quickly.

"A good question," Fred said, "but it really shouldn't be. The chances of you being struck are really low, unless a storm just goes banana-cakes. You're more likely to have a plane-triggered strike."

"Just another day at the office," she said with a smile. "And Dr. Y says he'd like us to record one of those anyway. Did any of the other cameras get that upward stroke?"

"The fucking starboard one flaked on me again," Fred

replied, "and it was the closest to being in the right spot, so no, it didn't. It's gonna be expensive, but we're swapping it out entirely for a new one so we don't have to worry about it failing again."

"Still, that was pretty amazing," Maribeth said.

"The Ghost would have slowed it down more than twice as much, with better resolution, and without moving all over the place. It would've been spectacular. I'm happy you got what you got, but we have to get it from the ground, too. We have to get lucky. Of course, you'd know all about that, wouldn't you?" Fred said to Jack as he clapped him on the shoulder. "Try to behave yourself. I'm going to go work on the camera swap."

"What was that about?" Jack asked as Fred left the room.

"He's such a goofus. He kind of knows about — you know. He guessed. And I'm no good at lying." The lightning video was still looping, the light flickering across her face.

He took one of her hands in both of his and kissed it. "You don't mind about last night, do you?" he asked.

"Mind?" She laughed. "Let's just say I surprised myself. But I — I am not unhappy that I did."

"Neither am I," Jack said, leaning in to kiss her. She tasted good. "Mmm, cinnamon."

"Now you know my real addiction. Hot mints."

"They've ruined many a life," Jack said.

"I know. I should take up something more healthy, like bourbon."

Oh, yeah. He liked her.

She turned to the keyboard, closed the video and starting browsing. "Fred said there was a video on here you should see. I think it's when Dr. Y was in the lightning tent."

"Oh, really?" In the rush to get out of the way of the

storm, Jack had forgotten about setting up video.

"Yeah. You used one of those wide-angle cameras in the bubble window, right? I love those things. Sometimes I mount one on my motorcycle when I'm riding at home. Or I used to."

"Get tired of the video?"

"No. I still have the camera," she said. "I sold the motor-cycle after I lost the TV job. Anyway, riding is a lot more dangerous than flying an airplane."

"Into tornadoes."

"Exactly," she said innocently. "Here it is, I think."

She'd opened a new video on the screen. The distorted, almost fisheye view of the camera showed the field of wind turbines under light rain and a diminutive, dark pillar shape in the middle of the frame.

"Is that it?" she asked.

"The tent. Yeah, that's it. I set up the camera after he already got in it."

They watched for a few minutes as lightning flashed off-camera and far away among the turbines. "Not much to look at," she said.

"Yeah, I don't think this part is what Fred was talking about," Jack said, feeling his anxiety build as the video put him back in that van, and then out of it, as he appeared on-screen, running toward the lightning tent.

"Oh, crap, that's you," Maribeth said, realizing what they were about to see.

"Yeah, that's me," Jack said darkly. "Being an idiot."

"Just doing your job. That makes it kind of heroic." She grinned at him, then turned back to the screen. "Why's it taking so long to get him out?"

"The absent-minded professor was stuck. He —" Jack stopped talking as a blinding flash overwhelmed the camera's sensor, nearly simultaneously with a loud *crack-boom*. As the camera compensated, a pulsing bolt could be seen just beyond Jack, so close it made him feel sick all over again, and in an instant, it was over.

"Flang," he said. "Shit, we were lucky."

"*You* were lucky," Maribeth said, turning to look at him, her eyes wide. "What did you just say? Before that?"

"Flang. Flash-bang. Something chasers say. When the lightning is that close, the thunder you hear is virtually simultaneous."

"That's a weapon, too, you know. A flash-bang. A stun grenade."

"A flang is nature's stun grenade," he said.

"Jesus, Jack. You almost got fried. *Flang*," she said, trying out the word. "I prefer 'zap bang.' "

"I'm starting to have a Pavlovian response to 'zap bang,' " he said, leaning over to kiss her.

"I don't recall saying 'zap bang' earlier when you did that," she murmured when he pulled back.

"There you go again." He leaned in to kiss her more thoroughly, cupping her neck with his hand. She relaxed into the kiss and put a hand on his knee, sending heat shooting up his thigh toward his groin. This was titillating but awkward. Damn office chairs. He didn't like office chairs.

Light flooded the room as the door opened, and they broke apart. "Oh, puh-leeze, no making out in the video lab," Fred said, but there was something in his voice that sounded absolutely delighted.

Maribeth looked mortified. "I've — got to go check on the plane," she said, making a hasty exit.

"Nice timing," Jack said after she left.

"You should talk," Fred said, sitting in the vacated chair. "I see you were watching your near-death experience."

"Don't remind me."

"It's good to be reminded once in a while," Fred said. "You know, Andreas, life is pretty fucking short. Don't screw around with it too long, or it'll bite you in the ass."

Jack didn't say anything, but he digested this bit of wisdom along with a bite of his ham sandwich as he reached over to the computer and hit replay.

MARIBETH SPENT some time sitting in the open cockpit, reminding herself that she was still a professional despite Fred's adolescent teasing. She stared at the dormant dials and touched the switches lightly, remembering when, as a girl, the controls of a plane had been one of the most intimidating things she'd ever seen. But she'd wanted to impress her dad, whose pictures and stories from his Air Force days intrigued her. She'd liked the look and sound of the planes, the hangars. She'd liked figuring out the puzzle of each cockpit, and she'd spent less and less time with the horses her mother trained and more and more time studying the planes in her father's modest fleet and hanging out with the guys who flew them. She played with a computer flight simulator and had her first lesson at twelve. Four years later, she took her first solo flight, on a sunny October day over north Texas, and from then on, she was hooked.

In college in Texas, when she fell in with other military students and was kicking around which direction to take, one of her ROTC instructors took her up for a couple of helicopter flights. She was a natural at the yoke, and with the right track, she realized, she could actually get into combat. That was before her mom got sick, when Maribeth thought she had all the time in the world, before she knew what loss was.

Now, she was glad to fly against a natural enemy rather than a human one. And she was free to think about the future, if she wanted, maybe even a future with a man.

But this was Jack. She might have been with him last night, and if she allowed it, maybe even tonight. But after he stole a few of her horses, she thought, chuckling at Fred's metaphor, he'd probably head for the next corral. The best thing to do was not think about it, she decided. Just go with it. She would let it happen, see if he was wearing a star or a black hat. For Christ's sake, she thought to herself, enough with the cowboy crap. Jack was about as close to a cowboy as Fred was to James Bond.

"Ms. Lisbon?" inquired Dr. Y, interrupting her reverie as he stood at the top of the pilot's ladder outside the cockpit. "Everything OK with my baby?"

She smiled. "She's just about ready for action. Fred's working on swapping out one of the cameras."

"That was my suggestion," he said. "I've spent this much; what's a hundred thousand more? So I'll have one less bottle of 1787 Chateau d'Yquem." He smiled and nodded, looking distracted. She'd known him long enough to see there was more on his mind, and she hoped it had nothing to do with what had been on hers.

"What's going on, doc?" she asked.

"May I speak to you in confidence, Maribeth?" he asked. Now she knew he was serious; he actually used her first name.

"Of course you can," she said. "But let me get out of this contraption."

She followed him down the ladder, and they ducked under the belly of the beast and beyond the tail, past the busy technicians.

"You see, my interest in lightning goes far beyond the science as it applies to our energy futures and cities," said Dr. Y. "It's also — I am also interested in how it affects people directly. And I have been trying for some time to locate a man who has been struck multiple times and has survived. I think he may be — quite valuable to my research and operations."

"How so?"

"That will come in time," he said. "For now, I just want to find him, and I think I'm close."

"He's here?"

"I do believe he is here, somewhere in the Great Plains, and that he may be among the storm chasers. In fact, I believe you may have met him yourself."

"We ran into a lot of storm chasers a couple of days ago, but I can't say we really talked to any of them," she said. "Except for a couple of guys involved with a TV show."

"No," Dr. Y said, "he's not a TV personality, though I did find one interview with him in my research. I believe he drives a food truck."

"Chuck's Wagon, maybe? You say he was struck by lightning?"

"More to the point, he's survived being struck by lightning, over and over," said Dr. Y. "I think he courts it. It might be in his interest if we can persuade him to stand down while we do our research. I doubt he's immune, but it would be interesting to find out."

"No doubt," said Maribeth. "What do you want me to do?"

"If you see him, I just want you to talk to him. Find out if he's the man I think he is, if he's been struck by lightning. See if he'll talk to me. And if I find him, of course, I will do the same, when I chase with the boys."

Jack's going to love that, she thought, but she nodded. She was willing to help, even if the request did sound a little strange. "Sure. He sounds like an intriguing case."

"One of the most compelling I've run across," said Dr. Y. The cloud seemed to lift from his brow. "There, now. Did you get lunch? These Kansans know how to cook." And he led her back toward the lounge, an enigmatic smile on his face.

❧

"I DON'T LIKE days off. That's when I get into trouble," Jack said, quaffing his third mega-margarita, as Fred nursed his second beer.

"I told you. Trouble," said Maribeth, who sat across from both of them at the Tex-Mex chain restaurant with her first glass of cabernet. She thought liquor might be a good thing to avoid tonight, at least during dinner.

She'd had a steak after Jack explained that storm chasers always had a steak after they saw a tornado. Despite her helicopter chasing, she wasn't versed in storm-chaser culture, which seemed to be a mix of superstitions, *Twister* quotes, encyclopedic recitations of storm reports, memories of horrible food and hotels, and references that only someone who spent a great deal of time perusing tornado videos would get.

"I didn't have a day off," Fred complained. "And I'm not feeling so hot after that enchilada."

"I told you, this is not the place to eat enchiladas," Maribeth said. "You need to go to Texas. They'll hook you up."

"It's probably also not the place to eat steak," Fred pointed out.

"Or really anything," Jack said, "but compared with most places on the road, this is pretty decent. And the drinks, while mediocre, definitely have alcohol in them." He took another swig and grinned.

"Especially the *Especiales*," Maribeth said. Jack had been ordering the biggest premium drinks all night.

"I'm sure the amount of alcohol is regulated by their corporate masters," Fred said.

"Why don't you get another beer?" Jack asked. "We have tomorrow off, too. I mean, we won't be chasing tomorrow."

"I'm bushed," Fred said. "And I know I can't keep up with you. If it's just the same to y'all, I'm going to head back to the hotel. You can get a cab, right?"

Jack and Maribeth exchanged a look. "Sure," Maribeth said.

Fred perked up a little at their momentary discomfort and smiled as he got up. "How much do I owe?"

"Dr. Y told me he's paying. I'll expense it," Maribeth said. "Good night, Fred."

"Good night, Ace," he said, "and Andreas." And he was gone.

Maribeth and Jack didn't say anything for a minute. There was a roar from the bar, where someone had been making a ruckus all evening.

"What are they doing over there?" she asked.

"Shots," Jack said. "I saw when I went to the bathroom. It's that TV crew we ran into on the road."

"That guy who flew in the tornado? The one you forecasted for?"

"Yeah, that guy," Jack said, derision in his voice.

"It's pretty crazy to fly into a tornado, but it takes guts."

"If only he had some." He took another sip and cocked his head as if listening for the next round of cheers.

Maribeth waited for him to say more. He didn't. "This is not a good place to drink you under the table," she finally said.

"Unfortunately, I have to agree with you," Jack said. "It lacks atmosphere."

"So we might have to actually talk."

"We talked last night."

"I don't remember much talking," Maribeth said.

"Just enough." Jack smiled.

"Ha!"

"It was perfect for last night," he said, "but this is good. I like talking with you. I feel like I'm getting to something real with you. Like you're connected to the world in a way I'm not."

Maribeth's brow creased. "I'd say we're all equally connected, only some people just don't know it and act accordingly."

"Maybe that was me," he said.

"Was?"

"Yeah, was," Jack said. "Change is in the wind."

"That's just the next storm system." She swirled the last sip of her wine and wondered where he was going.

"Look, I don't usually have unbridled amounts of optimism, so maybe we should just run with it," Jack said. "I'm telling you, you have something to do with it."

"You're teasing me."

"Seriously. I — like you, Ms. Lisbon," he said, using Dr. Y's appellation for her. "I think you are a badass and a gentlewoman."

"How romantic," she said, then immediately regretted it.

He gave her a look that would melt a locomotive. "Romance is easy," he said, "but saying this the way I want to say it is hard. I just want to tell you that I feel good spending time with you. I feel like I want to spend more time with the right people, and I think you're one of the right people."

"Miss Right Now?" she replied, her tone arch.

He laughed. "I want to be around smart people. Good people who know where they're going. Maybe it'll rub off. I like working with this team, even that nutbag Fred, and I have a good feeling about you. I just want you to know you have a fan. Though I still think Dr. Y may be crazy."

She wondered if he was actually expressing an emotion or just giving her a job review. "Dr. Y is a good man, too," she said. "Not that I'm — I'm not saying *I'm* good."

"I am."

"Once again, how can you — "

"I know you. I can't explain it, damn it, but I do." He sounded a little drunk, a little frustrated. He took another sip of the drink. "I'm not my old self on this trip," he said, "and it's really irritating. I would really love a cigarette."

"You smoke?"

"I did. Now I just eat pretzel sticks."

"It's the devil to give up," she said. "I smoked for a couple of years in the Army until — well, I just finally acknowledged that it was a bad idea."

"Until what?"

"What?"

"You said 'until,' " he said.

She didn't want to get into it. She shook her head. "It was a lot of things, but one of them was my mom dying of lung cancer."

"Oh, man. That sucks," Jack said.

"And it sucked even more because I wasn't there for most of it, for most of her last months and years on this earth, because I was halfway around the world." She could hear the anger in her voice, and she hadn't even wanted to talk about it.

Jack took a long sip of his drink. "That's not something you could help or change."

"Wasn't it? If I hadn't felt the need to prove myself in the fucking sandbox, maybe I would have been here for her."

"You did what you had to do," Jack said. "No shame in that. Though I know it hurts."

Maribeth finished her wine, remembering he'd said his mother was dead, too. "Nothing lasts," she said. "At least I've learned that."

"I have a confession to make. I haven't entirely given up smoking. Every once in a while, a cigar hits the spot."

"I give cigars a pass," she said, glad he'd changed the subject, "and I take a few puffs on occasion. That's how you know I'm really drunk."

"I thought I knew you were drunk last night when you set the bed on fire."

Jack was switching gears fast, pushing her into another space. She felt like being open with him. She'd given up on anything that might last, yet here she was, daring to let a dangerous idea grow.

"I liked it when you called me Mari," she said softly.

"What? Oh. Yeah." The corner of his mouth turned up, a wickedly handsome look.

"That's what my close friends call me. Mari."

"Does that mean we're friends?" He reached out and took her hand.

"Aren't we?" she asked uncertainly.

"At least," he said.

She thrilled to the thought of what he might be saying and just as immediately pushed the feeling down. But she wanted to find out. She wanted to be close to him again.

"Maybe we should go back to the hotel," she said.

He brightened. "Do you want to call the cab, or shall I?"

"I'll go outside and do it. There's no signal in here. And I'll call my dad while I'm waiting."

"Is he all right?"

"Oh, he's fine. I try to call him a couple of times a week, and I was thinking about visiting him. Maybe tomorrow, since I may have plans tonight." She smiled and let go of his hand, waved the waitress over and handed her a credit card.

"Mari?" he said.

She liked hearing it even more today. "Yes?"

"I just wanted to say it again. Friend."

"Right," she said, laughing this time. "Get another drink. I'll tell you when it's here. Last night they took, what, twenty minutes?"

"All I know," said Jack, "is that it seemed like forever."

❧

AURELIUS DIDN'T DO SHOTS, hadn't done them since the vicious hangover that followed a visit to a Yukon dive during his Arctic Circle expedition. But he sat at the bar, sipped a gin and tonic — top shelf since Brad was paying — and watched the others knock them back at a nearby table. It was interesting, staying relatively sober while the others got plastered. Danni was loquacious. Scooter was silly. Vinyl looked more stoned than ever. Tyler looked frustrated, Polly Ann was giddy, and Brad was totally focused on Polly Ann. Brad seemed to be drinking much less than the others, too, as he teased the blond bride, told her stories of his heroism, rubbed her back and encouraged her to drink another margarita. The conversation had become disjointed, rambling, loud, punctuated by cheers as they ordered and downed another round of tequila shots.

He became aware of another presence at his shoulder and turned to see who it was.

"I'll take one of those tequila shots," the man said to one of the bartenders, a buxom woman in a low-cut red T-shirt. The man didn't turn to observe the commotion; instead, he glanced up at the TV, where The Weather Channel was playing, his face impassive. That face — it looked familiar.

"You're the one," Aurelius said, causing him to turn. "You're the one who did the forecasting for the Bubble show. Remember, we just met again in the field a couple of days ago?"

"I remember," the man said. Aurelius couldn't recall the name. He was so bad with names that weren't his. So he reintroduced himself.

"Jack," the storm chaser said, sounding weary. The bartender put down the full shot glass, rimmed with salt and garnished with a slice of lime. Jack slapped some bills on the bar, licked the salt and downed the shot in one motion, then sucked on the lime. He sighed in satisfaction. "Always hits the spot."

"I'd like to know more about that extraordinary Bubble mission," Aurelius said.

"It was all in the TV show," said Jack, looking up at the TV, then nodding toward Brad. "You've got the source right there. Why don't you ask him?"

"He's — shy about discussing it."

"I'm sure he is," Jack said dryly. "I've got to go."

At that moment, a shriek split the air, and both men turned to look. It was Polly Ann, pushing Tyler away from Brad.

"You hit me!" said Brad, looking startled, rubbing his chin.

"You keep your hands off Polly Ann!" Tyler shouted.

"My hands weren't on her."

"Now Tyler," Polly Ann said, "he was just trying to get a bug off me."

"Off your boobies?" Tyler was red in the face and near detonation.

"You can be such a child sometimes," she said, crossing her arms and looking away.

"Is that what you think?" Tyler slammed his fist on the table. "Maybe you don't want to marry a *child*."

"Maybe I want to be with someone who treats me like I'm special and grown-up and not just the girl who carries his bowling ball. You do like playing with your balls!" she shouted.

Scooter and Vinyl looked at each other with a grimace and a low "Oooh."

Brad looked pleased at the chaos he'd caused. "Why don't you cool off," he told Tyler. "Go outside and walk around the parking lot."

"I am not listening to you, creep," Tyler said, lunging at him again as Scooter and Vinyl caught him by the arms.

Aurelius stepped forward. "Everyone out, now. Brad, settle up. We're going to go."

"I'm not going anywhere," said Polly Ann, who was somewhere between petulant and pissed off. "I'm having another drink."

"Bartender, a margarita for the lady," Brad called.

"Seriously?" Tyler cried, almost purple now. Aurelius thought he saw a tear in the poor boy's eye.

"Everyone out," Aurelius repeated. "Boys, take Tyler outside and walk him around." Scooter and Razor, not so steady themselves, guided the shorter man out the door, followed by Danni. Tyler looked stunned, as flattened as if he'd been run over by a steamroller.

The bartenders appeared relieved as Brad signed the check and presented Polly Ann with her margarita.

"Brad," said Aurelius.

Brad looked up like a lion interrupted in the middle of devouring his prey. "What?"

"Get out."

"You're kidding me." Brad was infuriatingly calm, though he rubbed his chin again where a red mark from Tyler's punch had begun to appear.

"I hate to pull rank," said Aurelius, drawing on all of his brawn and bass as he spoke, "but I'm co-producer. I don't care how much they're paying you. I'm your boss. Get out, or you're off the show."

Brad seemed to weigh his options, looking at Polly Ann, who'd perched herself on a barstool and was using a straw to suck down the drink at a rapid pace, and then at Aurelius. Then he noticed Jack at the bar and frowned.

"I'll go," Brad said, "but only because it's starting to stink in here." He caressed Polly Ann's back on his way out and left.

"Now, Polly Ann," said Aurelius, "this is all a big misunderstanding, and I want you to come with me."

"You get within three feet of me, I'll hit you with my self-defense moves!" she threatened. "They're the real thing! Stay back if you don't want to sing soprano!"

Aurelius was dismayed and modestly alarmed. He couldn't just leave her here. "Polly Ann," he said, resorting to pleading, "Tyler loves you, and we need you."

"GET OUT!" she screamed.

Jack tapped Aurelius on the shoulder. "Let me talk to her," he said. His detached demeanor was somehow reassuring.

"Really?"

"Go ahead. Give me five minutes." Jack's eyes took in every inch of their petite co-star. "I'll deliver her to you."

"All right," Aurelius said reluctantly. He hoped Jack would indeed deliver her. He just hoped it wasn't tomorrow morning.

❧

STANDING BY THE BAR, watching the squabble, Jack realized, remembering Maribeth's question last night, that he could use his powers for good or for evil. In this case, he thought, perhaps a bit of both. Polly Ann was a tasty little thing, a rosy-cheeked blonde with a perky figure and, obviously, a hell of a temper. And he liked a challenge.

As Aurelius left, Jack walked over to stand next to her.

"Men suck, don't they?" he said.

She looked up suspiciously before recognition dawned on her pretty face. "I know you," she said. "I watched that Bubble series, like, a thousand times. You were the forecaster! Jack, right?"

"Right," he said, smiling and shaking her hand, and he felt her relax at his touch.

"You're even better-looking in person." A look of embarrassment crossed her face. "Did I say that out loud?"

"I'm better in person in a lot of ways," Jack said, leaning against the bar next to her, still smiling.

She was bashful, suddenly, looking down and taking a sip through the straw. She looked up again. "I love your eyes," she said. "Once in a while you could see them on the TV show, when they did a close-up. But you weren't on that much, were you? I can't believe you got to work with Brad. How awesome was it?" Her anger had vanished, but her face was still pink, her sea-blue eyes tinged with red.

Jack leaned in closer. "Pretty awful," he said softly into her ear, as if sharing a secret. "He has a terrible way of getting entangled with girls and doing the wrong thing."

"What?" She was wide-eyed and disbelieving.

"Well, you know TV stars," he said, allowing the unsaid to fill her imagination.

Her eyes, her face betrayed her struggle as she worked through this unwanted revelation. "Is he really like that?" she asked.

Jack sat next to her, his voice barely above a whisper. "The worst kind of womanizer. He never met a woman he didn't try to sleep with."

"I — I thought he thought I was special," she said. "I mean, not that I don't love Tyler and all, but Brad — he acted like we might really have something. I mean, brave guys like him don't come along but maybe once a lifetime."

"Trust me. He's not all that brave," Jack said, putting a hand on her shoulder, rubbing it lightly. He saw her soften, calm. "You're a beautiful girl. You could be with anybody, you know."

"But he had this, I don't know, heroic quality on TV," she said. "I was wondering if maybe he was the handsome prince we all dream about. A real-life Mr. Right."

Miss Right Now, Jack thought, remembering Maribeth's joke. He pushed Polly Ann's hair back behind her ear and saw her almost lean into his hand, like a petted cat.

"I think you already found your prince," he said. He gave her his most earnest gaze and saw the attraction and bewilderment in her eyes. It would be so easy . . . "That guy you came with — he's your prince," Jack continued. "He looked like a real white knight, defending your honor. Those guys don't come along every day. He's the real thing."

Polly Ann seemed caught on a fulcrum, not sure which way to lean, a muddle of booze and frustration and desire, and then he saw her confusion melt away. She looked up at him and smiled. Ah, those blue eyes. There was a time he could have gone swimming in them. She got off the stool, stood on her tiptoes and kissed him on the cheek.

"Thank you, Jack," she said, her gaze bright again. "It's so great to meet you! Thank you again!" She turned and dashed out of the bar.

Jack sat back, laughing to himself at how he'd not only disrupted Brad's scheming, but did it by describing someone who easily could have been him. Could have been him tonight, if he'd wanted. But he didn't. He wanted Maribeth.

It was odd that she hadn't come to find him yet. He left the bar, now nearly empty, and headed out to the parking lot. All he saw was Aurelius Zane, directing the last of the crew into their vehicles, including that crazy wedding-cake car.

"Hey," Jack said, not really wanting to talk to him but not sure what else to do. "Have you seen a woman out here, brunette? She was probably talking on her cell phone."

"Oh, that pretty lady you had with you on the chase," said Aurelius. "Yes — she was talking with Brad, I believe, about five minutes ago, then went inside. Then she came out in kind of a hurry and got into a cab that had just arrived and took off."

"She left?" Jack was puzzled at first. Then, as he mulled the timing of her exit and what she might have seen inside the bar, his stomach did a slow roll. "Shit," he said.

"Need a ride? It's the least I can do," Aurelius said, coming closer and lowering his voice so the others wouldn't hear. "Polly Ann said you offered her some good advice. I'm just grateful she's back on board."

"Yeah — yes, a ride. I don't have to ride with Brad, do I?"

Aurelius smiled. "He's driving the crew van for tonight. Come along in the cake."

Jack got in the front, wanting to throttle Brad — Brad, the last one to talk to Maribeth before she went into the bar. He had a feeling it was no coincidence. It was a strange but quiet ride to the hotel, with Polly Ann and Tyler moving from whispers to making out and the two crew guys nodding off in the back while Aurelius drove. They dropped off Jack, and he took the elevator to the third floor and ran down the hall to Maribeth's door. He knocked.

"Mari!" he called. "You in there?"

There was no answer. He knocked again, then tried texting her.

After a moment, a door opened down the hall, and Fred stepped out in blue sweatpants and a white T-shirt. "Andreas, you're going to wake up every fucking person on the floor. What the hell do you want?"

"Maribeth."

"She's not here."

"How do you know?" Jack asked.

"Because she borrowed my car. Said she's going to visit her dad since we have tomorrow off."

"She's driving to Oklahoma City tonight?"

"No, you idiot," Fred said. "She's flying."

"Oh, shit," Jack said. He ran off down the hall to the elevator.

"Whatever it is, let her go, Andreas," Fred called after him.

Jack was too upset to listen. He got into the elevator and hit one. If he could just get to the hangar, to the airport, he might stop her. But he abruptly realized that despite his substantial tolerance, he was way too drunk to drive. He stopped the doors from closing and walked back to Fred's door, which had just shut. He knocked, and Fred opened it.

"What?" The engineer looked tired.

"Drive me to the airport."

"I told you, she took my rental."

"Drive my car," Jack said. "Please."

"I have a feeling this is a fool's errand," Fred said. "What's so urgent?"

"She wouldn't have just left like that unless something upset her," Jack said. "We have to hurry."

Fred crossed his arms and adopted a reproving tone. "And *did* you do something to upset her? Because that would also upset me."

"I didn't mean to," Jack said. "But I think I did anyway. I don't want to upset her. Ever," he insisted.

Fred took a moment and looked him in the eye, stroking his ruddy beard. "OK, goddamnit. But I know I'm going to regret it. Let me get my shoes."

The door closed, and a few seconds later, it opened again,

with Fred wearing flip-flops.

"Come on, fool, on your fool's errand," he said, but not unkindly.

A couple of minutes later in the hotel parking lot, Fred had trouble starting the wagon, and he pumped the pedal to no avail.

"Shit, I hope it's not the starter again," Jack said.

"I smell gas," said Fred.

"I think you flooded the engine. Get out and let me in there."

"There's no way you're driving. You smell like a moonshiner."

"I'm not going to drive," Jack said. "I'm just going to start it."

"You'll have to wait a few minutes."

"Don't you think I know that?" Jack said, walking around to the driver's side.

Fred got out and stood by the open door with his arms crossed as Jack got in. "Nice windshield." He nodded at the crack.

"I like them that way," Jack said from the driver's seat. "Pre-disastered."

"You're not going to catch her. Just wait a day or two. You can talk when she comes back."

Jack couldn't understand his own anxiety, but he didn't like the idea of Maribeth thinking badly of him, even for two days. "It has to be now," he said.

"It must've been pretty bad," Fred said. "What'd you do?"

"Nothing," Jack said, trying to be patient. "Nothing except a good deed that looked bad."

"There must have been a reason it looked bad. Nothing that looks bad is entirely good."

"That's one way to look at it," Jack said, remembering how he'd enjoyed playing on the blond girl's emotions. He turned the key, pressing the pedal just so, and the car started. "All yours," he said, getting out and running to the passenger side.

"Women are delicate," Fred said as he pulled out of the parking lot, "even the tough ones. Don't start something you can't finish, Andreas."

Jack watched the dark road vanishing under their tires, felt the night enveloping him, and wondered if he could finish anything.

There was little activity at the dark airport as the Volare pulled in. Jack ran out and waved his card in front of the security pad to get them through the gate.

"Let's check the hangar first," he said when he got back in.

"No one's there, except security," Fred said, rolling through the gate and threading among the buildings.

"Still."

"OK. Anything to get me out of this smelly car," Fred joked.

"Thanks," Jack said with sarcasm. They pulled up to their hangar, and he hopped out and went to the main door. It was locked. He looked around.

"Hey!" he said to the uniformed guard who was walking up from the back of the building. It was one of Dr. Y's hires. "Have you seen our pilot anywhere? Maribeth?"

"Just so happens I have," said the stocky, bald man. "She was headed for her plane and said to leave these keys for — oh, there you are," he said as Fred walked up. The guard handed over Fred's keys.

"The A-10?" Jack asked, confused. "It's still locked up, right?"

"No, *her* plane," the guard said.

"But where is she?" Jack asked, on the verge of punching someone.

"There," said the guard, pointing up as the drone of an engine came to their ears. It was a small plane, just airborne, lifting swiftly into the starry sky.

3

POINTS OF ATTACHMENT

When Maribeth awoke in the morning, she wasn't quite sure where she was. It was a feeling she was used to, even liked sometimes, when she was in a realm halfway between sleep and wakefulness, lost in a sunlit, waterfront place where she might be happy, with someone who made her happy, a fantasy from a dream. And then she would wake up for real and be back in the desert or Oklahoma or Kansas, in a tent or apartment or hotel room, and she was reminded again how unlikely it was that she would ever find that place of sun and love. In truth, she'd stopped looking.

This morning was different. Her fractured dreams were dark, and they slipped away quickly. She sat up in her bed in her modest apartment on the edge of Oklahoma City and looked at the clock. It was too early to visit her dad at the airport. Not too early to work out some of her angst.

She donned old running clothes from her half-empty dresser, put in her earbuds and hit the pavement, working out her stress through her legs and lungs. She took in the endless stream of chain restaurants and service stations, the little neighborhoods tucked between, the places she'd started to think of as fodder for tornadoes more than homes. Perhaps she thought that way because she hadn't put down roots herself.

Her apartment seemed even emptier after her three-mile run. Her work with her father and then Dr. Y kept her away more than she was here. Once she showered and dressed and walked around, she could read the signs of her absence. The bookcases, filled with history and stories of aviation and a few novels, were dusty, and even the cactus on the windowsill looked puckered. She gave it a little water and made herself black coffee. She didn't bother to forage for food; there wouldn't be any. This was not her home. No place really had been, since she'd left Texas all those years ago. She always had somewhere else to fly.

It had been so freeing, dashing into the skies in the C172 last night. Flying the Cessna was like flying a couch after the A-10 — cozy and comfortable, especially with no storms to make it interesting. Perfect flying. A perfect escape.

Maribeth tried not to think about Jack, tried to focus on the news on her tablet computer as she drank her coffee. Her chair by the window was comfortable, a thrift store find, like nearly all her other furnishings. She preferred to think of it as vintage. And disposable, if she had to move again. She did allow herself a few photographs on the bookcases: a couple of her mom and dad before her mom got sick, and one of her and a handful of the people she'd flown with in Iraq. It was taken on one of the good days, a quiet day, and they'd hammed it up for the camera. They all looked tan and boisterous and secretly homesick.

Weary of the news, most of it bad, she moved to her favorite weather data sites. There might be a few storms today in northern Colorado and far western Nebraska, and chances were much better tomorrow, but it wasn't clear whether the weather would reach the Nebraska wind farm. Or whether she'd be flying. And, she told herself, that was all she really ever wanted to do. Because staying on the ground meant nothing but strife.

What had she been thinking, getting involved with the nearest available man? There was no meaning in it. That was certainly clear after she saw him with his hands on the pretty blonde in the bar, whispering in her ear. Was anything he'd said true?

It bugged her, too, that she gave him this much thought. It was as if she'd invested something in him. Hope. It didn't help that her phone had pinged multiple times last night, messages from him, as if he actually had something to say. She'd just turned it off. She liked confronting problems as they happened, but this one was different. As Fred liked to say, there's no use wrestling with a pig. You just get dirty, and the pig likes it.

She caught herself staring out the window at nothing. The dregs of the coffee were cold. She got up, poured it down the kitchen sink, grabbed her satchel and headed out the door.

As much as she enjoyed flying, she had to admit that driving got a lot better once she was behind the wheel of her own car. It was an orange Challenger, a flashy model that nourished that facet of her personality that was best expressed through machines. The steering wheel felt good in her hands as she twisted through the back streets on her way to the airport and Casablanca Aviation. She liked the pulse of the engine, the alt-rock on the satellite radio. She liked driving when she felt this kind of control, a satisfying bond with a metallic creature of precisely engineered and assembled pieces that, as a whole, were greater than the sum of their parts.

She pulled up to the pretty glass, steel and concrete building that served as headquarters and immediately felt much more at home than she did in her apartment. This was where her father had moved the business after her mother died, and all the devotion he'd put into taking care of his wife now went into his planes and people. Not that his people ever got much less from him; they tended to come aboard and stay.

Those who were around waved and smiled as she got out of her car and walked toward the office. She loved it here, amid the smells and sounds of airplanes. She noted the Beech Bonanza was out, probably chartered. It was one of their luxury aircraft. The dozen-strong fleet was always in flux, in use for lessons or rentals or trips. Or the occasional indulgence of Ben Lisbon's daughter, who liked to fly the Cessna when she didn't want to drive.

She entered the small office building and took the stairs to the second floor, the top floor, where her dad's office had a decent view of the runways. She opened the door to the executive suite, and Karin, his German-born secretary, with a shock of short blond hair and chic red-framed glasses, greeted her with a cry of surprise and a hug. "Mari, Mari, quite contrary, always flying off without us!" she said in her gentle accent after reluctantly letting go of Maribeth.

"But always flying back to say hi," Maribeth said. "How are you? How's your son? Did he graduate yet?"

"This month. He's going to be an engineer. I'm so glad. He has job offers."

"Can't say that about too many careers these days," Maribeth said. "Tell him I said congrats."

"He still wants a flying lesson from you," said Karin.

"But he can have a flying lesson from anybody here."

"Yes, but he has a crush on you."

Maribeth waved her off. "Don't be silly," she said, though she'd seen the looks the young man had given her. He'd grow out of it any day, she thought, once he realized she was well on her way to becoming old and impossible. "Is Dad in?"

"Yes, and I think he's expecting you."

"He saw the Cessna," Maribeth said with a smile, walking to the inner door. "No surprising Dad."

She entered slowly, without knocking, and had a moment to take in her father at his messy desk, his silver-brown hair cropped close, his half glasses perched on his nose as he scribbled intently in a notebook. His computer sat next to him, barely used. As much as Maribeth loved technology, he loathed it, except when it made flying easier. On the wall behind him hung a large movie poster of *Casablanca,* surrounded by smaller photos of airplanes, some with him standing next to them, young and ready for anything; a sunset portrait of all of the pilots at Casablanca Aviation; and a couple of her, one as a teen after her first flight and another with her helicopter in Iraq.

He looked up at the intrusion, and a broad smile lit up his face. He dropped his pen and stood, coming around the desk to hug her. "I was wondering when you'd pop in to see me. No storms to chase?"

"Maybe tomorrow," Maribeth said.

"But you've had some."

"Oh, yeah, we've had some," she said, thinking of the close calls with the tornado and the hail.

"And you're not going to tell me about them." He looked at her quizzically, then waved his hand at her and sat on the edge of the desk. "Best not. I don't want to know the details. I just want you to be careful."

"I'm always careful, Dad."

"But you've got a streak in you. Like your mother."

"You're the fighter pilot!" she said, sitting in one of two comfy chairs that faced the desk.

"Was," he said. "Was. You know what I tell my students."

"Yes, Dad."

"There are old pilots and there are bold pilots, but there aren't many old, bold pilots," he recited.

She smiled. "I know."

"I knew your mother had a wild streak the day I met her." It was another story she'd heard many times, but she liked to hear him tell it. "I was crop dusting for a friend of mine out of an old country airstrip, and my job was done and I was just doing a circle or two, enjoying the day, and I see this girl on a horse far below me. So I decide I'll give her a little thrill, you know? Come up behind her and buzz her low, but not so I'd scare the horse." His blue eyes were alight with the memory. "And I go by her once and see her face as she looked up at me, and I see how beautiful she is, and I know I need to see her again. But how? So I decide to fly by her one more time, and as I get closer, she looks up again, laughing, and she starts galloping, racing me to the airstrip. I mean, there was no way she could beat me, but she was racing me! I hoped she would follow me all the way there, and you know what happened. She did. Got there just a few minutes after I did. Her horse was puffing, but she said he liked to gallop. And so did she. And that's how I met your mother." He looked happy for a moment, then wistful. He nodded toward the star sapphire on Maribeth's right hand. "You're still wearing her ring."

Maribeth nodded. She didn't need to say she missed her. Both of them did.

"You got anything that needs flying?" she asked instead.

"All booked up," her father said. "And by the way, I need the Cessna."

"You don't!"

"You'll have to drive back. It's only a few hours. Don't you get enough flying in that Warthog? I wouldn't mind a spin in that myself sometime."

"They've turned it into a camera with wings," Maribeth said, "but it's pretty cool."

"And how's everyone else? Dr. Y?"

"Trying to get himself struck by lightning."

"Good, good," her dad said, his dry humor coming through. "And that engineer — what's his name?"

"Fred. Burning holes in more eardrums every day."

"And Jack? The guy you kept mentioning when you were in Florida?"

"I did?" She didn't remember that at all. And she didn't want to talk about Jack.

"Yes, you did. I kind of got the impression that you found him interesting."

"That's one word for it," she said darkly.

"Hmm," Ben Lisbon said, "the plot thickens."

"There's no plot," she said. "He handles the ground operation and does most of the forecasting. I fly the plane."

"Then why are you all red?"

"Sunburn."

"And why did he call here and leave you a message this morning?" Ben asked, reaching behind him and plucking a scrap of paper from his desk.

Maribeth's mouth dropped open. "He what?"

"Apparently you weren't responding to his texts, and he was concerned you'd crashed into a barn somewhere."

"I would never crash into a barn," she said. "I'd have the decency to bounce in a field, at least."

"That's what I told him. Anyway, I set his mind at ease, but he said to give you a message."

Maribeth rolled her eyes. "I don't want it."

"I rather liked it, myself," he said.

"Then you keep it," she said. She couldn't help but be amused at her Dad's persistence.

"He said you have it all wrong. And he said to remind you that you said you didn't mind a reasonable amount of trouble."

"That's ballsy of him," said Maribeth, letting some of her anger slip out.

"Ah-ha. Interesting. And he likes *The Maltese Falcon,* does he? That's a point in his favor."

"I don't know if he likes it, but he can quote from it, I suppose," she said, regaining control.

"Then he can't be all bad." Ben put the note back on his desk and adopted a gentler tone. "If he is all bad, I'll help you kick his ass. But maybe he isn't. You've always been good at flying, honey, but it's OK to land, sometimes. He wants to talk to you. It might be worth listening." He smiled. "Let his horse catch up."

❦

THE ENTIRE *Zany Weddings* crew was yawning at 7 a.m. except Aurelius, who drove the cake this morning. Most were hung over, and nerves were still raw after last night's drunken quarrels. Brad sat quietly in the passenger seat, thumb-typing furiously into his smartphone, while Tyler and Polly Ann dozed in the back. The rest of the crew was in the support van, with Danni driving. They weren't so concerned with filming Tyler and Polly Ann right now, as the wedding they had to document today wasn't theirs.

They rolled into Alliance, Nebraska, at nearly 4 p.m., took a break and confirmed directions to Carhenge. The crew had come out the month before to film B-roll of the couple who were to be married; now, they had to film the ceremony and get into position for what looked to be good chasing the next day. There was a slight chance of storms this afternoon, too, and Aurelius eyed the sky warily as they left the brick streets of town and took a rural road toward the oddball tourist attraction.

"So what is a rockabilly pagan wedding anyway?" Brad asked.

"I'm not a hundred percent sure," Aurelius said, "but somehow rockabillies and pagans are involved. Or rockabilly-pagans. All I know is that I am not doing the ceremony this time."

"They have a preacher?"

"I think they have a witch."

"I thought somebody had burned all those by now," Brad said.

"It's not that kind of witch," Aurelius said.

Polly Ann piped up from the back. "I don't want to participate in anything that my pastor wouldn't approve of," she said.

"You won't be participating," Aurelius said. "In fact, I think we're going to hide you in the gift shop so we don't cross-pollinate episodes."

"Besides, I'm sure this is going to be a nice witch," Brad

said, his tone a touch patronizing now that he was, by all appearances, no longer pursuing Polly Ann. "Like the lady on TV who used to twitch her nose."

"I think I've heard of that," Polly Ann said vaguely. She was so young, Aurelius thought.

"We'll hang in the gift shop and write some postcards," Tyler assured her, "just in case God decides to strike them with lightning."

Aurelius looked in the rearview mirror and saw Tyler grinning. Good. A joke. He figured the young couple's version of God had better things to do, but he didn't like the idea of dodging lightning bolts.

He spotted the sign that pointed to Carhenge. The attraction stood opposite a farm in wide-open fields. The circle of gray-painted cars, set up to resemble Stonehenge, was visible from a distance. As they neared, he saw a small, gray building alongside the short driveway, which led them to a modest gravel parking lot that was already filled with cars, many of them classics or rat-rods, with shiny chrome trim, bold fins, exposed engines and pin-striping. Beyond, folks milled all over the field and the gentle hill nearby, among the Carhenge circle and other funky car-part sculptures.

After parking on the grass, the crew exited the vehicles, towing cameras and microphones, and Aurelius went looking for the bride.

The first thing he noticed was the tattoos. The second thing he noticed was the gorgeous women wearing them, with done-up hair, big black eyelashes, plucked eyebrows, bright red lips and colorful retro dresses that were not stingy with their décolletage. Finally, he noticed a cluster of three such women dressed all the same way, in black dresses sporting little red cherries and white lace trim. They were drinking bottles of beer.

"Bridesmaids," he said under his breath. He made his way over to them. "Hi. I'm Aurelius Zane."

"Oh, yes, you are," said one of the women, a brunette with heavily lined, dark brown eyes. She took his arm. "I've seen you on TV."

"Why, yes," said Aurelius, pleased someone finally recognized him, even if she seemed a little drunk. "I'm looking for the bride."

"Too bad," said the brunette, taking a swig of beer. "She's holed up in the gift shop, getting the last-minute touches. You should see her garters and stockings. So bridal. Hey, wait a minute, you should see *my* garters and stockings." She pulled up the hem of her dress, showing off a puffy red crinoline and a titillating glimpse of lace and thigh.

Aurelius withdrew his arm from hers immediately. "No need, no need! I'm working! Thank you, ladies."

"Too bad," the brunette said as he walked away. "I like 'em brawny and blond."

"And preferably dumb," he heard another of the women say with a laugh.

Aurelius had other things on his mind. Namely, getting their wedding-day interviews with the couple so they could get on with filming the ceremony. He heard a low rumble and looked up with apprehension. The clouds had nearly filled in, and far to the west, the sky looked even darker. Thunder. He consulted the radar app on his phone and saw just one small cell, but it was one more complication he didn't need. The crew was now interviewing guests and filming Carhenge itself, which looked especially dramatic under the clouds.

"Brad!" he called as he ran into their co-host chatting up another pretty girl, this one in a sailor dress.

"Yeah?" Brad asked, openly hostile.

"Did you find the groom?"

"He's in his pickup truck getting wasted with the best man."

"Well, un-waste him and get him out here. Ceremony's in fifteen minutes."

Brad sighed theatrically and whispered in the girl's ear. She giggled as he went off toward the other end of the parking lot. Aurelius ignored them and headed for the gift shop.

Outside the building, a three-piece band had set up — guitar, stand-up bass and drums — ready to play the bride down the aisle, which in this case was a dirt path someone had scattered with red rose petals.

Inside, drinking Pabst Blue Ribbon, the bride, a male hairdresser, a female photographer, a makeup girl, a few hangers-on and a rough-looking woman who was probably the bride's mother shared space with racks of snacks, souvenirs and postcards. Tyler and Polly Ann, looking dazed, hid behind the counter with the clerk, a teenage girl who sat on a stool, reading a fishing magazine and ignoring the whole affair.

The curvy bride, in updated 1950s style, wore a puffy white satin dress decorated with tulle and little red bows, with a wide and deep neckline and a red crinoline peeking from underneath the skirt. She resembled a coconut cake with cleavage, but quite delicious, Aurelius thought. She was a redhead, and he'd always been a sucker for redheads. He dismissed the thought of his latest email missive to Wynda last night. It was a swirl of jungle reminiscences, romantic storm metaphors, philosophical questions, culinary cravings and heartfelt apology. In the light of day, he blanched at the thought she might actually read it.

"Miss Waters?" he asked.

"For about ten more minutes!" she shouted, and the others cheered.

"I'm Aurelius Zane, with the *Zany Weddings* show. We'd like to interview you before the ceremony, if you don't mind."

"Let's get on with it," she said. "I'll never look as good as I do right now!"

Her support staff laughed, and Aurelius popped outside and waved down Scooter and Vinyl. He saw Danni interviewing the groom under a scraggly cluster of trees. He was a tall, lanky fellow with swooping black hair and big sideburns, wearing black pants and a red shirt complemented by black suspenders and bow tie.

Aurelius asked the questions, and they had the interview with the bride in the bag in five.

"And where is your officiant?" he asked.

"I think she's at the altar. Isn't Becky out at the altar?" she asked the crowd. "In the circle."

Outside, the sky looked gloomier. Trailed by Scooter and Vinyl, Aurelius strode inside the circle of gray cars, which were stuck vertically into the ground or supported horizontally by other cars to create the Stonehenge effect. There, slightly off-center, he found a white-linen-covered square table stocked with props, including a somewhat alarming knife. Overseeing the tableau was a handsome thirtysomething woman in a flowing black and silver gown and a headdress that reminded Aurelius of flashing coins.

"Becky?" he asked.

"The same," she said, shaking his hand. "The bride almost ready?"

"Yes, and not to be indelicate, but I wondered how long the ceremony is," he said, looking at the sky.

She followed his gaze and smiled. "The God and Goddess will take care of us," she said. "But don't worry. They wanted a short one. This handfasting is only ten minutes. You aren't a Wiccan, by chance, are you?"

"Not usually," Aurelius said, uncertain how to answer. As the camera and microphone quietly came around and into position, he asked her how she ended up officiating the wedding.

"I'm the groom's aunt," she said. "I came out from Omaha. They liked the idea of having someone in the family perform the ceremony. I would have preferred Beltane, but this was the day they were free. And the ritual is very adaptable."

Aurelius asked a few more questions about the ceremony, and Scooter got lots of shots of the ceremonial items as Aurelius spotted Danni waving frantically at him from the parking lot.

"Excuse me," he said, and made his way to her. "What is it?"

"The best man is completely passed out," she said. "The groom isn't much better, but at least we have him vertical and drinking coffee. What should we do?"

"How important is it?" Aurelius asked. "And what do we do about the knife?"

"What?" Danni asked, confused. "There are no other groomsmen. We really should have a best man. Maybe they'd be willing to have you or Brad do it. It would be great for the show."

A few minutes of negotiations later, and the crowd assembled in a semicircle inside the array of cars, with the table and Becky the Wiccan in front of them. The groom and Aurelius stood next to the table as she walked the Carhenge perimeter with the knife, calling on the four elements and the blessings of the God and Goddess. She drew no blood, to Aurelius's relief.

The band cranked up with a peppy version of Bill Haley's "Burn That Candle," with its apt references to a wedding, and played the bridesmaids and the bride out to the circle. The priestess bound the bride's left hand to the groom's right with a red cord. Vows and rings were exchanged, in a ceremony not unlike those Aurelius had seen at Christian churches.

With coaching, the couple invoked the elements. Low thunder rolled to equal rumbles from the crowd as the priestess blessed the wedding. Then she produced a rustic broomstick from under the table and walked around in front of the couple, beckoning Aurelius to hold the other end. She bent on one knee, and he did the same, wondering what came next.

"It's time for a leap of faith!" Becky called. The couple, who apparently had been warned, looked at each other with a grin and, still tethered at the wrist, ran forward and jumped over the stick — almost. The groom fell flat on his face, taking the bride halfway down with him before he leapt up, holding their hands aloft in triumph. The cheers were tremendous, and Aurelius, as he felt the first drops of rain on his face, felt strangely moved by his role in this odd little ceremony in the middle of nowhere. Here, amid an eternal circle and a hostile environment and a dubious support network, two young, crazy people were willing to tie their hands together for the little slice of eternity available to them.

And then it started pouring. With a whoop and a final blessing, they all ran off to their cars and to a party somewhere dry, warm and ordinary.

IT HAD BEEN LESS than two days since Jack last saw Maribeth, but it felt like an eternity, an epoch without light. Yesterday, especially, had been a very long day without her around, knowing she was pissed off at him and knowing why.

He'd thrown himself into his forecast in her absence. He knew that a potent system demanded they chase today, especially since it appeared the weather might encroach on the wind farm Dr. Y had instrumented in Nebraska. He also knew they would have to leave damn soon to make his initiation target of North Platte, which was, even the way he drove, probably four and a half hours away. His bag was in the van, ready to go. He didn't want to leave without seeing her. And yet, loitering in the hangar around the A-10 at 8:30 in the morning, he'd be damned if he'd ask about her.

"Hey, Fred," he called out as the engineer walked by, holding his giant coffee cup. "Is she coming?"

Fred paused and smiled a small, cheeky smile. "She'll be here."

Jack hesitated. "When?"

"Probably not till after we leave," Fred said. "She's driving up here."

"She has a car?"

"Of course she has a car, you idiot."

And then they turned toward the sound, a throaty growl with a backbeat of rock and roll. Through the wide-open hangar doors, Jack saw the flash of orange as the muscle car whipped into one of the spaces on the far side of the pavement.

She stepped out, her hair blowing in the wind, backlit by the morning sun, her figure accented by clingy jeans and one of those button-up blouses she favored, this one dark blue and skimming her curves. She was wearing sunglasses.

"Is she walking in slow motion, or am I just imagining it?" said Jack, who was almost uncomfortably turned on as she strode toward the hangar, a canvas bag over her shoulder. The car — the woman — she was *hot*.

"Shut up, Andreas," Fred said, but even he sounded a little awed. "Say what you gotta say. We have to get going."

"I know that as well as you," Jack said, never taking his eyes off Maribeth. "We have a few minutes."

She walked right past them with just a nod of greeting.

Fred shook his head. "I'm going to tell Dr. Y we're leaving in a half hour, OK?" He walked off toward the office before Jack could answer.

Jack turned and followed Maribeth, but at a distance. She went to the women's room first, and he hung around by the plane, waiting for her to emerge. Around him, a few techs attended to the instruments and servers in the Warthog's belly. This could be a big day for the study, and they wanted to make sure everything was working perfectly.

Maribeth emerged from the bathroom and headed to the lounge. She still wasn't looking at him. He couldn't just leave without talking to her. He walked over and headed in after her.

She was already seated on the couch, a cup of coffee in her hand, reading her tablet computer. She didn't look up when he entered, so he stood in the doorway and watched her, waiting for her to break and talk to him. Ms. Never Surrender.

"Mari," he said after two long minutes. She looked up at him with just a flash of emotion in those penetrating eyes, which quickly reset to cool gray-blue, this morning's color.

"Good morning, Jack," she said, turning back to her computer.

"Is it?"

She paused, lowered the tablet and looked up. "Going to fly today. That's always a good day. Looks like good storms, too."

"That's not what I mean."

"What do you mean?"

"Are you angry with me? Did you get my messages?"

"I see no reason why I would be angry with you," she said with studied indifference, but the icy blue in her eyes was cracking again.

She was going to make this hard. He could just blow it off, let her stew, let her despise him. But that notion was not acceptable. He hated to see her hurt, and he was struck with wonder that she might be.

"Let me tell you a little story," Jack said. "I was out drinking in a bar, and there was a pretty girl — not you — who was having a crisis. She was being seduced by a real jerk — not me — and she needed someone to tell her to go back to the man she really loved, her fiancé, even if they were going to be married on some stupid TV show. And that's exactly what I did. And then I came looking for you, and you were gone."

The emotions moved so quickly over her face, he couldn't read them. "That's an interesting interpretation of the situation."

"Fact, not interpretation."

"Jack, I always treat people like grown-ups until they prove me wrong," she said, running a finger around the edge of the tablet but not looking at it. "And I had the distinct impression that you'd proved me wrong. But it's pointless to discuss it. As I said, I don't know why it would matter."

"I think it did matter," Jack said, sitting next to her, feeling compelled to be next to her, saying more than he wanted to say. "It mattered to me. It mattered to me a lot that you left, and that whatever I did might have mattered to you."

A tiny smile crossed her lips. "What the hell are you talking about? You lost me on the fourth 'matter.' "

"This," he said, leaning in and kissing her hard on the mouth, grasping her around the waist, feeling her go limp under him as she opened her mouth against his and made a small, unintelligible sound. He ended the kiss with reluctance, placed a hand on her knee.

She caught her breath, searched his eyes.

"Are you fucking with me, Jack?" she finally asked in a small voice. "I'm not sure why I want to know, but I want to know."

This was a question Jack would have always answered with a no, no matter which woman was asking, no matter how slight his intentions. But something was taking over his brain, some sort of truth serum that came straight from her lips to his, and this time, his eyes boring into hers, he meant it.

"No," he said.

"Say it again."

"No, I am not fucking with you, Ms. Lisbon. Not everything is a battle, you know."

"Or maybe it is. And I'm a bad loser."

"Never that," he said, and he leaned over and kissed her again, more softly. Jack felt her hesitance melt into a tenuous and encouraging response, a sweet promise of more. If only they had time. He kissed her cheek, her neck.

She sat back, looked at him, saying nothing, saying much. He reached out and ran a finger along her cheekbone, behind her ear; he traced her lips, reddened and moist from their kiss.

"Mari," he whispered, kissing her again, and this time her response was more needful, the kiss more prolonged, more intense as she dropped her tablet and wrapped her arms around him. Their physical connection was undeniable, crackling between them, the current flowing through their bodies. He felt himself losing control, at least until the office door opened and she pulled away, flushed and working to school her expression.

"Oh, my, yes, indeed!" Dr. Y said. "Good to see you've joined us, Ms. Lisbon." His eyes were merry as she murmured, "Thanks."

"Yes, it is," echoed Fred, his amusement evident. "About ready to go, Andreas?"

Jack looked up at the men. "About ready for anything," he said. He turned back to Maribeth. "Maybe I'll see you tonight."

"Probably tomorrow." She sounded almost composed. "The plan is for me to land back here."

He looked up again at Dr. Y and Fred, who, with a touch of awkwardness, appeared to realize they might have better things to do and left for the hangar, closing the door behind them.

Jack looked back at Maribeth. He felt possessive of her, suddenly. Or maybe this was an addiction that only she could feed. A pleasant and wholesome one, he thought. An addiction for which he wanted no cure.

"We'll see if I can wait until tomorrow," he said, kissing her cheek with tenderness.

"Yeah, right," she said, her self-possession restored, the gate closed. "You'll find some honey-pie up in Nebraska. A girl in every port."

"And what about you? A guy in every airport," he said, a joke that engendered a pang of jealousy as he said it.

"They're lined up, Dr. Andreas," she said dryly.

"They should be," he said, hoping they weren't.

Her face remained impassive, but her eyes had lost their brittleness. They communicated a tentative and unidentifiable emotion, warm blue. "Be careful."

"It's not like I have to leave the ground."

"The probability of survival is equal to the angle of arrival," she quipped.

"What?" He laughed.

"Something my dad says. Get out of here."

Pushing down a frisson of concern at her joke, Jack brushed her hair back from her eyes and stood reluctantly. He gave her a rakish salute and one last smoldering glance and headed out the door.

SHIRTLESS AND SHOELESS, wearing baggy tan shorts, Charles let his bony toes sink into the sand under the lapping shallows of Lake McConaughy as the morning light cast the grasses and sloping banks around him in gold. Like the water stretching away from him, the green blades rippled in the fresh breeze, which carried moisture from far away, from another shore. A great blue heron stalked him in slow motion, wondering if this wading figure was a fisherman from whom he might grab an easy breakfast. An osprey above worked harder, crying in the morning light as it climbed. It entered a glide, gathering speed, scanning the water for a familiar shadow. It saw what it wanted and plummeted, shattering the surface and climbing again with a dripping, wriggling fish. A few other shorebirds wheeled overhead, bright white against the blue, hoping the osprey would fumble its prize.

At few places along the shore did trees obscure the view, and this spot was as open as any, allowing Charles to look up and scan the sky from horizon to horizon. Clouds were scant this early, but he knew from his years of storm-seeking that the atmosphere was ripe. Today it would yield vaporous and violent fruits, and he would be ready to harvest them. Always patient, he sensed a new urgency this morning. As the ingredients for storms came together with a perfection bordering on intention, he knew the global electric circuit had flowed around him to engineer his presence here in Nebraska. Timing was everything. Timing was luck. Timing was being in the right place at the right moment when lightning struck.

The hour was near when he would get into Chuck's Wagon, where he'd spent the night, and go east, perhaps to feed more souls before he again confronted his destiny. He was, he admitted to himself, tired. No prophet went untested, and the years had worn on his heart, had weathered his skin, had silvered his hair. But his soul was still lively, and at the prospect of entering a new dimension of joy and insight, it shimmered like the morning sun. It was time.

He crouched and reached his hands into the cool lake. He cupped water with his palms and rubbed it over his face and silver-haired chest. On his right arm, spreading like a fern from shoulder to wrist, a dark red tattoo branched over his skin where Nature had once made her mark. A similar pattern arced across his back, treelike, a twisting trunk that extended upward from the waistline of his shorts, with branches spreading across his shoulder blades, emblazoned where another charge had seared him. He'd had to get the tattoos quickly, before the divine drawing faded, but now he forever carried her fiery brand. Her first touch, when he was just a youth, he held only in his memory, but it had set him on his road of discovery, and for that, he was grateful.

He closed his eyes, bent again toward the water and swished his hands back and forth, greeting the anima he felt inside the waves, the female spirit speaking to its echo inside him, the unconscious archetype inside his mind's masculine master, always felt but unseen, the way a rough mussel shell hides the pearly pink and purple within. He'd known the ways of women once, but the spirit had quenched his sexual thirst, and now he communed with the feminine in this way, through Nature. While her touch wasn't usually as heated, sometimes she still gave him breakfast.

His left hand came up with a squirming fish, and then his right. The heron nearby lifted its head, alert, as he tossed a fish in its direction. The large bird snapped and grabbed the offering with its beak, and Charles stood with the other in his hand, saying a prayer for the life it was giving to sustain his own just one more day.

THE *Zany Weddings* cake car left the hotel in Sidney at 11 a.m., trailed by the silver crew van, heading east through southwest Nebraska to keep ahead of the developing surface low. That much of the forecast Aurelius had gleaned from online discussions and the National Weather Service. Brad rode shotgun again, but he just didn't seem all that into it, giving Aurelius a chance to play the star for once. Yet even the adventurer didn't feel like pouring on the charm for the cameras this morning. He'd stayed up late writing another

Quixotic love letter, and he was tired. Worse, he had trouble remembering why it had seemed so important to star in this show, but he wanted to get the job done well for their eager young couple. Tyler and Polly Ann seemed to have a new enthusiasm for getting married after seeing the rockabilly couple get hitched yesterday, though they basically watched it happen from the gift-shop windows.

"I don't see how you're going to film that rodeo wedding you were telling me about," Tyler said as they rolled east on I-80 toward North Platte.

"I'm going to dress as a rodeo clown, hide in a barrel and pop out to perform the ceremony," Aurelius said.

Brad looked up from his smartphone. "You're going to have to do it awfully fast if the couple are riding a bucking bull," he said.

"I will. The Church of the L.E.D. has a fantastic short version of the vows," Aurelius said as he drove. "I'll read most of it before they actually come out of the gate, and then I basically ask them for their 'I do's.' We can do it in twelve seconds. And the bull is apparently one of their nicer ones."

"But bull rides are only eight seconds," Tyler pointed out.

"Not this one," Aurelius said. "It's however long it takes."

"Then the bride better not have cold feet," said Polly Ann. She wasn't wearing her wedding dress yet, but it was in a bag under the seat, ready to go once the storms fired.

"I think just getting on the bull constitutes commitment," Aurelius said.

"And being nuts," Brad said.

"You flew into a tornado, didn't you?" noted Aurelius. "Was that nuts?"

"That was for science."

My ass, Aurelius thought. "Why don't you tell us a little

more about what it was really like?" he pressed Brad. "Was it bumpy? Did you run into debris? Did you get sick? How fast did the Bubble go?"

"I'm saving it for the book," Brad snapped.

"Then remind me of something that was in the show that I can't quite recall. The Bubble bounced, what, twenty times?"

Brad's face turned purple as two, three seconds ticked by, before Polly Ann jumped in.

"It was fifteen total, but the last few were small hops," she said. "I should know. I've seen that show so many times."

"Way too many times," Tyler said as he took her hand. In the rearview, Aurelius could see her smile ruefully. Good. She wasn't going gaga for Brad again.

"Anyway, it's not like this show is about me," Brad said to Aurelius with a puzzling touch of bitterness as he turned back to his phone, ignoring them all.

Aurelius digested his reaction with even more intense curiosity, then put it aside as he noted the field of clouds springing up above them. It cheered him.

"I have an idea. Let's get our own tornado today," he said to no one and everyone. He smiled into the nearest camera and pointed out the front window. "Looks like we're in the right place."

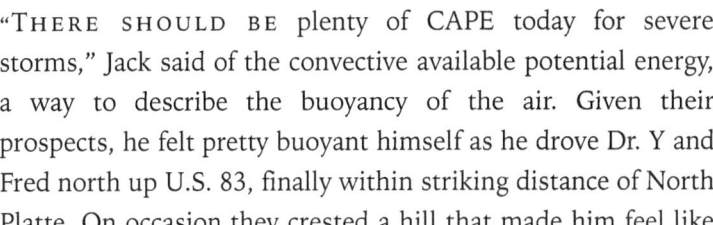

"THERE SHOULD BE plenty of CAPE today for severe storms," Jack said of the convective available potential energy, a way to describe the buoyancy of the air. Given their prospects, he felt pretty buoyant himself as he drove Dr. Y and Fred north up U.S. 83, finally within striking distance of North Platte. On occasion they crested a hill that made him feel like he was flying. Briefly, at each peak, he believed he could see the whole great state of Nebraska. At least he didn't expect to be chasing farther north in the rolling hills of Cherry County, legendary among chasers not for its beauty, which was abundant, but for its appalling lack of roads and cellular signals.

"I'm not so sure about tornado potential today," Jack continued, "but I think if things come together in just the right way, we might have an isolated bomb."

"How many times do I have to remind you, Andreas — we aren't here for the damn tornadoes," Fred said from the back.

"But that *would* make it exciting!" Dr. Y enthused from the passenger seat. "It has been a while since I've enjoyed a good tornado."

He made it sound like a steak or something. Which made Jack wonder if they'd see the food truck. He was ready to be spoiled with another good meal.

"There is that outflow boundary from last night's convection," Jack said, trying to forget how delicious the curried chicken salad had tasted. "That could make things interesting."

"Indeed!" said Dr. Y, baring his collection of tiny teeth in a large grin. "And by sunset, we can expect the low-level jet."

"That should enhance convergence as it develops," Jack said of the influx of strong wind that would transport more moisture from the Gulf of Mexico and inject energy into the volatile setup. "And there'll definitely be spin. So you agree with my forecast?"

"Of course," said Dr. Y. "I trust you completely. And North Platte's a fine place to start. They have quite a good Mexican restaurant there. But I made sure we have a cooler full of sandwiches as well."

The guy never stops thinking about food, Jack thought, even as his stomach rumbled.

"I was kind of hoping we'd run into that food truck," Fred said from the back, articulating what Jack was thinking.

"The food truck?" Dr. Y seemed more serious all of a sudden. "Do you think we might?"

"He has an uncanny way of showing up wherever we are," Jack said.

"Wherever the chasers are," Fred agreed. "He knows where his bread is buttered."

"That would be most fortuitous," Dr. Y said.

Jack caught something in his tone. "But we have sandwiches?" he probed, trying to get Dr. Y to say more.

"Yes. But, well — " The older man sighed. "I suppose I should confide in you fellows. We are facing the breach together, are we not?"

Jack focused on the road, almost not wanting to know.

"Sure," Fred said from the back. "Brothers in arms."

"We happy few," Dr. Y said with a strange chuckle. "Yes. Well. The truth is, I think I may know this food truck driver. When we saw him briefly the other day in the storm, I felt almost sure of it. But I must talk to him. He has changed greatly over the years. I'm afraid I told Ms. Lisbon a little fib when I said I thought he'd be good for my studies."

"What do you mean?" Jack asked. "She didn't mention this."

"Of course she didn't. She's an honorable creature and kept my confidence. Though I thought she might tell *you*," Dr. Y said.

Jack smiled, thinking of this morning's reconciliation with Maribeth.

"So who is this food truck guy?" Fred asked, leaning forward from his bench in the back.

"I told her I believed he'd been struck several times by lightning, and indeed, that's the case," Dr. Y said. "I actually saw it happen the first time. It was during one of our childhood idylls at our family vacation home in Florida. The experience started my lifelong obsession with lightning. Not long after, he disappeared from our lives, even changed his name, and I have longed to reach him ever since, to bring him back to us."

"But who is he?" Fred asked.

Dr. Y hesitated. "I believe this man is Charles Yzaguirre," he said. "My brother."

"No shit!" Fred exclaimed.

"Yes," said Dr. Y, settling back in his seat. "Actually, it's quite a relief to speak of it. I've spent a great deal of money and time over the years to bring him back into the fold. He's older than I am and has had a strange and wild life, from what I've been able to gather, but it's time for him to share in the family duties. My greatest concern is that he actually seeks out the lightning. I've tracked down acquaintances who say he's been struck no less than three times, and he's hoping to be struck again, perhaps to annihilate himself. Though I believe he sees it as a sort of spiritual communion. Finding him could very well save his life. And frankly, I need my brother. I need family now, with my parents gone. You're both young. Maybe you don't understand that." He paused and glanced at Jack. "Or perhaps you do. But I'll tell you, gentlemen. I will do anything to find him. And I feel that I have never been closer."

Jack had no idea what to say. Dr. Y's personal goals had a way of putting them into danger, and finding a long-lost brother was a lot more personal than testing a lightning tent.

This was a chase for lunatics. They were pursuing anything *but* tornadoes.

MARIBETH PACED the hangar more than long enough to make up for her lack of a run this morning. She'd arisen early to make the drive from Oklahoma City and, after the van left, took a nap in the lounge before changing into her boots and flight suit. As usual, she had a lot of waiting to do before she was given the green light to fly.

The scientific instruments were getting a once-over, and she did some final checks to satisfy herself that the plane was ready. But was she? She was unused to having anything significant to think about besides the flight, and she had a feeling that what Jack had told her this morning was significant. It mattered to him what she thought. And what he did mattered to her. She'd told herself her heated collision with him had been an outlet, a way to escape her routine, but now she had all these annoying notions, emotions, and she wasn't sure what would have happened if they'd had a locked door and five more minutes alone on that couch.

Worse for her state of mind, she had to acknowledge she felt more than chemistry when he was around. She saw a transformation in him, a dissolution of the cocky shell that he presented to the world. Near her, he seemed to come to earth, grounded, immediate and intense, becoming small and agile and able to slip through her defenses with the things he said and did. The things he did — she willed herself to stop thinking about that night in her suite, about this morning, but it came back to her when she least wanted to remember.

Damn this mooning, she thought. It was game time.

She stowed her bag in her locker and packed her pockets with the essentials. She rolled the A-10 out so it would be poised to fly. And then she waited.

To pass the time, she hovered near the plane outside so she could feel the quality of the air. She pulled out her phone and played games, interrupted by frequent glances at her radar app, online data and the sky. Cloud towers were going up just east of North Platte, satellite images showed, and the texts she got from Dr. Y told her the boys were watching them develop, hoping they would break the cap. She tried to be patient. She had farther to fly today and didn't want to waste time flying into the sun; she wanted to have plenty of fuel for the duration. But that didn't mean she enjoyed waiting around.

Her phone rang, finally, at 6:20 p.m. It was a video call from Dr. Y.

"Ms. Lisbon, are you ready?" he asked. His face looked flushed in the afternoon heat, and behind him, she could see Jack and Fred, looking at the sky.

"If there are storms, I'm ready," she said.

"We were starting to think they'd never break the cap, but we now have explosive development. Check radar, and you'll see what I'm talking about."

"Just a moment." She switched over to her radar app and saw a few showers on the dryline, but one cell gleamed at her like a red eye. The loop showed her it was growing rapidly in size and intensity. And it might even be on track to come into their wind farm. She switched back to the call and saw Jack looking over Dr. Y's shoulder. Seeing him was mildly disconcerting. *Focus.*

"That's blown up just in the last fifteen minutes," she said to Dr. Y. "Incredible."

"You should see it in person," Jack said, moving his face closer to the phone camera as Dr. Y shifted the angle of view. "It's like an exploding mountain of popcorn."

"With butter?"

"Better. With lightning." He grinned.

"Excellent," she said, wishing Dr. Y would take the call again — and wishing he wouldn't, just when he did.

"Time to fly, Ms. Lisbon," Dr. Y said with a broad smile. "We have high hopes it will head for ground zero. We'll see you in the domain!"

"Check six," she said automatically. She knew they'd watch one another's backs. It was up to her to watch her own.

She ended the call, noting with chagrin that she'd run her phone battery down almost to exhaustion. She turned it off and put it back into her pocket, used the restroom one more time, donned the complicated pieces of the G-suit over her flight suit and climbed the ladder to the place where she belonged: the snug cockpit, surrounded by the clear canopy that let her immerse herself in the sky. The ground crew stowed her ladder, and she went through her checklist, talked to the tower, taxied into position. She'd done this so many times, with plenty of crashes in the simulator and plenty of successful flights in reality, in good and bad weather. But this was only the second time she would deliberately fly into a storm. She would avoid the hail. She would focus. She would get the lightning data, she told herself. And she would come home safely with the goods.

The Warthog's familiar resistance was palpable as she lifted off, urging it to soar, and then it seemed to drop its chains and spring into the sky. She could already see distant convection on the horizon. The engines roared. The plane thrummed beneath and around her.

She was where she wanted to be, with the sun overhead and storms to the west. This wasn't the time to think about what might come later.

Anyway, after what she'd been through, after what she'd done, it was better to be alone.

She let her old friend envelop her, the wide, blue, white-dotted sky, and took in the changing colors in the bowl of infinity around her. She allowed herself to get just a little bit excited about the mission. The vector of their storm couldn't be more ideal. She had a chance to capture exactly what they needed, and she couldn't suppress the thrill she always felt when she left the ground — especially when her flight promised to be far from routine.

One thing Maribeth loved about flying was its speed. She would be at the target area, the wind farm east of Broken Bow, in less than an hour. If their supercell wasn't there yet, she'd fly out to greet it.

The west beckoned, where a roiling gray mass tinged with green and darkness consumed the deepening azure of early evening. Answering the call of the storm, she arced upward into Kansas airspace, heading for Nebraska.

AS THE BOUNDARIES between air masses — dry and moist, cold and warm — shifted during the day with the advancing low, so did Dr. Y's crew. Jack led them north and east of North Platte as Dr. Y became increasingly excited that any storms that formed might actually invade the wind farm.

They paused on the latest of a succession of dirt roads, this time west of Callaway, watching the towers build ahead of where the dryline met the warm front. They sweated, threw a Frisbee, checked data online, ate snacks and sandwiches from the cooler, checked more data, peed on hapless bushes. The clouds clambered up, skinny and stretching, bumped against the temperature inversion above them and collapsed, struggling. Jack wondered if they'd have a blue-sky bust as the magic hours of late afternoon wore on, but he felt in his gut that he'd get more than a sunburn today. The heat and dewpoints soared, and the towers were persistent in fighting their way upward, the clouds agitating for release. Something had to give.

While Jack eyed the cotton-candy mounds to the west, he watched on satellite imagery as a thin line of clouds — the outflow boundary left behind by yesterday evening's weak storms — drifted south toward them. It wandered in the warm sector, subtly shifting the winds, a wild card the atmosphere might play later.

When the first few towers of cloud did break through the cap, there was no question in Jack's mind that they were serious. The buttery early-evening light shone through and around them, illuminating the hard convection bubbling within the towers' corkscrewing walls. While a few of the cells sprouted anvils almost immediately — those discs of white at the storm tops that spread out to the east with the upper-level winds — one storm looked particularly vigorous. That's the one that prompted the call to Maribeth.

After Dr. Y ended the call, Jack felt a twinge, wishing she could be there with them to experience it, even if she hadn't seemed all that thrilled with the view from the ground. Then again, they'd almost been killed by a tornado. He'd see her soon enough, and with luck, all of them would be packing great video and data to share afterward. There was always luck to reckon with, that undeniable component of what they did, whether one called it fate or timing or fortune.

"Fred, is everything ready?" Dr. Y asked as he put his phone back in his pocket.

"Since two o'clock or so," said Fred, sounding irritated and nervous.

"Shall we go, then?" said their benefactor, the only one who looked at home in the heat, his large aloha shirt du jour dotted with colorful cocktails, palm trees, angry tiki gods and volcanoes that trailed clouds all over the ocean-blue background.

Jack took a moment to answer, watching the storms, especially the strongest one. He noticed bands of clouds streaming into it, not just from the lower levels — where what chasers called a beaver tail was starting to form — but at the mid-levels, too. It was sucking in fuel from all directions, its structure resembling not the stacked plates chasers longed to see but plates in mid-juggle, at crazy angles, with spokes of cloud shooting into the stack. Though its burgeoning rotation was only just starting to be evident, it had enormous potential.

"It's moving east-northeast according to radar," Jack said. "Still slow. Let's just move north a little and catch it. I want to get closer to Broken Bow."

"Why's that?" Fred asked as they got back into the van.

"Because that's where the outflow boundary is intersecting the front, and that extra helicity might make things really interesting. Plus, it's on the way to the wind farm."

Jack started up the van as the others strapped in. The storm shot a burst of lightning through its anvil that leapt outward with a bright strike to the ground not far to their west, well in front of the main updraft. The thunder followed, about eight seconds later — so the bolt hit about a mile and a half away, using the five-seconds-per-mile rule.

"A positive bolt, I do believe," Dr. Y said as Jack eased the van onto the dirt road and back toward the paved one.

"How can you tell?" Jack asked.

"Fewer branches, which of course would be much more visible in the high-speed video," said Dr. Y. "Negative leaders have more clear, pulsing steps. I've seen enough of these that I can usually just tell now."

"The lightning whisperer," Fred teased from the back.

"I like that!" said Dr. Y as they turned east on the road that would take them into town and to their north option. Within a few minutes, as they entered the small town's limits, they were caught in a stream of chaser vehicles.

"Not again," Fred moaned.

"Hazard of the job," said Jack, but he was annoyed, too. He missed the days when he could feel almost alone with a storm. Of course, he knew the generations before him cursed him at least as much as he resented the newest chasers, especially the ones with catchy team names and hats and T-shirts, whose screams mixed with braggadocio on their shaky videos.

"We can't speed through town, anyway," said Dr. Y as they passed a crowded gas station with ancient pumps that had probably never been this busy. "How's our fuel?"

"We filled up at the last town," said Jack.

"Oh, yes, that's right." Dr. Y seemed preoccupied as he looked around at the rolling crowds. A few antenna-clad vehicles were stopped, but there weren't many businesses to distract the chasers. Except one. It didn't seem to belong — a colorful food truck parked next to the tiny, one-story hospital.

"There it is!" Fred said. "Now why didn't he find us before

now? I'm stuffed with ham sandwiches when I could've had peanut butter, blueberry and bacon!"

"Where?" Dr. Y asked sharply, looking around. "Oh, there! Let's stop."

"I think —" Jack sighed. "OK, Dr. Y. I know this is important to you. But —"

"Pull over here," said Dr. Y, not really listening.

"If possible — well, just keep the storm in mind, sir. Especially with the chaser traffic jam," Jack finished lamely, but he knew his plea was futile. Dr. Y had already told him that finding Chuck's Wagon was paramount to a lifelong quest. The man was about to be reunited with his brother. Jack just hoped it wouldn't last all day.

Dr. Y surprised him by reaching over and patting him on the shoulder. "I know my duty, Dr. Andreas," he said. "But I've waited for this for a long time. And this may just be the first step in a long process. It's one I have to take." He smiled and jumped out of the van.

"Maybe I'll get a sandwich," Fred said idly.

"*No,*" Jack barked. "Oh, and look who's here." Now he was even more disgusted. Among the chase vehicles parked along the street were the *Zany Weddings* cake car and its support van. The crew, Aurelius Zane, Brad Treat and their engaged hostages milled among the dozen or so chasers hanging out, though the crowd was thinning fast as the weather geeks decided on their targets and took off.

"Well, I'm not going to miss the goddamn reunion of a lifetime," Fred said, opening the side door. "Get out of the van, Andreas. You can drag Dr. Y back if he gets too involved or decides to order prime rib or something."

Jack shook his head, reluctantly shut down the van and got out, his stress rising as he watched the growing, darkening storm to the west and wondered if Maribeth were airborne yet. Thunder rumbled. It was late in the day, it was time to chase, and he was trapped in a surreal traveling circus of chasers, eccentrics and reality TV stars. Brad caught his eye and shot him a look more blistering than a triggered lightning strike. Jack ignored him, choosing instead to play retainer to their ruler, Dr. Y, who walked toward the food truck with a gravity appropriate to a man about to meet a ghost.

AURELIUS IMPATIENTLY WATCHED the chaos washing around the food truck. He was ready to go, but they couldn't leave until Danni was satisfied with her shots.

"Shoot them getting in their cars and leaving!" she coached Scooter and Vinyl as chasers around them scattered, heading to their vehicles, goaded into action by a severe thunderstorm warning issued for the dominant supercell. The warning blared from the food truck's radio and pinged and beeped on cell phones and scanners all around them.

"Come on, Aurelius," Danni said. "Let's ask Mr. Smith what he thinks." The young producer seemed fascinated by the mystic, Aurelius was puzzled to note. Charles, he concluded, must have some magnetism that wasn't immediately obvious to men.

"We have to get out of here, too, you know," he said as they walked over to the truck's concession window, where Charles, clad in a colorful tie-dyed T-shirt, handed wrapped sandwiches to a couple of young guys wearing matching chase-team hats. The pair sprinted away as Aurelius and Danni approached, leaving Charles to gaze out over the counter, a faraway look in his eyes.

"Mr. Smith?" Danni called. "Mr. Smith, can we talk to you?"

But Charles Smith wasn't looking at them. He stared intently over their heads at a short, paunchy man who sported thin, reddish-blond curls, wire-frame glasses and a hideously loud shirt. Danni, driven by some innate sense for good television, held up her camera and started filming as a look of anticipation crossed Charles's face. Not surprise, Aurelius noted, but anticipation — and wonder.

"Percy?" Charles called out.

The shorter man, followed by Jack and that bearded fellow on their chase crew, seemed to lose a step. He put a hand to his heart, but before Aurelius had a chance to be alarmed, he just as quickly opened both his arms.

"Charles!" the short man called out in a voice laden with emotion. "Is it really you? Will you speak to me?"

"Percival, my dear little brother," said Charles, vanishing from the window and popping out the back of the truck in a flash. "Of course I will speak with you. It is time."

The wizened cook strode over to the shorter man, and they embraced, a hearty hug that spoke of years of separation. Aurelius glanced over at Danni, who smiled behind her camera. He noticed Scooter had joined her from another angle, shooting the reunion.

"Charles," said the shorter one. "I've spent years looking for you. Where have you been?"

"Planet Earth," Charles said, now holding his brother at arm's length, a grin on his face. "And the universe."

The shorter man looked around, noticed the onlookers and pulled his brother closer so he could speak quietly to him. Aurelius waved away Vinyl's microphone, to Danni's annoyance.

"They want some privacy," Aurelius whispered to her. She rolled her eyes, but she stepped back, still filming. Meanwhile, Aurelius subtly stepped forward; even if the cameras weren't going to capture the moment, he wanted to know what the men said. Out of the corner of his eye, he spotted Brad lurking on the far side of the crowd, poking around the vehicles, oblivious to the scene playing out before him, and wondered what he was up to.

"The company needs you," the shorter man was saying. "And I need you. You don't need to wander anymore. Come home, Charles."

"I wander because it has been my purpose," said the cook, crossing his arms. "My quest is not yet fulfilled. Nature is not done with me."

"You can't let nature be done with you," said his brother, his tone becoming more anxious. "Charles, you can't do what I think you're going to do."

"It's not up to me, my brother," Charles said softly. "She seeks me out. When she is done with me, I'll know."

"You can study lightning with me, you know. It's a huge part of my enterprise. You always had a great affinity for science."

"My mind has expanded much farther than science can reach," said Charles. "And I know what you've done. I'm proud of you. But I can't go with you. Not yet."

"Please," the short one said, now seriously distraught. "You can't go through with this."

"It's not my choice," said Charles, stoic. "I love you, Percy. If Nature is willing, I will see you again. But I think she may have a higher cause for me." He turned back toward his truck.

"No!" the shorter man said as Charles shut the back door behind him and closed the vending window.

"Dr. Y," said Jack, coming up behind the man, who took a gulping breath of air.

"I know," said the short man — Percy — Dr. Y. Aurelius wondered who this man really was. Who Charles really was. "This is a first step," said Dr. Y, his expression mournful. "I know. I know. I just hope it's not the last one."

Jack and the bearded fellow guided the shaken Dr. Y back to their van, and Aurelius elbowed Danni, who'd finally stopped filming.

"I suppose we should go," Aurelius said. "Tyler and Polly Ann are bored out of their minds, and I'm ready to get them hitched and home."

Danni looked flushed and excited. "Don't you know who that was?"

"Who? The little man?"

"He's a *big* man," Danni said, "if you've ever read anything about science and technology in this country. That's Percival Yzaguirre."

"Wait — the billionaire energy guy? The physicist? The weather researcher?"

"The lightning nut," Danni said, nodding. "And his brother drives a food truck!"

"We'll try to get an interview with him later so we can use the stuff you just shot," Aurelius said. "But I think we need to go." The white van with Dr. Y and his crew was already heading down the street, and the light around them had become dark and green, the air heavy, pregnant with the advancing storms.

"Yes, absolutely," Danni said, her celebrity-induced thrill fading. "Let's go, everybody!" she called out.

Aurelius waited outside the cake car until everyone was in and looked back toward the food truck. Charles had reappeared in the driver's seat and was looking his way. The mystic nodded at him and smiled. Aurelius nodded back, swallowing his apprehension as thunder echoed through the streets of Callaway, Nebraska.

MARIBETH HAD no trouble identifying the storm they were after, but Jack called her on Dr. Y's video connection to confirm its location.

"We're in Broken Bow, now, taking a quick break before it catches us," Jack said.

"Where's Dr. Y?" she couldn't help asking as she looked into Jack's face, strangely lit by the early-evening, storm-addled light, handsome, tense, framed by the tablet computer built into the cockpit.

"He asked me to make this call," Jack said neutrally, but she could hear something in his tone. "He'll contact you for an update." More quietly, he added: "Everything's OK. I'll tell you more later."

"Got it," she said, wondering what had happened. "I'm getting close. In fact, I think I see Broken Bow ahead of me now. I'm flying low enough — maybe you can see me?"

She saw him look up, the phone image spinning with him to show the van, Fred and a gas station before Jack's face appeared again. "I not only can see you, I can hear you. Damn, you're loud." He grinned.

"You may not see me as well later, once I start getting into the precip," she said.

"As long as I see you *later* later," he said.

"One thing at a time, Dr. Andreas. I've got to go now. I

want to stay out of the hail this time. But maybe I can trigger a little lightning for Dr. Y."

"What?"

"He said he's interested in plane-triggered lightning. It'll be fine. Planes do it all the time."

"I hope you know what you're doing," he said. "I take that back. I *know* you know what you're doing, but a little part of me wishes you weren't doing it. And I know the tornado chaser has no room to talk. Good luck," Jack said, holding the call open for a second longer than necessary. Then the image winked off.

"Thank god for that," Maribeth said to herself. That face was a dangerous distraction.

She scanned her instruments and banked the A-10 so she could get a closer look at the storm, taking in everything at once, looking back over her left shoulder at the wing, the tilting horizon. There were a few other storms, but they looked soft, disorganized. From the south, a line of towers fed into the dominant cell, which was large, mean and green. Crazy inflow bands poured into it from multiple directions. Its stout updraft seemed to become more cylindrical as she got closer. But it wasn't just her proximity, she realized; the rotation was tightening on the storm. As the supercell morphed into a spinning barrel of greenish-gray cloud, throwing out a ghostly white hail shaft just to her northwest, its lightning increased in intensity. So did its rain. She punched through a downpour with little warning, but she carefully avoided the hail shaft this time. It wasn't going to get her again.

The cameras and instruments were activated now, and something else was happening. Amid the multiple stimuli — the noisy rain, the flashing lightning, the increasing turbulence — something winked at her out of the corner of her eye.

She saw a hot pinpoint of light at the base of the canopy in front of her, and then a bright, forked flash in front of the curved window.

"St. Elmo's Fire," she breathed, watching the sparks dance back and forth, dueling pitchforks, exquisite lightning in miniature. Caused by static buildup as raindrops pelted the Warthog, it was exciting and generally harmless, but given her mission, a little unnerving. As she flew on into lighter rain, the sparking stopped, and she breathed a little sigh.

She knew the cameras below and around her were capturing the storm's frequent lightning, but she was anxious to get the plane into where it really counted: among the wind turbines, where there would be a real chance at shooting the upward lightning Dr. Y wanted.

Still, another swing through the storm might get him lightning triggered by the plane itself. She mentally plotted her pass, noting the dramatic striations forming in the super-cell and the pouchy mammatus extending through the anvil above her head. With an exhilarating feeling of being pressed into her seat by the warring forces of gravity and flight, she swept into the billowing curtains of rain.

"IT'S INTERACTING WITH THE BOUNDARY," Jack said to the others as he drove the van east of Broken Bow toward the wind farm. The supercell's rotation had cranked up visibly, producing a spinning lowering that had their attention before the wall cloud fell apart. Now the storm was cycling, Jack could tell, and more wall clouds, more lowerings were more than possible. He didn't want to say it, but so was a tornado, even if their primary mission was to capture lightning data.

He'd have to watch it closely. The storm was moving northeast toward them and would likely hit the wind farm directly, based on the map he'd memorized. But their stops in Callaway and Broken Bow had put them just behind where Jack wanted to be, and the continuing chaser traffic — now mercifully more scattered as the trucks and tanks and cars dispersed through the roads surrounding the storm — slowed them down.

Dr. Y had asked Fred and Jack to install the Ghost at their last stop so the camera would be ready for action when they got among the turbines. The subtext of his order: There would be no missing an upward bolt this time. Dr. Y seemed less distracted now, more focused on the mission, but not his usual jolly self. With each bolt, however — and the lightning increased at a dizzying rate as the storm intensified — his worries became less evident. By the time Jack spied the first turbines on hills to the northeast, Dr. Y exclaimed with excitement each time lightning struck nearby.

"Am I headed up there?" Jack asked, pointing toward the turbines on the horizon.

"No, we have a special gate to go through, with a perch on a hill," said Dr. Y. "We'll be able to see for miles."

"Sounds like we'll be a perfect target," Fred said from where he monitored the computer in the back.

"I do wish I'd brought the tent," said Dr. Y.

Jack looked in the rearview mirror and exchanged a look with Fred, who just shook his head.

They were getting into more hills here, rolling and serene, grassy slopes dotted with dark green trees. Above their heads, clouds streamed into their storm from multiple directions as it breathed, inhaling fuel — wind, warmth and moisture. The flanking line of convection to the south also produced rain and occasional lightning as it fed into their storm, a train chugging into a magnificent mountain that crushed the cloudy cars within its core. The strong surface winds buffeted the van, which hadn't been handling well for the last few miles. The vehicle seemed to be wallowing more than usual on the curves. That's what you get when you drive a box into a storm, Jack thought, but its hesitance bugged him. It hadn't driven like this before.

"Our turn is coming up," said Dr. Y. "On the left."

Here, several tall turbines were scattered across the hills. Jack turned onto the rough road, a mix of gravel and dirt with washboard-ridged sections that shook him to his teeth.

"The cameras, Andreas! Please!" Fred said as Jack navigated the curves.

"Talk to the guy who built the road," Jack said, wondering how far they would have to travel on it. Because, at some point, they'd have to drive back, possibly with an angry supercell on their tail.

"Here?" Jack asked as they approached a lane to the left that led to a turbine.

"Not yet," said Dr. Y. A lightning bolt hit nearby. "Oh, we must hurry."

"Trying," said Jack, but the van still felt weird, even more so on this rattling road. They kept going. And going. They finally neared a ranch house, where rows of large, round hay bales lay neatly rolled on both sides of the road. This must be it, Jack thought. The road has to end here.

But Dr. Y pushed them farther still. Now the road climbed toward a barn and more turbines in the distance. Jack wondered if they were going all the way to the horizon. He was relieved when, at the crest of the next hill, Dr. Y called on him to turn left. The red metal gate into the lane was wide open.

Signs on the fence posts next to it gave a speed limit of twenty-five and warned against trespassing. "T-0 thru T-13," another sign said, denoting the turbines in their immediate vicinity.

Jack made the turn, drove the short distance to the top of the hill and parked on the western side of the massive base of the nearest turbine, leaving the engine running. As Dr. Y promised, they were high enough to have a panoramic view of the ominous storm as it approached, not to mention the turbines on the hills around them, their huge white blades spinning slowly. Jack always forgot how big these things were until he got next to one. They were colossal structures; mythical, one-legged giants that dominated the sky.

"Crank it up!" Dr. Y called to Fred, who was already activating the Ghost. Jack and Dr. Y flipped open the large observation window on the passenger side of the van and got the cameras on the rail rolling. Dr. Y seemed to relax, then, as more thunder rolled around them. He sat back in the passenger seat, pulled out his phone and made a video call to the A-10.

Maribeth's face appeared on the screen. "Yes, sir," she said.

"Just checking in. We've deployed on the farm. You're all right?"

"Just about to come out of it again and reposition," she said, more terse now. "Wanted to see if I could trigger some lightning."

"Any luck?"

"Not yet. All's well. I'll update you later, if that's OK."

"Of course."

Jack couldn't help but look over Dr. Y's shoulder at the screen, and he thought he saw Maribeth's glance waver before the image winked off.

"I'm stepping outside, if that's OK," Jack said. "It's still at least five miles away. I want to get a look at the storm's structure before it eats us. If the hail misses us and the Ghost, you should be able to keep filming in the rain if you want, even if the storm goes overhead." And, he chose not to add, if there's no tornado.

"I don't like filming in the rain, but we'll see if we get something good before that happens," said Dr. Y. "Don't stay out too long, Dr. Andreas. It's not as if you have my lightning tent!"

Jack stepped onto the gravel and looked up and around. The wind, which had shifted to the east, blew stinging dust against his skin, and he turned away from it and toward the storm. While the turbines were giants, the storm was a mothership for giants, immense and otherworldly. The increasing rotation had shaped the updraft into a striated cylinder with a wildly expanding top that seemed to burst like an electrified hairdo into the anvil that spread far over their heads. Lightning shot through the mammatus in this cloudy ceiling, as well as from the storm's base; it crawled along the line of feeder cells and back and hit the ground near and far, followed by echoing reports of thunder.

Under this spiraling spacecraft, a new wall cloud had formed, a blocky lowering, large and rotating. After a few short minutes of mesmerizing motion — of the wall cloud organizing, growing, shooting spears of hot-white lightning at the ground — a tendril, then a funnel, pointed from its belly, utterly confident, smoothly spinning, lowering inexorably. In moments, it would likely be what Jack always sought, and yet, for once, did not want to see.

Now, he thought, it's time for some of that luck.

"WE NEED A VIEW *now*," Aurelius said. Brad drove them through the rolling hills just east of Broken Bow as Aurelius looked behind them at the spinning supercell. "It has a funnel. This is it."

"I need a turn that's not blocked by a damn gate," Brad said as he passed a closed road that would have taken them into the wind turbines.

Tyler and Polly Ann wiggled into the last of their wedding clothes as Scooter shot tasteful angles from the back. They had their quick-change down to a science, but Polly Ann's dress had not taken well to storm chasing. It had lost more sequins and, with its various smudges and wrinkles, could have been mistaken for bridal roadkill.

"I can't find my hatpins," she said, sounding nervous. "How can I wear my hat if I can't find my hatpins?"

"We'll figure it out, baby," Tyler reassured her, looking around the door cubbyholes and seat pockets for the hatpins.

"Aurelius," Danni's voice came over the radio. "It has a funnel!"

"I know," he radioed back. "We're looking for a turnoff."

"My GPS shows a farm road heading north in half a mile," she responded. "I think it's at the top of that hill. That'll be perfect — go there!"

"Why doesn't she drive?" Brad snapped.

"She's driving the van, genius," Aurelius said before answering "Copy" into the radio mike. Brad shot him a dirty look.

They made the turn. The road was little more than a dirt lane between two pastures, but it did lead to higher ground and a good view of the oncoming storm and its obvious funnel cloud.

"We definitely want to get out of here before this gets too muddy," Aurelius said.

"For once, I agree with you," Brad replied as he did a three-point turn and parked the cake car so it faced their escape route.

The support van rolled beyond them and also turned around. But to Aurelius's dismay, he saw another vehicle trundling up the lane toward them: Chuck's Wagon. It stopped some fifty yards away.

Danni's voice came over the radio: "He's going to be in our shot!"

"Don't worry," Aurelius said. "We're shooting west. We'll keep him out of it. Let's get set up fast!"

They started piling out, but Polly Ann wouldn't move. "My hat!" she wailed. "I had it specially made! I have to wear it! I need my hatpins! They had real rhinestones!"

"They must've gotten lost in all our moves and changes," said Tyler, sounding a bit desperate himself. "You look beautiful without it, honey."

"I need my hat!" Polly Ann screamed. She held the miniature top hat in her hands. Its lace flower was now torn, and more sequins were missing.

"I've got it," said Aurelius, "silver and everything." He jumped out and ran to the back of the cake car, followed by the couple and Scooter. Vinyl caught up with them with his boom mike. Aurelius opened the tailgate and unzipped a bag of tools, rummaging quickly. He pulled out a roll of the chaser's best friend. "Duct tape!"

Polly Ann crossed her arms, still clutching her hat. "You do not expect me to wear duct tape in my hair," she said flatly. "Not on my wedding day."

"It's on the ground!" Danni shouted. She was filming the tornado, which danced on the southwest horizon. "Get over here!"

"Oh, great," Aurelius said under his breath. He looked at the storm, where the funnel had become a tornado, sinuous and smooth and backlit, perfect for TV, if they could film the damn thing. And, not far away, Charles had exited his truck, seemingly oblivious to their presence, and stood on the edge of the field with his hands in the air, crooning a tune Aurelius couldn't quite hear.

Aurelius turned back to Polly Ann, assuming his deepest and most authoritative voice. "It's duct tape or no hat," he said. "And if you want to be a real storm chaser, you're going to have to accept that, sometimes, you just have to use duct tape."

Whether Polly Ann accepted his logic or simply gave in for the long-awaited chance to get married, she pouted, nodded and held out her hand. Aurelius tore off a couple of pieces of tape, which she took and slapped on either side of the tiny hat's brim. It was — well, it was effective. That was about the kindest thing he could say about it, so he didn't say anything. That hat wasn't going anywhere, even in the inflow winds, which were kicking up as the tornado ripped into the dirt. The twister was getting bigger, and lightning slammed the ground all around them.

"Now!" Danni screamed again.

Feeling her urgency and not a little unnerved by the lightning, all but Aurelius ran to her position on the edge of the field. He stopped to grab his leather book out of the cake car with the marriage rites of the L.E.D., and by the time he got to the wedding party, Danni had the couple positioned perfectly, with the tornado in the background and Brad next to them as best man.

Polly Ann looked nervously toward the churning cone, which grew thicker by the second, then back toward her fiancé. "Tyler?" she asked uncertainly.

Tyler kissed her quickly. "I do."

"Wait a minute," said Aurelius, and he started rushing through the rites, skipping the flowery bits but keeping in just enough formality so it sounded good for TV. The wind flapped his dashing jacket around him, and he raised his voice to be heard over the atmosphere's howl. After two minutes of speed reading, he got to the important part. "Tyler, do you take this woman to be yours in the eyes of the church of the Light-Emitting Deity, nature and humankind?"

"I do," Tyler said, louder this time.

"And Polly Ann, do you take this man to be yours in the eyes of the church of the L.E.D., nature" — a deafening flash-bang made them all jump — "and humankind?" Aurelius rushed through the last words so they sounded like one trick of his tongue.

"I do, I do, I do!" she shouted, her angst forgotten. She threw her arms around Tyler, who dipped her into a passionate kiss.

"You may kiss the bride," Aurelius smiled, mid-smooch. When they came up for air, another bolt hit the field beyond them with a sky-ripping crack-rattle of thunder. The ground glowed white hot for a moment, and smoke rose from the spot. They all cowered this time, and Aurelius looked up to see the tornado even larger, darker as it picked up more dirt and debris, a couple of miles away now. He thought he could see it lofting trees.

"We have to get out of here!" said Brad. "Now!"

"For once, I agree with *you*," said Aurelius.

He glanced at the swaying Charles just as another bolt struck the mystic himself.

"Oh, no!" Aurelius cried, stunned. The others looked around and realized what had happened as Charles crumpled to the ground and Aurelius ran at breakneck speed to the man's side.

Aurelius lifted the mystic's head and checked his mouth and pulse. Charles wasn't breathing, his heartbeat was undetectable, and his tie-dyed T-shirt was charred at the shoulder. Aurelius instantly went into cardiopulmonary resuscitation, a skill he'd considered essential for his expeditions. He counted as he compressed Charles's chest in rapid, even movements. He barely heard the others rushing to his side.

"We have to go now!" Brad shouted again, his voice wild.

"Shut up!" said Danni. "Is he OK?" she asked Aurelius.

"No," he said as he did more compressions, then tried to push air into Charles's lungs from his own, a couple of deep mouth-to-mouth breaths that appeared to have no effect. He resumed chest compressions and looked up at them and then at the tornado. Scooter was the only one still shooting, but Aurelius could tell it would be bad video. The cameraman was shaking like a leaf.

"Oh, lord," said Polly Ann. "This was going to be such a happy day."

Tyler just held her close, looking anxious.

"Listen," Brad declared, almost hysterical. "That tornado is coming this way. And I am going. I am going with or without you. And," he said directly to Danni, "if you want to keep your couple here in one piece, you might want to send them with me."

Aurelius breathed into Charles's mouth again, two forceful exhalations, and resumed the rhythm. He looked up at Danni. Distress had replaced her usual verve.

"You have to get them out of here," Aurelius said.

"But — maybe we can take him?" She nodded at Charles, who looked wan and lifeless, his long, gray hair splayed around his head.

"No time," said Aurelius, breathing harder, feeling the exertion of his work. "I need to try to revive him first. For as long as I can. Take our vehicles. It's OK. I can take the food truck when I get him breathing."

"There, see?" Brad said. "We're doing everything we can for him. Let's go."

Danni looked at him in disgust, then again at the tornado. "All right," she said, and the others sprinted toward the cars. "Aurelius?"

"I'm right behind you. Go." He smiled through his anxiety. "But make sure you stop to get your footage. That's a good tornado, and we went through a lot of crap to get it." He gave Charles two more big breaths but felt no response, and rain began to fall on the rough dirt road.

Danni put a hand on Aurelius's shoulder, squeezed once, then turned and ran like hell.

The two *Zany Weddings* vehicles blasted past Aurelius moments later, kicking up dirt as they skirted around him and his charge. The bride-and-groom hiker figurines on the top of the rolling cake wavered and bounced off the roof and into the field as the vehicle swerved off and onto the road. Aurelius coughed in the cloud of dust, finished his thirty compressions and tried again to blow air into Charles's lungs.

"Don't give up on me now," Aurelius told the man as he

made sharp pushes into his chest. "I need a guide, remember?"

But Charles's crystal-blue eyes remained wide and unseeing as Aurelius counted, pushed and breathed, while the tornado, sinister and violent, churned in their direction.

THE TORNADO WAS NOT SUPPOSED to be the main act for Jack, Dr. Y and Fred, but it threatened to upstage the prodigious lightning display that continued to escalate around them. Standing behind the van and out of the cameras' view, Jack had watched the funnel expand and darken for five minutes already before Dr. Y hopped out and joined him.

"Look at that, Dr. Andreas!" the physicist said. "A tornado! Why, I haven't seen one in person in more than a decade!"

"Yes, and you're going to see it up and close and personal in the near future," said Jack, "unless we can get our zingers and get out of here."

Dr. Y seemed unperturbed. "How long, do you think?"

"Fifteen minutes, tops. That's assuming it maintains its northeast track and speed. Few tornadoes last more than ten minutes, but that thing is getting stronger, so I think it will still be very much a tornado when it reaches us. Maybe a big one. The storm isn't moving that fast, but radar suggests it's accelerating."

"Hmm," mused Dr. Y. "Not ideal, but I don't want our van caught by a tornado. That's plenty of time to get our lightning."

The word "lightning" had barely escaped his lips when the turbine on the next hill took a direct strike, evident from a white-hot glow and a burst of fragments from one of the blades, followed closely by the concussion of thunder. Jack jumped a little, and Dr. Y whooped.

"The damage is regrettable, but that's going to look very nice on camera," Dr. Y said with satisfaction. "Now if only we can get an upward bolt."

Jack looked over at the van, where the cameras in the flip-open window were recording. The Ghost, protected in its bubble on top, was aimed at the heart of the storm, toward dozens of turbines to the west. A light caught his eye, a glimmer. He looked down. Something sparkled in the tread of a tire. A very flat tire.

"Shit," he whispered, dashing toward the rear driver's side and crouching next to it.

"What is it?" asked Dr. Y.

"We have a flat."

Dr. Y walked over and, in his sometimes oblivious manner, pointed at the passenger-side tire. "We certainly do! That's not good at all!"

"No, over here," Jack said, then looked at the other rear tire, which was even flatter than its twin. And glanced again at the tornado. And at the two tires. "Oh, fuck. That's not good."

"What? What?" Dr. Y had put it together. "Two flats? How on earth?"

"I don't think it was road debris," Jack said as he reached out and touched the object that had caught his eye. Sticking out of the tread, it sparkled like jewelry, a rhinestone-encrusted ball on the end of a thick, silver-colored pin, partially crushed but more than effective at causing their leak. It actually looked as if a couple of additional holes had been made around it, suggesting the puncture was no accident. Ignoring more thunder crashing around him, he moved to the passenger side, feeling around the tire until he found a matching bump near the ground on the inside wall. A glance underneath confirmed another rhinestone-topped spike. That was bad. A puncture in the sidewall could be catastrophic.

"What is it?"

"I don't know. Some kind of jewelry or something, with a point sharp and long enough to penetrate the tread. There's no way we just picked up two of those randomly," Jack said, thinking back to where they might have been sabotaged, remembering the *Zany Weddings* crew at the food truck. *Brad.*

"Take them out!" said Dr. Y.

"I don't think that would be wise."

"What wouldn't be wise?" asked Fred, who'd also come outside. "What are you two doing out here? You're going to get fried, and I want to be ready to leave," he said nervously, eyeing the tornado.

"I don't think it would be wise to remove the two objects that have punctured our two back tires," Jack said grimly. "I think that might accelerate the process.

Fred turned a whiter shade of pale and pulled on his beard in distress. "What?" He, too, took in the deflated tires. "They're already flat! We only have one spare!"

"We don't have time to change a goddamn tire anyway," Jack snapped. "Do you have a pump?"

"A what?" Fred asked.

"Something to inflate the tires. It might hold us long enough to get out of here. It took a little while for the tires to get into this state, at least if we picked these up where I think we did. If we can pump them up, we might be able get out of here."

"Where did we pick what up?" asked Fred.

"Some kind of pins."

"Pens?"

"No, pins."

"That's what I said. Oh, goddamn it, I *do* have an accent," Fred moaned.

"Fred," interjected Dr. Y. "There's an emergency kit in the back. In it, you will find a portable air compressor. I'll monitor the experiment while you hook the pump up to the power. Jack will fill up the tires. Won't you, Jack?" His voice was newly urgent.

"Yes, sir," Jack said. Scattered raindrops had started to fall on them, and the lightning was becoming even more frequent. And the tornado did not seem larger just because it was getting closer. What had started as a smoothly spinning elephant trunk had fattened into a stout, perfectly formed cone, with a cloud of whirling debris at its base and a thick, grungy, cottony collar of cloud rotating around the top, marking the tornado's transition upward into the stunning supercell that spawned it.

Any other time, he'd be glad to see such a marvel of nature. Any other time when he had a more assured means of eluding it and no friends in danger. Unconsciously, he looked up, imagining he heard the drone of the A-10 amid the sounds of the storm, and hoped Maribeth would avoid the vortex.

MARIBETH KNEW ENOUGH NOT to fly through an updraft that was producing a tornado, especially when the associated downdraft could cause her as much trouble as the twister itself, but she flew as close as she could while swinging near and far on her pattern. She hoped not just for upward light-ning, but to trigger some lightning herself. Airplanes were built to survive such lightning, with a metal skin and points of dissipation that led the charge away from their passengers. Her canopy, hardened with the fine metal mesh that would help distribute the charge from any strike, made her feel safe. And besides, the adrenaline of flying so close to this formidable storm had started to kick in.

She thought she spotted the research van atop a hill by one of the turbines, and though she flew relatively low, the vehicle seemed almost impossibly tiny next to the spinning white giant. All her senses were alive now as she felt the plane's speed and agility through the stick, heard the engines droning behind her and saw more and more lightning striking around her.

"Come on," she said, coaxing it as she had on her last flight.

A moment later, her plea worked.

A blast of light hit the ground, echoed by an upward flash from a turbine off her port side, a branched bolt launching into space. It was so fast, and yet, she knew, on the cameras it would dawdle beautifully, branch by branch, twig by twig. It was almost surreal, flying with that kind of power exploding just off her wing. It was like being in a 3D movie. Or war. Only this was nature, impartial and random, and she didn't have to make decisions that would impact anyone's life except her own. Yes, she liked this kind of flying a whole lot better. And they had an upward bolt. Surely the Ghost got it, too. A few more, and they'd have some real data to play with.

She felt a surge of confidence, even as she heard more static on her radio, charge building up around the Warthog. And then a slap above her, loud, unnerving, with a flash of light. She knew exactly what it was. The plane had triggered a strike! She quickly checked her instruments and grinned. Everything was working, and the cameras had almost certainly captured a bipolar leader. Dr. Y would be thrilled! She had to let him know, however quickly. Keeping in mind the position of the storm, the hail, and the now disturbingly large tornado, she made a video call with the tablet built into the panel.

Dr. Y's face came on. He was in the darkness of the van, she thought, and he looked harried. "Ms. Lisbon? Is everything all right?"

"Yes, sir!" she said. "I think you'll be happy!"

"Dr. Y," she heard Jack's voice in the background, "we have one done and are working on the other. A few more minutes. It's slow."

"That will have to be fast enough," Dr. Y said over his shoulder, then turned back to Maribeth. "What were you saying, my dear?"

She wondered what was happening in the van. Jack sounded stressed. But she wanted to tell them the good news. "Just a minute ago —"

Around her blossomed a dazzling light, the fireworks of angels. In an instant, five turbines lit up, throwing trees of lightning into the air, a forest of electricity birthed and burned in a blink. And there was a terrific bang, much louder than the earlier pop.

Dr. Y's face winked out, the tablet sparked and died, and the cockpit went dark.

"WHAT WAS THAT?" Jack asked, looking up from where he crouched next to the second tire. It was now almost as full as he could make it with the poky portable air compressor, plugged into the van's power.

"It was amazing," said Fred, who'd been watching the sky.

"Multiple upward flashes. Though it almost looked like —
naw, it couldn't have been."

"What?" asked Jack.

"I thought I saw the plane lit up against the clouds. Bright,
but just for an instant."

Jack reached for the easiest explanation. "Lightning probably illuminated her, like a flash bulb."

"Probably," said Fred, but he sounded uncertain.

"Boys, are we done?" came Dr. Y's voice. He'd emerged
from the van and had a strange look on his face.

"Did you get that?" Fred asked. "That was awesome!"

"I believe we got it," said Dr. Y, "but I'm a bit concerned. I
was on a call with Ms. Lisbon and then the connection just
flashed off. I can't raise her. Can you see her?"

Jack stood up instantly and scanned the sky. Their view
was obscured by increasingly congested clouds and rain.
Worse, the tornado was within a mile and a half of their position. He could hear the roar. Trees and pieces of structures
floated around it and crashed to the ground. Bits of insulation
from someone's hapless house had started to fall around
them.

"We don't see her," Fred said. "Not now, anyway."

"Let me try her," Jack said, pulling out his phone and
dialing her cell. It went to voicemail. Maybe she doesn't even
have it on, he thought, but worry unsettled him.

"Are you ready?" Dr. Y asked. Even he sounded nervous
now.

"Ready," Jack said, focusing on the task at hand. He
unplugged the compressor and spun the cap back on the tire
valve. He hoped the tires would hold long enough to get them
out of the path. They had to navigate the road from hell first.
"I'll drive."

"Leave the Ghost operating," said Dr. Y.

"You might get some super-slow-mo of flying debris," Jack said dryly, but he was thinking about Maribeth as he helped Fred quickly lock up the observation window. They piled into their places. "Everybody ready?"

"Go," said Dr. Y, not bubbly at all, as Jack tried to drive as fast and as gently as he could down the lane.

He turned right and began navigating the serpentine dirt and gravel road that would take them to pavement and escape. It was getting slippery. With the chilling approach of the voracious tornado, the van fought him in the screaming inflow winds. The big hay bales they'd passed on the way in were in attack mode; he had to swerve and thread the needle between them as the fat cylinders rolled and bounced in front of the van toward the twister. One caught a piece of their fender and burst apart on the other side of the road.

"I don't like this," Jack said as the tornado reached the first turbine. Before the darkest part of the funnel even touched it, the outermost winds shredded the nacelle and snapped off two of the blades, sending them flying.

"And you were worried about lightning damage," Fred said from the back as an enormous chunk of blade, twice as big as their van, crash-landed twenty yards to their right.

"Could you go a bit faster, Dr. Andreas?" Dr. Y asked in a deceptively calm voice.

"Talk to the guy who put the spikes in our tires," Jack said, but he tried to oblige, pressing toward the main road and their eastern escape route.

Another turbine succumbed to the tornado, all of its blades shattering, the bulky pieces dwarfed by the massive funnel. The twister hurled the white fragments around its churning center. The pieces winked in and out of view, riding the carousel, before smashing to the ground from a great height.

"Those are very expensive, you know," said Dr. Y.

Jack laughed, a bleak and humorless sound, as he hit a puddle and the van skidded. He wrestled it back onto the road and kept going. Wasn't he in this situation, what, five days ago? It seemed like a lifetime. But this was different; he was driving, and on debatable tires. No matter how bad they were, he had to keep pushing the van until they were out of the way of the tornado.

They entered the twister's path, and he stared it down as he pressed forward, willing it to wait just one more minute before it drew them in. More of a wedge than a cone, now, it lofted trees into the air like a fountain of deranged salad. A branch fell out of the sky and whacked their windshield before bouncing off the glass, instantly expanding the old hail-gener-ated crack into a web of gleaming veins. Jack could feel the twister's tug as he hit another rough patch of road, just before the stop sign that welcomed them back to pavement.

He turned east and pushed the accelerator hard as the hungry tornado chewed up the darkening world behind them, lumbering on their heels. The rear-flank downdraft winds slammed them, and a piece of debris took out one of the small back windows. Fred yelped. The van wavered but held to the road, and Jack, not one to ask the universe for anything, sent out a plea for just a little more luck, and not just for him.

A mile later, he could breathe again, though the tornado remained unnervingly close.

Still driving as fast as he dared, he pulled out his phone and hit redial, and the call again went to her voicemail.

"She's not answering," he said.

"Let me try," said Dr. Y. His video call failed.

Jack hit redial again. Still no luck.

"She's busy, Andreas," Fred said from the back, sounding more like his bombastic self now that they'd edged ahead of the tornado. "She doesn't want to talk to you. I don't think she even has the phone on when she's flying."

"But it's odd that the video call won't go through," said Dr. Y. "Let me try the hangar." He tapped in the number, a voice call this time, and spoke quietly to his contact on the other end. "Data transmission from the plane has stopped," he said when he got off the line, sounding perplexed. "I'm sure it can be explained. I mean, I'm sure she's fine."

Dr. Y's little moment of hesitation was what made Jack consciously acknowledge that she might not be fine. If the lightning had taken out her electronics, it might have done even worse.

"Would someone be tracking her?" Jack asked. "Radar?"

"Let me call someone at Kearney," said Dr. Y.

Jack looked over his shoulder at the tornado, which now paralleled their course. He tried to ignore Dr. Y's murmurs, but what he heard didn't sound good. Dr. Y ended the call and didn't say anything.

She'd survived war, for Christ's sake, Jack thought. She'd survived a helicopter crash in a storm. A stupid lightning strike wasn't going to take her down. Planes survived lightning all the time. She'd said it herself. But the dismal silence on Dr. Y's side of the van was suffocating.

Jack tried to stay focused, to make sure the van was driving OK, to make sure they were out of the path in case the tornado dived south. But he didn't like this terrible silence, its deadly implications. He didn't care what happened to himself. He didn't want to imagine a world without Maribeth.

AURELIUS CONTINUED through a few more cycles of CPR, his thoughts churning like the tornado to his southwest as he pressed Charles's chest.

Brad was a pussy. No, that was an insult to pussy. Brad was an outright coward, and how could a coward have flown in the Bubble? All the signs had been there — the Twister Tracker's reluctance to speak of it, his fury, even. If I make it out of here, Aurelius thought, that lad and I are going to have a talk.

The adventurer halted his ministrations for a moment as the tornado worked its way within almost a mile of his position. It might miss him. But as big as it was, even being within a mile of it was dangerous, and the wind whacked him with increasing amounts of dirt and grass as it got near. Too near. He looked down at Charles and noticed scorched lines in the ground radiating from where he lay, the mark of the strike.

"Old man, it's time," Aurelius said, reaching under Charles and picking him up. The mystic was surprisingly light. Had his life force left him? Aurelius feared the worst.

He got him to the truck and opened the back door with one hand, then hauled Charles in and found the pallet he slept on. He laid the man down and pulled a blanket up to his chin, looking one more time into the mystic's distant eyes. Did he feel a brush of breath against his cheek? Or was it the storm's winds pushing into the open door? There was no time to find out. Aurelius stepped back, slammed shut the rear doors and went to the front seat. The keys were in the ignition.

The truck seemed new and well-maintained. Perhaps Charles's connections had made his spiritual quest simpler; a trust fund went a long way toward bankrolling a quest. And a food truck. But on the first turn of the key, the engine didn't start. Aurelius had a horrible thought: What if the lightning strike had fried the truck's electronics, too? He tried again, and to his immense relief, the engine turned over immediately.

Aurelius began what became an agonizing five-point turn and got a very good look at the tornado as he tried to get pointed back toward the main road. The twister almost filled his windows, and small debris — branches, leaves, insulation — rained down around him. At least there were no falling fish.

He accelerated south. The surface of the road was slick with mud, but it hadn't gone full quicksand yet. He had to slow down to avoid sliding off into a ditch. In his rearview mirror, he saw a sudden upward flash of multiple lightning bolts from the wind farm and marveled at a universe that could make such wonder from such a machine of death. They were working together, he thought, the wonders and the destroyers, and acknowledging both, finding the center line, the balancing point — what did they call it? The razor's edge? — perhaps that was the path. Perhaps Charles was leading him there after all.

Charles. He hoped the poor man did have the spark of life in him, a fire he couldn't detect in those last few moments before they had to flee the tornado. He was, Aurelius realized, a friend.

THE LIGHTNING RESEARCH van made it four more labored miles when the back right tire blew. Jack barely maintained control as he heard the bang and the flapping sound of destroyed rubber and felt the van shudder. He clutched the wheel hard, slowly eased his foot off the accelerator and got them to the shoulder.

"Nicely done," Dr. Y said in a shaken voice.

Jack looked out his window to make sure the tornado wouldn't catch them. Radar showed it had shifted to a more eastern track, but it seemed it would scrape by.

"I think we're OK," he said.

"Fuck," was all Fred said from the back.

Jack hopped out to survey the damage. The right rear tire was in tatters; the left was almost completely flat, and its wounds had been aggravated by their rough travels. It wouldn't survive another inflation. Even with the spare, they could go no farther.

Jack silently cursed nature and Brad and lightning and bad luck, when he had so wanted just a bit of good. Just enough.

Fred, however, cursed aloud as he stowed the Ghost. Its dome sported one fine crack from debris, but the camera had survived.

Dr. Y called the auto club and discovered that no one from the next tiny town would be available to tow them, because the tornado had sideswiped the village and leveled the only garage. It would have to be a truck from farther away, and that meant a wait of at least forty-five minutes. He offered them sandwiches from the cooler that no one wanted, not even him, with his brother and his pilot on his mind.

Jack did take a root beer. He was desperately thirsty and would have preferred the real thing, but they were in the middle of fucking nowhere, and a bar was out of the question. He stood outside by the van and drank it. It was nearly dark, now, with an almost imperceptible orange glow edging the western horizon. Overhead, the stars had come out in the wake of the storm, a reminder of how infinitely small he was, how little his desires mattered, no matter how big his feelings had become.

He just knew he had lost someone precious tonight. Her easy insinuation into his consciousness had been so natural, he hadn't realized it until now. Or had been unwilling to acknowledge it. A friend who was also a lover. And more. He thought he'd been on the verge of this conviction before, but all that had been nothing. A wasteland of dalliances punctuated by flirtations with emotions that even he knew, deep down, were superficial and guided more by his dick than his heart. What a joke. His heart. He didn't have one. Hadn't until now. Could you lose something you never really had?

Occasionally a vehicle passed, including a few chasers who'd been caught on the wrong side of the storm. Distant flashes showed that the supercell continued rolling across Nebraska, though the tornado had lifted, according to the reports on his phone. Now the storm was lining out, joining with other cells that had generated after dark, creating a great wall of wind and rain that would sweep through the eastern half of the state, scraping the air clean with its power. He wanted to do the same thing with his mind. He was almost numb now, but not numb enough. He wanted a bottle of whiskey and a week in a dark hotel room. Make that a case of whiskey.

More headlights appeared in the east, this time accompanied by flashing yellow lights. It was the tow truck. The big flatbed Ford slowed in response to their blinkers, veered to their side of the road and backed in behind them.

Thirty minutes later, the van was on the truck, and Jack was folded into the tight back seat next to a child's car seat. Dr. Y and Fred were side by side in the front next to the driver, a pink, unshaven tobacco chewer wearing a Royals cap.

His name was Lenny, as indicated by the oval nametag sewn into his gray work shirt.

"Some storm tonight, huh?" Lenny commented as he drove east. "They got a lot of damage in Palladia. I saw a little of it when I drove through, but it was mostly on the north side of town."

"That's a shame," said Dr. Y.

"What are you people doing out here?" Lenny spit into a white foam cup, adding to the black swamp water that already half-filled it. "That van looks pretty interesting."

"Storm research," Dr. Y answered.

"You get anything good?"

"That remains to be seen," the physicist said, and his answer was so uncharacteristically cold that Lenny gave up his friendly questions. Fred stepped in and asked him about the truck's towing gear, the worst wrecks he'd seen and other cheerful topics, keeping him occupied as they drove through Palladia, where emergency vehicles were busy. They soon turned south toward the next town and the garage.

Jack leaned against the narrow window and closed his eyes, not wanting to think about what came next, wanting to be alone with his black thoughts. But he couldn't help over-hearing Fred and Lenny discover each had a toddler at home, and they compared notes on wives and day care and the quotidian joys and frustrations in which Jack had never felt the slightest interest. And yet he began to understand the attraction. They had a mission, these guys, that completely involved their minds and souls, even as they went about in the world. They had an investment in life Jack had never made.

"Poor bastard," Lenny said.

"What?" Fred asked.

"Hitchhiker back there. If I didn't have a full boat I'd pick him up. I've done a lot of hitchhiking in my time. Always good to pay it forward. Anyway, town's not far. We got a couple of motels if you're interested. One's right next to my garage. You gotta get this fixed tonight?"

"There's no point in doing it tonight," said Dr. Y. "We'll rest now, and if you can have the new tires mounted in the morning, that will be more than convenient."

"No problem," Lenny said, seemingly glad that the curly-haired leader was talking to him again. "I'll work on it for a little while tonight, anyway. I'm a night owl. Short sleeper, too. Stay up late, start early. Helps with the kid. I'm pretty sure I got those tires in stock, or the next best thing. I can even get my guy at the glass shop to come over first thing and replace your windows."

"That will be fine, sir, and we thank you for your efforts," said Dr. Y. "Please do lock up the van in your garage tonight, won't you? Our scientific equipment, you know."

"No problem," Lenny said again, exuding good-natured trustworthiness.

The truck's rhythm shifted, and Jack opened his eyes as it rumbled to a stop outside a gas station and garage lit with vaguely yellow, vibrating lights. An ugly place. It suited his mood. He robotically followed the others as they grabbed their bags from the van and walked over to the motel, a long, low, white building at least fifty years old punctuated by a stark row of green doors. A few cars were parked outside, and a pink neon sign declared "VACANCY" in the curtained office window. Dr. Y went inside as Fred and Jack waited in the gravel lot.

Fred dug his feet in the stones, kicking. "Did you try her again?"

"Several times when we were stopped back on the road.

And then I gave up. She would call us if she could. And she can't — because she can't."

"Jack, you don't know."

"You're not helping," Jack said, looking up as Dr. Y came out of the office with three keys, each attached to a large plastic burgundy tag adorned with gold-stamped room numbers. As he handed them over, he shook the men's hands in turn.

"Gentlemen, I am by nature a positive man. That is why I have been so successful. I approach my failures with the same positive attitude, because they lead to lessons and, ultimately, more success. I've also learned not to give up and not to assume the worst. I know what you're thinking, but our Ms. Lisbon is a resourceful woman, and we haven't heard any bad news. When airplanes are involved, bad news travels fast. My people are calling every airport in Nebraska, and I think we will have good news tomorrow, at least on that front. And then we can continue our quest."

"Thanks, Dr. Y," Fred said. Jack was silent, but he felt the wisdom of the words, even if, in his current desperate state, they offered little comfort.

AFTER THE CONCUSSIVE BOOM, Maribeth could barely hear with her stunned ears. It was dusk now, the shadows deepened by the storm sucking the sun away from the western sky. The dark panel in front of her chilled her to the bone. She looked back to see if she still had engines.

First: The plane was airborne. Second: She was flying. There was no doubt of it. But the radio was dead. Her father's words went through her mind: *Aviate, navigate, then communi-*

cate. She had to assess, to fly to safety, if she could still fly. There was no ejector seat in the research plane. If she was able to land, then she'd worry about little things like talking to her team.

Another small part of her brain wondered exactly what had happened. This wasn't like the lightning triggered by the aircraft. She had to assume she'd been struck by an upward bolt. Nothing like turning yourself into a guinea pig twice.

She reached into a pocket, found her small LED flashlight and pressed the button with her thumb. The beam of light seemed barely bright enough, especially after the eye-searing lightning. But it let her look at the main attitude indicator. It was clearly out. That left the small peanut gauge, independently powered, but not for long. She moved the beam and found the gauge. Working. Good. She had, what? Thirty minutes, tops? She needed an airport, fast.

The airspeed and altitude indicators still worked, and they showed she was OK. A few other indicators were working, too, and they verified what her senses told her was true: The engines were operating. That fact was kind of important and made her feel just a wee bit better. But the storm was way too close, and even in the lowering evening, she could see the large tornado continuing to rampage east-northeast. That narrowed her escape routes considerably. She didn't want to land at an airport about to be consumed by a monster, and she didn't want to plow through the storm on the way to North Platte. Lightning flashed again nearby, underscoring the urgency of her situation.

Maribeth popped the circuit breaker panel and allowed herself sixty seconds of resets to see if she could get any joy. Nope. Still dark. Time to plot a course, preferably east or southeast. She knew some of the bigger airports, but with her radio fried, she'd rather go in somewhere traffic wouldn't be a problem. And she didn't have the luxury of time.

She pulled out her notebook to confirm the idea forming in the back of her mind. She didn't want to go as far as Grand Island or Kearney and certainly not back to Salina. But nearby, there was a small-town airport unlikely to have any traffic this time of day, in this kind of weather. It was worth a try. She'd head southeast to Loup City. She noted the coordinates she'd recorded in the notebook and entered them into her pocket GPS to make sure she was on track. She knew the airport was near a memorable bend in the riverbed. And it would take only a few minutes to get there.

She flew south first to get out of the storm, mentally chiding herself for the relief she felt to be in clear air again, and then chiding herself for being an fool. Liking a challenge was one thing. Wanting to die was quite another.

It was less dark here, out of the realm of the supercell. The rain diminished as she let the flanking line pass her, revealing one of those long, low twilights Nebraska enjoyed this time of year, with hints of orange still on the western horizon. The colors cheered her. This was the sky. This was where she loved to be. But now, she wanted to be on the ground. That's where she wanted to *live*.

The Loup City Municipal Airport looked tiny, even from the lower altitude she'd adopted in emergency mode. One lighted runway, or at least one paved one. It wasn't a great time to go barreling into a field if she could help it, no matter how good the turf strip was. She circled the field twice, examining it thoroughly as she banked the Warthog just to be sure there weren't any obstacles. She noted trees around it, but the paved runway looked clear. Time to go.

Keeping an eye on her tiny backup attitude gauge and her

airspeed, she let instinct — a byproduct of a ridiculous number of training hours — kick in as she brought the plane in.

She turned the A-10 so she could land into the wind and dropped her gear. It worked. Good.

"Doin' it old-school," she murmured as she pushed the plane into its descent, watching her pitch and speed as she closed with the runway.

She pulled the nose up slightly: Flare. Touchdown. Brake. She felt the tough tires grip the runway as she slowed down. She turned and rolled the Warthog to a stop outside a small cluster of buildings and went through her shutdown with the help of the flashlight.

In the ensuing quiet, she took a deep breath, pulled off her helmet, leaned back and closed her eyes, letting the tension seep out of her body. She was aware of everything, her senses still on hyper-alert — her heartbeat, the cockpit around her, the night. The elation of being alive. The hollowness of being alone.

Two minutes later, she was ready to move. But first, she'd better call the team. She hoped the cameras weren't fried, too. That was news she didn't want to deliver to Dr. Y.

She pulled the cell phone out of her pocket and turned it on, waited for it to pick up a signal. She should call Dr. Y. She knew that. But she wanted to call Jack. The impulse was strangely urgent. She fought it, almost gave in, resisted again. *No.* Dr. Y first. She went into her contacts to dial the number, and as soon as she tapped it, the phone's screen blacked out with the spinning spiral of death. Dead battery. The long afternoon had done it in.

"Shit," she said, resigning herself to the fact that she'd have to find another way to call.

She put a few things in her pockets — the flashlight, her GPS, an energy bar from her cockpit stash — and popped a hot mint into her mouth. She pressed the button to extend the boarding ladder — at least that worked, she noted with relief — opened the canopy and climbed down to the tarmac.

It was a bit darker now. The pavement felt hard beneath her boots. She took a few minutes to take off her heavy G-suit, unraveling the zippers and buckles of the trousers, the complex vest, leaving her in just her green flight suit. Much more comfortable. She rolled up the bundle of garments, stowed it by the front wheel and looked around.

Just a couple of buildings sat alongside the runway. The trees stood shoulder-to-shoulder, gloomy sentinels around the tiny airport. There were a couple of lights. After the cacophony of the day, it was eerily quiet. Far to the north, distant flashes on the horizon suggested her storm still rampaged. She spent a moment looking around, marveled at the emptiness, noted a few stars winking at her, listened to the insects. Curiosity replaced relief. What had happened? Planes were usually well-shielded, though she'd heard of lightning research mishaps before — radar domes exploding, radios cooked, that kind of thing. Perhaps the scientific team had introduced a vulnerability when they were rewiring everything. She walked around the Warthog, looking for damage. The lights weren't bright enough to show her what she wanted to know. Needed to know. The snarling face on the plane's nose seemed to grin a little more at her as she eyed it in the semi-darkness. *A little lightning won't get me down,* it seemed to say.

We'll get it right next time, she thought. They'd figure out the problem, and she'd fly it again. But that could be a long way down the road.

Maribeth walked over to the cluster of buildings, looking for a pay phone, not expecting to find such an ancient relic. After several minutes of exploring, she didn't. Doors were locked. Windows were dark. No one was home.

She pulled out the energy bar, unwrapped it and ate it, enjoying the feeling of the warm night falling around her, considering her options. She figured there was only one, unless she wanted to wait here until morning. So she consulted her GPS and headed on foot for the gravel lane, on her way to Route 58 and the mile or so it would take to walk into town.

JACK'S overnight bag always held an escape. As soon as he got into the room, he rummaged through the few clothes in the canvas bag and found it: the bottle. He set it on the chipped laminate desk, then sat on the edge of the bed and stared at it dully for a couple of minutes. Finally, he got up and grabbed the square plastic ice bucket and left the room to find the machine.

It was halfway down the long building in a breezeway. As he pressed the bucket up against the button and heard the familiar, almost comforting rattle of the cubes hitting the bottom, he felt a buzz in his pocket. Probably Fred or Dr. Y. He didn't want to talk to them, and he dared not hope it was someone else. But he should look. Just in case.

"Are you really here?" said the message.

A message from Maribeth. He looked at it with mistrust.

Here? What could it mean?

"Is it really you?" he typed back, his thumbs bumbling through the words, misspelling them and retyping till he got it right. His brain was thick as hot taffy. He pressed send and waited an excruciating minute for the answer.

"Yes. OK. In Loup City. Where are you?"

Yes. Yes, she was alive. And so nonchalant. And she wanted to know where he was. This seemed like such a practical question, and yet he was almost too overcome to answer it. *She was alive.* In Loup City, wherever that was. It dawned on him that he had no idea what town they were in. He'd done his best to shut out the world on the way to the garage.

"A motel in middle of nowhere as usual," he typed. "Will find out."

A few moments later came her reply: "I wondered because am looking at Y's van right now."

It took half a second for this information to work its way through the taffy and jump across his neurons into comprehension. He left the ice bucket under the spout and sprinted out of the breezeway and down the length of the motel toward the garage next door. The lights were still on — Lenny working late — and the garage was wide open, the van up on the lift. Lenny was affixing a new tire with a noisy power tool and looked up at him expectantly, between lug nuts.

"Where is she?" Jack asked, breathless.

Lenny looked confused, then smiled. "Our hitchhiker?" He nodded toward the office.

Jack saw the door, ran over, threw it open. It banged against the wall. Maribeth leaned sideways against the counter in her flight suit, tapping on her phone. She flinched, looked up at the racket and dropped her phone on the counter. Across her tired, lovely face came the most glowing grin he'd ever seen.

In two strides, he was at her side, hugging her hard, twirling her, setting her on her feet and holding her face between his hands and kissing her with all the reborn fire that had cooled to mournful embers in the past couple of hours, a conflagration that traveled from his core outward, around her, through his mouth to hers, drinking of her life, her cool waters, fire quenched by rain, burning all the brighter still. He felt her arms wrap around his waist, felt her answer his passion. But after a heated suspension of time, she let go. He took her withdrawal as a sign to release her. He let his arms drop to his sides and stared at her, lost in the unreal moment, still shocked to find her here.

"Well," she said, a hitch in her voice, "hello to you, too."

"I thought you were dead."

"For a second, so did I."

"Do the others know?"

"I called Dr. Y," she said. "He said he found his brother today? You'll have to tell me more about that. He was going to call Fred and the hangar. I — I told him I wanted to call you."

"Why didn't you call earlier? Text? We were freaking out."

"I never have the phone on when I'm flying, and I had other issues. Like landing the goddamn thing." He saw her reliving whatever she'd gone through up there. "It's a good plane. The electronics took a hit — lightning fried the tablet and radio, too — but it got me home. To earth, that is. Just up the road. Dr. Y's sending a crew tomorrow to give it the once-over. Once we make sure it's safe to fly, I'll get it back to the hangar for a full analysis."

"But you didn't call!" Jack said, still marveling at her presence in this little office, the faint smell of tires, the bulletin board covered with cartoons and ads and work orders, the retro pinup calendar, the flickering fluorescent lights, her gray-green eyes.

"My phone was dead. And I don't know if you noticed, but

that airfield isn't exactly DFW. I had to walk into town. I was glad Lenny had a power cord." She glanced over at the phone plugged into the nest of cables on the counter and looked up at him, smiled. "Though a pay phone would've been OK. I still have your card in my wallet."

"So my card really is lucky."

"I'm sure it's the only reason I'm alive," she deadpanned, but beneath the humor, she seemed troubled and uncertain. She looked at him as if seeing him for the first time. "I was so happy you were really here."

"*We* are really here," he said, putting his arms around her waist.

Maribeth rested her hands on his arms but didn't hug him back.

"I need a room," she said. "Think that can be arranged?"

"You don't need a room." He smiled, but her expression was unreadable. "Do you have a bag?" he asked.

"What you see is what you get."

"More than enough for me." He bent down and kissed her below her ear. "But what a shame you don't have any clothes," he whispered, kissing her neck again, slowly. He thought he felt her sigh. He took her by the hand. "Come on."

Maribeth remained still, her feet planted, searching his eyes. He took a step away from her, pulling her toward him, wanting badly for her to assent. And then stepped forward, fell in with him, heading out the office door into the garage. He felt an astonishing lightness carry him into the fragile night, fueled by an exquisite energy that traveled from her hand to his.

"I'll pick up my phone tomorrow, OK?" she called to Lenny, who waved as she and Jack walked out the open garage door and across the barely lit parking lot toward the motel, still holding hands. They didn't say anything. Jack had run out of words. He needed new ones, but he didn't know the language. This was foreign territory, a newfound land. He took her by the breezeway, grabbed the ice bucket and led her the rest of the way to his room, using the old key to let them inside.

"Not much to welcome you," Jack finally said as she stood in the middle of the room, arms crossed, in the dim light of a 1970s-era lamp. It barely illuminated the gold-and-navy pattern on the bedspread and the coordinating gold carpet.

"After what happened today," she said, "it looks pretty damn good to me."

"Bourbon?"

"Water first," she said. "I'm dehydrated. I don't drink much while I'm flying."

"Just tap water, but there are cups in the bathroom."

"Thanks." She seemed to relax a little, moved toward the bathroom, came out a few minutes later with a clear plastic cup of water. He gestured toward the bed, and she gave him an odd look.

"Sit down," he said. He wanted her in his bed for other reasons, but she was as tense as a cat on a raft. "You've had a long day."

Maribeth looked visibly relieved at this bit of normalcy, sat, closed her eyes and drank down the cup of water. He took it from her, scooped ice from the bucket and added bourbon, handed it back to her. He got another cup and made himself a drink, too, and sat near the end of the bed, next to her.

He eyed her feet, the tough flowered footwear. "Sexy boots."

"Made for walkin'," she quipped.

"Which you did. Shit, Maribeth, you scared me to death."

She took a long sip of her drink, looked at him. "I have a feeling your van story is going to scare me, too."

"Like you're ever scared." He elbowed her.

"Of course not," she said. "But I saw the hatpins."

"What hatpins?"

"Lenny showed me. The things he pulled out of your tires. Hatpins. Pretty fancy."

"Who the fuck uses hatpins anymore?"

"You tell me," she said. "One was still hung up in what was left of the shredded tire."

He drank down half his cup. "I think someone spiked the tires. Would a bride use hatpins?"

"I suppose she might," Maribeth said. "Are you a runaway groom?"

Jack laughed. "No, but we ran into the *Zany Weddings* TV crew again and my old buddy Brad."

"He told me some things about you that I didn't want to believe, that night I flew to Oklahoma City," she said.

"All lies."

She shot him a questioning look. "You think he did it? Why do you two hate each other so much?"

"I don't hate him. I don't even think about him," Jack said. "But apparently, he hates me."

"Why?"

"You're the only one I'll ever tell," he said. "But not tonight." He reached behind her, leaned over and set his now-empty cup on the nightstand; on the way back, he gently pushed a lock of her hair behind her ear.

Maribeth took another sip, appearing not to notice. "Tell me about the van." She was deflecting him. He didn't know why. As he answered her, he took her left hand and unclasped her chunky pilot's watch, tossed it behind him and massaged her wrist.

"We found the pins and the flat tires while we were parked," he said, "filming the lightning."

"And you saw the tornado?"

"Oh, yeah. We saw the tornado. Almost didn't make it out. But we're OK. Just like you." He let go of her wrist, put a hand on the small of her back, leaned in, planted kisses up her jawline. "Finish your drink," he whispered.

"I don't know," she said, but she knocked it back, as any pilot might who'd just escaped death, and put down the cup, turning those eyes to him, skeptical, strong, stubborn. All the things he loved. He cupped her chin with one hand and kissed her with a light, tender touch of his lips. She shivered but did not move to embrace him, to engage him as she'd done earlier.

"Mari," he murmured with an assurance he'd never felt before. "This is right."

"I don't know."

"You *do* know," Jack said, kissing her neck, enfolding her, moving to the zipper of her flight suit. He tugged it down a few inches.

"Wait." She put a hand on his chest, keeping him at bay.

"You want me."

"Yes." She was clear on that point, at least.

"I want you. I more than want you, Mari. I'll always want you." He kissed her mouth and marveled at how deeply he meant it. She started to melt into him before she pushed him back again.

"I can't." But her voice wavered.

"You said that before. You can do anything you want."

Her eyes were moist. "You don't understand."

"You've had a hard day," he said, trying to soothe her, but she just seemed more upset.

"Yes. No." She became more forceful, her voice raw. "You don't understand. You don't understand what I've gone through to get to this point, this point in my life where I'm not feeling the pain all the time. Where I'm not always imagining the faces of the people I killed. Where I'm not constantly looking over my shoulder."

It was more than she'd ever said about her past. Jack could see her trying to quell the darkness. He hoped he had enough strength to help her through it, because he needed her strength, too. It was part of what drew him to her.

He put an arm around her shoulders. "I'll be with you," he said.

"You don't get it. I've lost so much. So many. I can't lose anyone else. I can't do this."

"You won't lose me."

She shook her head. "There are no guarantees. I can't just throw away the life I've built."

"Then you're way ahead of me. I just figured out that I haven't had much of a life until now." Jack's laugh held a touch of bitterness. He finally saw what he wanted, and she was trapped in her own fortress. "Tell me about this life of yours," he goaded her. "What are you protecting? I'm serious. Tell me."

She took a deep breath, her head down like that of a runner about to sprint, and he saw she was working to regain control, her damn control, the walls going back up. Her brown hair, lank and rough after all she'd been through, hid her eyes.

He hated to see her like this. He knelt in front of her, held both her hands, kissed them and looked up at her. "Listen.

You don't have to surrender, Mari. You'll never have to surrender to me. I surrender. *I surrender.*"

She slowly lifted her gaze, wary, hopeful. The walls weren't finished yet. "How do I know? Nothing is forever."

"We have a long time before forever," he said. "I'll be here for at least that long. I knew it today. Didn't you hear me? You don't have to surrender."

"But I think I do," she said. "And I don't know if I can."

"You can do anything you want," he said lightly. "You rock."

Maribeth laughed suddenly, and that expansive, bitter-sweet, unexpected sound chased away the shadows and lifted his spirits.

"You are making it hard for me to ignore you," she said.

"That's my plan. Don't you trust me?"

"Every impulse of my brain tells me not to," she said. He raised his eyebrows. "I mean, come on, Jack, I can see the effect you have on women. But I know you now. I have to admit that every part of my — everything else says I do — I want to trust you."

"Every part of your body? No. I know that's not what you mean. Though I know it's that, too."

Her face turned pink, illuminating her freckles like a faint dusting of stars on either side of her nose.

"Your heart. Your heart knows," Jack said. "It's a hard word to say. I couldn't even say it in Cheerios."

"You gave me a lightning bolt instead," she said, giving him a half smile at the mention of his breakfast message that morning in Salina.

"It was a heart first. Before you saw it."

"Not sure that counts," she said.

"I wish I had a do-over." He still held her hands, hoping she wouldn't let go.

Maribeth shook her head. "Mutual surrender? That's hard for a soldier."

"It'll be easy with me." He could barely stand the suspense as she stared him down, the hair's-breadth distance between them, between now and the rest of their lives.

"Too easy," she finally said, and she leaned in and kissed him, as hungry for him as he was for her. He felt his blood pound through his veins as she whispered: "I think I Cheerio you, Dr. Andreas."

MARIBETH'S HEAD spun from an overload of emotions, feelings she was used to putting away in a locker at an airport, leaving on the ground as she soared into the sky, packing away in a trunk or a disused apartment. She felt a wrenching transformation in her heart, her armored heart, and a commensurate surge of need in her body. And, with it all, a flare of joy.

Jack pulled at the zipper of her flight suit, pulled it all the way down, reached to her boots and loosened the laces and yanked them and her socks off, and she reached down and unzipped the ankles of the suit and stood so they could wrestle her out of it as quickly as possible. And then, still in her bra and underpants — simple black cotton today — she helped pulled his clothes off him, his black T-shirt, his high-tops and socks and jeans, his briefs, until he was beautiful and naked before her. A man could be beautiful, she thought, especially this man. She never expected it. Never expected to feel this way about any man, and especially about a man like this, whose dissolute and winding road was not one that should have led to her buttoned-up, dutiful self. Did she believe they could take the road together? Incredibly, she did. She looked into his green eyes, blazing with yearning and something else, a depth of feeling she not only believed but *knew* was there, the way she knew aerodynamics could make her fly.

His hands roamed over her, pulling down one strap of her bra, one cup, revealing one breast that he gently kissed; he sucked at her nipple, unhooked the bra and pulled it off in one motion.

"Beautiful," he whispered, echoing her thoughts as he leaned down over the other peak, played with it with his tongue till the sensation nearly made her mad. All her dams were breaking, and yes, *beautiful, beautiful,* he was beautiful, the night was beautiful, this ugly hotel room was beautiful. Inside, she was beautiful, too, in the heated circle of his love.

Love. It was a word she dared not say, yet, but she felt it as she spun him and pushed him back on the bed, straddling him, still in her underpants. He grinned at her, that impish grin. She wasn't ready to be completely naked, yet; she wanted suddenly to feel his surrender beneath her, to feel him respond to her, to hang on to a vestige of control. She rubbed her hands over his taut chest and kissed his nipples in turn, and he groaned as she nibbled and kissed her way down his belly. She felt his erection pushing against her middle, and she let it slide between her breasts, up and down once, twice to tease him, to see him growl and give her a scorching look of longing. She touched his shaft with one hand and lightly stroked it as she kissed his thighs, prolonging his agony, then took him in her mouth, knowing his pleasure, taking pleasure in it. He moaned as she took him deeper, drawing him deliberately with her lips until she tasted the first drops of his desire. Then she pulled away, touching him lightly again, stroking him, looking into his eyes.

"You can't torture me forever," he said hoarsely, sitting up and grabbing her by the waist, rolling her, pushing her against the bed. She laughed, a laugh of relief as much as of delight, of sudden freedom, as she lay back. "Mutual surrender," he said, that smile turned devilish. He put one hand under the waistband of her underpants, exploring, finding the place where she knew she was wet and ready for him. His eyes showed he knew it, too. With both hands, he pulled her underwear off, then stood and reached on the floor for his jeans, his wallet, a condom.

"Always prepared, aren't you?" she said, irrepressibly sardonic even as she wanted him.

"I wasn't prepared for you," he said as he rolled it on. He reached under her knees and pulled her almost to the edge of the bed. He pushed her legs open and she acquiesced with anticipation as he leaned over her, deftly stroking her with his fingers, focusing on his ministrations, bringing her to the brink.

"Now, Jack," she whispered, clutching the blanket beneath her. He lifted his gaze back to hers and rested his hands on her hips, positioning himself. She gasped as he pushed his tip just inside her, tantalizing her, and withdrew slightly, hovering there. She could feel him at the gates as he toyed with her bud with his thumb until she groaned. "Now. *Now*," she implored him.

"Say please," he said with mock seriousness.

"Don't push your luck," she hissed through rapid breaths.

He gave her one of his smoldering stares as he ran his hands over her body. "I like surrendering to you," he said. He grasped her hips, eased himself inside her with a delicious fullness and then pushed hard, a rocket into her hot center.

She gasped and lifted her hips to take him in, pushing against him as he thrust harder and faster, an exhilarating, pounding rhythm, and she felt a silver fire wash over her, pour out from within, a lightning bolt of connection, certainty, ecstasy. She felt him convulse inside her as her own shock wave enveloped him, and she pulled him close as they rocked against each other, each crying out with the aftershocks of their pain and pleasure until they quieted in each other's arms. As their breathing eased, they lay against the bed and explored with their hands as if they'd never touched before, caressing their bodies as if one skin flowed into the other until they slowed and stopped, like a boulder finishing its headlong rush down a mountain, at rest in a green field, the wildflowers crushed and fragrant beneath.

"Come here," Jack said after disposing of the condom, coaxing her up to the head of the bed and the pillows. He pulled the covers down and pulled her to him under the sheet, brushed her hair out of her eyes. "Are you OK?"

"Sweet of you to ask. And yes. I think I am."

"I keep feeling like it's some kind of miracle you're here."

"What about you?" Maribeth asked. "Do you try to get killed by tornadoes during every chase?"

"I think tornadoes are attracted to me," he said, touching her cheek. "Anyway, you should talk. You're getting pretty good at crash landings."

"You know," she said with chagrin, "to a pilot, that's not really a compliment."

His eyes twinkled as he moved in to kiss her, a slow, sensual kiss that burned to her core. She had an almost scary hunch that she would never get enough of those kisses.

"I just hope," she added when he'd released her, "that Dr. Y's experiments are OK."

"Leave tomorrow to tomorrow," Jack said, kissing her ear, her neck, melting away her worries. "Tonight, you're with me."

"And tomorrow?"

"And tomorrow," he whispered, kissing her again. "And tomorrow."

🖋

"I HEAR Percival Yzaguirre has a research plane holed up in Loup City," Danni said, drinking her coffee at the counter at Tommy's in Grand Island. "This might be our chance to interview him about his brother, tie up that story."

Aurelius nodded, sipping tea and enjoying the last of his apple pie. He was grateful the story wasn't over. He and Danni had just come from visiting Charles in the hospital. The doctors were keeping him for a few extra neurological tests — perhaps, Aurelius thought, because they couldn't find enough wrong with him. They were all fascinated by the man who had survived his fourth lightning strike.

The mystic himself was tired, more from the sleep deprivation of the hospital than any injury, a fading red branching pattern visible on his shoulder and chest under his blue gown. He'd been glad to see them. Before he'd drifted off, he'd held Aurelius's hand and thanked him and said they would meet again. What a hell of a night it had been. Was it just three days before? When Aurelius had escaped the tornado with the food truck and his unconscious charge, certain it was too late, he'd found himself in Palladia amid flashing emergency lights and flagged down an ambulance. The town had mostly property damage, few injuries and EMTs to spare, so they took Charles from him, confirmed that he was breathing and, with sirens screaming, hauled him away to Grand Island for treatment.

Aurelius caught up with his team there, leaving the food truck in the hospital parking lot, and together, late the next day, they'd delivered Tyler and Polly Ann back to their bunker home. They'd filmed the groom carrying her over the threshold and eagerly shooing them out the door. And after the crew spent a night in an Enid hotel, they'd driven back up to Nebraska at Aurelius's insistence. He had to be sure Charles was all right. He and Danni had managed one quick visit yesterday afternoon while Charles was sleeping before returning to the hospital this morning.

Now, behind them in one of the tan and red leather booths, Brad told tales of his adventures to Scooter and Vinyl, who appeared too hung over after their night off to pay much attention. Brad was more smug than ever after the tornado encounter, as if none of them had noticed that he was a spineless bastard. Aurelius hadn't had a chance to confront him yet, but he felt sure the Twister Tracker of fame and fortune was not anything like the Brad he knew.

"We can head up to the airfield after breakfast," Aurelius told Danni. "The worst Yzaguirre can do is say no."

"I think he'll be happy to talk to us," she said. "I had a word with his assistant in Florida this morning — she has a seriously cool Jamaican accent — and she seemed totally thrilled to know where Charles is. She implied we'd be greeted with open arms if we cared to stop by. Apparently Yzaguirre has been looking for him for years."

An hour and a half later, the cake car, with Aurelius and Danni, and the crew van, with Brad and the guys, pulled into the tiny Loup City Municipal Airport. They struggled to find a spot to park. The place was crawling with vehicles, equipment and personnel, all surrounding an open circus tent of sorts that had been set up over a snarling A-10 Warthog.

"Let me check in before you start filming," Danni cautioned them when they'd piled out with their gear. She dashed toward the tent, looking for someone in charge.

Brad wandered off, and Aurelius followed him, unobserved, anxious to speak with him. Aurelius waited until Brad paused near the corner of the massive tent and stopped. The technicians were conferring with that woman they'd seen at the restaurant in Salina. She was wearing a flight suit. Brad scanned the crowd, and Aurelius wondered what he was looking for. And then they both saw Jack, who'd helped Aurelius with Polly Ann's meltdown that same night. Aurelius watched Brad's fists tighten, his face twist into a scowl.

"What are you thinking, Brad?" Aurelius asked.

Brad whirled in surprise. "None of your business."

"Well, I've been thinking," said Aurelius, strolling over to stand next to him. "I've been thinking that there's no way a guy who was so terrified by a tornado that he had to leave a dying man could have possibly flown in the Bubble."

"Maybe I have post-traumatic stress," Brad said.

"Maybe," said Aurelius, "but I think something else is going on. Oh, look, and here's your colleague." Jack walked toward them. "He doesn't seem to want to talk about the Bubble, either."

"He can't," said Brad, who abruptly bit his lip, as if he'd said something he oughtn't.

Jack, in blue jeans and a black T-shirt, reached them, nodded to Aurelius and spoke to Brad. "The only reason I'm not throwing you out of here is that Dr. Y wants to talk with you for some reason."

"Maybe because we saved his brother's life!" Brad retorted.

"*We?*" Aurelius was aghast.

"I have something of yours," Jack said to Brad, reaching into his back pocket. "When I saw you, I knew I had to return them." He held out two long, deadly sharp, sparkling pins. Aurelius struggled to figure out what they meant. Polly Ann's hatpins?

Brad looked flustered. "Those aren't mine."

"Are you sure?" Jack said. "They almost did the job on our tires, but I think you should have them. You'd look so pretty in them."

Brad leapt forward, as if to attack Jack, but Aurelius stepped in and gave the Twister Tracker a hard push in the chest.

Brad stumbled backward and turned his fury on Jack: "You should have died in that tornado!"

Jack eyed him with cold regard. "Which one?"

Aurelius gaped. He looked at Jack, who smiled, gave him a casual salute and walked away.

Aurelius turned on Brad. "You never did fly in the Bubble," he breathed.

"The world knows I did," said Brad. He straightened his "I fly into tornadoes" T-shirt and got himself under control. "And for what I have planned, that's all that matters."

AN HOUR LATER, Jack watched the *Zany Weddings* crew depart, fat and happy after their interview with the illustrious Dr. Y. Their short benefactor stood near the Warthog in a

tomato-red Hawaiian shirt, watching as Maribeth, in the
pilot's seat, went through preflight checks. It was almost time.
Jack dreaded her flying the plane again, but they'd repaired
the electronics system, and there would be no storms today.
The scientific instruments, including the cameras, had almost
entirely avoided the effects of the strike. Fred, who was
running around with the technicians, had tried to explain it to
him — separated, shielded systems had preserved their func-
tion and data. The team had extraordinary high-speed footage
of multiple upward lightning strikes, including the one that
had hit the Warthog. But Jack knew Dr. Y was mortified that
their design modifications might have led to the plane's
dangerous failure. A half-inch hole in the plane's body and
scoring around it showed the lightning shared at least some of
the blame.

Jack walked over to Dr. Y and tapped him on the
shoulder.

"Ready?" Jack asked.

"I feel absolutely confident that she'll be back in Salina this
afternoon," said a smiling Dr. Y. "I mean, the plane *and* Ms.
Lisbon, of course. We'll finish analysis there and harden the
A-10 before we fly it again into a storm. We're already
working on new protections and redundancies. Fear not, Dr.
Andreas." Dr. Y looked at him keenly. Jack knew he and Maribeth had acted differently with each other since the emergency
landing, and Dr. Y wasn't stupid.

"I know she'll be OK," Jack said. "But knowing a thing and
feeling a thing are not the same."

"Of course," Dr. Y said with empathy. "It's been a challenging week for all of us. But I do have good news. My
brother Charles is recuperating from a lightning strike in
Grand Island. That TV crew saved his life. Can you imagine it?

I'm going to see him this afternoon. I hope I can talk him into returning to the fold."

"That's amazing," Jack said. "Good luck."

"We're a lucky family," said Dr. Y, "in different ways. I think we can double our luck together. And I'm sharing a little of my good fortune with that young man who stars in the TV show. The one who flew in the Bubble — but, of course, you know all about it."

"Brad?" Jack tried not to let his revulsion show. "What do you mean?"

"He's going into politics. Apparently his father is an influential man in Texas, and young Mr. Treat's fame could take him far. I told him I'd support his campaign."

"But —" Jack wasn't sure what to say. He didn't want Dr. Y to know all the reasons for his and Brad's mutual antipathy. It would mean explaining too much. "Are you sure?" he finally asked. "You don't know that much about him."

"His team helped save my brother," Dr. Y said simply. He observed Jack for a moment. "I feel I am a fairly good judge of character, and perhaps your concerns are not invalid," he added, "but I have motives of my own. It never hurts to have friends in Texas politics. They tend to end up in high places." He winked at Jack, then walked off to confer with Fred, who was flagging him down with a clipboard.

Jack looked up and saw Maribeth climbing down the pilot's ladder to the tarmac. She walked toward him in her green flight suit. Though other clothes had been delivered for her to wear in the past couple of days as they worked on the plane, he felt a tiny thrill at seeing her in the suit again. He smiled as she came near, strong and capable and beautiful, vulnerable and true. He didn't care what anyone thought. He reached his arms around her waist and kissed her. She responded with equal heat before she stepped back, in professional mode, smiling a secret smile.

"It's time," she said.

"I know. How about I drive you. Fred can fly the plane."

She laughed as she looked over at Fred, who, chatting amiably with Dr. Y, was taking a hearty gulp from his giant coffee mug. Techs scattered, leaving the plane, fueled and checked out and ready, a clear path to the runway.

"Now they have to shut down the circus," she said.

"I never did get why they didn't just use the hangar here."

"Dr. Y didn't want to inconvenience the locals," Maribeth said. "And I think he enjoyed the attention. He's kind of a showman, you know."

"And you're the daredevil act."

"Absolutely not," she said, grabbing him by the hand. "I'll see you tonight."

"Promise?"

"You doubt my word?"

"If only this morning's fog had stuck around," said Jack, "we could reenact that scene from *Casablanca*."

"Except that I'll be there tonight," she said. "I promise."

"I'll be there, too," he said.

She squeezed and released his hand and walked back to the plane. A tech handed her the pieces of her G-suit, which she donned as final preparations were made. With the others, Jack stepped farther back as she climbed aboard, put on her helmet, did her checks, started the howling turbofan engines, tested the flaps, watched the ground crew stow the ladder and, finally, closed the canopy and rolled the A-10 forward and out of the tent. Jack felt better watching it move, seeing its sturdy square tail and its robust fuselage and the engines that would bring her home to him as she taxied into position. He could see why she loved it, loved all aircraft, the almost magical machines that could take her up into the sky where the weather happened, the same place where he virtually lived his most exhilarating moments.

In position to fly at the end of the runway, the plane seemed a formidable force. The Warthog's engines made the air tremble as it accelerated down the strip of pavement and lifted off the ground, roaring into the blue. The team burst into applause. Jack clapped, too, but he was too worried to rejoice.

Fred's voice at his side startled him. "The van's packed," said the engineer, who looked tired but happy. "These guys can tear down the big top. Wanna drive to Salina?"

Jack grinned. "You're a good friend despite being such a freak," he said, and shook Fred's hand. Together, they walked toward the van — chasers, scientists, the usual suspects — ready for the road on a bright, fogless afternoon.

AT A PRAIRIE CROSSROADS outside the town of Pancake, Kansas, a food truck parked in the sun, under the passing shadows of clouds. It was late June, and storm season was almost over, but chasers, travelers and residents alike enjoyed a taste of something new. Chuck's Wagon was always happy to oblige.

The latest customers had been a happy couple, he tall with curly hair, chasing after a bouncy little dog; she blue-eyed with blond braids, pregnant and toting a camera, on their way to a former baseball field they had turned into a hybrid art project and lightning experiment. They chatted briefly with the chef, finding they had interests in common, and went on their way, excited about the day, hoping for supercells.

When the white van pulled up, the lunch crowd was long gone. They were TV people, judging from the logo on the doors. The driver of the food truck was used to TV people, but he wanted to get a look at them, first, and make sure they weren't more of those paparazzi who had come along after the lightning strike drama. He stayed in the shadows, waiting for them to approach.

The redhead came to the window first, ordering the two guys accompanying her to hang back.

"Is this Chuck's van?" she called out in an English accent. "Or have I been misinformed?"

The chef emerged from the shadows and approached the window, a broad-shouldered man with floppy, dirty-blond hair, wearing a brown apron over his white, button-up shirt, its sleeves rolled up. He made the apron look surprisingly dashing.

He greeted his visitor with a wide, handsome smile.

"There's no Chuck here," he said in a deep voice. "I run this business now. It was a gift from a friend."

"And what do they call you, sir?" she asked in a playful tone.

"Aurelius Zane."

"Aurelius," mused the redhead, who cocked her head and looked at him with a glint in her eye. "I knew an Aurelius once. Quite an obnoxious fellow. World adventurer."

"I knew him once, too," said Aurelius. "He still loves adventure, but he's also aspiring to be a philosopher. And a cook." He leaned forward, elbows on the counter. "Wynda! What brings you to Kansas?"

"Another weather documentary. Always in demand.

Besides, it was almost as if I'd been summoned." She raised one eyebrow as a brief look of discomfiture crossed Aurelius's features. "I never fancied I'd see you in an apron," she continued. "Do you really cook?"

"My dear, I am going to make you the best sandwich you've ever tasted."

Aurelius worked quickly, extracting his own variation on chicken salad from the fridge. He'd blended the roasted chicken with garlic, lemon, seasonings and a touch of Worcestershire sauce. He spread the salad on sesame-seed bread, added fresh arugula and tomato and scooped up some of his homemade potato chips, dusted with the secret spices Charles had taught him to make before the mystic joined his brother's company. Charles, it turned out, had a master's in philosophy *and* a doctorate in atmospheric sciences.

Aurelius wrapped the sandwich and handed it to Wynda on a cardboard tray with the chips.

"Judging from the pile of emails I received," she said, "you can offer quite a bit more than a sandwich."

Aurelius bowed, his embarrassment forgotten in the presence of his ex-paramour. "My dear, I meant every word. Are you in town long?"

"Town? No. But I've set up a production company in Austin," she said, "to meet the American demand. And sometimes, you know, I get quite hungry."

"There's more where that came from," he said with a smile. "And I deliver."

Wynda took a bite and savored it, closing her eyes. "Bloody hell, that's good," she said. She beckoned her crew, then looked up at Aurelius as they walked over. "I hated you for a while," she said. "But then I sort of missed you. Especially after I read all those letters. They were quite — stirring. You've been on a journey, you have."

Aurelius reached out to her, and after a moment's hesitation, she let him take her hand.

"The universe works in mysterious ways," he said. "Let me tell you all about it."

As MARIBETH awoke, she wasn't quite sure where she was or whether she was still in the dream. The warm sun shone on her face, dawn in a strange place, and she opened her eyes to a room full of light. Beams danced off the waves she could see through the glass doors, splashing them with diamonds, shooting their brilliance into the room. She shifted in the warm bed, knowing, now, that this wasn't a dream. She rolled over and looked at the man sleeping next to her, the face she'd come to know so well, the complex heart she'd learned to trust as well as her own.

Jack's eyes opened slowly, slits at first, then wider, emerald green this morning in the ocean light, taking her in as if he'd felt her thoughts. He smiled.

"Ready for your beach run already?" he asked softly, reaching out to pull her to him.

"Depends on my options," she said, kissing him.

"Oh, you have options," he said, plying her with more kisses, touching her, leading her into another sweet awakening, heated and soulful and absolutely real. When they were sated, they lay back against the pillows, nestled together, and watched the light glisten on the waves and reflect on the ceiling of the Cocoa Beach condo. They were halfway through a two-week vacation. Soon, Maribeth would be back with

Casablanca Aviation, as well as on call for Dr. Y. Jack had taken a job with Dr. Y's research division with promises of many chases to come and a challenging analysis of their lightning research.

"It's beautiful here," Maribeth said.

"You make it beautiful," Jack replied.

"Oh, stop."

"It was never this beautiful," he said. "I never really saw the beauty in it. I don't think I understood it until you came along."

"How can you stay in a place like this for as much time as you have and not see its beauty?" She was entranced by the beach, by its golden mornings and fragile seashells and afternoon thunderstorms.

"I was wearing dark glasses." He smiled, but she could see an old ache flash in his eyes and disappear.

"I'm not sure I could have imagined being in a place this beautiful," Maribeth said. "I used to dream about it. I didn't think it was possible."

He pulled her closer. "I wish we could stay like this forever," he said. "Or until next storm season."

She laughed. "That's a long time. You know I'll always have to go up again."

"And I'll always be waiting, on the ground."

"Probably in a tornado," Maribeth joked.

"Fuck, I hope so." Jack grinned. "That reminds me. I have something for you." He reached over to his nightstand, opened the drawer and pulled out a small, square box wrapped in blue paper spangled with silver stars. He handed it over. "Just a little token. For now."

She wasted no time in ripping off the paper and opening the box. Inside, nestled in white tissue paper, was a dark blue velvet bag. She lifted it out, tugged open the drawstring, turned the bag upside down and let its treasure slip into her palm: a clear, smooth disk about two inches across with what looked like lightning etched inside it. She held it up to the light. The branches of the bolt glistened as she turned it.

"It's gorgeous," she said. "What is it?"

"A Lichtenberg figure. Captured, manmade lightning. A good-luck charm to take with you when you're flying."

"My luck just keeps getting better." She kissed his nose. "Thank you."

"Come on," Jack said. "Let's go get our feet wet. And then we'll get breakfast and drink ourselves silly and wait for the lightning storms."

"Have I not been zapped enough for you?"

"This research project is going to take a lifetime," he said, kissing her cheek. "I may never understand this equation. Add two hardheaded opposites — "

"One plus one equals one?" Maribeth interrupted him.

He returned her smile, his eyes as light as she'd ever seen them.

"Let me check your math," he whispered, finding her lips again, and his kiss told her she was right.

NOTES AND THANKS

Zap Bang, like *Funnel Vision* and *Tornado Pinball* before it, is inspired by my experiences as a storm chaser, but its characters and situations are fictional. Though I have sought to be authentic in all aspects of the story, I have manipulated geography and technology when it suited me.

While many of the cities are real, a few are fictional; I thought it might be kinder if my tornadoes didn't target real towns. The hotels, bars and restaurants may have roots in reality, but they are mostly invented. However, Tommy's is a very cool diner in Grand Island, Nebraska. And Carhenge is absolutely real. You must go.

As for technology, the National Science Foundation is refurbishing an A-10 for storm research, but it will not focus on lightning like the plane in *Zap Bang.* And the high-speed cameras are very close to reality in their capabilities.

I am deeply grateful to several people for the inspiration and expertise that helped me in writing this book. I alone hold the responsibility for any inaccuracies, but their guidance was invaluable in what became an epic research project.

Tom Warner (ztresearch.com), a lightning researcher, pilot and longtime chaser friend, gave me crucial insights into the latest questions in lightning research and the mysteries of upward lightning. He also answered my naive questions about what it's like to fly a research airplane into a lightning storm.

Monica Foley was very generous in sharing her experiences

as an Army helicopter pilot in Iraq. She helped me understand what it was like to be a woman serving in that role and what many veterans faced when they left.

Airline pilot Dennis "Fish" Prokopowicz answered a taxing number of questions about the A-10 Warthog, a plane he used to fly. He was enormously patient with my continuing queries about St. Elmo's Fire, helmets, ladders, pockets and other trivia, and I'm thankful.

Thanks to author and retired fighter pilot Bob Harvey (viperpilotpress.com) for connecting me with Fish. Kudos to the Cape Canaveral Chapter of the American Meteorological Society for its continuing presentations on weather research, which often gave me inspiration. Also thank you to Danny Morris, pilot and surf guitarist deluxe, for a helpful answer to my question about the Cessna 172.

Thanks to my friends at *Florida Today* for their continuing support, including Suzy Fleming Leonard and Christina LaFortune, and to other publications in my part of Florida that continue to write about authors and books, *The Beachside Resident* and *SpaceCoast Living*.

I can't thank my storm-chasing friends enough for their aid and companionship on the road through hail, tornadoes, thousands of miles of driving and frequently terrible food. They've offered humor when the situation was bleak and comfort when we lost some of our own. I'd also like to thank the storm chasers and other folks who have been kind enough to read the *Storm Seekers* books.

I owe George Jenkins much for his unflagging encouragement and support of my writing, photography, storm chasing and other mildly crazy obsessions. I'd mix him a Manhattan, but he already makes the best one around.

For great conversations and martinis by the water, cheers to writers Susan Hubbard and Dianne Marcum.

Finally, I must toast the talented scribes of the Harbaugh Literary Salon for their feedback and friendship as I wrote this book: Pam and John Harbaugh, Rachel Wilkerson, Annette Clifford, Billy Cox and especially Cathy Mathias for her patient reading of the manuscript, sharp pencil and excellent notes.

As the proprietor of Chuck's Wagon might say, if Alfred Painter hadn't already: "Saying thank you is more than good manners. It is good spirituality."

Thank you all.

BOOKS BY CHRIS KRIDLER

The STORM SEEKERS Series

Writing as Chris Kridler

FUNNEL VISION

TORNADO PINBALL

ZAP BANG

Storm Seekers Series Boxed Set: Books 1-3

BOHEMIA BARTENDERS MYSTERIES

Writing as Lucy Lakestone

These funny mysteries star Pepper Revelle and a team of mixologists who travel to colorful events where life is a cocktail of fun — until it's shaken into madcap mayhem ... and murder.

RISKY WHISKEY

BAFFLED BY BITTERS ~ *story free to subscribers*

WRECKED BY RUM

VEXED BY VODKA

JIGGERED BY GIN

BEGUILED BY BOURBON

SHOCKED BY CHAMPAGNE

WHY OH RYE?

BOHEMIA BARTENDERS COCKTAIL COLORING BOOK

The BOHEMIA BEACH Series

Writing as Lucy Lakestone

Award-winning hot contemporary romance

In a beautiful small city on Florida's east coast, artists meet, create, laugh and love. Where restless hearts are fueled by secrets and imagination, romance is impossible to resist. Welcome to the seductive tropical escape that's home to drama, humor and lots of heat – Bohemia Beach.

BOHEMIA BEACH

BOHEMIA LIGHT

BOHEMIA BLUES

BOHEMIA HEAT

BOHEMIA NIGHTS

BACK TO BOHEMIA ~ *story free to subscribers*

BOHEMIA BELLS

BOHEMIA CHILLS

Bohemia Beach Series Boxed Sets:

Books 1-3 | Books 4-7

ABOUT THE AUTHOR

Chris Kridler is an award-winning writer, photographer and storm chaser who lives in Florida. She travels every year to Tornado Alley in search of the perfect storm. She also writes mysteries and romances as Lucy Lakestone. Learn more about her work and travels at ChrisKridler.com.

www.ingramcontent.com/pod-product-compliance
Lightning Source LLC
Chambersburg PA
CBHW070221260626
47160CB00002B/637